THE
ISLAND

OTHER NOVELS BY PAUL FINCH

Detective Sergeant Mark Heckenburg

Stalkers
Sacrifice
The Killing Club
Dead Man Walking
Hunted
Ashes to Ashes
Kiss of Death
Rogue

Detective Constable Lucy Clayburn

Strangers
Shadows
Stolen

Standalones

Crime/Thriller
One Eye Open
Never Seen Again

Historical/Adventure
Usurper
Battle Lord

Fantasy
Stronghold
Dark North

THE ISLAND

PAUL FINCH

This is a work of fiction. Names, characters, organizations, places, events, and incidents are either products of the author's imagination or are used fictitiously. Any resemblance to actual persons, living or dead, or actual events is purely coincidental.

Text copyright © 2025 by Paul Finch
All rights reserved.

No part of this book may be reproduced, or stored in a retrieval system, or transmitted in any form or by any means, electronic, mechanical, photocopying, recording, or otherwise, without express written permission of the publisher.

Published by Thomas & Mercer, Seattle

www.apub.com

Amazon, the Amazon logo, and Thomas & Mercer are trademarks of Amazon.com, Inc., or its affiliates.

EU Product Safety contact:
Amazon Publishing, Amazon Media EU S.à r.l.
38, avenue John F. Kennedy, L-1855 Luxembourg
amazonpublishing-gpsr@amazon.com

ISBN-13: 9781662526329
eISBN: 9781662526336

Cover design by Dominic Forbes
Cover image: © Nic Skerten / ArcAngel

Printed in the United States of America

For all my family, friends and colleagues who've encouraged my writing over so many years

1: WOLF IN THE FOLD

One

Everything about Cookham bespoke gentrification. It had never been dirt poor, though as a village on the outskirts of Manchester it had once boasted a pit and a couple of textile mills, and there were still a few terraced streets left. But mostly these days it was new housing estates, swish restaurants, and pubs that had once been street-corner boozers but now were wine bars serving Asian fusion food. The modern Cookham was pleasant and suburban, and the people seemed nice.

Of course, that made it harder for Charlie and Lennie, who'd known from the outset that they'd need to blend in, and so had come dressed in smart casuals, their faces shaved and hair cut neatly, but who still felt conspicuous.

'Once a crim always a crim,' Peter Quincannon had said, choking on his beer when they'd told him the plan. 'You think you desperadoes could ever look like anything else?'

It was true. Charlie was tall and rangy, and though he might once have passed for handsome, with one eye green and another blue (a punch-up at school) and a white scar bisecting his left cheek horizontally (a more recent altercation), those days were past. Lennie meanwhile was shorter, dumpier and ape-like, which suited his sloped forehead, his too-close eyes and his flattened nose.

But the time of day ought to help them. It was mid-evening on a Thursday. Not the busiest part of the week, though things were picking up for the weekend. The customers in the pubs and bars were getting a little more oiled than they would on a Tuesday or Wednesday and would be more inclined to overlook any guys they didn't know. On top of that, Cookham was situated in the extreme north-east of the Manchester borough called Crowley, which, further in, had significant levels of urban deprivation, so people who looked like they didn't belong often came drifting through.

'Wouldn't have been my first choice, doing him round here,' Charlie murmured, as they installed themselves in the vault of The Dog and Partridge. 'But he's not dumb enough to come on to our manor, is he.'

Lennie sipped his pint of lager and stared at the object of their interest, who stood with his back turned, watching the news on a big TV screen.

He was outstandingly ordinary-looking. Somewhere in his late thirties, a good ten years older than either of them, wearing jeans, a polo shirt and a suede jacket. He had dark, curly hair, lean, serious features and stood to just under six feet, with a trim build and athletic aura, though there was nothing about him that suggested he was a tough guy. It was interesting, of course, that he was standing alone, that he hadn't in fact interacted with anyone since they'd latched on to him half an hour ago.

'Even his own bastards don't want him anymore,' Lennie had chuckled.

'Who wants a dodgy ex-cop?' Charlie had replied.

When the dodgy ex-cop moved on, Charlie and Lennie moved on as well, though they gave him a minute or so first, so as not to stand out on any of Cookham's security cameras. That said, they were fairly certain that, whatever happened to the ex-cop before the night ended, he'd keep his mouth shut. There was no love lost between him and the Greater Manchester Police.

They kept pace, but stayed at least a hundred yards behind, ambling along the main road into the village. There was another pub coming up, The Old George. The ex-cop went inside, but instead of sliding furtively in after him, they crossed the road and entered a kebab shop, where Charlie ordered a burger and Lennie a doner. They sat at a table in the window.

'Do you ever think about having some lamb with your chilli sauce?' Charlie asked.

Lennie frowned. 'Uh?'

'State of that thing.' Charlie nodded disgustedly at Lennie's plate, where crimson goo oozed from all sides of the folded pitta bread.

'I like chilli sauce.'

'Goes through me like shit through a goose.'

Lennie made the sort of grunt that implied this was only to be expected.

'What's that supposed to mean?' Charlie asked him.

'What?'

'That fucking noise you just made?'

'Just like chilli, that's all.'

Charlie eyed him suspiciously, the pair almost jumping from their chairs when the pub door across the road suddenly banged open. But it was only a bunch of lads. They settled down again.

'What I love is the way the scumbag thinks it's perfectly okay,' Charlie said. 'Like he's done what he's done . . . he's basically got away with it, and now he's wandering around his own patch like the big "I am".'

'His life's turned to shit, though,' Lennie said.

'It's going to.'

Charlie felt under his zip-up jacket, to ensure his spring-loaded cosh was there, and then at his trouser pocket for his cut-throat razor. Lennie was carrying a Stanley knife and a lug-wrench. They'd have brought shooters, but Pete had come down on that firmly.

'You'll give the pigs no fucking option,' he'd said. 'You can still do a job and leave him alive. And they'll be less arsed about that.'

The ex-cop re-emerged as they finished. They wiped their fingers and scrunched their napkins, letting him get ahead again, then exited the premises. Considering he must have had two or three by now, the guy was still walking steadily. But he'd put a pair of shades on, which they thought was funny. It was May and the sun had been out all day, but it was setting now.

'Doesn't want to get recognised, does he?' Charlie snorted. 'Worried he might meet people he knows.'

'They'll know him whether he's got shades on or not.'

'Probably makes him think he's a hard-arse. You know, Clint Eastwood. Thinks they won't say, "Hey, you're that bent bastard who was doing this, that and the other." Worried he might lay 'em out if they do.'

Lennie looked troubled. 'Don't like the idea of him meeting people he knows. Where we going to take him?'

'Stick with him for the time being. We'll get a chance.'

They were now in the centre of the village, which offered a range of hostelries: one of the aforementioned wine bars, called The Stocks, a more traditional pub, The Legs of Man, and The Billy Flynn, which had a rough and rugged air, as if it had been there long before the place got tidied up.

Their target avoided The Billy Flynn and went first into The Legs and later into The Stocks. Charlie and Lennie watched from The Billy Flynn's front window. When he finally reappeared it was shortly after ten-thirty.

The timing couldn't have been better. They didn't need to be quite as careful now. For one thing, the guy had had a skinful, and while he wasn't exactly stumbling, he was heading home slowly. For another, they were able to tag along a little closer, forty or fifty yards away, instead of a hundred; there were lots of deep shadows they could step into should he glance behind, which he never did. However, they were uneasy about jumping him on the main road and he seemed to conscientiously avoid any other route. There was a convenient shortcut around the back of the local community gym: he didn't take it. A car park servicing Cookham Parish Church backed on to a small patch of woodland, which would have reduced his journey time: he didn't take it.

Finally they followed him into his home neighbourhood, one of those tidy housing estates. They were more likely to be spotted here, but it was dark now and that helped. The elm trees lining the avenues were in full leaf, which blotted out most of the street lighting. On top of that, Rutland Drive, where the ex-cop lived, ran down the east side of a small park, which was unlit. This gave them an opportunity like no other. As their target lumbered around the corner on to his home straight, they didn't even bother following him, but instead nipped through the open park gates, from where they could get ahead of him without being seen.

'Shit,' Lennie grunted as they sprinted across the kiddies' playground. 'This doesn't work with beer and kebab meat in your gut.'

Charlie hissed at him to shut it. A single belt of trees and bushes lay between themselves and the road. The ex-cop was on the other side of it, and the last thing they needed was for him to overhear them. They'd gone maybe two hundred yards when they halted, Lennie doubling over, looking like he was going to puke, Charlie sidling into the foliage until he was in a position to peek out.

The ploy had partly worked.

They'd overtaken their target. He was still forty yards down the road, but he'd crossed to the other side, where the houses were. That didn't matter. His own address, number 28, was just opposite the point where Charlie was now waiting. The moment the bastard turned on to his drive, all they had to do was scurry over, slug him from behind and drag him back here and out of sight.

'What's he doing?' Lennie muttered, stepping closer.

'Just get ready.'

They backed into the leafage a little. The guy had been drinking all night. But an ex-cop was still an ex-cop. Eyes like a shit-house rat.

Charlie felt for his cosh. Its lead weight wasn't much larger than a golf ball, but at the end of that short spring, it didn't half deliver a whack. He gripped the handle, the hard, moulded plastic slick with sweat.

'Fuck!' Lennie breathed.

A car had turned in at the far end, the dazzling blots of its headlamps advancing towards them. They watched, frustrated, as it decelerated.

'Fuck's wrong with him?' Charlie muttered.

The driver was presumably looking for an address. At this snail's pace, he was going to pass them just as their target reached his drive.

'Crap!' Charlie said, almost too loudly.

Lennie grabbed his arm, to make sure he didn't do something stupid like dash out there. 'We can always come back.'

The car cruised past, revealing the ex-cop at the top of his drive.

'Can you believe that?' Charlie hissed.

'We'll come back.'

But then something unexpected happened. The target didn't let himself in through the front door of his semi-detached, but instead approached the double doors to his garage. He opened the one on the right and slid into the darkness beyond.

'Lost his front door key?' Lennie wondered. 'Fucking piss-artist.'

'He's left it open.' Charlie's scarred features glistened with sweat. 'We're going in.'

'You sure? I mean . . .'

'We're going the fuck in!'

Lennie's primary role in the firm was muscle. He wasn't renowned as a thinker, but he too knew when they were being offered something on a plate. They lurched out of their cover, running across the road and up the drive, each covering his face with his hand.

Seeing that the right-hand garage door was indeed still open, they dug into their pockets and pulled their gloves on. If they were going indoors, it meant lots of flat, smooth surfaces.

Weapons in hand – Charlie his cosh, Lennie his wrench – they eased their way into the garage. It was pretty dark in there, so they couldn't go blundering around. They'd knock stuff over and alert even a drunken dipstick like this guy. They halted at the rear of a parked vehicle. Lennie placed the wrench on the car as he fiddled with his iPhone, which wasn't easy with gloved fingers.

'Come on, come on,' Charlie urged him. All they needed was a bit of light, so they could find the internal door.

But they got more than that.

A pair of strip-bulbs suspended in the middle of the ceiling came on together with a *bang*. Charlie jolted sideways into Lennie, knocking his iPhone to the floor.

'What are you fucking clowns up to?' a voice demanded.

They spun around, angry, scared. It was the ex-cop, but he didn't seem quite as drunk as before, and that was probably a good thing, because it meant that the sawn-off Remington 12-bore he was levelling at them was rock-steady.

Two

The ex-cop pulled the garage door closed. He'd already removed his shades, a pair of steely grey eyes riveted on the intruders.

'Seriously? You dickheads thought you could come to my *house?*'

'Nowhere's off-limits now, pal,' Charlie said.

'You reckon?' The ex-cop clicked both hammers back and pointed the Remington's double-barrelled muzzle straight at his face. 'You born stupid, or do you work at it?'

Charlie cracked a cocky, confident grin. 'You're not using that.'

'What's gonna stop me?'

'You can't.'

'Why not?' The ex-cop smiled. 'Rules of engagement? I play by my own rules these days. So first off . . .' he indicated the cosh, 'drop that penis extension.'

Charlie had no choice and the weapon clattered to the garage floor.

'Kick it over here,' the ex-cop said. '*You* . . . ape-man! Move away from the wrench.'

Scowling, Lennie complied.

'Got anything else on you?' When they didn't reply, the ex-cop nodded. 'That means you have. Let's see. Nice and slow.'

They dipped into their pockets and produced the Stanley and the razor.

The ex-cop gave a low whistle. 'Suppose I should be flattered. Drop 'em and kick 'em.'

Again, they complied. The ex-cop now noticed Lennie's iPhone lying on the floor. 'This yours?' He clomped down on it with his cowboy boot heel. 'Sorry, it broke.' Lennie gazed at him in disbelief. 'I'm going to ask you this one time. Who are you, and what are you doing here?'

'You don't remember us?' Charlie said.

The ex-cop shrugged. 'Seen a lot of shit in my time. Sorry if your faces didn't stick.'

'We're not telling you who we are,' Lennie snarled. 'You're not going to shoot us.'

The ex-cop appraised him. 'It's really not smart to keep tempting a guy who's got nothing to live for. But now you mention it, *your* caveman mug rings a bell. You're Lennie Hargreaves, aren't you?' He glanced at Charlie. 'Which means you must be Charlie Quincannon. I sent your Paddy down, didn't I?'

'He got twenty years!' Charlie snapped. 'Just for dealing smack to a bunch of shit-bag junkies who were already at death's door.'

Or alternatively, the ex-cop thought, *managing a heroin distribution business that covered half the Greater Manchester area, and netted hundreds of thousands each year.*

He sniffed. 'Your old man sent you, did he? Must be losing his marbles trusting a job like this to a pair of wank-stains like you two. Unless he wants to shed some ballast. Suppose that's possible . . .'

'You corrupt bastard,' Charlie said. 'If that judge had known what you were, he'd have chucked the case out.'

'Cry me a fucking river. Your Paddy was good for twenty just for being who he was. Now, it sounds like we're done. So open that door and get the fuck out.'

They followed his orders, opening the garage and edging out on to the drive. He followed them, Remington still levelled.

'You're fair game, mate,' Charlie said. 'You haven't twigged that yet?'

'Course not. I carry this to live out my Arnold Schwarzenegger fantasies. Keep going.'

They retreated down the drive towards the road.

'You'll be seeing us again,' Charlie warned.

'More than can be said for your Paddy. Least, not till he's pushing a Zimmer.' The ex-cop backed them on to the pavement. 'Now do one . . . the pair of you. I see you round here again, it's the last time anyone'll see you.'

Jack closed the garage and locked it, before going into the house through the front door.

He didn't consider it a victory. Not over a couple of wannabes like those two, who'd now feel they had even more to prove. Okay, he'd seen them off. But this wasn't the end of it. And when the next time came, they'd know he'd be packing heat. So, they'd do the same thing.

What would happen then?

He wandered into his living room, hit a few lamp switches and cracked open the Remington, emptying the shells into his jacket pocket. His head swam a little, the last of the booze wearing off as he stood in the emptiness of his home. Tiredly, he dug the phone from his pocket. He checked it as a matter of routine – almost no one called him these days – but rather to his surprise, he saw that it was registering a voicemail. Intrigued, he hit play.

'Jack, it's me.' Claudia. She sounded tired and stressed. 'Just reminding you that it's my mum's funeral tomorrow and you're invited. I mean, I understand if you don't want to come along . . . but I could use a friendly face.'

The line went dead.

Jack stood thinking. Old Mrs Crayford's funeral.

'Okay, yeah,' he said to no one in particular.

It wasn't like he had anything else to do.

Three

A former DI in Greater Manchester Police's Anti-Gang Intelligence unit, Jack McGurn had dealt with some of the most dangerous organised criminals in northern England. He also knew several colleagues who'd died in the line of duty, and had subsequently attended far too many funerals. But this one would be a particular challenge.

That was why he had turned up late to St Abigail's Church in Crowley. Black suit, black tie, standing at the back, as unobtrusive as possible.

The old lady's coffin sat at the front, before the altar, various friends and family members going up to the podium to speak. Jack couldn't help noticing that Claudia didn't. She was in the front pew with the other family members, a slender figure, wearing a black skirt-suit and black high heels, her fair hair tied in a bun. She didn't once look round.

When the pallbearers brought the coffin down the aisle at the end of the service, Jack had already gone outside. On the church forecourt, he melted into the waiting crowd. After exchanging a few brave words with well-wishers, the Crayford family climbed into four funeral cars. It pleased Jack that Claudia went in the first one, as it indicated that she hadn't been totally ostracised. As the vehicles moved in slow procession towards the forecourt gates, he caught her eye. He saw the recognition there, but that was all.

The crowd now dispersed, heading for their own cars, following to the cemetery in slow cavalcade. Jack's BMW was parked on a side street. He waited a good ten minutes before setting off.

As he drove through the mid-Friday traffic, it struck him that old Mrs Crayford's funeral hadn't been an especially sad one. Her departure wasn't unexpected. That wouldn't make Claudia's situation any easier, of course. Her mother, ravaged by dementia for years, had never known of the disgrace that had befallen her youngest daughter, which was undoubtedly a good thing, but conversely it meant that the old lady had been the only person who'd held no enmity towards Claudia – and now she was gone.

Crowley municipal cemetery had an atmosphere of peaceful repose, headstones and monuments ranging far and wide. Jack kept to the rear of the hushed gathering, while the vicar worked his way through the final prayers, the coffin was lowered, and the family went forward to deposit clumps of earth on its shiny lid. Only belatedly did it occur to Jack that an event like this, which had merited some mention in the local press, might prove attractive to the odd unsavoury character. He glanced furtively at his fellow mourners.

Most were respectfully dressed, standing quiet and thoughtful. There were no scars on view, no telltale neck tattoos, no cheap and nasty bling. But he chided himself for thinking in these terms. He'd been a cop for seventeen years, a detective for twelve, and for eight years the mid-rank supervisor of a special investigations unit. He knew better than anyone that the worst felons generally didn't look like Charlie Quincannon and Lennie Hargreaves. Murderers who drew no attention were by far the most dangerous. As his eyes roved the cemetery, they came to rest on the boundary fence and a single male figure standing on the other side of it, watching.

A lone fixture far out on the periphery of events, he might not have caught Jack's attention, except that, fleetingly, he seemed familiar.

He was tall, about six-foot-four, of lean build, with grey hair. He wore jeans and a brown leather jacket, and his attitude was one of only casual interest. But he stayed put, continuing to watch. There was no harm in that in itself, Jack supposed, but funeral-spotting wasn't the sort of thing you usually indulged in while out for a midday stroll. He wondered what it was about the guy that he thought he recognised, but he couldn't quite pin it down . . .

'Oh my God, what are you doing here?' said a harsh voice.

Jack swung around. He'd been so preoccupied that he hadn't noticed the graveside service had ended and the entire party were now heading back to their cars.

The voice had come from Claudia's older sister, Judy Denton, a tall, angular woman wearing a fitted black trouser-suit, her long fair hair scooped back untidily.

'Came to pay my respects.'

She glared at him. 'Isn't it enough that you've brought shame on our family, without reminding everyone about it, and on a day like this!'

'Judy,' he said quietly.

'Are you going to hang around our family's neck for the rest of our lives?'

'Come on, love,' her husband, Tom, said. He was quite a bit older than she was, balding, bulky and mournful looking. He tried to lead her away. 'There's no point getting upset.'

Jack glanced around awkwardly. Most of the mourners were climbing back into their cars, though here and there they'd turned to look. Claudia, engaged in conversation with someone else, made a hurried apology and walked towards them.

'You disgust me!' Judy said, giving Jack a look of utter contempt. 'That's all I have to say.'

I wish it was, Jack thought to himself.

'Do we have to do this here?' Claudia was made up nicely but looked tired and careworn.

'We're going,' Tom said apologetically. 'It's all right.'

'It's hardly all right,' his wife retorted.

'Judy, let's not make things worse than they already are,' Claudia said.

'You'd have trouble doing that, my girl.'

'Come on, let's think about Mum.'

'Oh yes, let's think about Mum. It's a bit late for that now, though, don't you think? For *you*, I mean.'

'For God's sake,' Claudia said.

'Judy, come on,' Tom pleaded.

'You two deserve each other.' Judy fixed Jack with a belligerent stare. 'This is the last time I'm going to say this to you, Mr McGurn. What's done is done and it can't be changed, but we still don't want you in our lives.'

At least we agree on that, Jack thought.

'In fact, if you show your face around us again, I'm going to report you to your superiors.'

Forgotten already? I don't have any.

Rather grandly, Judy allowed her husband to steer her away.

'Sorry about that,' Claudia said, watching them go.

'It doesn't matter,' Jack said.

'It *does* matter. We've been through this crap already. We don't need it again. Especially not today.'

They ambled side by side towards the cars.

'Look . . .' Jack tried not to appear as sheepish as he felt. 'I was going to come to the wake, but after all that, it's probably for the best if I don't.'

She stopped in her tracks. 'For God's sake, Jack! Don't do that to me!'

He was surprised. 'You want me there?'

'Course I want you there. I'll need some kind of friend.'

'I'm just likely to make things worse.'

'Oh, pish! Judy's no angel herself, you know.'

'I know.'

Claudia sniffled. 'I only took that money so I could afford to keep Mum in that private care home.'

Jack nodded. He knew this too. Even on a detective sergeant's wages, Claudia couldn't have afforded it otherwise. But he thought it best not to say anything. Because that was probably the most painful irony of all. For Claudia at least. Her mum suddenly dying, just as they were dismissed from the service, meant that she'd pocketed all that illicit cash, and then had no one to spend it on.

'Judy and Tom could easily have afforded to help with Mum's care,' Claudia said, 'but they were always pleading poverty, even if it meant chucking her on the social.'

'Don't beat yourself up about it.'

'Look, Jack . . . you've got to come to the do.' There was a genuine plea in her voice.

He glanced around again. Most of the others were now in their vehicles, many already heading for the cemetery gates, but a few more heads had swivelled in their direction. None as openly hostile as Judy, but none of them friendly either.

What are those two criminal bastards up to this time? they'd all be thinking. *Talk about peas in a pod. Thick as thieves, that pair* . . .

'If you don't, I'll be stuck in the middle of it on my own,' Claudia said. 'You're not going to do that to me, are you?'

'Course not,' he replied.

Before climbing into his BMW, he turned and glanced across the graves towards the boundary fence.

'What's the matter?' she asked.

There was no one there now, so he shrugged. 'Nothing. Thought I saw someone I knew.'

'Anyone important?'

'No. Couldn't even remember his name.'

'Okay, well . . .' She backed off. 'I'll see you at The Waterwheel, yeah?'

'Sure.'

'It's going to be hell, of course.'

'After everything *we've* been through together . . . It'll be a doddle.'

Four

The Waterwheel had two main bar areas: downstairs, for public use, and upstairs, which was reserved for private events. This being late on a Friday afternoon, plenty of patrons were already coming and going as the funeral party arrived. The spacious upstairs function room had a long bar and a well-stocked buffet table, but there were many more guests than Jack had expected. He got himself a pint of Diet Coke and stood in a corner, though already he was conscious that glances were being thrown in his direction, accompanied by none-too-complimentary muttering. Pretending he didn't know what they were saying, he affected an air of insouciance, at the same time keeping an eye on Claudia as she made the rounds of her guests.

In some ways it was easier for her. After all, she was one of theirs. They loved her, even cherished her. None of this could really be her fault. Doubtless she'd been led astray by him. But it was still hard for her to face them, shaking hands, offering hugs. She looked strained to breaking point. Some of them remained stiff and unsmiling as they returned her greetings; others just looked troubled and confused, as if they couldn't believe what their beloved little Claudi had done.

'I don't wish to cause any offence . . .' someone said quietly, 'but I don't think it's a good idea, you being here.' Jack glanced around to see Tom, Judy's husband. He looked pale. Standing up to a bad-ass bent cop clearly frightened him. No doubt Judy had sent him over.

Jack finished his drink and laid it on a shelf. 'If Claudia asks for me, tell her I've gone downstairs.'

'Certainly, of course.'

As he trudged down to the lower bar, Jack was relieved.

In truth, he wanted to go home, but he'd promised Claudia he'd be here, so . . .

He ambled to the counter with hands in pockets and ordered a lager. There were plenty of other customers present, but down here no one was paying attention to him. He was on his second when Claudia climbed on to the next bar stool.

'Pint or half?' he asked.

'What do you think?'

He bought her a pint.

'Sorry,' he said. 'But I was really catching it up there.'

'I know. I saw.'

They sipped disconsolately.

'Won't you be missed?' he wondered.

'Well . . . they hate me when I'm there, and they hate me when I'm not.'

'I'm sure they don't *hate* you. None of those people up there suffered because of what you did. They're just embarrassed by it.'

'Maybe.' She offered her own credit card as more brimming pints came over the bar top. 'How's it for you?'

'Well, my family weren't talking to me anyway, so . . .'

'Anyone from the job been in touch?'

He snorted beer. 'No chance of that, is there? Guilt by association. You?'

'Same.' She became thoughtful. 'Funny, isn't it? It's almost like a bereavement. Like a huge part of your life has disappeared overnight. One day they're all there for you, the next they're not.'

'Maybe they were never really there for you in the first place.'

'There we go again,' she said, 'blaming others.'

'I certainly blame that bastard, Jesperson.'

Claudia pulled a face. 'That was our fault too, Jack. Getting involved with a nut-bag like Jesperson. Anyway . . . on happier subjects, I'm thinking of moving.'

'Yeah?'

'Now Mum's gone, there's nothing to keep me here, is there?'

'Starting afresh?'

'If I can.' She eyed him quizzically. 'No thoughts on that?'

In truth, Jack *did* have a thought on it. He hadn't yet mentioned the previous evening's visit to his house by the Quincannon firm. He'd handled them without too much stress, mainly because he'd spotted them earlier in the evening and had had plenty of time to prepare. But in reality, it hadn't been a minor thing. And it certainly wouldn't be a minor thing in Claudia's mind. She'd been his DS back in Anti-Gang Intelligence. She could handle herself. But now that she was a civie, with no backup to call, ongoing attention from the underworld would be an alarming prospect. Especially as she lived alone. He didn't want to frighten her, but he didn't want to hold back on warning her, either.

'No comment?' she said.

'Erm . . . no.' He made a casual gesture. 'I think moving away's a good idea.'

'Just like that?'

'Why not? Like you say, nothing keeping you. Look at somewhere nice. The Cotswolds, Cornwall. Why struggle on in the miserable north when you don't need to?'

She eyed him. 'Sounds like you've got similar plans.'

'Crossed my mind. I mean it's bad enough living in Crowley without being unemployed and unemployable.'

She sighed. 'Where did it all go wrong, Jack?'

'Jesperson, obviously.'

'No, I mean before then. How did we end up making such a total cock-up? We had it all, didn't we?'

That much was true. They'd only been two of numerous hard-working detectives in AGI, their primary role to tackle medium-range drug-dealing across the Greater Manchester force area. But Jack's team had been particularly successful, their intel-led raids taking down a number of mid-level firms, seizing weapons and narcotics of considerable street value and securing lengthy jail terms for hundreds of Manchester gangsters.

Jack swilled his lager. 'All looked great on paper, babes. You can't beat being the toast of the Serious Crimes Division press office. But what they never tell the public is how crap your take-home is. I had my mortgage and child maintenance, you had your mum's care to worry about.'

'We should have put in for more overtime.'

He snorted again. 'No one logged more overtime than us. And every minute of it well spent. Which is more than you can say for a dozen other specialist teams I could mention.'

'Let's not go there, Jack.'

'Where?'

'Painting ourselves as misunderstood heroes. We weren't.'

There was no arguing with that, of course. Looking back on it, it was difficult to recall at which point they'd actually crossed over, but they'd both been struggling with their respective money problems for years before they started boosting their incomes by dipping into the proceeds of their busts. At the time it had seemed supremely clever, not to mention foolproof. Squirrel away a couple of packets of whichever illegal substance it happened to be, heroin, coke or speed, never declare it as part of the haul and sell it back to its original owners for half the price. It was an arrangement that worked for everyone. The losses were never such that they'd easily be noticed, the mobsters tolerated it as it meant they were able to recover some of their lost merchandise at less than the going rate, while Jack and Claudia could more comfortably cope with those horrendous debts.

'I know it looked bad . . .'

'It *was* bad,' she said.

'But we're not genuine criminals. We didn't enjoy what we did. We didn't plan it long-term. We were driven to it by unavoidable circumstances . . .'

They were both startled by a scornful chuckle. They spun around.

They hadn't noticed another drinker pull up a stool, close enough to overhear them.

'I've never met a corrupt cop yet,' he said, 'who'll one hundred per cent accept that he'd stopped being a solution to crime . . . and instead had become part of it.'

The guy turned to face them.

Jack wasn't sure what surprised him more. That this was the same tall, grey-haired man in the brown leather jacket who'd been watching from over the cemetery fence. Or that it was someone he now clearly recognised.

Because the word 'infamous' didn't even come close to describing Harry Wayland.

Five

'You look uncomfortable, Jack,' Wayland said. 'You got some idea that, any minute now, the press pack is going to jump out and start snapping us? And then tomorrow they're going to run a story that says: *Look at this . . . McGurn and Crayford caught in company with Harry Wayland. They were bent after all. What further proof do we need?* Well . . . newsflash, kids. They *don't* need any further proof. They know damn well you're bent.'

Wayland was nearly sixty with iron-grey unruly hair and thick sideburns. His once wolfish looks were leathery and seamed, battered both by age and considerable experience. But he'd taken off his leather jacket and underneath that was wearing a white T-shirt. His physique, while lean, was sinewy. He looked strong and fit.

'Just to be clear, Harry,' Jack replied, 'we weren't actually convicted of anything.'

'You used up your entire lifetime's supply of luck when that decision was reached. And you know it. The sole reason CPS didn't prosecute you is because the only witness they had was a drug-addled chemist called Ronald Jesperson, who'd been helping you check the quality of the gear but who still grassed you up as soon as he was facing other charges. But Jesperson was in such a state by then that putting someone like him on the witness stand would have been comedy value only.'

'Okay, we were lucky.' Claudia shrugged. 'Doesn't feel like it, I can tell you.'

'You don't need to tell me anything, Claudia. I know.'

They'd found a quiet corner for themselves in The Waterwheel's downstairs bar. Neither Jack nor Claudia had been personally acquainted with Harry Wayland, formerly DCI Wayland of the Major Incident Team, but there was no Greater Manchester Police officer, past or present, who didn't know about him.

It was Harry Wayland who'd led the enquiry that eventually brought Jimmy Cornwallis, aka 'the Dogman', to book. A self-styled urban guerrilla and infamous serial killer, Cornwallis, who chose his own nickname, inspired by his own 'dogged nature', was a shell-shocked ex-para with strong right-wing leanings, who on returning to Britain from the army, found it a crime-ridden mess, and undertook to clean things up by stalking and killing the prostitutes, pimps and drug-dealers infesting many of those north-west English towns he considered his home. A very dangerous individual indeed, he'd clocked up thirty victims, using a variety of crude weapons – knives, clubs, neck-wires – before being cornered by Wayland, who'd shot and killed him while he was resisting arrest.

However, despite Harry Wayland's high-level police skills, he was also corrupt. It later transpired that many of the murder enquiries he undertook – Wayland was regarded as a homicide expert – he diverted when it looked as though they were leading towards his underworld paymasters. This often resulted in the conviction and imprisonment of innocent men. They may have been criminals, undesirable specimens, but none were guilty of the murders for which they were jailed.

Wayland had taken down some of the worst of the worst, but he had also gone to great pains to jail the innocent, often for life, purely for money, the real killers left to roam the Earth with impunity.

Perhaps inevitably in Wayland's case, the Professional Standards people had fought hard for a jail term. Despite his previously stellar career, he served seven years of a ten-stretch. Just surviving that, as a former copper who'd sent villains down whether they deserved it or not, was impressive. And yet here he was now with a nonchalant air and philosophical attitude. He sat back, swilling from a bottle of lager.

'Society's changed gears these last few years,' he said. 'We're deep into a new age of pious intolerance. The eighties, which was when I started . . . fuck, feels like a lifetime ago. There are no likeable rogues anymore. We don't have loose cannons or Jack the Lads. All we have now are the thoroughly despicable, the low lifes who are beyond redemption, the out and out reprobates who need exposing, vilifying, rooting out. I'm talking coppers, of course, not normal folk. Look at a secretary the wrong way these days, and you're on a charge. Lay a finger on some shit-house who's been battering old ladies and you're out of a job.'

'There's no point trying to convince us we didn't do something wrong,' Claudia said. 'We know we did.'

Wayland glanced at Jack. 'She always this contrite?'

Jack shrugged. 'Doesn't pay to be anything else.'

'Doesn't pay to be remorseful either. Listen up, fellas . . .' Wayland leaned forward. No one else was earwigging, but he lowered his voice anyway. 'This shit's going to drag on. There's no respite for the likes of us, no forgiveness. And you know who's behind that. The metropolitan elite.' He spat the words, as if they were poisonous to him. 'That's right . . . those cosy middle-class wankers whose lifestyles we protected by taking so many villains off the street. None of that counts for anything now, you see. All the collars you felt, all the risks you ran, all that stress . . . all that falling out with your missus, every night, Jack, because each time you came home and your head wouldn't stop pounding after the teenage OD victims you'd pulled out of the drains that afternoon, or the little 'uns you'd found beaten to crap and dumped in a pond by their drunken mum's dog turd of a boyfriend, Claudia—'

'I thought you just said we were *part* of the problem?' Jack interrupted.

Wayland sat back again. 'You are. Or were. We all were. Doesn't mean *we* didn't get fucked over too.'

'Strangely enough,' Jack said, 'none of this is cheering us up.'

Wayland swilled more lager. 'I know something that might.'

He laid a business card on the table. It was beige and printed only on one side. It read:

DAMNED RANKERS

Underneath it, there was a telephone number.

'Damned Rankers?' Claudia said.

Wayland smiled. 'You think your world has ended. But I'm telling you it hasn't.'

Jack looked the card over. 'What is this?'

'In short . . . a support group. For discredited ex-officers.'

Claudia arched an eyebrow. 'Never heard of it.'

'Course you haven't. It's all done on the hush-hush. Imagine the fuss if the metro luvvies found out.'

'A support group?' she said. 'And you're part of it?'

He crooked a half-smile. 'I'm its official rep.'

'A support group for dirty cops?' Jack said.

'You look as if that's some kind of joke.'

'Isn't it?'

Wayland finished his bottle. 'Look, you did wrong. But you've paid for it. You've lost your careers, your reputations. Is it right you keep on paying for it just because the metro elite says you should?'

'Harry . . . cut the conspiracy crap,' Claudia said. 'We committed serious criminal offences. Like you said, it's a miracle we didn't do time.'

He eyed her. 'Perhaps if you *had* . . . like me and a few others, you wouldn't be so dismissive.'

'A few others? How many are there?'

'Enough.' He got to his feet, but a minute later, had returned to the table with a bottle of lager for himself and pints for Jack and Claudia.

'It's seriously called Damned Rankers?' Jack said.

'Catchy, eh?'

'Catchier than Bent Bastards, I suppose.'

'Or Damaged Goods,' Claudia said.

Wayland shook his head. 'You two are a right pair.' He glanced at Claudia, '*You're* acting like you'd voluntarily go inside,' then at Jack, 'and you're giving it the tough-guy routine, pretending you don't give a shit, which is a sure sign you do. It's bollocks. Your lives need to go on.' He tapped the card. 'And this is the key.'

Claudia picked up the card. 'What is Damned Rankers?'

'What I've told you. The circumstances you'll now have to live the rest of your lives in are not unique. But they are unusual. And no one knows about that better than the handful of others in the same place.'

'Who are these others?'

'Uh-uh. No private info until I know if you're in or out.'

Claudia put the card down. 'And if we're in, what benefits are there?'

'We offer friendship, advice, guidance. Sometimes a bit more.'

'A bit more?' Jack said.

'Well . . .' Wayland lowered his voice again. 'I imagine you two have got quite a bit stashed away. You didn't do the things you did for nothing. But you're not going to find decent jobs easily from now on, so at some point, that money will run out.'

'Financial assistance?'

'Maybe.' Wayland swilled from his bottle again. 'You know, most people I've approached have snatched my hand off by now. But seeing as you're playing hard to get, I'll humour you a little longer.' He looked thoughtful. 'Damned Rankers was the brainchild of a very private British-born billionaire, one of whose younger relatives was a student at uni down south. One night – no dates, sorry – she was attacked on her way home from a party, raped and strangled. The investigation made ground quickly. They closed in on a good suspect, a real weirdo who'd been causing nothing but trouble for women and girls in his neighbourhood for years, but who was reputed to have possession of a loaded pistol. A specialist firearms team moved in to arrest him in the early hours. The team leader went in first, called out a warning but almost immediately had cause to open fire. One shot went into the suspect's chest, the other into his head—'

'Damon Banks,' Jack interrupted.

Wayland shrugged. 'Maybe.'

'Give it a rest with the maybes, Harry. It was Damon Banks.' Jack glanced at Claudia. 'Tactical Firearms inspector, Sussex. He attempted to arrest Kenneth Renfrew, a Brighton resident who was also a registered sex offender and a suspect in three murders of local women. The arrest went haywire when Renfrew supposedly reached for a weapon on his bedside table and Banks shot him dead. In fact, alarmed by the intrusion, Renfrew had been reaching for the bedside light. A subsequent search of the property revealed strong evidence linking him to the murders, but no sign of a firearm, loaded or otherwise.'

Claudia nodded. 'I remember now . . . 2010-ish? Banks was charged with murder and convicted. He even lost his appeal, which infuriated the Federation and *Sun* and *Daily Mail* readers all over the country.' She looked at Wayland. 'I believe he's still in custody, still contesting his life sentence.'

'And let me guess,' Jack said, 'his campaign is now being bankrolled by this reclusive billionaire.'

Wayland shrugged. 'No stone will be left unturned in the quest to get Banks out. A highly decorated officer, who made one mistake . . . the only outcome of which was the removal from this world of a worthless toerag to whom females of any age were nothing more than playthings.'

'And now this billionaire, whose identity I suspect we could learn for ourselves if we dug deep enough . . .'

'I wouldn't count on that.'

'Whatever . . . he's now expanded his campaign to assisting other officers whom he considers have also got the shit end of the stick?'

'Harry . . .' Claudia shook her head. 'What does this new boss of yours not understand about *our* particular position? In contrast, for example, to Damon Banks?'

'In your case . . . and *mine*, there's no miscarriage of justice to be overturned. So . . . to us, all he offers is support. Friends help each other. There's nothing illegal about it. It's not even iffy. Look, he's doing a good thing. Getting ex-cops who went off the rails back into society, making them useful to their fellow men again.'

Jack and Claudia sat, pondering.

'Ultimately,' Jack said, 'it's all going to boil down to a bunch of us in hardbacked chairs in a draughty church hall, isn't it?'

Wayland smiled. 'Or first-class holiday accommodation in the Scilly Isles.'

Claudia looked puzzled. 'Come again?'

'Our next official get-together is mid-June. A week-long break, all costs and expenses paid, at Porth West, a new but exclusive resort on St Dunstan in the Isles of Scilly.'

'A holiday?' Jack said.

'You think you don't deserve one?'

Jack and Claudia glanced at each other. This was the last thing they'd expected. Jack shook his head. 'Sorry, Harry. Count me out.'

Wayland shrugged again. 'Up to you, but this could be the biggest miscalculation you've made since putting your life and career in the hands of Ronald Jesperson.' He turned to Claudia. 'How about you?'

'I'll be honest . . .' She flushed a little. 'I was thinking of starting again. Moving away.'

'We can help with that. The guy in charge has limitless funds. We can help you sort your mortgage out, get a new job, open a new bank account. All that stuff.'

'It's tempting. I won't deny it. But I don't know, Harry . . . I just want to be through with all this. Put it behind me.'

'You don't want any connection to your old life?'

'Correct.'

'We can arrange that too. We can sort a name change for you . . . hell, if it comes to it, we even know a few good plastic surgeons who'll give you a discount.'

'I thought this wasn't something iffy,' Jack cut in.

Wayland eyed him with irritation. 'It isn't. Jack, will you get it into your head, the guy who's paying for this thing is worth more than everyone else you know put together, times five thousand. You don't reach that level of economic superiority if you don't know how to play a few angles. But that doesn't mean you're a crim. Quite the opposite. You make the system work, you don't try and buck it. But listen, it's up to you.' He emptied his bottle and stood up.

'Where do we get in touch with you if we change our minds?' Claudia said.

'You've got the card.' He sidled round the table. 'But don't leave it long. That number will change.'

'Why?' Jack asked.

'Try using your noggin. The new puritans and their virtue-signalling mates in the media find out about this, it'll be the kind of coverage our benefactor doesn't need.'

'Perhaps *we* should sell them to the press?' Jack said, after Wayland had left. 'Our last big payday.'

Claudia looked round, accusation in her face. 'Why would you want to do that?'

'Come on, Claudi.' He fingered the card. 'This thing's got dodgy written all over it.'

She jumped to her feet. 'Well, *you* ought to know.'

'Wait up, what's the matter?'

She was halfway to the bar, but now came back. 'You're really going to turn your nose up at the one chance we might get to live something approaching a normal life again?'

'How will this give us a normal life? A new social circle, maybe, the odd interest-free loan.'

'Jesus, Jack! Even that'd be better than what we're facing now.'

'Claudia, you're your own person,' he said when she returned with fresh drinks. He slid the card towards her. 'You must do what you think's best. But one thing I don't reckon either of us needs at this moment is a week in the Isles of Scilly.'

She looked at him. 'Do you know anything about the Isles of Scilly?'

'Well, I mean . . . they're . . .'

'They're supposed to be really nice.'

'And is *nice* what we need?'

'Well, if *not nice* is what you need . . . do nothing. Stick around here.' Sulky again, she sank some lager. 'And suck it up.'

Six

It was just before ten and those still present at the wake in The Waterwheel were mostly the worse for wear. And it wasn't pleasant.

Claudia stood in the porch alongside her sister to say goodbye to all those on their way home. Not knowing how to react, many decided to blank her. She responded by blanking them back. But one or two caustic comments were made.

'Look at you . . . like butter wouldn't melt.'

'To think how proud we all were of you.'

'You know our Maggie's eldest girl died from an overdose?'

'No one's surprised, Claudia. We all thought it a bit weird that you got into the cops. You're a slip of a lass. You wouldn't know one end of a truncheon from the other. Unless it's the end where the batteries go, eh?'

She replied to that last one by calling the loutish younger nephew of one of her maiden aunts 'a fucking dickhead!' and told him to step outside where she'd show him 'the end of the pavement'. At which point, Jack steered her back into the bar. Minutes later, Judy came in and reiterated that they were a total disgrace. She never wanted to see either of them again and hoped they'd both get what was due to them.

'You see?' Claudia slurred, as she and Jack traipsed back through the town centre. 'See now why I want to disappear to the other end of the country?'

'You don't need to go that far,' he replied. 'Just shut them out. Shouldn't be hard. I mean, no disrespect to your family, Claudi, but if half of that lot had a brain cell, it'd top itself through sheer loneliness.'

'I've got to get away from here, Jack. Everything about this place reminds me, you know.'

They trudged on, the pub and bar district falling behind them. There were few pedestrians around now, and fewer cars, the only sound the fast clicking of Claudia's heels.

'I'm thinking of ringing the number on that card,' she said.

He shrugged. 'Your call.'

'And what will you do?'

'I don't know. I was seventeen years a cop. There's nothing else I want to do even if I could.'

'If you're working round to talking about doing yourself in again, I'm not buying.'

He'd alluded to this one time only, several weeks earlier, while muttering that he finally understood why certain folk considered ending it all a viable option.

'I wasn't totally serious about that.'

'You're not forty yet. There are loads of things you could do.'

'I'll find something, don't worry. But it'll be at a time and place of my own choosing.'

'Your problem, Jack, is you were always a control freak . . . always had to be in charge of everything.'

He was determined not to get vexed with her. She'd had a rough day, she was drunk, plus she was the only friend he had left. 'You never objected to my management style back in the day.'

Claudia became thoughtful as she wobbled along. 'You took *me* into your confidence more than anyone else. So, maybe I didn't have reason to . . . maybe that's where it all went wrong.'

'There was only you I ever trusted.'

'Pity. Because you had a good team under you.'

He snorted. 'Dropped us right in it when the time came, didn't they?'

'They didn't exactly drop us in it.'

Jack didn't reply. It was difficult not to harbour some level of resentment against their former colleagues, but what Claudia said was essentially true. Despite Ronald Jesperson's statement, there'd been no hard proof against either of them, though examination of their financial records had revealed anomalies – increased earnings failing to marry up with official salaries, overtime, and so forth – and when pressure was put on the rest of his team, a couple of younger members had cracked and admitted that drug hauls seized during raids always seemed lighter when being logged into evidence than they'd appeared to be on seizure. It hadn't been sufficient for the CPS to open full proceedings, but it had been more than enough for the pair of them to be dragged in front of a misconduct hearing.

'They could have been more vocal in their suspicions than they were,' Claudia added.

'Why mention any suspicions at all?'

'Because they didn't want to go down themselves, did they? They hadn't done anything wrong and had careers to think about. You surely don't blame them?'

Jack grunted. 'Look . . . I know I'm the one who fouled up.'

'Wasn't just you.'

'That's kind, but if it hadn't been for me, you'd still be on a fast track to the top floor. Look, I know I act like some kind of loner who can tough anything out . . . But . . .'

At which moment, with a screech of tyres, a silver-grey Saab veered across the road towards them – for half a second, they were rabbits in headlights – before mounting the kerb and blocking further access along the pavement.

The Saab's two front doors clattered open, and Charlie Quincannon and Lennie Hargreaves emerged, the former grinning as he stood facing them, the latter circling round the vehicle on to the pavement, cutting off any potential backward flight. Both wore dark waterproofs, zipped up tight, and dark gloves. A spanner slid into view from Charlie Quincannon's left sleeve. Hargreaves meanwhile hefted a ball bat to his shoulder.

Jack and Claudia backed towards the nearest shopfront.

'How you doing, piglets?' Hargreaves shouted. 'Or should that be ex-piglets?'

'Bacon sarnies, I'd say,' Charlie chuckled.

Sweat beaded on Jack's brow as he risked a glance behind them. There was a recessed doorway, but no escape. The shop was closed and locked, the recess grilled off.

He glanced back. 'Take it easy, eh?'

'Take it easy?' Charlie smacked the spanner into his gloved hand.

'Not got your shotgun with you?' Hargreaves said. 'That's a shame.'

The shop window now stood at their backs, preventing any further retreat.

Oddly though, despite there only being three or four yards between them, it now became a stand-off rather than the blitz assault Jack had expected.

'Told you we'd catch up with you,' Charlie said.

'You think you'll get away with this?' Jack replied.

'Let me see . . . two ex-coppers, bent as fuck, who no one likes anymore, with no influence whatsoever. And then us two . . .'

'Who no one likes either,' Claudia said.

Charlie gave her a grouchy look. 'Maybe, but we've still got lots of influence. Besides, we go to jail, so what? Nice little holiday with a few of our mates.'

'You two are nobodies,' she retorted, drawing more courage from her semi-drunkenness. 'Gofers at best. You don't even qualify as muscle . . .'

'Easy, eh?' Jack murmured.

'All that may be true,' another voice said. 'But it's not just *them* you're dealing with.'

A third party had climbed from the Saab's back seat. He was a great sagging block of a man, an ungainly mass squashed into a three-piece suit. His head was round and hairless, a pair of circular metal-framed glasses perched on his stubby nose.

'Tell you what, though . . .' He ambled on to the pavement, hands in his trouser pockets. 'You've got a mouth on you, girl. I was thinking of letting you walk . . . But now I've changed my mind.'

'We're civies now, Pete,' Jack said.

The new guy looked startled. 'So, you just get a pass?'

'Look . . . it was a game we all played. You knew the rules.'

'The problem is *you* didn't play by them.'

'I think you're just embarrassed because your firm's a joke,' Claudia said. 'Because we just dismantled you instead of doing business with you.'

'Christ's sake, Claudi!' Jack hissed. Most likely it was the combo of booze and everything else bad that had happened to her in recent months. But hell, why stir the pot?

Peter Quincannon eyed her long and hard. 'You didn't get this one as well trained as you should have, ex-DI McGurn. She's gonna cop it now. Alongside you.'

'Dirty Peter!' someone else said, sounding delighted. 'How the hell are you?'

All five of them turned, surprised, as Harry Wayland stepped out from the unlit alley alongside the shop, phone held upright. 'Still coming the big boss, Pete? Talking like you're Crowley's own Bugsy Siegel?'

Peter Quincannon regarded him with confusion, then recognition, then distaste. 'Three in one go. Fuck me. Must be my lucky day.'

'Or maybe not.' Wayland indicated his phone. 'I've been filming you for the last two minutes. Caught every word you and your goons have just said. I've even looped in a couple of mates I've still got in the job. So, if anything happens to these two people, or me – not just tonight, but basically ever again – they'll know exactly whose door to knock on.'

Peter Quincannon snorted with amusement, but it didn't reach his myopic little eyes. 'You think it's that simple?'

'I know it is.' Harry strode up to them, still filming. 'I also know the only way you're going to get your lard-arse out of this one is to take it far from here. Very far. Right now. And take your comic relief with you.'

Charlie Quincannon looked almost too startled to respond. 'You don't . . . you don't talk to us like that.'

'Talk to who? *Him?*' Wayland pointed at the older Quincannon. '*Dirty* Peter?'

'All right, Wayland!' the older gangster warned.

'Bet you've never heard about the stuff he got up to when he was younger, eh?' Wayland laughed. He tapped his phone. 'We're still on the live feed, by the way.'

'I said *ENOUGH!*' Peter Quincannon barked.

Harry's smile faded. 'In that case, pack up your circus and go home.' His voice was quieter, softer, but with an undercurrent of edged steel. 'There's nothing for you here, Pete . . . and there never will be.'

The stand-off dragged on for several taut seconds, the gangster trembling with impotent rage. 'Get in the car,' he finally told his underlings.

'Fuck's sake, Dad!' Charlie complained.

'Get in the fucking car! And *you*!' The gangland patriarch rounded on Hargreaves. 'Both you fucks, move it! *NOW!*'

He glared at the three ex-cops one more time, before climbing in himself, the vehicle rocketing out on to the road, tyres smoking as it pulled a fast three-point and tore away.

Slowly, the trio on the pavement let out their breaths.

'You've still got mates in the job?' Claudia asked.

'Like hell.' Wayland showed them his phone. It wasn't even recording. 'But I've still got those two most crucial police skills of all. Bullshit and bluster.'

'God's sake, Harry!' Jack said. 'What the hell are you playing at?'

Wayland eyed him. 'I think the words you're looking for, Jack, are thanks very much for saving our undeserving backsides from a right royal kicking.'

'Why are you following us round?'

'Well, no one else had your backs. Clearly.'

'You knew we were in trouble?' Claudia asked.

Wayland gave her a pitying stare. 'Really must have lost your edge if *you* didn't.' He turned to Jack. '*You* knew, didn't you?'

Jack yanked at his collar. 'Bollocks . . . I don't know.'

'What're we talking about?' Claudia glanced from one to the other.

'Those two clowns,' Jack admitted. 'Charlie Quincannon and Lennie Hargreaves. They had a go at me last night.'

Her eyebrows lifted. 'And you never mentioned it?'

'Don't worry about it,' Wayland cut in. 'They won't be coming back. Dirty Peter's lucky he only got a year when you busted his firm. He won't do anything else that might screw his life over.'

'He was pretty pissed off about their Paddy,' Jack said.

'Yeah, but not so much that he didn't let him take the full rap. Besides, he's got sons all over the north-west. Most from underage mums, I'm guessing.'

'How did you know they came to visit me last night?'

Wayland shrugged. 'Didn't. Saw them obbing the funeral today. They were keeping their distance, though not so much that I didn't spot them straight off.'

'Well, *I'm* grateful even if Jack isn't,' Claudia said.

Wayland zipped his top. 'All part of the service.'

'We haven't signed up for any service,' Jack replied.

'Bet you're thinking about it now, though, eh? Look . . . this is a perfect example of what Damned Rankers can offer. All alone, we don't have a hope. But together, we can go places.'

'You on some kind of bonus for everyone you recruit?' Claudia wondered.

Wayland laughed. 'The one bonus I get is helping out people in the same predicament as me. But listen . . . don't take my word for it. Take our benefactor's.'

Jack frowned. 'This mystery billionaire?'

'Since we met in the bar earlier, I've learned that he's going to make a personal appearance. On St Dunstan, no less.'

'This guy's actually going to be there?' Jack said.

'Wants to get to know you all personally. See for himself what's needed to help you out.'

Jack and Claudia exchanged bewildered glances. This whole thing was happening so fast. Could it be that somewhere in this world that hated them they might have a friend after all? A powerful friend.

Wayland grinned. 'You think you've got no one left in your corner, kids. But you are so, so wrong.'

Seven

'Well, this was always going to be the most uncomfortable part of the week,' the woman in the puffer jacket and jeans said. 'So, let's get it over with. I'm Cheryl Baxter.'

Jack and Claudia introduced themselves in return, shaking her hand, though it felt awkward. But at least she'd come over to them. The three other people waiting on the small stone quayside at Porth Conger were keeping themselves to themselves. Cheryl Baxter was probably in her late forties. Her short, light-blonde hair fell into natural ringlets; she was bright-eyed, pert-nosed and full-lipped. She'd attempted to be pleasant, but hadn't given much away.

In the past whenever Jack and Claudia had met cops they didn't know, at a Federation bash or whatever, they could ask them which force they hailed from, but that was a no-no today. Better to let these people volunteer any personal information in their own time.

However, Jack couldn't help wondering about Cheryl Baxter, who had now crossed back over the quay and was speaking with one of the others, a young girl of Indian heritage. From Baxter's accent, he suspected she hailed from a Yorkshire force. But wherever it was, she didn't seem the type to have got up to no good. There was something too wholesome about her.

'Penny for your thoughts?' Claudia asked quietly.

He nudged at his travel bag with his foot, to ensure it was still close (though there was nobody around to steal it). 'Can't believe you got me here.'

'*I* didn't get you here. It was the promise of meeting our new benefactor.'

'What are we really expecting?'

'A million quid each.'

He arched an eyebrow. 'Yeah, right.'

'I'm joking.'

'You don't say.'

She got huffy. 'If nothing else, we're going on holiday. You're allowed to smile.'

'Going on holiday.' He shook his head. 'Like this whole deal isn't weird enough.'

With a hefty *clank*, the boat waiting at the dock lowered its gangway. There was a gate fixed at the end, so it wasn't time to board just yet, but a surly-looking crewman was visible on deck, preparing everything. The other passengers, Cheryl Baxter among them, grabbed their luggage and shuffled towards it.

'I mean, how will it look,' Jack said in a low voice, 'if we do end up monetising this situation?'

'Monetising?'

'Making a bob or two. From being corrupt police officers.'

'You mean a bob or two more than we did when we actually *were* corrupt police officers?'

Now the gate had been lifted and the gangway opened. It was only narrow and one by one their fellow travellers were balancing their way up it.

'Nobody's seriously thinking about monetising anything,' Claudia said. 'This guy just wants to help us out.'

She picked her pack up, but Jack hung back.

'Damon Banks shot and killed a sex murderer,' he said. 'Which right-thinking member of society wouldn't have tacitly approved? But *we* were on the take. How are these things similar?'

She looked frustrated. And cross. 'We've got ourselves a supporter. That's all you need to know. Now, if you're not going to enjoy yourself, fine. But don't throw a wet blanket on it for me.' She headed to the gangplank. With some degree of reluctance, Jack followed.

◆ ◆ ◆

The trip from St Agnes to St Dunstan had a holiday atmosphere. The sky a cloudless blue, the sea calm. The midsummer sun rode high, but there was a stiff Atlantic breeze, so they were glad of their jumpers and waterproofs.

It was a fifty-minute voyage, but this wasn't the luxury superyacht they'd half expected. It was a private charter, paid for in advance, but it had the appearance of a converted fishing boat, its storm-battered hull and the metal barrier along its gunwales in need of a paint job. The skipper and his single crewman, unsavoury individuals, installed themselves in the pilot's cabin at the vessel's stern and didn't reappear for the remainder of the journey. The rest of the main deck, about fifty or sixty square feet in total, was open to the elements, and any other bits of equipment, its antennae or boom mast, or any additional housing that had once been there, had long gone, replaced by passenger benches, some located around the bulwarks, some in the middle, facing frontward.

That said, it was spacious enough with only the six of them on board, excluding the crew.

Jack and Claudia had settled themselves on the portside bench when Cheryl Baxter came over with the young Indian girl, whose name was Varada Rathour. She seemed too mousy and petite to have been a serving police officer, at least for long enough to fall into the sort of bad habits that had landed everyone else here. She was in her early twenties, pretty, with smooth schoolgirl features, dark eyes and shoulder-length black hair currently being tossed in the sea breeze.

No doubt Cheryl Baxter had meant well when she'd brought her over, but the poor girl seemed embarrassed.

Glad it's not just me, Jack thought.

All they had in common with these people were the extreme betrayals of trust they were each responsible for. Some kind of kinship, that was.

'Been to the Scilly Isles before, Varada?' Claudia asked.

'I've never even been to Cornwall before.'

'Are we still in Cornwall?' Jack said.

'The Duchy of Cornwall,' Cheryl Baxter replied.

'There's not much on the islands themselves,' Claudia said. 'Mainly tourists. I've been checking it out on YouTube. But in summer they're supposed to be beautiful.'

After that, the stilted conversation dried up.

Sod it, Jack thought. They were going to have to break the ice at some point.

'What force were you with, Varada?' he asked.

'Oh . . . *oh*!' Her eyes widened. 'I wasn't a police officer.'

'You weren't?' he replied, unsurprised.

'I was civilian staff . . . Operational Support. TacOps, as we called it.'

'That's Lancashire, isn't it?' Claudia said.

'Yes, Lancashire Constabulary.' Rathour looked apologetic. 'That's where I *was*. I'm not there now, obviously.'

Jack glanced along the bench to Cheryl Baxter, who'd stiffened a little at the turn in the conversation. 'West Yorkshire,' she said curtly.

'We were GMP,' he replied.

'All northern forces,' Claudia observed.

Wasn't it a little odd that everyone they'd met so far came from the same region?

'I don't think *he* was.' Baxter nodded over to the starboard gunwale, where one of the other passengers stood alone. 'I tried to speak to him earlier, but he'd only mutter. I think his name is Jonas Pugh.'

Pugh was a nervous, twitchy sort in his mid-fifties with an unruly mop of red-grey hair and a thick matching moustache. He stood by the barrier, swigging from a hip flask, seemingly unconcerned whether anyone noticed.

'Did he say where he was from?' Claudia asked.

'No, but he has a slight Welsh accent.' Baxter nodded to where the final other passenger was seated alone. 'I don't know about him. We exchanged pleasantries but that's about all.'

Sensing that he was under discussion, this second object of interest glanced around, made eye contact and with a bland smile, stood up and ambled over.

'Sorry, I've not introduced myself.' He offered his hand. 'Alan Rothermere.'

Jack was the last to shake with him. 'Jack McGurn.'

Rothermere nodded and smiled again.

There was something about this chap that put Jack on guard. It was that copper's sixth sense. Sometimes you just knew when you were in the presence of a bad egg, and yet there was nothing especially unlikeable about Alan Rothermere. He was somewhere in his late forties, with fair hair, greying around the edges. About five-nine and chubby, he wore a gabardine overcoat over a V-necked sweater and a shirt and tie. Everything about him was prim and proper.

He didn't stay to make small talk but went back to his seat, dug into his holdall, extracted a paperback and commenced reading.

It bemused Jack that he'd taken such an immediate dislike to the guy. Was it because he knew that Rothermere could only be here because he'd done something wrong? It was the same with everyone else on the boat.

He stole another glance at Pugh, who was drinking again. Was *that* the problem in his case? Pugh glanced casually over and Jack averted his gaze.

What about Cheryl Baxter? Varada Rathour? Jack checked Rothermere out again, furtively. The guy continued reading, smiling to himself. He looked as innocent as they came. Your regular Mr Average. An inoffensive, upstanding citizen.

Which again, he obviously wasn't.

Eight

'Why does that phrase seem familiar?' Jack said.

They stared across the harbour at the large, broad-fronted pub. It was built from whitewashed stone, its woodwork painted green, and along the boarding above the front door, in ornate gold lettering, were the words:

THE SALMON OF KNOWLEDGE

'Was a character in that horror film, *The Wicker Man*,' Harry Wayland replied. 'This guy dressed himself up in a fish costume for the village festival. Bit of a rum character. Well, they all were, weren't they?'

'Hang on,' Jack said. 'Didn't that film finish up with a copper getting burned in a ritual sacrifice?'

'He was a serving cop,' Wayland said, grinning. 'Not an ex-cop. And that was a key plot point, you see. He went to that island with the power of a king. You haven't got that anymore, so you're safe.' He turned to Claudia. 'Good journey?'

'Long one,' she replied. 'An eight-hour train ride to Penzance, then a boat to St Mary's, then a boat to St Agnes, then a boat here.'

'All booked for you, though. All paid for by our benefactor.'

She couldn't deny that all this had made it easier, their tickets posted to their home addresses. All they'd had to do was sit back and enjoy the journey. And now that they were here, it looked as if it might have been worth it.

The island had seemed like any other as they approached. Except for Porth West, it was uninhabited, which always wove a slight air of mystery about a place. The June sunshine and the cerulean seascape added to its photogenic allure, and now that they'd docked, the quaint harbour was charming. Marked near its entrance by a single buoy, it was perhaps two hundred yards across, horseshoe-shaped and hemmed in by the stone quay on its south side, where they now stood, and a long timber jetty on the north. A semi-circle of fishermen's cottages partly enclosed it, also whitewashed, along with a couple of shops. Some were terraced, others separated by narrow, cobbled alleyways. Apparently, there were no roads in Porth West, only footways. In fact, there were no roads anywhere on the island, though a paved esplanade occupied the harbour's landward side, The Salmon of Knowledge situated on the other side of this, facing out to sea.

With its hanging nets, mooring posts and the like, it was the picture-postcard Cornish experience, though aside from the ferry, they could see no other boats there. Porth West was actually a new facility, designed to look *old world* when it was almost entirely fake.

Not that this detracted from it.

The waters in the harbour lay crystal-clear, schools of fish zigzagging over a white sand bottom. Apparently, the sea encircling the Scillies was famously clean owing to the islands lacking any natural water sources, which meant no rivers of any significance depositing silt around their coastlines. Inland meanwhile, visible beyond the rooftops, the land rose upward. There was nothing you'd call a mountain on St Dunstan, but its verdant, wooded heathland was leafy and green, splashed gold with sunlight.

Two palm trees were visible over the top of the cottages opposite, reminding Jack that the Isles of Scilly were so deep in the Gulf Stream that it wasn't unusual for such fragments of exotica as coconuts to wash up on the beaches.

Wayland had been conversing with a white-bearded Cornishman wearing a button-up seaman's jacket and a skipper's cap, who'd already been introduced as Ted Pasco, the Porth West harbourmaster. The elderly chap had now finished his paperwork with the captain of the ferry and was trudging up behind.

'Must be honest,' Wayland said to Jack. 'Didn't think we were going to get *you* here.'

Jack shrugged. 'Free holiday, isn't it?'

'You've changed your tune.'

'I'd like to say I made him see sense,' Claudia chipped in.

They had discussed it repeatedly, Claudia taking the position that they had nothing to lose, Jack unable to counter that assertion, and increasingly wondering why he was even trying.

'The thought of meeting your rich mate appeals to me,' Jack said.

'I don't know him,' Wayland said.

'He must know *you*, though. And he must know *us*. And he won't have heard anything good.'

'He'll have heard plenty good,' Wayland replied. 'He has all the intel he needs. You two, me, everyone on this island . . . We all did our bit in the war on crime before things went wrong for us. *More* than our bit. And this guy, he fucking hates crims.'

They rounded the harbour's southern corner and were now on the esplanade, where the other passengers milled about uncertainly.

Wayland raised his voice. 'Okay, folks! Here we are. Porth West. You're at liberty to do anything you want, of course. But let me at least give you a rough idea of what's what. You're seeing lots of pretty cottages and shops. You might be a bit bemused by that, seeing as you've been advised there is no resident population on St Dunstan, apart from the staff of course. Well, once the shops are open, they'll sell all the usual trinkets you get in tourist towns, while the cottages will be used as higher-priced accommodation. But most of them are not finished yet. Still need their interiors doing, not even hooked up to the generators. So, they're not open at present. But the pub and the hotel, The Culraven Arms, about five minutes' walk from here, are both fully functioning, so that's where you'll all be put up.

'Unfortunately, the forecast isn't great. We've got stormy weather Monday through till Wednesday, but a bit of rain shouldn't stop you taking advantage of the Quad Track, which speaks for itself. It's for quad biking and circles the entire island and is free to use. If you fancy a bit of hill trekking you can stride out now if it suits you. Near enough all of St Dunstan exists in its natural state, so it won't be like many other woodlands you've explored in the UK. To start with, I've never been anywhere else as peaceful as this . . .'

That much appeared to be true. Since the ferry had cut its engines, the only things they could hear were the gulls and the gentle lapping of waves on the harbour pilings.

'The main thing,' Wayland said, 'is avail yourselves of the luxurious accommodation and the masses of drink and food that'll be provided, all of it gratis. The first boatload of guests arrived earlier today, and they're already doing that, trust me. So, why don't you catch them up?'

'What about the guy we have to thank for all this?' Alan Rothermere asked. 'When does he arrive?'

The others waited with interest for an answer, but Wayland shrugged. 'I'm reliably informed he's definitely going to show, but that's all I know. Now, I'll just nip up to the hotel to find out who's staying where. Why not pop into the boozer in the meantime? It's all free. We'll reconvene there in half an hour's time anyway, so I can allocate your rooms.'

'All seems a bit disorganised,' Jack said, as they humped their bags to their shoulders and strolled along the esplanade.

'What's there to organise?' Claudia asked.

He eyed the closed doors and curtained windows belonging to the shops and cottages. 'There don't seem to be many staff around.'

'There's Pasco.'

'Well, I suppose there'd *have* to be a harbourmaster.'

'There must be people working in the pub and the hotel.' She grabbed his arm. 'So let's find out.'

As he entered The Salmon of Knowledge, Jack had a moment of déjà vu. Right back to his earliest days in the job, when he was a young uniform called to incidents on Friday and Saturday nights. It didn't matter how cute the interior was with its low beams and crooked timber pillars, its horse brasses, hanging tankards, huge real-flame gas fire, and wall-mounted nautical instruments, all he heard was the braying laughter, the drunken shouting.

Two men at opposite ends of a pool table were loudly deriding each other.

'You fucking distracted me!' the younger one said.

'As if,' the older one replied.

'Chalking your cue while I was lining up my shot. You always used to do that.'

'You never said anything back then.'

'You fucking outranked me back then.'

'I fucking outrank you now, you twat.' The older one pushed a pair of thick-rimmed glasses back up his sweat-greased nose. 'Always did, always will.'

'I should have known,' Jack said under his breath.

Ex-Detective Superintendent Ray Donaldson leaned on his cue, looking amused. 'Fuck me sideways. Machine Gun Jack McGurn. So, the real gangsters are finally arriving.'

He had to be in his sixties, but Donaldson was every inch the yob he'd always been. He was wearing a polo shirt and cargo pants rather than the scruffy suit that had become his trademark during his Robbery Squad days, but his ale gut still swung over his belt buckle, the iron-grey hair was still brushed back wetly, long, straggling and yellowing at its ends. His face remained a map of the inner Manchester he'd once terrorised: grey, bleak, hard. The younger one, ex-Detective Sergeant Declan O'Hare, was Donaldson's enforcer back when they'd ruled the roost. Only in his thirties, he still resembled the former heavyweight prizefighter he'd once been. Six-foot-six and broad as a bullock, he had deep-set eyes, a dented nose and a dense black beard and moustache.

Claudia didn't know them personally, but she knew of them. How could she not? GMP's finest turned into two of its very worst.

'Well, well.' Donaldson eyed her brazenly. 'She's a nifty little piece. Well done, Machine Gun. Done all right for yourself there.'

'Excuse me,' Claudia replied. '*She* happens to be an actual person.'

Donaldson switched his attention back to Jack. 'This'll be the party to end all fucking parties,' he said, though from the range of empties on the tabletops around them, it looked as though the party had begun some time ago.

'What you standing there for like a gormless prick?' Declan O'Hare shouted. 'It's lager and shots for the whole rest of the fucking week. Get 'em in.'

Jack and Claudia approached the bar in the sort of numb, careful, overly sober fashion you tend to adopt when you've just had a brutal reality check.

Claudia sighed. 'Maybe this wasn't the best idea after all.'

Nine

'I made it very clear,' Alan Rothermere said loudly, 'that I would not be attending if those two creatures were going to be here as well.'

Harry Wayland sat on a bar stool in The Salmon, a bottle of lager in hand. 'I'm a guest,' he said, 'just like you. I have no control over who's invited.'

The rest of the guests were also present, including Gabby Milburn, a tall, athletic black woman in jeans and a T-shirt, and Sally Jakeman, a slim, attractive white woman in a summer dress. They had all gathered in the pub taproom to be allocated their accommodation, but had walked into an argument. The only two who seemed relaxed were Donaldson and O'Hare, who watched from the pool table.

'Christ's sake, Wayland!' Rothermere had gone pink. 'If I'd known they were going to be here, I wouldn't have come.'

'Nonce,' Ray Donaldson chuckled.

'You hear that!' Rothermere pointed at him.

'He called you a nonce because you *are* a nonce,' Declan O'Hare added. 'Still denying it?'

'I want you to call that boatman back. I'm leaving.'

'Don't be hasty, Alan,' Cheryl Baxter put in.

'Stay out of this, if you don't mind. Listen, Wayland . . . those two ruined my career.'

'You ruined your own career, mate,' Donaldson said, 'when you downloaded compromising footage of underage boys.'

Rothermere glared at him. 'You *know* that material was planted. And you *know* who was behind it, if you weren't behind it yourselves.'

'Prove it.'

'I don't need to prove it because everyone already knows that you two are out-and-out villains!'

'We're all villains in here, Alan,' Jack said.

Rothermere stared at him. 'Except me. I was *framed*.'

'If you're so innocent, why did you even come?' O'Hare wondered, sidling to the bar. 'No one forced you.'

'Because I want help.' Rothermere turned from one to the other. 'I want to restore my reputation and I thought maybe our so-called benefactor could play a part.'

Donaldson snickered. 'Pretty ironic, I'll admit. Me and Dekko are only here because ex-Inspector Rothermere . . . *uniform* inspector, by the way, another of these clock-watching bureaucrats who now infest the job, another middle-class twat who hadn't locked anyone up for four or five years, blew the whistle on us.'

'You were selling intel to criminals,' Rothermere stated.

'And we don't deny it. And we got suitably punished. Either way, our benefactor's got a sense of humour, hasn't he, bringing us here with you?'

'You're very glib about it, Donaldson, considering some of your grasses disappeared without trace. Almost certainly because you two named names.'

Donaldson smirked. 'And you're very cocky for someone who got caught noncing.'

'I'll prove you and your mates fitted me up. I'll make it my life's work—'

'All right, enough!' Wayland placed his bottle on the bar top and got down from his stool.

Rothermere rounded on him. 'Are you going to call that boatman back?'

'That boatman has a timetable to keep,' Wayland said. 'We're a long way out in case you hadn't noticed. Six miles from St Agnes, the nearest island, and thirty-five miles from the mainland. All of it across open sea.'

'He must be coming back soon?'

'The end of the week. When he's been booked to take you all home.'

'For Christ's sake! Can't you at least ask?'

'If only I could.'

'There's no phone signal on St Dunstan, Alan,' Cheryl Baxter tried to explain.

'And no Wi-Fi,' Donaldson chuckled.

'So we're just marooned here?'

'It's only a week,' Gabby Milburn said.

'A week's a long time in company like this!'

'Look,' Wayland said. 'Maybe I can speak to Pasco, the harbourmaster. He's got a marine VHF radio in his cottage. He can ask on your behalf. But I can't promise anything.'

'He's already on a promise,' O'Hare laughed, handing Donaldson a fresh pint, along with a shot of bourbon. 'Some rent boy back in Manchester.'

'I said enough of that bollocks!' Wayland shouted.

O'Hare snorted, plunging his face into the froth of his brimming pint.

'Just get him to call someone,' Rothermere said. 'Because this is a snake pit, and I want no further part in it . . .'

'Hey, whoa.' Wayland eyed him coolly. 'As things stand, you got convicted, you got sacked, and you did time. Until proven otherwise, you're no better than the rest of us.'

'What?' Jonas Pugh spluttered through his own glass of Scotch. It was the first time he'd spoken, but he suddenly seemed agitated. 'He's a damn sight worse. Unless you're saying there're other kiddie-fiddlers here.'

Donaldson guffawed. 'Least everyone knows me and Dekko aren't.'

An explosion of voices followed, everyone expressing strong denials. Rothermere glanced around at them like a hunted man.

'Okay, okay!' Wayland raised his hands. 'I thought it might come to this. I hoped it wouldn't, but I had a feeling. So, let's get on with it, clear the air.' He nodded at Rothermere. 'You all know what *he* did. *Allegedly.*' Then at Donaldson and O'Hare. 'You all know what these two did. You all know what *I* did – it was well publicised. So, let's hear from the rest of you. Just so there's no further confusion.'

Wary glances were cast at the barmaid. Apparently, her name was Ledina, and she was one of three Albanian women, the other two her mother and sister, who comprised the bulk of the staff at Porth West. She was pretty, with long, black hair, and wore a colourful cheesecloth top. But she returned their stares blankly.

'Ledina doesn't speak English,' Wayland explained. 'Just enough to get by serving beer and cooking breakfasts. So, let's not pretend her presence is a problem.' He threw a sideways glance at Pugh. 'Want to start the ball rolling, Jonas?'

Pugh looked startled. He lowered his glass, his moustache sodden with whisky.

'Might as well,' Jack said. 'Be in your best interests.'

'My best bloody interests?' Pugh looked even more surprised.

'Before Mr Pugh starts,' Wayland said, 'you should all know that he's a rarity among us. Despite originating from the Valleys, he's formerly of Essex Police. Which means he's the only one here who didn't work up north. Why that's the case, I don't know. I didn't choose the guest list. Maybe he can enlighten us? Floor's yours, pal.'

'I . . .' Pugh looked from one to the other, taking another hard swallow of spirit. 'I don't bloody know if I want to!' The expectant silence lingered. 'All right, then . . . all bloody right!' Pugh's face had reddened to almost match his hair. 'Jonas Pugh, Essex Police. Detective Inspector. CSI. I . . . well, I had debts, you see . . . and—'

'Didn't we all,' Donaldson interrupted. 'Get to the juicy bit.'

Pugh glared at him. 'I misused my position to . . . well . . . I contaminated crime scenes, see. Not all the time, you understand, but . . .'

'When it suited your paymasters?' Milburn said. 'When they wanted you to direct an investigation somewhere else?'

Pugh shrugged.

'Sneaky.' O'Hare sounded impressed.

'Clever too,' Donaldson said.

'I'm not proud of it,' Pugh admitted.

'Good thing, too, I'd say,' Sally Jakeman said.

'Would you?' Wayland looked at her. 'How virtuous of you. So, what's your story, Miss Jakeman?'

She was good-looking in a conventional way: bright green eyes, a wild array of red hair. But there was something hard and defiant about her that wasn't endearing.

'If you want the truth,' she said, 'I never wanted to be a police officer.'

'That's the job all over these days,' Donaldson snorted. 'Used to be a killer just getting to the interview stage. Now you can luck your way into it without even wanting to.'

'I was told it would be a lucrative career,' she added. 'Just didn't expect—'

'Didn't expect to have to do any police work?' the ex-super interrupted again. 'Don't worry, love, you're not alone in that anymore.'

'Ray, will you shut the fuck up?' Wayland cut in. 'Give her a chance.'

Donaldson feigned contrition, still enjoying himself.

'I realised I had to get up the ladder,' Jakeman said simply. 'I didn't have the qualifications to get fast-tracked. Hadn't done much to catch the eye in my day-to-day work either, but I found a way.'

'And what rank were you?' Milburn wondered.

'Just a PC. I'd done the odd bit of plain-clothes work, but no eye-catching arrests fell into my lap.'

'You tend to have to look for them,' Claudia said.

'Anyway, that's it.' Jakeman shrugged. 'That's all you're getting.'

'I don't think so,' Wayland said. 'Sally here sent out certain vibes, shall we say . . . designed to attract the attention of certain senior officers.'

'You tried to sleep your way to the top?' Baxter seemed genuinely disgusted.

Jakeman shrugged again, resolutely unembarrassed.

'It wasn't quite that simple,' Wayland said. 'Once she'd got their interest, she attempted blackmail. And when that didn't work, filed false allegations of sexual harassment, even assault.'

'Seriously?' Milburn looked furious. 'Like we don't have to put up with that shit all the time . . . and then you go and encourage it, and try to make a payday out of it.'

For the first time, Jakeman tinged pink. 'It takes two to tango . . .'

'The upshot,' Wayland said, 'was that a few senior ranks got suspended pending several months of internal investigation.'

'And several high-level enquiries in the Lancashire Constabulary got delayed,' Jack added, 'if not completely scuppered.'

'Know about this one, eh?' Wayland asked him.

'I do. But before I get cocky, me and Claudia are not squeaky clean.'

He told them about the allegations they had taken drugs and guns from underworld stashes, selling them back to the original owners. Claudia remained stoney-faced, eyes filled with shame. Jack stuck to the line that these were the reasons given for their brutal expulsion from the service, carefully avoiding any admission of guilt. Just because no charges had been pressed, that didn't mean there wasn't still a chance they might be.

Donaldson gave a short whistle. 'That was low, Machine Gun. Especially for a glory boy like you.'

'At least no one died,' Jack said.

'That we know of,' Milburn replied.

'That's the voice of experience, is it?' Claudia asked.

'Not in my case, thank God.' Milburn straightened up, which was impressive in itself. She was in her mid-thirties, fit, strong, very statuesque. When she spoke, she had a slight Liverpudlian accent. 'I was an SFO on Merseyside.'

'Rank?' O'Hare asked.

'Is it going to offend you if I say sergeant?' She hit him with a bold stare. 'A black chick with stripes on her arm? Terrible, eh?'

'Let's hear what you did first.' Donaldson was still having fun.

'Most of you lot got greedy,' she said. 'But that wasn't me. I just wanted to stick it to the brass. Eight years I was in Specialist Firearms, for whom I also worked as a martial arts instructor. I partook in more live-fire jobs than I can count. I went in where the bullets were literally flying . . .'

'And let me guess,' Donaldson sneered, 'you never got promoted? And all because you're an ethnic?'

She regarded him coolly. 'Partly.'

'Not because you weren't that good?' O'Hare wondered.

'My record was second to none. And yet every time an inspector's slot came available, some knuckle-dragging . . .'

'White boy?' Donaldson snickered again.

'Whatever the colour of his skin, he got the nod ahead of me.'

Baxter looked puzzled. 'I'd have thought in the modern era they'd have gone out of their way to promote you.'

'Well, you thought wrong. I passed every test, my performance on duty was exemplary. I've probably been in more shoot-outs than the rest of you lot put together—'

'So, what did you do?' Jack interrupted.

Milburn smirked but without humour. 'I heard that certain people would pay for tip-offs about upcoming dig-outs. Big stuff, you know, major operations . . . but, frankly, I'd reached a stage by then where I'd have ratted our lot out even if I hadn't been paid—'

'You know this is all very moving,' Rothermere cut across them, his voice dripping with sarcasm, 'and I'm sure it's good for your souls, unburdening like this. But that boat is getting further and further away. And I'd imagine that means my chances of turning it around are diminishing by the second. So, Mr Wayland, would you please go down to the harbourmaster's office, get on the radio and get me a ride off this island?'

Wayland sighed. 'I suppose we can put things on hold for the moment. I'm telling you though, Rothermere . . . don't get your hopes up. They won't be coming back. Not today. And maybe not tomorrow with this storm due.'

Rothermere waited and watched Wayland as he pulled on his leather jacket and sauntered out of the pub. The others glanced round at each other, not quite sure how they all ought to respond now their shameful secrets were in the open.

'Lucky for you,' Donaldson said to Varada Rathour. 'Just as your turn was coming up.'

She sat alone at a table, her bag alongside her. She hadn't even taken her coat off yet.

'Pity,' he added. 'I'd love to know what it was.'

'Let me guess,' O'Hare said. 'You were giving blowjobs to the bosses and decided to up your fee.'

Rathour jumped to her feet. 'I was selling intel, that's all.'

'That's all?' Donaldson and O'Hare roared with laughter.

'I was technical support,' she said, eyes glimmering with tears. 'I had access to classified info. I abused my position, yes. But I don't know why you have to make everything so dirty.'

'They make it dirty, love,' Claudia said, 'because they get off on it.' She glanced at the ex-Robbery Squad contingent. 'You two are a fucking joke, by the way.'

Donaldson laughed again.

'The demonic duo living up to their reputation,' she said, as the mismatched group broke up.

Baxter shook her head. 'They make me sick.' She raised her voice. 'You two make me sick.'

Donaldson and O'Hare had gone back to playing pool. The latter glanced casually over. 'Like anyone cares. I mean, when did hurt feelings become a problem? Not when I was a probie. Got the shit ripped out of me everywhere I looked.'

'Probably deserved it,' Baxter muttered. 'What a pair of neanderthals. It's like the last thirty years never happened.'

'Or like someone's just rolled them back,' Jack said.

'I should talk to Alan.' Baxter nodded across the room to where Rothermere sat on his own. 'He must be feeling pretty lonely.'

'Can't roll back time, Jack,' Claudia said, when she'd gone. 'Much as bastards like those two might wish it.'

'You sure?' Jack was noncommittal. 'I mean, we're a bit of a lawless crew out here.'

'We're only in the Scilly Isles. Not the end of the world.'

He headed to the bar. 'Let's see what this storm's like, eh? Then we can make a judgement on that.'

Ten

'Any joy?' Jack asked.

Wayland looked puzzled. 'Joy?'

Jack and Claudia were leaning on the harbour-side barrier, enjoying the midday heat, when he came strolling towards them from the harbourmaster's cottage.

'Getting a boat for Rothermere.' Wayland didn't look hopeful. 'Pasco's trying to get in touch. But I know what the result will be.'

'They're pretty busy, eh?' Jack couldn't resist showing how sceptical he felt about that.

The harbour was empty of any boats, the waves rolling into it still lapping gently. Further out, the sea was equally devoid of craft.

'You wouldn't know it to look at them,' Wayland said. 'But that's the whole Cornwall-Scilly Isles culture. Next to the Caribbean, it's got to be the most laid-back place on Earth. They'll get to Rothermere eventually, but it won't be any time soon.'

'I thought there'd be more boatmen,' Claudia said.

'It's the smallness of the islands that's the problem.' Wayland indicated they should walk. 'Or rather the smallness of the population. St Mary's is the most populous and there are only about one and a half thousand permanent residents there. There're only about one hundred and fifty on St Martin's, and none at all on St Dunstan, except the staff at Porth West, who are currently no more than a skeleton crew. How many pro standard skippers do you think you can get out of that? Follow me, anyway . . . I'll take you up to The Culraven Arms, the hotel. We've booked you two in there.'

Jack was relieved by that, seeing as Donaldson and O'Hare had made camp in The Salmon. They took a side passage, a paved footway snaking between several rows of empty cottages.

'Was Rothermere framed by Donaldson and O'Hare?' Claudia wondered.

Wayland blew out a long breath. 'Damned if I know. He's always said he was. Not by those two specifically, but I suppose they're good candidates, him being the whistleblower who sent them down.'

'Hardly a harmonious start to the week,' Jack said.

'There were always going to be teething problems. This sort of thing's never been attempted before.'

Now that they were away from the harbour front, more of the layout of Porth West became apparent, though there wasn't a great deal of it. Wayland explained how, seeing as there were no official roads here, the only way that food and drink supplies, laundry bags and other bulky deliveries could make their way up to the hotel from the harbour was via what was called the Back Lane, which was basically a tarmac track. It commenced at the landward end of the jetty, weaving its way around the back of the cottages, though not without looping in again and calling at the rear of The Salmon. Goods transportation was provided by a small fleet of trolley-cars. One was currently parked in the pub's yard. It looked like a four-seater golf buggy with a trailer attached.

'Get in,' Wayland said. 'I'll give you a ride to the hotel.'

He slid behind the wheel, while they threw their bags into the trailer and climbed aboard. Wayland hit a button and the small electronic vehicle juddered to life. He drove from the yard and on to the Back Lane.

'You don't think it was wrong of me?' Wayland asked. 'Making everyone confess?'

'Served a purpose,' Jack replied.

'None of us can take the moral high ground,' Claudia said. 'Aside from Mr Rothermere, who's apparently as pure as the driven snow.'

'The court decided otherwise,' Wayland countered. 'He did three years of a five-year sentence. He can consider himself lucky, some of the stuff they lifted from his laptop.'

The Back Lane had now ascended the grassy slope sufficiently to join the Quad Track, which on this side of the island passed the hotel's open front gates. The Quad Track was a firm but sandy path running in a mostly straight line, curving only slightly as it dwindled away in front of them. On the left, a wrought-iron railing bordered the hotel grounds, a lushly wooded slope rising beyond it.

'You say this track circles the whole island?' Jack said.

Wayland nodded. 'Mainly, it follows the coastline. So, it's pretty scenic. And exhilarating. The ATVs are in a shed back there. Take one any time you want. The key to the shed is held at the hotel reception, and the machines are all kept fully fuelled. It's good fun, trust me. Just don't go off the track. There are gullies and the like, and there are no rescue services on St Dunstan. The quad bikes go a lot faster than this bloody thing, of course.' They were doing about fifteen miles per hour. 'These fucking eco-twats get their way, and you'll be travelling at this speed everywhere.'

'Come on, Harry,' Claudia said.

'Chill,' Wayland laughed. 'Out here you can say what you really think.'

'Who decided who's in the hotel and who's in the pub?' Jack asked.

'Don't know. Probably just pot luck.'

Wayland swung the vehicle left between two tall, granite gateposts, each surmounted with the bronze figure of a bearded merman, one blowing a horn, the other wielding a trident. The hotel itself was about two hundred yards ahead, on higher ground and surrounded by handsome terraced gardens.

'Don't worry about that crap down in the pub,' Wayland said as they passed tidy lawns, flower beds and sculpted topiary.

'I was hoping for a holiday, not a brawl,' Claudia replied.

'Donaldson and O'Hare are prize dickheads. Wherever they go, there's argy-bargy. The rest of us, though . . . we need to support each other, because let's be honest . . . we're all we've got.'

'Let's hope it gets easier,' Jack said. 'Seeing as we're stuck here now.'

'Look . . . check it out . . .' Wayland gestured, and through breaks in the trees, they glimpsed the coastline lying south of Porth West, dense gorse thickets giving way to sand dunes, and at sea level an unspoiled beach so white and smooth that it could have been formed from talcum powder. It was an intoxicating view, enriched by the clear sky, hot sun and sparkling blueness of the sea. Not a soul was in sight, nor a speck of litter.

'Don't think of it as being stuck here,' Wayland said. 'There are plenty of things to enjoy on St Dunstan.'

'When does our benefactor arrive?' Jack asked.

'It'll happen when it happens. None of us will see it coming, or so I've been told. By the way, that's a ruined castle down there.' He pointed to a distant grey, tooth-like outline. 'Built during the Spanish Armada era. You should steer well clear of it. No one's done any preservation work on it since the sixteenth century, which means it's unsafe . . . and I mean very unsafe. They'll definitely need to sort that before the general public arrive. Anyway, we're here.' He braked on the hotel's paved forecourt. 'You'd best get out so I can go down and scoop a few of the others up. Don't want them thinking I'm playing favourites.'

They climbed out and grabbed their bags.

'The chef here is Mariela,' Wayland said. 'Ledina's mum. By all accounts, she's superb. Pop back down to the pub when you've eaten and we'll make a night of it, yeah?'

Then he swung the small, simple vehicle around and trundled away downhill.

'So . . .' Jack said. 'A beautiful island, but we're marooned with a bunch of people who hate each other's guts.'

'Some of them. Not all.'

'We've only just arrived, Claudi. There's plenty of time.'

The hotel looked typically Cornish: a handsome whitewashed structure standing four storeys high with huge bay windows on the ground floor and red pantiled roofs. A single revolving door admitted Jack and Claudia to a small porch, where a brass signpost requested that any muddy footwear be removed at this point. A set of motion-sensitive doors then slid open. The hotel vestibule was all pile carpets, polished wood and gleaming chrome. Pastel shades were favoured, pale silk wallpaper, framed images on the walls, paintings and photographs of Scillonian or Cornish settings.

On the right was the hotel restaurant, on the left the reception desk. Directly ahead, the vestibule became a broad corridor, again hung with pictures, but with recesses on either side, containing comfortable furniture and crammed bookcases.

'Welcome everyone,' a smooth voice said. 'Do I have the pleasure of addressing Mr Jack McGurn and Miss Claudia Crayford?'

A tall young man approached them from reception. He was in his late thirties, handsome with fair hair and bright blue eyes. He wore a light blue blazer and a scarlet tie. On his left breast pocket, a gold badge proclaimed him:

Lucas Beck
Manager

He seemed genuinely pleased to see them. 'I hope you've had a pleasant journey. Your rooms are ready. You'll find coffee and tea in there, plus a minibar. It's all paid for already, as I'm sure you know.' Beck was well spoken with a slight Afrikaans accent. 'We have en-suite bathrooms and plenty of hot water. May I take your luggage?'

Jack and Claudia followed him into a lift. On the third floor he led them along a corridor to their rooms, 36 and 38, where he supplied both guests with card keys.

The accommodation was pleasant enough, each room containing a double bed, an armchair, a writing desk, a satellite television and double doors opening on to twin balconies overlooking the harbour.

Claudia went out first and stared at the cobalt-blue seascape, broken here and there with crests of white. St Agnes lay north of St Dunstan by several miles, but now they were facing west no land was in sight at all.

'Next stop the US of A,' Jack said, coming out on to his own balcony.

'When it's finished, this'll be an amazing place for a holiday.'

'When it's finished.' Jack sipped from a small can of Pepsi. 'Surprised to learn there're only three permanent members of staff in the entire hotel.'

After Beck the manager, and Mariela the cook, Mariela's other daughter, Eliza, apparently did everything else.

'Well, there's only a handful of guests,' Claudia replied.

They cast their gaze downward, the small semi-circle of buildings around the harbour looking chocolate-box pretty.

'The quaintness is certainly a selling point,' Jack said.

'The weather and view aren't half bad either.'

That was undeniable. The palms and other exotic flora in the hotel gardens helped create a pseudo-Mediterranean feel, added to by a sun more intense than anything they'd been used to in northern England. Its heat seeped through them.

North of the village, the coastline was a series of rocky coves and outcrops, mostly tree-lined down to the water's edge. Southward, the beach lay in all its glory. The Quad Track was clearly visible too: a narrow, sandy ribbon just inland from the beach, running parallel for a while before vanishing into the bright greenery of the interior. From this vantage, the ruined castle was more than just a distant outline. It might have been crumbling to pieces, but it looked almost elegant up on the wooded headland.

'Imagine being posted all the way out here during Queen Elizabeth's time,' Claudia said.

'Could've been worse. At least you'd be a long way from any real wars.'

'That would suit me.'

Jack sipped his Pepsi. 'We can always hope.'

Eleven

Claudia put a white robe over her one-piece swimsuit, slipped on a pair of towel flip-flops, left her room and descended the main staircase into the deserted vestibule. Following the signs, she walked along to its furthest end, turned left and headed through into the gymnasium.

This brand-new exercise area had an 'old world' feel. It was spacious and airy, with a high, vaulted ceiling. At the edge was the swimming pool, and beyond that, a pair of ornate French doors, which opened out on to an extensive lawn. Conversely, the exercise equipment was state of the art. First though, she went left, taking a tiled passage towards the Male and Female changing areas. Having stowed everything she had in her locker, she bound her hair, then went back to the pool. She normally enjoyed a good workout in the gym, but swimming was her passion. A schoolgirl champion, she'd never taken a holiday where there wasn't regular good access to clean blue water.

This pool was about forty metres long and fifteen wide, and according to a safety notice, eight feet deep at its furthest end. Pleased to have so much room to herself, Claudia stepped down into the shallow end, wading ahead until the level rose to her chest, diving under, and when she resurfaced, striking forward at an easy crawl. She'd done maybe ten lengths and was just commencing her eleventh when she glimpsed – or thought she glimpsed – a figure standing outside the French doors, watching.

Watching *her*.

She still had water in her eyes, and came to a quick halt, mopping at them with her forearm – only for her hair, which had come loose, to fall over her face. By the time she'd whipped it out of the way, there was no one on the other side of the glass.

She trod water, wondering who it might have been and what they'd been up to. Her vision had been blurred and she'd only caught a fleeting glimpse. She wasn't quite sure what she'd seen, but whoever it was, they'd gone.

Swimming to the nearest stepladder, she clambered out, and with arms folded, walked to the French doors. There was no one on the other side. Just open lawns, flower beds and more well-pruned shrubbery. She angled round, looking left and right. No one. Had someone really been watching her? Whoever it was, she thought they'd been wearing green, and by their shape and size she was pretty sure it had been a man.

Ill at ease, Claudia decided to stop at ten lengths. That would give her time to go up and get ready for dinner, at least. Earlier that evening, a menu card had been pushed under her room door. Booking a table for eight o'clock that evening, Jack had ordered steak and chips, Claudia opting for seafood linguine.

There wasn't going to be anything romantic about it. She'd been firm on that. She and Jack hadn't been amorous for quite some time and had been pulling apart in social terms; they were only back together now as friends of convenience. It wasn't that she didn't still fancy him, but since the disastrous route they'd taken together she'd realised what a cowboy he was at heart. She'd often told him to grow up, but she suspected he never would. Jack always did his own thing. Plus, he had an aggressive streak, which meant he was a player by nature, a real competitor. He went at things all guns blazing. She supposed that was what made him such a productive DI in an anti-organised crime outfit. But it had got him into trouble as well, more than once, and that wasn't the sort of bloke you ought to fall for, not if you wanted a quiet, orderly life. She'd had to find out the hard way.

She went back into the female changing room, stripped her costume off and entered one of the cubicles. The lush, hot spray was refreshing and invigorating.

Then something *clunked* in the changing area.

She placed a hand over the showerhead.

Another *clunk* sounded.

She turned the shower off, stepped out of the cubicle, and grabbed her towel from the wall hook, wrapping herself in it.

The changing area was just around the corner, and now she could hear movement. A rustling of cloth. Another wooden *clunk*. The lockers were made of wood.

Good luck finding anything valuable, she thought. What would they steal: her slippers, her bathrobe?

How about your room-key, dufus?

She was about to go round the corner when some inner voice told her to take a beat.

That guy looking through the French doors. Were those doors locked?

She cursed herself for not checking. It had gone quiet in the changing room – too quiet? suspiciously quiet? – as if whoever was there had heard her? And was lying in wait?

But who? The island was uninhabited. Everyone here knew everyone else. But then again, the people who *were* here weren't the best examples of humanity. And after twelve years as a serving police officer, Claudia knew her limitations. She was five-foot-six and slim of build. Yes, she was reasonably fit, but she'd long ago realised she couldn't mix it in a slugging match with some burly street guy. Her contribution to the job had been brain rather than brawn, but that wouldn't be much use in this situation.

She listened again, hearing nothing.

Was whoever it was lurking just around the corner?

She fancied she could hear them holding their breath, and glanced down at the wet tiled floor as if a telltale shadow might be lying there. Inevitably, there was nothing, but now she was thinking about their face-off with the Quincannons. Had those hoodlums followed them all the way out here? Nobody knew they were coming here. They'd been told to keep it a secret to avoid press interest.

But what if one of them had been tailed?

She chided herself for letting her imagination run riot. There was one boat service and it had made only two trips so far, and Harry Wayland had supervised both.

How about someone with their own boat?

She pondered that, before kicking it aside, and going determinedly round the corner, making out as if drying her hair was her only priority.

There was no one there.

All the lockers were closed, including her own.

She opened hers anyway, but everything was as she'd left it. Then she heard a sound from the gym. A prolonged creak, followed by a hefty *clank*.

She slipped into her robe and slippers, grabbed her costume, and went warily forward.

The exercise area was empty, as was the pool. She pivoted, peering into every corner. Still no one. She went to the French doors, to test them. They were escape doors, equipped with a push-down bar. She didn't bother trying in case they activated an alarm. The main take-away here was that they couldn't be opened from the outside. That was one concern put to bed.

Keep up with this, girl, and you'll end up a paranoid wreck, she told herself, walking past the pool and threading back through the gym.

At which point someone stepped right into her path, causing her to yelp with fright.

Gabby Milburn looked equally surprised. She'd just come around the cross-trainer, behind which she'd been squatting to root in her gym bag. Her hair was tied in a tight bun, and she looked stunning, her tall ebony form sleek and muscular in a cream sports bra and leggings.

'Sorry,' Claudia said. 'Didn't hear you.'

'No problem.' Milburn went past her to the first of the rowing machines, where she accommodated herself on the slide-seat, fitting her sneakered feet into the stirrups.

'Finally got bored at The Salmon?'

Milburn chuckled without humour. 'All there is to do down there is drink.'

'They still at it?'

Milburn punched keys to set the resistance level. 'O'Hare and Donaldson are. They'll have heads on them tomorrow. Sally Jakeman seems to be getting matey with them too.'

'She is aware they can't advance her career anymore?'

'Think she's just a natural-born party girl. Harry's with them. When I left, they were all comparing war stories.'

'Suppose they'll have a few to tell, between them.'

'I could've chipped in with some of my own, but I don't think they count for much anymore.'

'I know the feeling,' Claudia said.

It was a glum note, which made her feel even more inadequate as she stood there in her robe, watching while the other woman, a picture of tensile strength, commenced rowing in strong, sure fashion. She wasn't personally acquainted with Gabby Milburn, yet she had a sudden urge to confide in her.

'Glad you came here?' Claudia asked.

'Hardly.' Milburn grunted with effort. 'Not exactly peace in the valley, is it?'

'I agree, but once our . . . well, our *new owner* arrives, things might be different.'

'New owner?' Milburn forced a smile, sweat gathering on her brow. 'Let's see what he's offering first.'

'You got plans?'

'Nothing certain. Might be viable to stay in the security world, or it might not. Depends if there's any mileage in this new identity malarkey.'

'There's a downside to that,' Claudia said. 'Moving back and forth between two different worlds.'

Milburn took a breather, rubbing at her neck and face with a hand towel. 'I'll be moving back and forth as little as possible, trust me.'

'People at home giving you a hard time?'

'No more than the rest of you, I'm sure.'

'Sorry if that was a personal question, but I always assumed the black community would be closer knit than ours. The National Black Police Association's supposed to be an excellent support group.'

'Yeah, but I'm not a police officer anymore. And home? Well . . .' Milburn looked thoughtful. 'I don't want to talk in clichés, but the background I come from . . . well, lots of guys and girls join the job now. There's no stigma in it. But that wasn't always the case, as you know. And . . . well, that's what kept me safe inside. I've got cousins who've got cousins, if you know what I mean.' She clambered off the rower, walking to the next piece of kit, which, to Claudia's eyes looked like some kind of hi-tech torture device, but in fact was one of those ultra-new pulldown weight machines. Milburn adjusted the weights, organised herself on the seat, then drew the overhead handlebar down, and commenced a vigorous series of reps. 'The downside of course is that there are a few people, some quite close to me, who kind of hoped it wouldn't work out . . . and now they feel vindicated, and they can't stop saying it.'

Claudia understood that perfectly but was now paying more attention to what Milburn was actually doing. Again, she sat solidly upright, her midsection tight as a drum, her sinewy arms and shoulders visibly straining as she worked the handlebar up and down. Some 210 lbs of weights rose and fell in tandem.

'Wow . . . you can really pump iron.'

Milburn grunted, unable to respond easily. Her supple body gleamed with fresh sweat.

'You didn't try to come in through the French doors earlier?'

The ex-Merseyside cop threw a distracted gaze at Claudia. 'No . . . why?'

'Nothing. Thought I saw someone watching me while I was swimming.'

Milburn released the bar, extricated her legs from under the pad and swivelled around. She glanced at the French doors. 'Someone was watching you? Who?'

'Not sure. Might have been someone passing by. Could even have been Mr Beck.'

Milburn snorted with disappointment. 'Be a damn shame if *he* turned out to be a peeper. With looks like his.' She towelled herself again. 'Speaking of which, you and his nibs . . . Jack? You two a thing?'

'Once. Not anymore. We decided it was getting in the way of our professionalism. Jesus . . .' Claudia felt as though she could cry at some of the choices she'd made. 'Our *professionalism*. There's a joke in there, somewhere.'

'Just shows, eh?' Milburn swung back into place. 'There's always a bigger mess round the corner.'

Claudia backed away. 'Those French doors can't be opened from the outside. Just in case you're worried.'

Milburn strenuously worked the handlebar. 'I'm not.'

Jack and Claudia met for dinner in the restaurant, ate a satisfying meal and then discussed whether or not to go and join the rest of the crowd in The Salmon.

'I wonder how far gone Donaldson and O'Hare are by now,' Jack said.

'To think blokes like that used to be the rule in the job, not the exception,' Claudia replied.

'Bit of an exaggeration there.'

'Either way, I don't fancy it.'

'Let's have a nip or two here instead.'

'Now that's a plan.'

They went into the hotel bar and got comfy on a pair of bar stools while Lucas Beck mixed them some excellent cocktails, at the same time offering polite small talk.

He'd been with the hotel chain for several years, he said, but had moved around from one resort to the next, though mainly on the Cornwall/Devonshire peninsula. He explained that he came from South Africa originally but was careful not to ask specifically about Jack or Claudia's backgrounds.

There was no sign of any of the other hotel guests until around nine-thirty, when Alan Rothermere came trudging through the vestibule. He was headed straight for the lifts, but when Jack called to him he entered the bar, regarding them with weary mistrust. He looked sallow-cheeked and dishevelled.

'So, what's the story with the boat?' Jack asked.

'Is it coming back?' Claudia said.

'Erm . . . not for, well, four or five days at least.'

'Four or five days?'

'This storm that's supposed to be coming.'

'I imagine storms out here can get pretty bad,' Jack said. 'And it was only a small boat.'

'You'll just have to put up with us,' Claudia added.

Rothermere's expression hardened. 'You're not funny.'

'I'm not trying to be.'

'Look, I'm not claiming to be better than anyone else here . . .'

'That's not what you said earlier,' Jack retorted.

'Only inasmuch as I'm innocent and none of the rest of you are . . . by your own admission.'

'We admitted nothing.'

'No, of course not.' Rothermere gave a knowing, humourless smile. 'You were very careful about that, I noticed. But neither did you contest the IOPC's decision to get rid of you both. Which is in sharp contrast to me. Because once I get a bit of cash behind me, I'm going to contest my public disgrace very forcefully indeed.' He backed towards the door. 'And an awful lot of people are going to finish up with egg on their faces. Goodnight.'

He traipsed from the bar, without looking back.

'Maybe he *is* innocent,' Claudia said.

'On the basis that he's being bolshy about it?' Jack chuckled. 'Course, if he is, it was a bastard of a thing to do to him.'

'Professional Standards will have investigated, though, won't they?' she said. 'They did with us.'

'Yeah, but Donaldson and O'Hare aren't amateurs.'

'God.' She sipped her Long Island iced tea. 'This is one messed-up bunch of people.'

'Going to be a fun few days.' Jack downed his old-fashioned. 'Feels to me like anything could happen.'

Twelve

The sun was still high the following morning, the sky mostly clear of cloud, but there was a slightly different atmosphere. No haze hung over the ocean, strong wind buffeting the waves into whitecaps. Jack watched from his balcony as rollers came ashore along the beach. The harbour was choppy too, foam bursting over the jetty and quayside.

'Feels a bit more like a British summer,' he told Claudia over breakfast.

This first meal of the day was a very civilised affair, Mariela having laid out platters of scrambled eggs, sausages, bacon, mushrooms and grilled tomatoes on the sideboard, along with jugs of juice. There was also a tea and coffee-making machine, a toaster, and a mountain of sliced bread.

Gabby Milburn and Varada Rathour were at separate tables, spaced well apart, but there was no sign of Alan Rothermere. Claudia commented on that.

'I feel certain St Dunstan's newly appointed mother hen will invite him to sit with her when he finally shows,' Jack said quietly, nodding to where Cheryl Baxter was placing slices of watermelon on her plate.

'Don't be mean.'

'You don't think it's a bit weird that she seemed to feel sorry for him?'

'She probably doesn't like seeing people ganged up on.'

'Come on, Claudi,' he said, 'he's the one among us who's *most* offended against society.'

'Loath though I am to speak in defence of a convicted paedophile, it's still the case that we're none of us in a position to throw stones.'

He made an exasperated gesture. 'Some of us have done worse things than others, but like you say, we're all of us bad eggs. And if that's the only thing we've got in common, this private club's creaking already . . . You want the truth? I'm enjoying the free food and the free booze, and I'm very intrigued about our new benefactor, but . . . let's not make out we're enjoying each other's company.' He scrubbed a hand through his hair. 'Fancy a refill on that coffee?'

'No.' She got to her feet. 'You know, Jack, good things don't happen to people routinely. Maybe you should think about that.'

She'd made no effort to lower her voice, and he glanced around the room awkwardly. No one else was paying attention, except Gabby Milburn, who'd registered only vague interest.

'I'll see you in the vestibule in twenty,' Claudia said.

'Why? Where we going?'

'For a walk.'

'A walk?'

'We're on a beautiful island, so let's take it in while the sun's still shining.'

'What if miladdo rocks up . . . our benefactor?'

'I'm sure he'll still be here when we get back,' she said. 'And what fun that'll be. Because then all our problems will be solved.'

◆ ◆ ◆

Jack suggested they take a couple of quad bikes, but Claudia said she'd rather have peace and quiet. That was what St Dunstan was going to be famous for: the solitude, the tranquillity. Frankly, she couldn't understand why the hoteliers had even bothered with the quad bikes. When the resort was thronging with customers, they'd be a noisy nuisance.

Initially though, they walked south along the Quad Track, looking down over yards of gorse thickets, dunes tufted with spiky marram grass, and then the beach itself and the thundering waves. It was bracing, a stiff, salty breeze blowing. Jack was soon wondering if a T-shirt, tennis shorts and a pair of well-worn trainers had been a good idea. Claudia zipped up her tracksuit top.

'See,' she said, 'this is lovely.'

'Pity we don't surf.'

'You can always learn.'

'You've really got one on you today.'

'I'm not letting you drag me down, Jack. No more than you already have.'

'Ouch. That was low.'

'A low blow was called for. We have to commence the next period of our lives sometime. It might as well be now.'

They strolled on, the distant battlements of the castle gradually becoming clearer, though well before then, they climbed a stile and took a leafy pathway inland between wild hedgerows and were soon in a completely different environment, the wind no longer ruffling their hair, the heat intensifying. The further in they penetrated, the deeper and richer the greenery. The path intersected with others, earth and pebble footways winding through wiry undergrowth. Clearly, St Dunstan's unspoiled nature was its most obvious asset. Once again, the ubiquitous palm trees raised their heads amid the more traditional English foliage, lilac, hazel and willow. There were colourful butterflies everywhere and, briefly, the call of a cuckoo. The roar of the sea became a distant sigh.

'Is this place the best-kept secret, or what?' Claudia said after forty minutes of aimless wandering.

Jack grunted, slapping at the gnats leaving multiple bites on his sweaty limbs.

'Ah, you're here!' a voice said.

Cheryl Baxter came clambering over a stile wearing a broad-brimmed hat with her grey sweats. She looked hot and flustered.

Claudia strolled towards her. 'What's up?'

'It's probably not an emergency,' she said, 'but . . .'

'What is it?' Jack asked, still swatting insects.

'Have you seen Alan at all . . . during your travels?'

Jack and Claudia glanced at each other and shook their heads.

'In that case, it seems he's gone missing.'

'Missing?' Claudia said.

'He's vanished.'

There was a brief silence, before Jack said, 'What do you want *us* to do about it?'

Baxter stiffened. 'Perhaps help me look for him, if you don't mind.'

'He can hardly have gone missing,' Claudia said. 'It's not a big island and most of the buildings are closed.'

'I assure you he's gone missing. The rest of us . . . well . . .' briefly, she looked cross, '*most* of the rest of us have been looking for him for the last half-hour. But now Harry Wayland's sent me to find you, to bring you back to the village so we can mount a proper search.'

'Have you checked his room?' Jack said.

'Of course I have. He's not there.'

'There are other guest facilities in the hotel,' Claudia said. 'The gym, the swimming pool . . .'

'I've looked there too.'

'The Salmon?' Jack suggested.

'He's hardly likely to go there, is he?' Baxter said tersely.

'What about the harbourmaster?' Claudia asked. 'He must know all the secret places.'

'Harry Wayland's already spoken to the harbourmaster. He hasn't seen Alan anywhere. Nobody has.'

'I think there's another boatshed on the other side of the jetty,' Claudia said. 'There's also the bike shed near the hotel. Has anyone looked there?'

'We have,' Baxter replied. 'He's not in any of those places.'

Jack mused. 'Well, hanging around in a shed on a nice summer's day would seem a bit peculiar.'

'Mr McGurn!' Baxter snapped. 'This is not the time for joking around.'

'Harry wants us back in Porth West, you say?' Claudia cut in.

'Straight away. He's trying to organise a search of the entire island.'

'The entire island?' Jack whistled. 'That could take a while.' Baxter gave him another reproachful glance. 'All I'm saying is there are no roads . . . it's all countryside.'

'I'm sure that sometime during your service, ex-Detective Inspector, you must have been involved in line-searches over open ground in far worse conditions than these.'

Baxter didn't wait to hear more but headed back the way she'd come. They followed, climbing the stile, and wading after her through rivers of rainbow-coloured flowers.

'Maybe Rothermere's so pissed off about the boat not coming that he tried to swim to the next island,' Jack said quietly.

'Don't even joke about that,' Claudia hissed.

'How do you know I'm joking?'

'He's a fellow human being, Jack, and he might be in trouble.'

'He's not in trouble.' A holly blue butterfly fluttered lazily across their path. 'Even Rothermere couldn't get in trouble in a place like this.'

'Yeah, well Harry clearly doesn't think so.'

Jack had no smart comeback to that. Wayland was as seasoned as they came. He didn't get fazed or spooked easily. So, on reflection, maybe – just maybe – Cheryl Baxter was right. This wasn't a time for jokes.

Thirteen

When they got back to the hotel, Harry Wayland was waiting on the forecourt with Gabby Milburn and Varada Rathour. They were all wearing rugged outdoor gear, as if expecting a tough ramble.

'Glad at least you two could make it,' Wayland said to Jack and Claudia. He seemed uncharacteristically agitated. 'Jonas Pugh's being a total wanker.'

Jack was puzzled. 'What use would he be? He's a piss-artist.'

'What use?' Wayland looked at him askance. 'He was top-level CSI . . . a crime scene specialist. And he won't even get out of bed to come and look at Rothermere's bedroom.'

'What's his bedroom got to do with it?' Claudia asked.

'Seems Rothermere never kept his breakfast date with Cheryl Baxter this morning. She finally went up, and he wasn't there . . . but his bedroom door was open. A bit unusual, I'm sure you'll agree?'

'Unless he'd just nipped down the corridor for something.'

'It's still open. He hasn't been back, and he hasn't been seen.'

'Bedroom in disarray?' Jack asked.

'Not especially,' Wayland admitted. 'Looks like he's unpacked, put everything away, made himself a brew. But that's about all.'

'Had the bed been slept in?'

'Yep. Not been made yet, because I told Eliza to stay out. But it's the little things we might be missing.'

Gabby Milburn sidled up to them. 'I can go and grab Pugh, if you want,' she said. 'Drag him up from The Salmon by that crappy tash of his.'

'Not for the moment,' Wayland replied. 'We need peace on this island. For all our sakes.'

As they were the only ex-detectives present, it was decided that Wayland, Jack and Claudia should go and appraise the room again.

'No sign, Lucas?' the former asked the hotel manager as they passed through reception.

'I'm afraid not, Mr Wayland,' Beck replied from behind his desk.

'Have you asked your staff?'

'I have. They haven't seen any sign of Mr Rothermere.'

'Perhaps we should speak to Eliza ourselves?' Claudia said. 'She's the one who does the bedrooms.'

'Eliza's also the only waitress,' Wayland replied. 'She's not been upstairs today. She was run off her feet clearing up after breakfast.'

'Cameras?' Jack suggested.

'They're not up and running yet.'

They ascended in the lift together, Claudia noting the genuine concern on Wayland's leathery features. 'You think something bad's happened to him?'

'Bloody hope not,' he muttered. 'Be the first and last nail in the Damned Rankers' coffin, if it has.'

When they got to Rothermere's room on the first floor, the door was ajar. They stared in but didn't enter. The bedclothes were rumpled and there was a dirty teacup on the bedside cabinet, but otherwise everything was tidy.

'Those clothes on the luggage rack.' Claudia pointed out a small pile of neatly folded garments. 'Weren't those the ones he was wearing last night, when he came in?'

'Looks like it,' Jack said.

'You saw him last night?' Wayland asked.

'After dinner,' Claudia said. 'Ten-ish. Think he was going up to bed.'

'Anything off with him?'

'You mean apart from him being furious there wasn't a boat coming?'

'This is fucked,' Wayland said under his breath.

'Well, there's clearly not been a struggle in here,' Jack said.

'Unless someone went to the trouble of tidying up behind them,' Claudia replied.

'But didn't go to the trouble of closing the door?'

She couldn't argue with that.

'Let's get back down,' Wayland said. 'I'll tell Beck this place is out of bounds.'

Downstairs, he stopped at reception, while Jack and Claudia went outside to join the others on the forecourt. Sally Jakeman had arrived in a light anorak and shorts, but didn't look especially motivated.

'Any sign of him?' Jack asked.

'Nothing,' Baxter replied.

'We're all going to look a bit silly if he turns up now, aren't we?' Jakeman said.

No one responded.

'What about Donaldson and O'Hare?' Jack asked.

'Those two pigs,' Baxter spat. 'What use would they be?'

'If nothing else, they'll be extra bodies,' Wayland said, emerging from the hotel.

Milburn snorted. 'The way they're going at it, they'll literally be that . . . bodies.'

'They're drinking already?' Claudia said. 'It's not eleven o'clock yet.'

'That's what they're here for, apparently.' Milburn had adopted a rough Manchester brogue. 'They're on their holidays.'

'I've had enough of this bollocks.' Wayland set off down the hotel drive.

Jack hurried to catch up. 'I'll come with you.'

'Don't waste your time,' Baxter called after them. 'They're not interested in anyone else . . . especially not someone like Alan.'

'Taking it a bit personally, isn't she?' Jack said.

'In her case, it *is* personal,' Wayland replied. 'Take it you've not heard her story yet?'

'She hasn't volunteered it.'

'I'm not surprised.' Wayland got his thoughts in order as they strode quickly downhill. 'Cheryl was an inspector in West Yorkshire. Did Traffic for a while, but mostly Division.' They turned right along the Quad Track. 'By all accounts, she was good as gold. Total straight bat. Then, one day, her entire world fell apart. Her son, Tyrone, was arrested for kiddie-fiddling. Not pictures or videos. The real thing.'

'Shit,' Jack said. 'But why did it cost her her job?'

'It didn't. It was what happened after.' They descended the steps into the village. 'Tyrone drew a twenty-stretch. Sounds like he's a soft-arse. Cheryl reckoned he wouldn't stand a chance inside, especially going in as a nonce. So, she bought him some protection.'

'How?'

'Went to see her local crime bosses. Made a bargain. If they could guarantee no one would lay a finger on Tyrone while he was doing time, she'd hand over some names.'

'Names?'

'Police informants. And not just a few. She might have been in uniform all her career, but she'd done two and a half decades. She knew a lot of people.'

'And it worked?'

'Seems to have . . . till she got caught. It also seems to have skewed her thinking. She didn't help herself while she was under investigation by expressing sympathy towards the nonces of the world. She reckons they're sick . . . you know, in the head. That it's not their fault.'

'Hence her fondness for Rothermere?'

They'd now reached the rear of The Salmon, where they halted. 'Depressing what the job can do to people, isn't it?' Wayland said.

'What about the grasses she put names to?'

'What do you think? Those who didn't make it into hiding are dead.'

'Jesus. And there was me, thinking her some kind of mother figure.'

'There are mothers and mothers.' Wayland headed through the pub's open back door. 'There's the kind, cute, cuddly mum. And then there's the she-wolf who'll kill to protect her cubs.'

They found Donaldson and O'Hare in the pool area, in garish holiday gear of Bermuda shorts and Hawaiian shirts, tucking into egg, sausage, chips and beans and swilling from brimming pints of lager.

'Thought you'd have had your brekky by now,' Wayland said.

'This is our second brekky,' Donaldson mumbled. 'We're on our—'

'Yeah, you're on your holidays,' Jack cut in.

'You're aware we've got a problem?' Wayland said.

Donaldson forced a laugh, spraying food fragments. 'The nonce'll turn up. What's the panic?'

'The panic is, Ray, that if he doesn't, it's not going to look good,' Jack said. 'Not least because of all the enemies he's got on this island.'

Donaldson eyed him. '"Ray", is it? You my mate now, Machine Gun?'

'If Rothermere doesn't show up, you're going to need all the mates you can get.'

Donaldson's eyes narrowed behind his pebble-thick glasses. 'Sounds like a threat.'

'What do *you* think's going to happen?' Wayland asked him. 'Who are the two tossers who had words with him yesterday in front of everyone else? Who are the two tossers who he's openly accused of setting him up on those kiddie-porn charges?'

'Not to mention he's the one who snitched on you,' Jack said. 'You two have got way more reason than anyone else on this island to punch Rothermere's ticket.'

'Which also means you've got more reason to help us find him,' Wayland added.

Donaldson's hostile expression slackened. He swallowed more food and took a huge slurp of lager.

'All right,' he said. 'We'll come. But me and Dekko are getting pretty comfy here. This is our corner of the pub. And we aren't going to be happy if we drag our arses all over this fucking rock and end up finding Rothermere sunbathing nude or whatever other pervy thing he does.'

O'Hare looked dismayed, his attention torn between his unfinished second breakfast, his beer, and his former boss, who was getting to his feet. 'We're really going with them?'

'Course we are,' Donaldson said irritably. 'Leave that slop and get some proper gear on.'

As the pair of them lumbered upstairs to their rooms, Jack glanced across to the bar, where Ledina stood pale-faced behind the pumps. How much English did she understand? He followed Wayland out and joined him on the esplanade.

'What's all this "Machine Gun" crap?' the ex-homicide guy asked.

Jack snorted. '"Machine Gun Jack McGurn". Prohibition-era mobster. Donaldson always thought it was funny.'

'Suppose it is, given how things turned out.'

'And yet mysteriously, I'm not laughing,' Jack said. 'Primarily though, that's because I'm concerned we might be going at this like a bull at a gate. What if Rothermere really is taking a nature walk or something?'

Wayland considered the blue sky and even bluer sea. 'It may not feel like it, but the weather's turning,' he said. 'If we end up having to call a helicopter from the mainland, we'll need to contact them sooner rather than later.'

'You don't think it's that bad? I mean the guy's not in his room, that's all.'

Wayland nodded at the pub. 'It's those two in there who are worrying me. They really fucking hate him, Jack. And that squad they were part of . . . they were a serious heavy mob back in the day. You're right, he could still turn up. But mate, I was a murder detective for over twenty years. Sometimes you can just feel these things in your gut.'

Fourteen

The boatshed was situated on the north side of the jetty, at the end of its own short pier. About the size of a suburban garage and built from clapboard, it didn't look as though it was intended to be a permanent structure. Inside was a grey rubber dinghy, fully inflated, with a motor-driven propellor at the back. It sloshed about on its tether, as the sea, which came in through the opening at the front, rose and fell heavily.

'One way to get off the island if all else fails,' Ray Donaldson said.

'With a storm like this brewing?' Jack replied. 'You'd be lucky if they found your body.'

'And what would you know about it?' Donaldson sneered. 'Unless you traded some of those drugs you sold back to the Crew for a course in basic seamanship.'

'One thing's certain,' Claudia said. 'Alan Rothermere hasn't tried it.'

O'Hare grunted something about that being a damn shame, which drew a warning glare from Donaldson. The boatshed didn't contain much else: a coil of rope, some netting, three petrol canisters, a couple of weed-encrusted life belts. Waves meanwhile surged forcefully in, spraying them with foam.

They returned along the short pier, circled around the harbourmaster's cottage on to the esplanade, and began searching Porth West itself.

Harry Wayland had divided them into four groups allocated to different quadrants. Jack, Claudia, Donaldson and O'Hare pattern-searched the harbour, while Wayland, Gabby Milburn and Sally Jakeman covered the shoreline south of the village, primarily the gorse bushes and then the beach. Cheryl Baxter and Varada Rathour went north, checking the rocky coves and coastal woodland under the guidance of harbourmaster Pasco. As the only person on St Dunstan who was anything like a local, his knowledge of the terrain ought to have proved useful.

Jack and Claudia's group was the largest and had the most work to do. Once they'd cleared the town, they had the hotel gardens to investigate: a dozen acres of lawns, flower beds and shady walks ending at potting sheds and greenhouses packed with tropical plants, or secluded arbours containing summerhouses and kissing benches.

All in all, it looked like more than a day's work.

At least Donaldson and O'Hare were doing their bit. They might be surly and dishevelled, but as they moved from cottage to cottage and shop to shop, they tested every door and window.

'The terrible twosome suddenly seem keen to assist,' Claudia commented quietly.

'Wouldn't you be?' Jack said. 'If you were top of the suspect list?'

He checked the next building. 'Course, just because these two are helping now doesn't mean they're innocent. But if they'd done something to Rothermere, don't you think they'd have put this act on from the beginning?'

'What about the man himself?' she wondered.

Jack pondered. 'I don't know Alan Rothermere. First impression . . . bit of a prig. But doesn't seem the sort to go off and hide.'

'There's still a chance he fancied a walk.'

Jack was now doubtful of that. 'Bloody long one. If he disappeared before breakfast, he's been gone a good few hours now.'

'Well, okay . . . but if someone marched him out of his hotel room, it would have to be during the night. Less chance of being seen. How do you do that without causing a ruckus?'

'All you need is a gun and a gag. Maybe a pair of cuffs . . . a piece of rope.'

They tested the next building's front door and windows, then went round to the rear, vaulting over the wall into the back garden. As with the others, there was nothing there yet but freshly laid turf.

'Suppose it isn't Donaldson or O'Hare?' Claudia asked. 'Who would have something to gain?'

He grinned, as they climbed back out. 'Are we playing whodunnit now?'

'Someone's got to.'

'If we're running our own enquiry, the most obvious person to take point is Harry.'

'Except that Harry has to be a suspect too.'

'Everyone's a suspect except us. But Harry's solved dozens of murders as SIO, whereas we only worked murders peripherally.' They'd now emerged inland of the village, where they followed Donaldson and O'Hare up the steps to the Quad Track.

'Granted, he'd be useful,' Claudia said, 'but we don't clear him of suspicion just because he once had a sparkling record. He's done bad things since.'

Up on the Track, Donaldson and O'Hare had already moved out of sight, heading south towards the hotel gate. Jack and Claudia dallied a little, peering across the harbour. Beyond it, the sea was turning grey, the waves rushing inshore. Further out lay a vast, rolling landscape of exploding foam.

'Okay . . .' Jack said. 'Well, assuming the terrible twosome had most reason to harm Rothermere, but at present we can't prove anything against them, let's look at Harry as our first next suspect. What could his motive be?'

Claudia shrugged. 'No one likes a nonce.'

'But most people, as in ninety-nine per cent, aren't so rabid about it that they'd kill. Add to that Harry's worried this may mean the end of Damned Rankers before it's even started. Seems to me he has a good motive *not* to have done anything.'

'Okay. But bear in mind that Harry knows every ex-cop here. There may be a history between him and Rothermere we aren't aware of.'

'You could say the same for everyone.'

She nodded past him. 'What about our favourite mother hen?'

About forty yards north, Cheryl Baxter had also appeared on the Quad Track, and was waiting with arms folded outside a small wooden shed-like structure set back amid the inland foliage.

'Just because her son's a child abuser, would that make her empathise with child abusers in general?' Claudia sounded sceptical. 'She must know the human wreckage those bastards leave behind.'

Jack considered. 'It's a good point, but it's not helping us narrow things down.'

'I still think Rothermere's going to turn up. Don't you? Seriously? Come on, Jack . . . half of this lot have already done time. They're hardly likely to commit murder now they're out.'

Jack mulled it over. Superficially, it made sense. But here they were, on the extreme fringe of the UK. There was literally no one else around. Their only medical facility was the first-aid kit behind reception. There was nothing. No lifeboat team, no police office. And then there were the people gathered here. Not the worst of the worst, but they'd stand out in a crowd. For God's sake, he and Claudia alone had done deals with drug gangs affiliated to the Crew, the overarching criminal power in the whole of northern England. In no sense of the word were he and Claudia ordinary. And the same could be said of all the others.

Cheryl Baxter – trading the names of police informers to keep her son safe in jail.

Jonas Pugh – misdirecting murder enquiries to keep gangland gunmen on the street.

Sally Jakeman – a walking-talking honey trap, her sights set on the biggest names in the job.

Was it really such a leap that among a group like this there might be someone who'd decided Alan Rothermere didn't deserve to live?

'The woods along the northern shore are all thorns and undergrowth,' Cheryl Baxter said as they approached. She pointed to where Ted Pasco, looking red-faced and tired, came limping into view. 'The ground's very steep, very uneven. With our man here in tow, we were having trouble making progress. He suggested we come up here and get one of the quad bikes, then he at least could ride along the Track. Supervise from above. Varada's gone to the hotel to get the key to the bike shed.'

Right on cue, Varada Rathour rounded the bend.

Baxter took the key, unlocked the double doors at the front of the shed and flung them open. It was dim inside and smelled of oil and fresh-cut timber. There were eight quad bikes in different colours. Their keys hung on the wall. Pasco, still huffing and puffing, now joined them.

'You okay?' Jack enquired.

'Not as young as I was, zurrr,' the harbourmaster replied. His Cornish accent was almost exaggeratedly strong. 'Hoped oi'd be more good to you than this.'

'What's the top speed these machines do?' Claudia asked.

Pasco scratched under his seaman's cap. 'Oi believe they've run these things up to fifty miles per hour.'

Claudia was impressed. 'Perhaps we should all take one.'

'They're not much good if you go off the Track, miss,' he replied.

'So we've been told . . .'

Before they could say more, a wild shouting came from down in Porth West. It sounded like a woman. They hurried across the Track to the top of the slope, immediately halting, in fact shunting into each other, at the sight of some sort of object – something floating – which appeared to have entered the harbour.

'Is it a boat?' Claudia said, squinting over the rooftops.

Jack didn't reply. It looked like a rowing boat, minus oars and with some kind of structure on top . . .

'Oh my God,' Rathour said slowly. The youngest there, she had the best eyesight. '*Oh my God!*'

'Is that . . . is that Alan?' Cheryl Baxter stuttered.

Pasco, for all that he was old, stiff and tired, was already hobbling along the Track to the top of the steps. He was harbourmaster, after all. Nothing could enter and dock without his permission. Not that this was his prime concern at present.

Jack hastened in pursuit, Claudia in close attendance, the other women behind.

They'd overtaken the older man by the time they entered the esplanade. Ledina, the barmaid, and the source of the frantic shouting, was standing by the harbour's edge as she gazed across the waters, now rising and falling with force, foam shooting upward. Such was the strength of the incoming tide that the vessel was already close enough for them to see it clearly, along with the cargo it carried: two hefty pieces of timber, each about seven feet in length, laid across each other, forming an X and fixed in the centre, presumably with nails, then laid flat atop the boat and fastened in place again.

But this was not the whole story.

On top of this crude saltire, limbs akimbo, was a naked man.

Even from a distance of fifty yards, they could see he had been slashed open. Not once or twice, but over and over: the torso and the arms and legs, and presumably the face, though as the head hung backward into the belly of the boat, it was impossible to be sure of the latter. Even if they could have seen it, it likely would have been coated in sticky crimson. Just like the rest of the tortured figure, like the cross itself, just like the boat as it drifted steadily to the harbour wall.

Fifteen

Recovery of the corpse proved problematic. Any basic rules about contaminating crime scene evidence had to be discarded, because the boat soon reached the harbour wall, where it was tossed about like matchwood and in danger of overturning.

Pasco managed to snare it with a boathook, and with Claudia's help was able to lug it along the wall to the first set of steps, which were under heavy spray and treacherously slippery. Despite this, Jack, on the end of a makeshift safety line – the coil of rope they'd found in the boatshed – descended to the water. Cheryl Baxter, Varada Rathour and Ledina were on the other end, though Rathour wasn't being especially useful. A former civilian analyst, she was the only one among the island's guests who'd never seen a real-life murder victim, and could only clutch the rope loosely, her eyes locked on the mutilated form, which, with water now sluicing over it, washing away the clotted gore, was becoming ever more identifiable as Alan Rothermere. A couple of times, when Jack almost lost his footing, and once when he actually did, a wave thudding into him, swamping him to his chest, Baxter and Ledina found themselves taking all the slack.

'For Christ's sake, Varada!' Baxter shouted.

With no option, Claudia took over from her, and despatched the terrified girl to grab herself a quad bike and go and fetch the others. This meant that Jack, who'd scrambled his way back up the steps for safety, was able to go chest-deep again and work his way to the front of the boat, which continually turned and tilted, grab its tethering line, and throw it upward, so that it could be secured to a mooring post.

This freed up Pasco to hobble back to the boatshed, where he could unfasten the towline from the rubber dinghy and bring that back too. It was a narrow cord made from polypropylene, but it would suffice. He was badly out of breath when he returned, his face knotted into a scarlet mask, but he still dropped one end down to Jack, who tied it around an iron hook at the boat's stern, while Pasco looped it around another mooring post some twenty yards south of the first. This drew the boat flush alongside the bottom of the steps and held it there.

The next problem was retrieval of the corpse. Because while the X-shaped cross had been nailed down, so had Alan Rothermere.

In an almost biblical act, iron spikes had been pounded through his wrists and ankles. If he'd been alive when this had been done, he'd have been completely immobilised, and when Jack was able to get on board he could see why it had been necessary for the assailant to do this – because the victim had then been repeatedly and extensively gashed by some kind of blade, the wounds so deep and washed so clean he could glimpse bone and internal organs beneath them. Up close, there was similar horrific damage to Rothermere's face.

Harry Wayland now returned, having commandeered the quad bike that Rathour had used and found a way to ride down on to the esplanade itself. Shouting that the others weren't far behind, he descended the steps recklessly, even though he wore no safety line, plunging in up to his waist as he steadied the boat, which continued to rock and sway.

'Christ almighty!' he exclaimed.

'We're going to need a pair of pliers!' Jack shouted.

Wayland nodded dumbly. 'There'll be no concealing this from the boss. This is a right fucking mess. In more ways than one.'

'Look . . . anyone thinks we did *that*, they want their heads examining!' Ray Donaldson yelled. The rest of the pub sat in steadfast silence. His cheeks were pale, his glasses askew, his hair hanging unkempt and stringy. 'You *know* we didn't do it.'

'How the hell do we *know*?' Cheryl Baxter asked with a shaking voice. 'Who had more reason than you two?'

'Not surprised you stayed a woodentop!' Declan O'Hare was on his feet as well. 'You can't *prove* a damn thing.'

Another silence followed, the gas fire hissing, light from its flames flickering on the brass telescopes, the antique sextants, the pirate cutlasses. Otherwise though, The Salmon's interior was unlit and filled with lurking, late-afternoon shadow. The others were scattered in their ones and twos, their expressions blank and tired.

'Way to go, Declan,' Claudia finally said. 'Make it *sound* like you're guilty, why don't you?'

'This is bollocks!' O'Hare glared at them all. 'We're not on trial here.'

'Damn right they're not,' Sally Jakeman said, getting to her feet. 'None of us are.' With the exception of Varada Rathour, Jakeman seemed the most shaken. 'Instead of all this finger-pointing,' she said, 'why don't we try to find a way off this damn island? I can't believe we're stuck here.'

'You *have* heard what's going on out there?' Gabby Milburn asked her. In answer, the window and doors rattled, surf roaring beyond the esplanade.

'We're supposed to be living in the twenty-first century,' Jakeman retorted. 'Has nobody heard of air-sea rescue?'

'Harry's talking to Pasco now.' Jack nodded towards the harbour-side windows, beyond which Harry Wayland could still be seen in conflab with the harbourmaster, the pair of them buffeted by the steadily strengthening wind.

'Why don't they just call someone?'

Jack, who was still saturated, tried to straighten on his seat, but it hurt badly. He was close on forty and his escapade in the water had taken it out of him. His back and muscles ached, and his limbs throbbed where the waves had beaten him on the stonework.

'He's going to,' he said, 'but it still may take a while to get someone out here, and in the meantime, "Did one of us do it, or is some other nutcase hiding on this island?" is a pertinent question to ask.'

Outside, Pasco lurched away, leaning into the gale, while Wayland also moved out of sight. Jack assumed that he'd go first to the pub's rear, to check in the outside storehouse where they'd laid Alan Rothermere on a canvas sheet. Even Jonas Pugh had been disturbed by the ruckus and had finally come outside. It hadn't been as hard as Jack had expected to persuade him to look the body over once they'd got it under shelter, primarily because even *he* had been jolted on first sight of it. Despite this – and Pugh was still in there, suggesting he was giving it more than a quick once-over – Wayland came in through the front.

'Right,' he said. 'Pasco reckons it was the late afternoon tide brought the body into the harbour. Says it's not uncommon for items that go into the water north of Porth West to be carried in at this time of day, especially during high seas. There's a headland up there. Hangman's Point. Seems there was a gibbet there once . . .'

'A gibbet!' Donaldson blurted. 'For Christ's sake!'

'Great fucking place for a holiday, this!' O'Hare declared.

Wayland eyed them irritably. 'Pasco says it was erected by the Surveyor of the Royal Works . . . same bloke who built the castle. It was a warning to Spanish infiltrators. Main thing is, if something went into the water there, it would definitely have floated round into the harbour.'

'Hangman's Point?' Claudia said. 'Should we check it out?'

Donaldson gawked at her. 'What're you talking about?'

'If that's where the murder took place, that's where the murderer may be,' she replied.

'You seriously think he'll still be there?'

'If nothing else, there could be a crime scene to preserve.'

The ex-super snorted. 'In which case, be our guest. You go and sort it.'

Claudia shook her head. 'This the inspirational leadership you showed in the Robbery Squad, Ray?'

'Newsflash, babes . . . we're not coppers anymore. We don't get paid to do that stuff. Though maybe *you* should. You're obviously still keen. Plus, *you're* the one who saw the bastard . . . saw him and didn't say anything.'

Claudia was about to respond sharply, but Jakeman interjected.

'Why don't we just cut the crap. We're nobodies now. We should leave this whole thing to the regular authorities.'

'As we speak, Pasco's gone back to his cottage to try and radio Devon and Cornwall,' Wayland replied, crouching by the fire. 'They'll have to take it from there. I'm still not sure anyone'll get here in the next couple of days, though.'

'How's Pugh doing?' Jack asked.

'Well, it's sobered him.' Wayland stood up again.

'Do you trust him with a job like that?' Milburn wondered.

Wayland shrugged. 'He's not a medical examiner, but he's got more experience than the rest of us.'

'You should be in there too,' Jack said. 'You're the murder man.'

Wayland's response to that was to slump on to a seat. His clothes were still damp too and he looked grey-faced and drained. 'All I can say is that whoever it was . . . they did a real number on the poor bastard. There was serious hatred in that killing.'

'Yes, and we all know who that points to.' Baxter directed another venomous glare at Donaldson, who'd now sidled behind the bar, which was unoccupied since Wayland had sent Ledina up to the hotel.

The ex-super rolled his eyes. 'For Christ's sake . . .'

'Do you think getting drunk is a good idea, Ray?' Milburn asked. 'At a time like this?'

Donaldson rooted under the counter. 'For your info, darling, I'm looking for some snacks. We've none of us eaten since breakfast.'

'They'll do food for us up at the hotel,' Wayland said, 'but it'll only be basic stuff. Sandwiches and that. I've told Beck and his staff that they need to lock themselves into their accommodation once everyone's got sorted.'

'Perhaps *we* should do the same, eh?' Milburn suggested.

Wayland shrugged. 'I'm not giving that order. Firstly, I'm not in a position to give orders. Secondly, it's up to you guys . . . but we've got a couple of days ahead of us yet, at least, and personally I'd rather be proactive.' The response to this was muted. Wayland turned to Claudia. 'This peeper you saw outside the gym . . . can you describe him again?'

'There isn't much,' she replied. 'Male . . . I'm pretty sure it was a guy. Wearing green.'

'Height?' Milburn asked. 'Body shape?'

'You can keep asking me the same things over and over,' Claudia said, 'but it was a very fleeting glimpse, and it was blurred.'

Wayland glanced at Milburn. 'He defo didn't come back when *you* were in there on your own?'

'Didn't see anyone.'

'You sure it couldn't have been one of us?' Jack asked Claudia.

'I've already said that, haven't I!' She tried not to sound truculent, but guilt was gnawing at her, and she still felt nettled by Donaldson's caustic comments. 'It wasn't necessarily a stranger, but . . .'

'But?' Wayland asked.

'He was hovering there, you know. I mean . . . with intent. Whether he was one of us or not, it didn't feel like he'd just happened by and was interested in the gym.'

'He was spying on you?' Baxter cast further furtive glances at Donaldson and O'Hare.

'I thought so, yeah.'

'Like Ray said . . . pity you didn't mention this before someone died,' Jakeman snapped.

'All right,' Jack cut in.

'No, she's right,' Claudia said. 'My instinct at the time was to look into it more, but I wanted to keep all that at arm's length because I wanted to have a holiday. And it was wrong of me.' She got to her feet. 'Which is why I'm not going to sit around and do nothing for the next few days, either. Quad bike still outside, Harry?'

'Key's in the ignition.'

She headed for the door.

Jack jumped to his feet. 'Where you going?'

'Hangman's Point, if I can find it.'

'Apparently you go north along the Quad Track,' Wayland said. 'Only a few hundred yards. There's a path leading down. But it's rough going once you're off the Track.'

'I'll be careful.'

'Wait a minute,' Jack said. Claudia was now in the doorway but glanced back. 'Okay, you feel guilty,' he said, 'but you sure you want to do this?'

'Why not?'

'A few things spring to mind. One's lying in the storeroom out back.'

'Jesus, what a melodrama,' Jakeman snorted. She stared at Claudia. 'Seriously? What're you trying to prove?'

'Nothing. Maybe I just can't get used to the fact this isn't what I do anymore.'

'Then more fool you!' Donaldson called from behind the bar. Despite his intent to forage for snacks, he'd found himself a large Scotch and was in the process of pouring one for O'Hare.

'I'll come with you.' Jack walked over.

'Don't go straight away, Jack,' Wayland said. 'We need to talk first.'

'I'll be fine,' Claudia said. 'If the perp was there, the chances are he'll be gone. You don't hang around at your own crime scene, do you.' She eyed the rest of the room, adding quietly, 'He could even be in here with us, right now.'

'Claudia, I . . .'

She put a hand on Jack's forearm. 'What did we say about control freakery? You're not in charge anymore. I've told you I'll be fine!'

'Jack,' Wayland called across the pub again. 'Need a chat, mate.'

Jack looked back at Claudia, but she'd already left.

Sixteen

'Wanted a private chinwag,' Wayland said, 'because I have to trust someone to help me out.'

He and Jack were standing alone in the dimness of the pub's rear corridor. At the far end of it, a door opened out into the unloading yard, while two side doors faced each other: the entrances to the Gents and the Ladies. No one was in either at present, but Wayland was speaking quietly, his tall, lean form hunched forward.

'You mean help you to investigate this crime?' Jack said.

'Look, Jack, in a few days we're all going to be suspects. As if the world doesn't hate us enough already. The only way to offset that is to make some headway of our own.'

'How do you know you can trust *me*?' Jack asked.

'I don't. Not entirely, but I've made a calculated gamble that you're my best bet.'

'Any particular reason?'

'Not very flattering, I'm afraid. Donaldson and O'Hare are obviously both out. Pugh's helping for now, but once a pisshead always a pisshead. Varada and Sally are so inexperienced as to be next to useless. Cheryl's already decided who the guilty party is with no evidence whatsoever, and while Gabby would be good, she's probably the most physically adept among us . . .'

'And therefore, the one most capable of overpowering a fully grown man and nailing him to a cross?'

'Correct, and while you and Claudia could probably manage that too, you come as a team, and I consider it much less likely that *two* of you could have gone to the dark side.'

'But you don't know for sure?'

'Like I say, it's a calculated gamble.'

'A gamble our benefactor will approve of?'

'We won't see him till this storm clears. But under the circs, that's probably a good thing.'

Jack had to concur.

'In the meantime,' Wayland said, 'we have to assume that whoever the perp is, he or she is armed.'

'I've already mentioned that to Claudi.'

'Which begs the question why didn't they just shoot Rothermere dead?'

'The obvious answer is the manner of the killing. The hideous nature of it was purposeful.'

'My reading too,' Wayland agreed. 'Yet you don't commit a crime like that without having a screw loose of your own. Sorry for the non-technical terminology, but that was sick stuff, and it'd take a sick puppy to pull it off. And yet . . . you saw that no one had forced entry to Rothermere's hotel room?'

'Which means he let them in.'

'Correct again. Presumably late last night.'

Jack pondered. 'So, it *is* one of us?'

'Well . . .' Wayland raised a warning hand. 'I've investigated dozens of murders, and you can't take anything at face value. Rothermere could have been half asleep when he opened the door, and a stranger just jammed a gun in his face. It's not impossible, though I concede the evidence suggests otherwise.'

'Either way, it rules out Donaldson and O'Hare,' Jack said.

Wayland didn't reply because he clearly agreed. Even if Rothermere had answered his door bog-eyed with sleepiness, there was no question that the sight of one or both of his two most hated opponents would likely have triggered an immediate response, probably to slam the door in their faces.

'Seriously?' someone said from further along the passage.

They swung round and saw that Cheryl Baxter had come quietly upon them.

'Seriously?' she said again. 'You're already discounting those two bastards?'

'Look . . .' Wayland began.

'No one else here even knew Alan,' she asserted. 'And like *you* said, Harry . . . that murder had feeling behind it. That was torture, humiliation.'

'Cheryl . . .'

'So the suspects are armed, yes? That's also what you just said.'

'It's a possibility,' Wayland mumbled.

'How many of us here are experienced with firearms?'

The two men glanced at each other, resigned to the fact she'd earwigged everything.

'Gabby was an SFO,' Wayland said. 'I was authorised, but not a specialist.'

'Same for me and Claudia,' Jack admitted.

'And so were our two ex-Robbery Squad detectives, I imagine?' she said.

Jack shook his head. 'You don't need to be experienced with firearms to point them at people, Cheryl.'

'But maybe you do to know how to get hold of one in the first place.'

'Come on,' Jack said, 'there's some wild supposition going on here. We've got to be professional in our response.'

Her brow furrowed with fury. 'That's so what a modern copper would say. "Let's be professional, let's not overreach ourselves, let's not rush to any conclusions." When I joined up, you arrested your suspects, leaned on them to get your lead, and slung them in the traps. That was the top and bottom of it. And it worked.' She turned and stormed back into the pub.

'That's the first time I've ever been called a modern copper,' Jack admitted.

The outside door now banged open, and Pugh came in. He had no disposable latex gloves, so he'd donned the next best thing: a pair of heavy-duty gauntlets that one of the builders had left in the outhouse. He stripped them off and tossed them away.

'Any thoughts on cause of death?' Wayland asked.

Pugh ran a limp hand through his mop of hair. He looked weary and haggard. 'Dunno the correct terminology these days. Massive blood loss, massive tissue damage, shock, cardiac arrest . . . take your pick.'

'Anything that *we* . . . or rather the investigation team can actually move with?'

The former CSI sniffed, his unruly moustache twitching. 'Evidence of recent *antemortem* tissue damage. Would suggest his wrists were bound not long before death.'

'Bound together?' Jack asked.

'Probably behind his back. He was gagged too.'

'Perhaps to make it easier to march him away from the hotel?' Jack said.

'Most likely.' Pugh thought about it as they went into the taproom. 'He was barefoot . . . I can tell you that much. There are injuries to the soles of his feet, consistent with stones, twigs, that sort of thing. There's a heavy contusion to the back of his head. To stun him, I'd say.'

'So . . . what's the hypothesis?' Milburn asked. She and the others had now come forward. 'The bastard clubbed him from behind when he'd finally got him to the murder scene?'

Pugh shrugged. 'What I saw would align with that.'

'And then, when he was stunned, he was nailed?' she asked.

Pugh shrugged again.

Jack pondered the ugliness of that thought. 'So, he *was* crucified alive?'

Milburn frowned. 'And the blade assault was to ensure he'd be dead by the time he got here?'

'Either that, or whoever it was didn't feel that beating him up and nailing him down was punishment enough,' Rathour said, sounding stunned.

'I don't suppose you were able to isolate any forensic traces relating to the assailant?' Wayland asked.

Pugh glanced at him. 'Without any kit?'

'Even without kit, you could've checked his fingernails and his teeth,' Jack said.

Pugh stared at him angrily. 'Poor bugger hasn't got any teeth left. And his fingernails are clean. Christ, I need a bloody drink.' Pugh lurched towards the bar, where Donaldson looked ready and willing to serve him. Only when he'd swilled down half a tumbler of malt whisky did the ex-CSI look round again. 'There could be minute traces there. Under his nails. But as I say, I haven't got the gear for that.'

'Time of death?' Jack wondered.

'I'm not a doctor, for Christ's sake.'

'Anything to suggest there was more than one assailant?' Wayland asked.

Surprisingly, Pugh seemed to give this question serious consideration. 'If he was unconscious, or even semi-conscious when he was crucified . . . one offender could manage that alone, probably. They'd need to be pretty robust though. Manipulating someone who's inert . . . and a dead weight . . .' He swilled more Scotch. 'But holding him in place and nailing him to a chunk of timber? That'd take strength and determination, for sure.'

'I take it there's no indication of sexual activity?' Wayland said.

Pugh wiped his moustache with his bony wrist. 'Can't be sure . . . he was immersed repeatedly in seawater. But there's no damage down there. None that I could see.'

Milburn glanced at Jack. 'Seems odd, doesn't it?'

'What do you mean?' Jack asked.

'The guy's been mutilated to death as punishment for being a sex offender, and yet his genitals are left unharmed.'

'God almighty!' Sally Jakeman stamped forward. 'I seriously can't believe we're having this conversation. I mean, who's going to thank us for it?' She rounded on the rest of them. 'Have you actually considered that when the real cops get here, *we'll* be in the frame? Even if we weren't who we are, they'll assume everything we tell them is a lie.'

'In which case trying to reconstruct the crime and assemble some leads can only work in our favour,' Jack said.

She shook her head. 'Why make it easier for them? After what they did to us?'

Before they could say more, Pasco staggered in through the pub's front door, red-faced, grunting. He made a beeline for Harry Wayland. 'Moi cottage! Broken into while we were out searching. The marine VHF . . . vandalised.'

'Vandalised?' Wayland repeated.

'Someone's smashed it.'

'What the hell are you saying?' Jakeman demanded.

'He's saying we're stuck here till the next scheduled boat arrives,' Jack said.

'But that's several days off.'

'Wait a mo, grandad!' Donaldson shouted from behind the bar. 'Someone's vandalised your radio? You sure you haven't just broken it because you don't know what you're doing?'

Pasco glared at him. 'Oi know my business, zurr.'

Wayland placed a hand on him to calm him. 'You're saying it can't be fixed?'

'Oi . . . oi . . .' The harbourmaster shook his head. He almost seemed tearful. 'Oi can try, but oi can't promise anything.'

'What the hell do we do?' Jakeman demanded. 'How do we get a message out?'

Wayland frowned. 'We can't.'

Pugh snorted through his whisky. 'What're you talking about, boy? We *have* to. We've got a murder victim here.'

'On the contrary, Jonas, all we have to do now is look after ourselves,' Jack said. 'Watch your backs, keep your bedroom doors locked.'

'He isn't finished?' Milburn said. 'The killer, I mean?'

'No,' Wayland replied. 'Plainly, he isn't.'

Seventeen

Claudia had never ridden a quad bike or ATV before, but they were famous for being easy to handle. The machine that Wayland had brought down from the Track had bright blue livery, but was dented and scraped around its lower edges, spattered with mud and sand. However, a key hung in the ignition, as he'd said, and when she climbed aboard, it was a straightforward exercise, the throttle lever located under the right handlebar, while the four-wheel drive button and the brakes spoke for themselves.

She shifted into automatic, and gunned the vehicle to life. Keeping a steady pace, she guided it through the village to the foot of the grassy slope. Here, she halted for a second, the powerful engine rumbling as she glanced down at her tyres, which had deep off-road treads. Feeling certain they'd give her the traction she needed, she throttled the bike, leaning forward and accelerating as she ascended the slope, the ride levelling out as she attained the Quad Track.

She decelerated again, and braked, glancing around.

The bike shed stood open, its double doors swinging in the wind. The sea, meanwhile, looked seriously rough, the sky a mass of dark, scudding cloud. For mid-June it was cool and damp, and Claudia was still only wearing running gear. Presumably there'd be some overalls around for guests seeking to ride the ATVs, not to mention helmets, goggles and gloves. But going up to the hotel felt like a potential distraction. Deciding that she wouldn't be long on the bike – Wayland had said the path down to Hangman's Point was only a few hundred yards away – she opted to endure the elements, accelerating northward.

The hotel fell behind her, and briefly she even lost sight of the Atlantic as trees sprang up on the trackside, only for it to come back into view on her left, though it now seemed further down than before, suggesting the Track had elevated.

According to her watch, it was just after six. So, a good three and a half hours of daylight remained, though with no actual sunshine there was an aura of encroaching darkness and danger. It was difficult to quantify how differently she now felt about St Dunstan compared to the night before. As she rode north, she was careful not to approach any kind of serious speed. The Track was firm and level, but that didn't mean branches and the like hadn't been deposited on it by the wind. The last thing she needed was to be thrown from the saddle while travelling at thirty-plus. Not when there were no hospital facilities here.

She glanced left again. The ocean seemed to have receded further downward, along with the upper reaches of trees, which left the topmost section of slope to scrub vegetation, in the centre of which Claudia suddenly spotted a break that almost looked manmade.

She pulled the machine to a halt, pocketed the key, and dismounted.

The break was indeed a path, which tumbled away downhill. Almost certainly, it was the same one Wayland had mentioned, but it was steep and rocky, the soil itself loose. Thick, prickly vegetation – yet more of this semi-Mediterranean flora the Scillies seemed to specialise in – inundated the slope's upper section, overhanging the path from either side.

Claudia was clawed and spiked as she descended. All the while of course, the wall of trees further down was rising toward her, their upper boughs clashing and clattering in the wind. If the perp was still down there, and she needed to run, it wouldn't be easy scrambling back up. More than once, she glanced behind her. The path wasn't so much steep now as teetering. It was like looking up a cliff face. She'd only travelled a couple of hundred yards down and she couldn't see the road, never mind the quad bike. The time to go back was now, if that was what she was thinking, but hell, she'd already come this far.

She continued down, and gradually, the closer she came to the trees, the easier it proved. Not so much because the path levelled out, which it didn't, but because the vegetation on either side thinned. She peered down through widely spaced trunks of myrtle, pine and elm, and spied the sea at the bottom, explosions of foam where it collided with the rocky shore.

Once inside the wood, she halted, eyes attuning to the half-light. The woodland floor still tilted steeply, but now was cluttered with dried leaves, twigs and cones. Given the waves of motion rolling through, it was difficult to be certain, at least from this perspective, that there was no one else down there. However, one thing she *did* spot, far below but clearly visible, was a small, ramshackle building.

Which gave her pause for thought.

With no one supposedly having lived on St Dunstan before, it seemed odd, bewildering even. But of course, there were paths all over the island. And the castle. There might never have been what you'd call permanent habitation, but lots of visitors had clearly had cause to stay here at one time or another.

Claudia proceeded down, moving from trunk to trunk. The path had all but disappeared, though it wasn't needed now with the ground suddenly bare of cover. An echoing *crack* sounded somewhere to the right.

She halted and glanced over that way.

There was nothing obviously suspicious. The noise had likely been innocent enough, an upper bough splintering in the gale. The sea breeze stiffened, dead leaves swirling. Overhead, more branches clacked and clattered. She recommenced her descent, the gradient reducing, the small structure coming more clearly into view. It was built from wood, with a roof possibly made from tarpaper, though sections of this had collapsed. Location-wise, it was almost on the water's edge, which made her think that it might be another boatshed.

With an ear-piercing shriek, a sizeable object swooped past the top of Claudia's head. Cursing, she ducked, then stared up wide-eyed, seeing an over-large seagull flapping strenuously away, soaring upward through the trees, and in the same motion, as her gaze tracked after it, catching movement on the slope itself about thirty yards to her left.

Claudia spun in that direction, certain she'd just glimpsed a figure clambering away along that higher section of slope, vanishing amid the trunks.

She held that position for several seconds, still in a crouch, eyes straining.

There was no sign of movement now, which had to be weird. If there'd *really* been someone walking away, wouldn't she spy them again? A bit further afield?

Unless they've stopped, an inner voice told her. *Because they're not leaving, and now they've found a hiding place close by.*

She rose to her feet, eyes still locked on that high, distant place, which was difficult to penetrate with any accuracy of vision. It wasn't just the dimness of the fading day; it was the tossing foliage.

It didn't obscure much; it obscured nearly everything. But that didn't mean there was someone there.

Boldly, she went on down the slope.

Near the bottom, the trees thinned completely, and the ground levelled itself into a natural platform before plunging again, this time over razor-edged rocks into heaving, boiling surf. It was on this platform where the shed rested, about thirty yards below her, and it was every bit as dilapidated as she'd first thought. In fact, it visibly shifted in the wind, creaking and thudding as its rusted screws jiggled between age-old joists.

She'd also been right that it wasn't just a shed, but a boatshed, for as she approached it from behind, Claudia saw that it had been erected face-on to the sea, and while there were no windows or other apertures at the back or on either of its sides, when she made her way round, she spotted where a slipway had been cleared down to the water's edge and laid with a ramp made of planks, though all were now rotten and had gaps in between. At the front of course, the structure stood wide open.

Claudia halted at the building's north-west corner. Directly below, the sea bludgeoned the shoreline, spray shooting skyward. It was difficult to imagine that any craft could have been launched from here without immediately capsizing. But what was it Ted Pasco had said? If a boat should enter the water here at a certain time of day, it would eventually find its way into the harbour. Did this mean the boat carrying Rothermere's body had been launched several hours ago? They were already working on the basis he'd been abducted and maybe killed during the night, which would have given his funeral barge ample time to round the headlands south of here, before the seriously heavy waves came in.

Deciding it best not to set foot on the ramp's upper platform, which looked perilously slippery, she sidled into the interior, but didn't go fully in until her eyesight had adjusted to the gloom.

At which point she went cold.

Despite her twelve years a cop, she'd never been a dedicated murder investigator. But as a divisional CID officer and later as part of an anti-organised crime taskforce, she'd attended numerous murder scenes. And what she was seeing now was too obviously one of those.

The interior was strewn with crinkled leaves, seabird feathers and roof fragments. But there were other things too: several offcuts of freshly sawn wood, a range of discarded tools including a hammer and a scattering of nails, a jar with a brush stuck in it containing some kind of gum-like resin, possibly epoxy, and, last but not least, a pile of man-size pyjamas: scrunched, filthy and liberally stained with blood.

Claudia fought to keep her thoughts on track, and of course, ensure that she didn't stray another foot on to the crime scene. On one hand she was thankful that it was already sheltered from above: that meant the forensics would last a little bit longer. Plus, it would be easy enough to declare this place out of bounds to everyone else on the island. However, it reinforced in her mind the savagery of what had been done to Alan Rothermere.

Hammers and nails were crude, simple tools, hardwearing and heavy-duty.

And hellish when you pitted them against human flesh.

That said, this was evidently where the carpentry had taken place, the epoxy implying that the boat itself, which had probably lain abandoned in here for uncountable years, had needed patching up, while the cross had been constructed from whatever spare parts the killer had found when he or she had first recced the site. Of course, all of that suggested advanced planning, and a knowledge of the island and its tidal currents. As far as Claudia was aware, they themselves, aka the Damned Rankers, had only arrived yesterday, though that didn't mean it was the first time they'd all of them been here.

But even with a significant amount of pre-planning, this wouldn't have been easy. If the killer, having abducted his target in the middle of the night, had brought him here by quad bike – if such a thing was even possible, and Claudia didn't see how it could be – the noise would surely have woken someone in the hotel. In which case Rothermere came here on foot.

She also found that near-enough incredible, but what alternative was there?

The killer had marched his prisoner down to the Quad Track from the hotel, along the Track and down the path to here. All told, that whole journey on foot must have taken a minimum of twenty-five minutes to half an hour. That certainly demonstrated discipline on the killer's part. In addition, it *proved* Jack's theory that he or she was armed. How else would they have been able to control their captive? Even then it would have required real determination, real strength of purpose. And almost straight away, Claudia struggled to see Ray Donaldson and Declan O'Hare fitting that bill. Okay, they hated Rothermere with a passion, but most of their time on St Dunstan they'd spent in vacation mode, drunk, overeating, taking nothing seriously.

The wind changed direction, moaning through the high trees. Below the boatshed another hefty wave pounded the shoreline. The shed gave a long, arthritic creak. Claudia glanced above and around, checking the stability of the old, weathered structure.

Which was when she saw it.

The eye.

Red-rimmed and hideous.

Goggling in at her through a notch in the woodwork.

Eighteen

Claudia spun around, a yelp of fear trapped in her throat.

Immediately, the eye was gone, only dim woodland visible beyond the spyhole. But she didn't hear the sound of feet thrashing off through the brambly undergrowth. She remained fixed to the spot, reaching slowly down with a shaking hand, grabbing the hammer.

The wind picked up again, the ocean booming and roaring, making it impossible to detect any other movement outside. She backed down the length of the shed, veering warily towards the notch in the right-hand wall, only to restrain herself at the last moment. She'd seen enough horror movies to know there'd be nothing to stop some long, sharp instrument from being rammed through just as she peeked out. She continued retreating until she reached the rear wall, where she halted. Beyond the opening at the front, she saw only tumultuous grey cloud, and a rumbling, exploding seascape.

He couldn't let her leave, of course.

Not now that she'd discovered the crime scene.

Once a team of examiners got in here, it was over for him.

She strained her ears for telltale sounds beyond the flimsy woodwork. Hearing only the creaking and groaning of long-decayed joints.

How long before Jack came to see where she was? Under normal circumstances, perhaps it would be soon, but when they'd parted, she'd been obstinate with him, insisting that she wanted to do this on her own, that she didn't need his help.

Still, only sky and sea lurked beyond the opening. Briefly, crazily, she wondered about dashing out there, sliding down the slipway, taking a chance in the ocean. At which point a particularly immense wave detonated on the coastline rocks, spraying even the boatshed's interior with spume. *Maybe not*, she corrected herself.

There was only one thing for it. She had to make a break back up through the woods and along that terribly steep path to the road. It would be hard going, but it would be hard going for anyone chasing as well. And if he caught up with her, she had a weapon.

She regarded the hammer in her fist. It was a simple claw hammer, something any workman would keep in his toolbox. But it would pack a punch.

The boatshed shifted sideways, the timbers at her back juddering.

Despite everything – the sweat soaking her body, the speed of her racing pulse – she shouted, 'What are you waiting for? You know I saw you! Come on in! Let's do it!'

It was madness of course, to provoke him, to challenge him. A madness fuelled by tension and terror. And only now did she remember that, whoever he was, he most likely had a gun, which now that he'd heard her shouting, could enable him to pinpoint her exactly. He might be aiming at the woodwork directly behind her even as she stood here.

She lurched forward, stumbling the length of the interior, only halting a couple of feet before the slipway platform. The dank sea air caressed her; more spray hit her face. She glanced back, expecting the rear wall to explode inward as a hail of slugs tore through. But that didn't happen.

'Shit!' She fought to get her nerves under control.

Okay, he was out there. But what if he'd got spooked on learning that his murder den had been discovered? What if he'd simply legged it?

He has to get rid of you, you dumb mare! He needs to clean this place up, so there'll be no sign you were ever here.

Though that was the way an organised offender would work. Not necessarily one who was disorganised. Disorganised killers were great for stalking and slashing their prey, but when it came to covering their tracks, that was often where they fell down.

Christ almighty! Who do you think you are, some God damned behavioural scientist? All that matters is getting the hell out of here.

She struggled to moderate her breathing, to calm herself.

Clearly, he didn't want to come in. Did he genuinely not fancy hand-to-hand combat with someone who'd been forewarned? It wouldn't be cowardly of him, as much as smart – anything could happen in a fight – but in that case why didn't he just come in and shoot her? Maybe he didn't have a gun after all?

Again, she chided herself for trying to work out details without solid evidence. Her one priority now was to leave this place in one piece.

If he was out there still – and she had to work on the basis he was – he'd either be the first thing she'd see when she finally risked it, or he'd be hiding, the purpose of the latter presumably to launch an ambush. That wouldn't be easy, owing to the lack of ground cover in this lower portion of the woods, and while it always worked in the movies, standing behind a tree trunk rarely worked in real life.

But suppose he was lurking at the back of the shed? Because when she went out, either to left or right, she'd still need to pass the hidden space at the rear before commencing the uphill trek. That was surely the point where he'd jump her. Whatever the case, she couldn't stay here. It was already dark enough in these woods without night falling.

Claudia steeled herself for the dash to freedom. Some dash. The mere thought of charging up that exhausting hill was onerous.

She took a couple of deep breaths, gripped the hammer tightly, and darted out to the right. For half a nightmarish second, she skidded on the sodden platform at the top of the slipway, but then stepped clear of it on to the woodland floor, where she found herself staring along the north side of the boatshed. No one was visible. She glanced leftward into the woods. Again nothing, apart from the stirrings caused by the wind. Of course, there was still the rear of the structure. The ambush point.

She walked stiffly forward but veering away, giving the boatshed a wide berth. Again, no attack came. She bypassed the rear and there was nobody there. Striking uphill, she found new energy, though she continually looked around and behind. Always, the woods remained apparently deserted.

'Okay,' she said, encouraged, 'okay . . .'

Not that it would be easy, even if the path back remained clear, the gradient torturing her with its terrible angle. She jogged rather than ran, hoping to conserve her energy in case a burst of genuine speed was suddenly required. Again, she glanced back, though it was harder to see now, her vision tunnelling down through darkening, cavorting trees.

He's here somewhere. You know he is.

She increased her speed. The adrenaline kept her going, but her lungs were already working overtime, spittle gathering in her mouth, legs and arms throbbing.

Strangely, it was only when she broke from the cover of the wood, the path slanting even more steeply, that the fear really seized her. As she stumbled upward, her breath rasping like a saw in her chest, she glanced back again and again, each time expecting to see a masked figure scrambling in energised pursuit, perhaps clad all over in black . . . or maybe green, as she'd seen at the gym.

He watched you there, took in your form, salivated over you . . .

'Shut up!' she tried to scream, but it came out a gagging cough. She was almost at the top now. Survival was in reach.

So, this was the moment when the massive hand would clutch her collar from behind. Or where steel would rip through her, or a gun would jam in her ear and a gloating voice whisper obscenities as she was marched back downhill to where the nails and timbers waited.

In truth, there was no one more surprised than Claudia when she tottered on to the Quad Track, wobbling on legs made of rubber. Shoving the hammer into her tracksuit pouch, she straddled the quad bike, slotted the key into the ignition, gunned the machine to life and swinging it round in a tight U-turn, raced back the way she'd come.

Even then it was impossible not to think that some hulking figure had come up on to the Track behind her and now was standing there, watching as she hared away.

So frantic was she that, as she swerved off the Track and down the grassy slope to Porth West, the machine tilted on to two wheels and for a couple of seconds, she descended at what felt like fifty miles per hour, veering crazily along the muddy furrows cut by Harry Wayland. She hit the paved path below at too tight an angle, but just about made the turn. Gasping, hunched over the handlebars, she rode through the mini network of footways, and finally into The Salmon's rear yard, where she sat limply, head drooped, sweat dripping.

She was so physically exhausted that she could only dismount awkwardly. She went wearily through the pub's back entrance, thankful beyond words that she could hear voices in the bar. It was only as she hobbled towards them that she realised someone else was in the darkened rear passage. First, it was the soft *click* of the door to the Ladies closing just behind her. Then the harder, more metallic click of a weapon cocking.

She stopped rigid, ice-cold shivers passing through her.

Claudia only needed to turn her head slightly to see the muzzle of a Beretta 92.

Nineteen

Jack was in mid-conversation with Harry Wayland when the door to the pub's rear corridor swung open, and Claudia, pink-faced and dishevelled, came stiffly in. The others in the taproom barely noticed at first. Jakeman and Pugh were on bar stools, drinking whisky, Donaldson and O'Hare still behind the bar, revelling in the attention a redheaded looker like Jakeman was again paying them. Gabby Milburn was shooting pool on her own. She *did* glance around, and then straightened up, cue in hand.

Because Claudia wasn't alone. Cheryl Baxter was just behind, levelling a Beretta pistol on the back of her skull.

Jack didn't realise what was happening until Baxter had pushed Claudia away and advanced on the bar, her weapon now aimed two-handed at Donaldson and O'Hare, the latter of whom dropped the pint he was swilling from, glass shattering at his feet.

'What's this?' Jack shouted, lurching across the pub.

'No one panic!' Baxter ordered them, eyes fixed on the startled faces of the two ex-Robbery Squad men. 'No one do anything stupid. Don't try it, O'Hare!' The big guy froze before he could slip through into the stockroom. '*You're* the one I'm here for! And *you*, Donaldson!' She threw a half-glance at Claudia. 'Sorry about that, but I didn't know where everyone would be when I came in here and I might've needed some kind of shield.'

'Gee, thanks,' Claudia replied.

Jack edged forward again. 'Cheryl . . .'

'Stay where you are, Jack!'

He froze, as did Wayland, who'd also been encroaching. Pugh and Jakeman remained on their stools, eyes wide, though Pugh was struggling to get his in focus. 'What in the name of . . . ?' he slurred.

'Shut up!' she retorted, still fixated on her two main targets. 'You bloody sot!'

An ear-pummelling silence filled the pub, broken only by the soft hissing of the gas fire. Donaldson tried to smile, but failed.

'You really are a nutty bitch.'

Baxter's face was eerily expressionless. 'Still trying to brazen it out?'

'Fellas . . .' He threw sideways glances at Jack and Harry. 'Some help, yeah?'

'I said no one move,' Baxter snapped at them. 'You're a good actor, Donaldson, I'll give you that. Pretending you don't recognise this weapon.'

His attention shifted to the Beretta. 'I've never seen it before.'

'Even though I've just found it in one of the bags in your room?'

Donaldson's eyes narrowed. 'You've been in my room?'

'They left their balcony windows open,' she told the pub in general. 'It was no problem getting in through them . . . all I had to do was climb on to the outhouse roof.'

Wayland edged forward again. 'Cheryl,' he said gently, 'what are you saying?'

Her gaze burned into her two targets, both of whom, with no other option, had raised their hands. The gun remained levelled, unwavering.

'They might have pulled the wool over all the rest of your eyes,' she said, 'and I'm particularly surprised at *you*, Harry Wayland, but they didn't mine. And at least now we *know* these two are the guilty parties.'

'You went up there and searched?' Wayland asked.

'An illegal search, of course. Me not having a warrant, and all that. But thankfully I don't need one these days, because I'm not a police officer.'

Donaldson glanced again at the rest of them. His flabby features had paled under the overhanging strands of sweaty hair. 'You guys can't seriously be buying this?'

O'Hare sidled again towards the stockroom door. 'Look . . . if you didn't find anything in *my* room, this is nothing to do with—'

'Stay where you are!' she shrieked. 'Last time I'll tell you, O'Hare. You and him are two halves of the same whole. You *both* went to jail because of Alan. You *both* had more reason than anyone else to do what you did to him.'

'Mind if *I* move, at least?' Sally Jakeman slipped down from her bar stool and manoeuvred herself out of the firing line. 'I mean, this place is great, isn't it? Come and have a well-earned holiday. Put your feet up with some kindred spirits. It's more like a fucking looney bin.'

'You can shut your yap too,' Baxter spat, still aiming at Donaldson and O'Hare. 'I've noticed *you've* got pretty thick with these two killers.'

'Cheryl . . . put the gun down, eh?' Jack urged her.

'The hell I will!'

'It'll end up going off.'

Baxter scowled at Donaldson. 'And if it does, the world will be rid of a truly disgusting piece of trash.'

Milburn had now come into the taproom. She still carried her cue but held it down by her side. 'Cheryl, come on,' she said. 'We don't want any more deaths.'

'Look, the fact they had a gun in their luggage . . .' Jack said.

'That wasn't in my luggage,' Donaldson interjected. 'Someone's planted it.'

'It doesn't prove anything,' Jack said. 'Just put it down, yeah? It can be checked for prints when we get it to the mainland.'

'And then you'll see that neither of us even touched it,' O'Hare said.

'But that won't matter if you've already shot us, will it?' Donaldson added.

She glowered all the more. 'Don't tempt me.'

'Isn't it about time you got your head round it?' Jakeman said, having retreated to the entrance to the snug, a small room off the main bar area. 'Alan Rothermere was *not* your son, okay?'

'Luckily for these two.'

Jack glanced covertly at Milburn, who'd ventured forward until she was about three feet to Baxter's left, while he and Wayland were maybe four feet away on the right. She caught him looking, and shook her head tautly.

He got the message. After everything Baxter had been through, she was under monumental strain. What kind of horrific fate had she envisaged befalling her son that she'd been driven to negotiate with gangsters to buy his safety? And now it couldn't even be written off as a frantic mother's overwrought imagination because she'd seen what had happened to Alan Rothermere. If they interfered with her now, she might genuinely start shooting.

All that said, for the first time Baxter seemed distracted. 'There's too much . . . too much injustice in the world.' Her voice had changed. Was suddenly less defiant, almost querulous. 'Alan paid his debt to society the same way you did.' She glared even harder at Donaldson. 'You seriously think you can do that to him, and walk away?'

'Cheryl,' Jack said calmly, 'Ray and Declan searched for Alan alongside us.'

'The same way a whole bunch of other killers have injected themselves into investigations all through history, to pretend they care.'

'What do you propose we do?' Jack asked her. 'We can't get them to a police station for the next five days. You going to stand here and point that at them for the whole rest of this week?'

'I . . .' She struggled. 'For God's sake, you've seen what these men are like.'

'Sure,' Wayland replied. 'A pair of boorish, pig-ignorant slobs. But that doesn't make them murderers.'

Milburn edged nearer. 'Cheryl, how many likely suspects have turned out to be innocent?'

Baxter threw a fleeting glance at her. 'Are you mad? I found *this* in their luggage.'

'So, hand it to me,' Jack said. He was the closest, one hand now resting on the bar top. 'They're not going anywhere, and we'll probably all be arrested anyway when this week ends. Then we can each put our suspicions to the investigation team.'

Her face twisted with doubt.

'What happened to Alan Rothermere was unconscionable,' Wayland said. 'Even if he was guilty as charged. We don't nail people to crosses in this country. But we don't shoot them either.'

She swallowed. Sweat glinted on her forehead.

'I just . . . I just wanted you all to know . . . to see what I found.'

'And now we have,' Jack said. 'So, hand it over, yeah?'

She glanced sidelong at him. Their eyes locked, but she still seemed distant. Even so, after a lengthy deep breath, she lowered the firearm and handed it to him grip first.

There was a grunt of relief from the rest of the pub. Apart from Donaldson and O'Hare, the former of whom snatched down the knobbly-headed shillelagh hanging behind the bar. 'You crazy bitch, you could have—'

'Enough!' Jack shouted, dragging Baxter back and levelling the pistol on them himself.

Again, Donaldson froze. 'Have *you* lost it too?'

'Keep your hands where I can see them, both of you.'

'Jack?' Wayland said uneasily. 'Mate?'

Jack turned slightly, so that no one could come up on him from behind, but he kept the weapon trained on the two barmen. 'They *had* this gun, Harry. We can't just ignore it.'

'I already told you,' Donaldson shouted, 'someone's framed me.'

'Maybe. But that's a chance I don't want to take.'

'Okay, okay . . .' Wayland, still looking happier that Jack had the gun rather than Baxter, circled round into the middle of the taproom. 'So, what do you want to do?'

Jack shrugged. 'Lock 'em up. Just till someone comes.'

'For the whole rest of this week?' Donaldson exploded. 'Are you nuts?'

'It won't necessarily be that long,' Jack said. 'Once Pasco fixes the radio, we'll get through to someone . . . even if it's only the Coastguard. They can't just sit on their arses complaining about the storm now we've got a murder to deal with.'

Donaldson threw his arms out. 'Are the rest of you hearing this?'

'We are,' Milburn said. 'And he's got a point.' She looked at the others. 'We wouldn't let this go on the street. Any unexplained firearm would lead to an arrest, especially if we've reason to believe it's just been used in a violent crime.'

Wayland pondered. 'Okay. So where do we lock them up? Their rooms here?'

'No way!' Baxter protested. 'That means we'd have to stay here too . . . give up our cosy accommodation at The Culraven.'

Jack watched Donaldson and O'Hare warily. 'I suggest we walk them up to the hotel. Beck might have a storeroom or something.'

'A storeroom!' Donaldson blurted. 'Fuck's sake, McGurn!'

'You don't get to talk!' Baxter jabbed a finger at him. 'Not after what you did.'

'Taking them up there now?' Wayland asked.

'I reckon,' Jack replied. 'I know this whole thing's screwed up, but we've got to do what we think's best.'

But the two suspects remained in place behind the bar.

'That geriatric pillock, Pasco, said the radio got smashed while we were all searching,' Donaldson said. 'But all that time, me and Dekko were never out of your eyesight.'

Jack wondered about this, but now Claudia joined the conversation.

'That's not strictly true.' She shouldered her way in among them. 'Sometimes you were. We were all doing different parts of the village.'

'What would *you* do, Ray?' Wayland asked the ex-super. 'Let the prime suspect wander around, free to go wherever he likes, do whatever he wants?'

'Like some wolf in the fold?' Baxter added.

Donaldson threw her a brief, baleful glance. 'What crap is that? If me and Dekko had done Rothermere, that'd be it. What beef would we have with the rest of you?'

'Maybe you'd want to get rid of some witnesses,' Claudia suggested.

'We'd have some explaining to do when the cavalry finally arrived and there was only us two left.'

'Enough talking.' Wayland lifted the bar flap. 'Let's get up the hill, get this thing over and done with.'

Donaldson and O'Hare glanced at each other one final time, as if they might resist further. But in truth, all the brutishness had drained out of them. They seemed exasperated but tired. And what were they going to do, exactly? Fight with everyone here? Even if it was only Harry Wayland and Jack McGurn, it wouldn't work in their favour. Not with McGurn packing a gun.

Doggedly, they trooped out.

Jack turned an expression of relief to Claudia, but her own face remained inscrutable.

Twenty

'How did *your* investigation go?' Jack asked quietly.

Claudia didn't reply at first. They were walking up the drive towards the hotel, the two prisoners trudging ahead, Harry Wayland on the left of them, Gabby Milburn on the right.

'Well, I found the crime scene,' Claudia replied, equally quiet.

'Yeah?' Jack still had the gun in his hand but was unsure how to carry it. Even in these circumstances, it had felt plain wrong to level it on the backs of two former comrades, so he kept it lowered.

'Pretty certain,' she said.

'Okay? Managed to preserve it?'

'Didn't really get the chance.'

'Did it tell you anything, though?'

'First, answer me this, Jack. All the time I was away, was everyone else in the pub with you?'

'Hard to be sure. Cheryl wasn't, obviously. She was busy breaking into bedrooms upstairs.'

'What about the others?'

He threw his thoughts back, but mostly while Claudia had been away he'd been deep in conversation with Wayland. The rest of the pub interior, meanwhile, had gradually filled with shadows and flickery firelight, so it wouldn't have been easy keeping tabs on everyone anyway. All he could do was shrug.

'Who are the ones you're certain were in there?' she asked.

'Harry,' Jack replied. 'These two.' He nodded at Donaldson and O'Hare. 'They never came out from behind the bar.'

'Shit,' she hissed.

They'd reached the hotel and made a solemn procession as they entered. Beck was still behind reception, beating a tattoo on its counter with his fingers. This ceased when he saw them approaching, the two prisoners at the front, Jack close behind wielding a firearm.

Harry Wayland explained as best he could. It was a surreal moment, even for the ex-cops, so it must have been even stranger for Lucas Beck.

His eyes darted from one to the next, as if he hadn't heard properly. 'You wish me to find a room in which these two guests can be confined?'

'It's called a citizen's arrest,' Wayland replied. 'I assure you it's entirely legal.'

The hotelier glanced again at the Beretta.

'We'll take full responsibility,' Wayland said. 'You probably know something of our background. If not, I'm sorry. You're just going to have to trust us.'

Beck still seemed bewildered, and not a little bit upset, but he was clearly wary of the gun.

'Unfortunately, none of our guest rooms can be secured from the outside,' he said. 'It's a standard safety precaution, you see. In the event of fire.'

'You must have something,' Jack said. 'Closets and the like.'

Donaldson snorted, as if to say they'd play hell trying to get him into a closet.

'I suppose there's the attic,' Beck suggested. 'It's on the top floor of the hotel. It's very spacious and airy, because there are windows in which small panes can be opened.'

Donaldson shook his head. 'You're seriously going to put us in the fucking loft?'

'As I say, sir,' Beck replied. 'Technically speaking, it's an attic. It has a floor, and there are sundry items stored up there already. Spare furniture and the like . . . nothing unpleasant.'

Jack glanced at Claudia, then at Wayland. Wayland glanced at Milburn, who shrugged.

'The attic it is,' Wayland said.

'And it can be locked from the outside?' Claudia sought to confirm.

'It's a storage space, so yes it can, ma'am.'

'You mentioned there are windows?' Milburn said.

Beck shrugged. 'There are, ma'am. But they'd be a poor form of egress. They're eighty feet from the ground.'

'So, who's keeping the gun?' Milburn asked, as the four of them descended the hotel drive.

It was getting dark, the wind intensifying, though the rain had held off. But it was no time for turning in yet; Wayland had already organised another conflab in The Salmon and had sent Varada Rathour to find out how Pasco was proceeding with his repair job.

'I'll keep it,' Jack replied. 'It's already got Cheryl's prints on it as well as the actual killer's. And now it's got mine too. We don't want to add any more.'

No one argued with that. Jack halted, checking the safety was on, and tucking the weapon away inside his anorak. Claudia waited with him, watching as Wayland and Milburn continued down the drive.

'You know,' she said. 'Donaldson might have a point when he says that if only him and O'Hare were left alive on the island, it would be the end of them.'

Jack shook his head. 'I'm increasingly sure it wasn't Donaldson or O'Hare.'

'Okay . . . ?'

'It's not just the fact they're too obvious a pair of suspects. They didn't know Rothermere was going to be on the island any more than we did. So they wouldn't have had time to plan anything, make themselves au fait with the tides, the coastal currents and that. There's something else too.' He slapped his anorak. 'This Beretta's not loaded.'

'What?'

'The clip's empty. I sussed it as soon as I took charge of it. Too light. You want proof?'

He took the pistol out again, ejected the magazine and showed her.

'But Donaldson and O'Hare put their hands up,' Claudia said.

'Correct. Which means . . .'

'It isn't their gun.'

He headed down the drive again.

She followed him. 'So, it *was* planted?'

'Feels like the obvious explanation.'

'Why have we locked them up?'

Jack grimaced, troubled. 'Because they're still the most likely suspects. They aggressively despised Rothermere, and made no secret of it. Just because it isn't their gun, that's no guarantee they didn't murder him.'

'When were you planning to share this info about the gun with the others?'

'When you say the others, who do you mean? Because if Donaldson and O'Hare didn't do it, who did?'

'Surely you trust Gabby and Harry?'

'I don't know,' he said. Ahead of them, the aforementioned twosome had now vanished through the hotel gate. 'Harry knows this island a bit better than the rest of us. He *could* have done some pre-planning. And Gabby, well . . . she's *physically* capable of killing someone.'

'It doesn't make sense,' Claudia said. 'But if nothing else, at least now that we're alone, I can fill you in on what happened at the crime scene.'

Jack looked round as they walked, Claudia describing everything: the scene inside the boatshed, the person she thought she'd glimpsed, the eye glaring in at her.

'I didn't say anything when I first got back to the pub, because, first of all, I had a gun on me and my focus was elsewhere. But also, because, like you just said, even if there's a third party on St Dunstan, that doesn't necessarily put everyone else in the clear.'

'More than one of them, eh?' Jack muttered. 'There's a cheery thought.'

They descended through the gate on to the Quad Track and headed north.

'The problem,' Claudia said, 'is that if we treat everyone else as a suspect, we're not going to win many friends at a time when we could really use some.'

He pondered. 'We'll make it known about the mysterious other person at the crime scene. Say you delayed mentioning it because you were so shaken up. But let's keep the intel about the gun not being loaded between us.'

The top of the steps down to the village came in sight. Varada Rathour stood there, wrapped in her coat, in tense conversation with Milburn and Wayland.

The latter turned to face them as they approached.

'Pasco's not in the harbourmaster's cottage,' he said simply. 'Not only that, the radio's still in pieces . . . there's no sign he's done any repair work at all.'

Twenty-One

Raindrops flew like bullets when Jack, Claudia and Harry Wayland pulled up on their quad bikes at the point where the path plunged down to Hangman's Point.

'Down the bottom here?' Wayland said, huddled in his waterproof as he peered down the precipitous footway. Night had fallen properly, and as well as soaking wet, it was pitch-dark.

'Several hundred yards down,' Claudia said.

'Like gazing over the edge of hell,' Wayland mumbled.

To Jack's eye, it was a bottomless void, roaring and screaming as the sea wind tore through the shoreline woods, the thundering echoes of invisible waves an assault on their very ears.

'You say you didn't see very much of this fella?' Wayland asked. He had to shout just to be heard.

'Nothing at all really,' Claudia said.

'He didn't follow you up the path when you came back to the road?'

'No, but . . . well, just because I didn't see him, doesn't mean he wasn't there.'

'Seems weird he let you go,' Wayland said. 'Unless he knew this storm was coming and it would wash everything away.'

'I'm not sure it will,' she said. 'I mean, that boatshed was decades old. Must have stood through Atlantic storms before.'

'Either way, it's out of bounds at present.' Wayland stepped back from the edge. 'Unless you two fancy going down? I know I don't . . . not now we've got rain as well.'

Claudia glanced at Jack, who'd said nothing so far.

He shrugged. 'No sense putting ourselves in greater danger than we already are. We can come back in the morning, or whenever the storm's blown itself out. See what's left then.'

As they rode back, the rain intensified, drenching them in sheets. It was so heavy that, by the time they reached the village, they only rode down the grassy slope, now slick as glass, with extreme caution. The storm was no less fierce on the esplanade, waves pounding the seafront, erupting like volcanoes of foam, the wind-powered rain lashing over them as they convened with Milburn and Rathour.

'Where's everyone else?' Wayland shouted.

'Jonas is in The Salmon, drunk as a mop,' Milburn replied. 'Cheryl and Sally have gone up to the hotel, to lock themselves into their rooms.'

'Bloody great!' Claudia retorted.

Milburn shrugged. 'I sent them up there. Look at this, it's impossible . . .'

'What about Pasco?' Jack asked.

'No sign. I mean, it's difficult searching in these conditions, but he's definitely not in the harbourmaster's cottage . . . or anywhere around the harbour.'

'There may be somewhere else on the island he could have gone,' Claudia said. 'He might just be scared.'

No one immediately responded, their hooded heads bowed against the blows of the rain.

'The boat with the cross on it has gone, by the way,' Milburn said.

'Gone?' Jack said.

'Smashed to pieces on the steps. Don't even think of going over there to look. I did and I almost got swept in.'

'Only a matter of time,' Wayland replied.

'That's one way of looking at it,' Jack said, surprised at how calmly their resident murder detective was taking it. 'Another is that all the evidence anything bad ever happened here is disappearing as fast as we are.'

'Okay, listen.' Wayland held up a hand for calm. 'We've got *one* casualty so far. That's all.'

'One casualty we know about,' Claudia said.

'Either way, chin up.' Rain swept them again, rivulets running from the hoods of their waterproofs. 'Look . . . whatever's happening here, we're not some bunch of *Sleepaway Camp* numb-nuts just waiting to get carved. We'll sort this.'

Another blast of intense wind drove the rain into them sideways.

'God!' Milburn shouted.

Wayland started edging towards The Salmon. 'Look . . . we'll reconvene at the hotel tomorrow morning. Nine for nine-thirty, yeah? We'll have some breakfast and if Pasco still hasn't shown up, we'll make a plan.'

Jack wasn't happy. 'Shouldn't we all spend the night in close proximity? You and Pugh down here at the pub alone, the rest of us up there at the hotel? Is that wise?'

Wayland gave a shrug. 'Trying to prise Pugh from the pub is a laughable concept. As for me, the bedrooms down here lock up just as tight as they do up there. We'll be fine.'

Milburn and Rathour needed no second telling. They were already lumbering off through the downpour. Jack and Claudia bumped fists with Wayland and followed them. Even the short distance to the hotel was a struggle, especially as they went on foot, having opted not to chance the uphill grass on the quad bikes, but within a few minutes they'd rounded the gatepost on to its stately drive. High above them, the building remained its elegant self, beautifully lit, palm trees now thrashing about in front of it.

'Look at that,' Jack said. 'Straight out of *Murder in Paradise*.'

But Claudia's thoughts were elsewhere. 'You know,' she said, 'so far, we've given the staff here a bit of a pass. I mean, we've been talking suspects and never even mentioned them.'

Jack pondered that. 'Beck's worked hotels all over Cornwall and the West Country. I'm sure his credentials were easy enough to check before he was appointed.'

'Do we know anything about the three Albanians?'

'A mother and two daughters? Not normally the stuff maniacs are made of.'

'The Albanian syndicate's been pretty active these last few years.'

'Mainly in the south-east. We're northern coppers. Why would they have an issue with us?'

'Shit!' Claudia came to a dead stop. 'The place is open.'

They'd now ascended to the hotel forecourt, and indeed, the revolving door at the building's main entrance stood turning of its own accord. It was obviously because of the gale, but it wasn't comforting to see it.

'Beck and his staff were told to lock themselves in their quarters, which are in a separate building.' Jack went forward. 'So, this place had to be left unlocked for us.'

Claudia followed. 'That means Pasco could be in *here* somewhere.'

'Or someone else.'

'Jeez, Jack . . . you really know how to cheer a girl up.'

They entered the porch area, Claudia pulling her hood back, standing dripping while Jack applied the revolving door's upper and lower bolts.

From there, they regarded the hotel's well-lit interior. Suddenly, there was an eeriness about its pristine state. Not just after the furious weather outside, but seeing how empty it was, how quiet, how bereft of fellow human beings and thus how purposeless all this luxury seemed to be. They proceeded along the vestibule, passing reception, now unmanned of course, peering through open doors. Chrome and polish glinted, the rich carpets as yet untrampled by the passage of multiple feet. Outside, the storm raged on, windows rattling, raindrops machine-gunning the panes.

'Only a couple of times in the job did I ever think I was in danger, myself,' Claudia said quietly. 'It insulated you, didn't it? You always knew that *they* knew that if someone injured a copper, a heavy mob would come down on them like ten tons of granite.'

'Didn't worry some I could name,' Jack replied.

'Maybe it gave us a false sense of security. But it meant we could keep doing it . . .'

'Don't kid yourself. Takes a special kind of person to be a career copper.'

Claudia jumped as a door thudded somewhere upstairs. It was nothing to panic about, she was sure. Milburn, Baxter, Rathour and Jakeman were already up there.

'I'm not feeling very special at the moment,' she said.

'Look . . . there's probably no safe place on this island at present. But we lock ourselves in our rooms tonight and that's as good security as any of us are going to get.'

'Sure,' she replied. 'But we've got to get up there first.'

'I've got the gun, remember.'

'Yeah, which isn't loaded.'

Despite that, they made it safely to the lifts, the one on the left standing open.

'What's going on here, Jack?' Claudia asked, as they went in and hit the button for the third floor. The door slid closed. 'I mean, one minute we're invited to rediscover ourselves, all fees paid in advance, hot sun, lovely location . . . the next thing, it's lashing rain and there are bodies nailed to crosses.'

'Well . . .' he mused. 'I always thought it was too good to be true.'

'What do you mean . . . this Damned Rankers thing?'

He shrugged.

'Jack, what do you mean?'

'Nothing,' he replied. 'I hope.'

Twenty-Two

'You know what pisses me off most about this, Dekko?' Ray Donaldson said.

He sat forward on an upside-down packing case, his hair a hank of rat tails hanging over a face hidden in shadow.

Declan O'Hare, seated opposite, shrugged. 'We haven't got a free bar anymore.'

'I'm being serious,' Donaldson grated.

'So am I.'

The attic where they'd been imprisoned was every bit as spacious as Lucas Beck had promised, perhaps forty feet by fifty, but divided into several sections by partition walls, unlit, and filled, also as promised, with junk. Windows were fitted on two of its sides, but only small panels in each could be opened, and both were currently closed to keep the weather out, though that didn't prevent the wind groaning through the dust-thick rafters or the rainwater reflecting in black trickles across the entire dim-lit interior.

'You can be a right pillock sometimes,' Donaldson growled.

'Cheers, boss.'

'Think about it. We're being served up for this.' Donaldson let that thought hang. 'We made it crystal clear that we hated that ponce's guts. And now someone's done him in. Not only that . . .

if nothing else happens on this island, now that *we've* been banged up, they'll take that as extra proof.'

O'Hare raised his head. 'What about the forensics and that?'

'What fucking forensics? Listen to that storm. If that bastard Rothermere got nailed to his cross outside, there'll not be a speck of evidence left. And it's not like the world'll want to hear *our* side of the story!'

'Same for the others. They could just as easily get blamed.'

'You reckon? Look at us, Dekko, and look at them. What do you see?'

'Corrupt police.'

'But there are different kinds of corrupt, aren't there? Me and you are the sort the wider world expects to be corrupt. We're the old-schoolers, the lads' club. We're the ones who used to drink with the villains. Even when we weren't on the blaggers' payroll, we were a bit too matey with them.'

'The others were doing near enough the same.'

'New model coppers,' Donaldson spat. 'They might have been bent, but they kept up appearances. Woke bastards. Even if they didn't believe any of it, they always said the right things. Compared to that shower, blokes like us were just dinosaurs.'

O'Hare shrugged. 'We kept the job going. Yeah, we were dirty, but we did our bit. We kicked doors down, banged heads . . . all right, not very politically correct, but we got results. The brass'll know that even if the rest of the world doesn't.'

'The brass knows no such fucking thing. The brass are the problem, Dekko. Half of them came straight from university, the other half never walked a fucking beat. They don't know the first fucking thing about coppering. *Real* coppering. And now suddenly, they're in charge. No wonder the entire job's going down the shitpan.' Donaldson paused for effect. 'They're going to send us down, pal. Nothing surer. We'll get life.'

'What else can we do?'

'First of all, we can get out of *here*.'

'I've already tried the door. It's double-locked.'

'What about *that*?' Donaldson said, nodding.

Ten yards away, just beyond the open doorway connecting with the next section of attic, a square of glass, a skylight, was visible in the leeward side of the roof. Thanks to a steady drip of water at its lower end, the ex-super had already spotted that it was open by a couple of inches. Most likely it had been closed earlier but not locked, and the wind had done the rest.

O'Hare stared incredulously. 'You want to get on the roof?'

'Not me,' Donaldson replied in a don't-be-daft tone. 'I'm too old and too fat. But you could manage it.'

'I can't reach that window. It's got to be ten feet up.'

'There's all sorts in here. Boxes, furniture. That'll be all you need.'

O'Hare walked underneath the glazed aperture. It was hinged, and about three feet by three, so he could more than likely get through it. But that wasn't the real problem.

'Ray,' he said, 'you can't send me out on the bloody roof. Not in this weather.'

'What you afraid of?'

'What do you bloody think?'

'There'll be a fire escape down to the ground.'

O'Hare looked doubtful. 'Didn't see one from outside.'

'We didn't look round the back, did we? Anyway, if there isn't, you just get back in here. It's not a major problem.'

The big guy scratched nervously at his beard. 'Suppose there is a fire escape and I get down. What do I do then?'

'Come back inside and let me out.'

'After that where do we go?'

'I'll think of something.' Donaldson moved around, hauling crates and bits of sturdy furniture forward, so they could build a tower. 'There's that rubber boat, to start with.'

O'Hare's eyes almost popped. 'We're not taking that out in *this*!'

'Storms don't last forever. If we can hunker down somewhere, we can commandeer it later. It's only six miles to the next island.'

'They'll have a BOLO on us by then.'

Donaldson shrugged. 'Who's going to nab us? No one lives out here. God's sake, Dekko. All we need to do is get back to the mainland. Between us, we know enough people who can make us disappear till such time as we can get a decent solicitor to represent our case . . . guarantee us a fair trial. The alternative is we go back to jail, and you know how shite that was.'

O'Hare didn't need reminding. Though he and Ray Donaldson had served their time in different prisons, which meant they hadn't been able to team up, they had both been held on vulnerable-prisoner wings, which had technically meant they'd be safer, but they'd still had ten-by-six cells to live in, from which they could view a narrow slice of the world through windows the size of shoeboxes, and they had only been permitted socialisation with men who were either sex offenders or mentally ill. The unpleasantness hadn't ended there. They'd still had to eat food that was prepared in the main kitchens by other inmates, who rumour always held might sometimes taint it with snot, spittle or urine. On at least one occasion in O'Hare's experience there'd been a two-day riot, which the guards had struggled to control, the ringleaders almost making it into the protected units – it was anyone's guess what would have happened then.

He too commenced sorting through junk, selecting and stacking those heavier items that would give greater stability when he climbed. 'If there's no way down, I'm coming straight back in.'

'Deal.'

O'Hare turned to look at him before clambering up. 'If I fall off this roof, Ray, I've had it.'

'You fall off this roof, Dekko, and we've both had it.'

Jack ensured that Claudia was back in her room, and her door locked, before retreating to his own. Before closing his own door behind him, he glanced along the third-floor corridor. It might have been his imagination, he supposed, that the lights seemed weaker, the passage dwindling off into dimness. But it was the stillness that got to him, not to mention the knowledge that behind those many doors lay empty blackness. He'd never found hotels worrying, and he'd stayed in some absolute kennels in his time, but knowing you were there with many others always took the edge off the discomfort. The Culraven Arms though, was like a ghost ship. There *were* other people here, yes, but they were distributed widely, while the staff quarters were apparently a good four hundred yards away from the main hotel. The vast bulk of the place remained spookily deserted, and the constant sighing and thudding of the storm added to its air of menace.

Back in his room, he ensured the catch was in place before stripping off his wet clothes. Outside, the tempest raged on. More water streamed down the window, the wind buffeting the side of the building.

He opened the minibar, and poured himself a double JD over ice, and stood drinking it while he gazed out into turbulent nothingness. After that, he hit the shower for a good ten minutes.

In all Jack's police experience, he'd never known a scenario like this. It was the incommunicado nature of it that stymied him. When he'd first joined the job, there were still some old sweats hanging around, forty-year men, who claimed they remembered a time before personal radios, when everyone worked alone and could only summon help by whistle. The mere thought of that had always bemused him. In an age when the cops had every form of transmission device conceivable, it was mind-boggling, as if some inner mechanism prevented you believing it. And yet here they were now, not only unable to contact anyone, but so far out of reach that no one could get here to help them anyway, and all the while they were on unfamiliar terrain, and with a killer in their midst. He grabbed a towel from the heated rack, rubbed himself down, and went back into his room, where he dressed in a clean pair of undershorts and his tracksuit, and then delved into his travel bag, hooking up the false bottom, and taking out the sawn-off Remington with which he'd warded off Charlie Quincannon and his mate a few weeks ago.

It was holstered in a leather shoulder-rig and unloaded. He slid it out, broke it open, rummaged around at the bottom of his bag again, and retrieved the five cartridges he'd brought, slotting two in and snapping the weapon closed. In truth, if someone had asked him why he'd brought the wretched thing here, he couldn't have told them. Something about never again believing that good things happened simply because they happened. But even now he honestly didn't know what he was going to do with it. If he went out with this in the morning and pushed people around, demanding answers, they'd draw the obvious conclusion.

So, you had a firearm you wouldn't admit to? Maybe you're the one who marched Alan Rothermere to his death.

And it wasn't as if he was going to seriously threaten to shoot people. A gun was only ever as effective as the bluffer wielding it, and these were all street-hardened former cops. They wouldn't be cowed by bullshit.

Even so, he re-holstered the weapon and laid it on the writing desk near the bed. Not so close that he could accidentally reach out in the middle of the night and set the damn thing off, but close enough that he could jump out and grab it if he needed to.

That was what it boiled down to.

It was only to be used if he needed it. But if he *did* need it, he would.

Because like it or not, someone on St Dunstan was killing people, and Jack McGurn was damn sure that he wasn't going to be one of them.

He poured himself another drink, this time a Glenfiddich; there was just enough ice left to fill the tumbler. Over the last few weeks, he hadn't intimated to Claudia that he was contemplating suicide purely to win her concern. He'd been halfway there for real. It had niggled constantly in the back of his mind that, when it finally struck him what he'd done to his life and how nothing at all remained of it, he might take the final logical step. But the visit to his home by the Quincannon firm had roused some slumbering dog inside him, some latent fighting spirit that he'd thought all but leached away, but which maybe – just maybe – might signal a pathway back to self-respect.

And then *this* had happened. If nothing else, it was interesting. Because this was all that and much more. He wondered how the press would headline it:

TERROR IN THE ISLES

THE STORM-CLOUD MURDERS

THE PORTH WEST HORROR

A HOLIDAY FROM HELL

There'd only been one murder so far, he reminded himself. Though he didn't hold out much hope for Pasco, if he was honest.

He supposed he ought to stop thinking in Agatha Christie terms, and more along the lines of the current British media. In which case it would be something like:

THERE IS A GOD AFTER ALL
FINALLY, THEY GOT WHAT THEY DESERVED

'Yeah, well not me.' He placed his empty glass down and stood by the window again. Maybe there was nothing better for dragging a man out of a suicidal stupor than someone else threatening to do the deed for him.

At which point, a muffled shriek tore across the upper floor of the hotel, followed by another, and another.

And another . . .

Twenty-Three

Clambering out on the roof in weather like this had been an idea that verged on insanity. Declan O'Hare had run into trouble almost immediately, the structure he and Ray Donaldson had built from old boxes and sticks of leftover furniture swaying precariously.

Only with monumental effort did he manage to force the skylight open wide enough to get his ox-like shoulders through, primarily because of the elements battering against it. The roof itself, slanted of course but not especially steep, proved hazardous because it was smoothly tiled and now slick with rainwater. O'Hare, a huge, clumsy oaf of a bloke, struggled to gain any kind of perch and straight away found himself sliding downhill. The storm hammered him, not just drenching him, but, because it was blowing west to east, driving him remorselessly towards the nearest drop. His shouts for help were initially lost as he scrabbled both with hands and feet, finding nothing to latch on to. It crossed his mind to stand up and walk back to the apex, using all his strength and weight to lean into the gale, but a quick afterthought advised that if he exposed even more of himself to the wind's devilish power, it would be inviting death.

O'Hare's frantic shouts only became full-on, chest-deep screams when he spied the edge of the roof rushing up towards him. When he slid over and dropped, the terror was mind-numbing, the rain-filled void below looking bottomless. As he grabbed wildly for any handhold, it was more by luck than design that his fingers hooked the steel guttering below the eaves.

The breath caught in his throat as he swung over an abyss, his heart thumping his ribs, his fingers burning as the slim metal edge bit into them like a blade.

He shrieked and shrieked as his enormous weight bore on him, the guttering itself creaking and groaning, jolting downward as a bracket sprang free.

'Christ!' he howled. 'Someone help me, please . . . *for God's sake . . .*'

Every muscle stretched to breaking point as he clung there, an icy torrent gushing over his head and face as the guttering sagged ever further downward. When he kicked at the wall with the toes of his training shoes, he met only brickwork.

'Here!' someone shouted.

He glanced around and two feet to his left, saw that another window had opened. A dark, featureless figure leaned out, beckoning.

O'Hare swung himself sideways, convinced his purchase would break first, either his grip or the entire length of metal guttering, sending him plummeting.

But somehow, that didn't happen.

Within inches of the open aperture, the entire panel of which had been pushed outward, so that his saviour could reach towards him, a gloved hand caught the waistband of his pants and strenuously hauled him in.

'Careful!' O'Hare shrieked. '*Careful!*'

The open window did not extend down the full length of his body, so he couldn't just poke a foot towards it and find a flat surface to plant his weight on. It came to about mid-thigh, so he had to swing his legs forward and up, bending them at the knee, which was additional torture on hands so agonised that he could barely feel them, and still the horizontal steelwork supporting him creaked and contorted, and with an echoing clank, lurched down again as more anchors broke loose.

The hand clasping his belt, and the strong arm behind it, gave invaluable assistance, though the last part of the rescue was the worst. When O'Hare managed to get both feet on the sill, his body slanted backward at a terrifying angle. Momentarily, he didn't dare let go of the guttering, though he knew he had no choice. With an echoing clunk, another bracket sprang loose. The steel sagged downward again, now bowing in the middle.

Shouting wildly, he released it with his left hand, clawing inward towards his would-be saviour, who still gripped him by the waistband but now lunged forward with his other hand, catching the big guy's left wrist. Gravity tugged O'Hare backward and down, but his rescuer retreated into the darkness behind the window, exerting huge strength as he pulled the ex-cop upward and through.

O'Hare landed on his knees on a thick pile carpet, saturated both by rain and sweat. He slumped down, his forehead touching the rich fabric, his fingers burrowing into it.

'Th-thank God,' he stuttered. 'Thank God for you . . .'

'What's going on?' Claudia shouted, as she barged into the hotel corridor.

'I don't know.' Jack stared around, trying to pinpoint the direction of the cries.

She hurried towards him. 'What was that screaming?'

He shook his head, still pivoting. Whatever that clamour had been, it had stopped now.

'Jack!' Claudia suddenly sounded even more astonished. 'What is *that*?'

She pointed at the Remington, which, almost unconsciously, he'd brought out with him.

'If you don't ask, I won't need to lie to you.' He lurched down the passage.

'Wait a minute.' She was barefoot and wearing only shorts and a zipped-up running top, but she ran nimbly after him. 'Jack, what the hell is that?'

'Bit of extra insurance I collected.' He reached the first junction, glancing left and right.

'During one of our raids?' For some reason, she seemed shocked by that possibility.

'Claudi!' He eyed her with bemusement. 'Most weapons we found, we turned in as evidence, including Uzi sub-machine guns and Armalite battle-rifles. Meanwhile, we pocketed rafts and rafts of illegal narcotics . . . and you've got a problem with *this*?'

'No, I . . .' She never finished the sentence, puzzled that it had even surprised her.

Maybe it was because she'd gradually started feeling like a police officer again. Whatever, it was possession of a loaded shotgun in a public place without legal authority, while any shotgun with its barrel length sawn down to less than thirty centimetres was an offence in itself. It was a bitter reminder that they were still on the opposite side of the law.

'Just don't shoot the wrong person,' she said, as they approached the lifts.

They now heard another noise, this one reverberating down from the ceiling. They glanced up. It was a forceful, angry yelling rather than the wild screaming of before. A series of thunderous impacts, a fist pounding wood perhaps, accompanied it.

'What are those lunatics up to?' Jack groaned.

They darted along a corridor leading towards the rear of the building, where they banged their way through a fire door and ascended a narrow set of uncarpeted stairs to a single door, which Lucas Beck had fastened with both a Yale lock and a padlock. Thankfully, both keys were on the windowsill next to it.

On the other side, Donaldson continued to bellow and hammer with his fist.

Jack handed Claudia the keys while he stepped back, shotgun levelled at chest height.

'Fuck's sake!' Donaldson pounded again. 'Open this fucking door. I think there's just been an accident.'

Claudia first unfastened the padlock and then the Yale. The door was yanked inward before she could push it. Jack hustled forward, aiming the shotgun squarely at Donaldson's red, sweat-soaked face.

The ex-super was in such a state that he didn't even register the weapon. 'What the fuck are you clowns playing at?' he shouted. 'You didn't hear that racket on the roof?'

'What are you talking about?' Jack retorted.

Only now did Donaldson spot the Remington, his eyes widening. He backed into the attic, hands partly raised.

'What's going on?' Jack demanded 'Where's O'Hare?'

'He went on the roof . . . climbed through the skylight. Think he might have fallen off.'

'Shit!' Claudia spun round and scampered down the stairs.

'You had him climb out on the roof for you?' Jack said in disbelief.

'It was only a recce . . .'

'A recce! In a fucking hurricane!'

Seeing that he wasn't going to be shot, Donaldson lowered his hands. That old pig-like sneer returned. 'If *you* were facing life imprisonment, Machine Gun, I wonder what you'd do? You might be yet . . . if you get trigger-happy with that thing. I'd love to know where you got it from, by the way. Regular wolf in sheep's clothing, aren't you?'

'Jack!' Claudia called from down the stairs.

Jack descended. 'Stay up here, Ray. If O'Hare's fallen off that roof and killed himself, you're going to be in it deeper than squid shit.'

Down in the corridor, he found Claudia in company with Gabby Milburn and Varada Rathour, the former back in her gym gear, the latter bare-legged but wearing the same heavy overcoat she'd worn on the crossing from St Agnes.

'Nice bit of hardware.' Milburn eyed the sawn-off. 'You didn't find that here, I'm guessing?'

'Long story,' he replied. 'For the moment, just say I like to be prepared.'

'What's going on?' another voice intruded.

Cheryl Baxter approached along the passage, wearing pyjamas, slippers and a dressing gown. They explained as they hastened towards the lifts.

'My God!' she said.

'What took you so long to respond?' Claudia asked. 'You're on the same floor as Gabby and Varada.'

'I was in the bath,' Baxter said, and indeed, her hair was tousled and damp.

'Where's Jakeman?' Milburn asked.

Baxter shook her head. 'All I can think is she's on the first floor, so she might not have heard anything . . .'

They returned to the lifts, but before they could summon one, some ten yards along the corridor on the other side, a door creaked open. About half a foot or so, where it came to rest.

They stared at it, specifically at the slab of blackness behind it.

'That one of the bedrooms?' Claudia asked quietly.

With a moan of wind, the door slammed closed.

'That *was* the wind, yeah?' Rathour said.

Jack and Milburn glanced at each other, then ventured towards the door in question. The others went too, but slowly, warily. On reaching it, they stopped and listened. There was no number, nor apparently a lock. Just a closet then, or some other storage space.

It rattled in its frame.

Again, it could have been the wind.

As before, Jack assumed the position, Remington levelled.

Milburn moved to the door, the others backing away. She sidled to the left, so that she was shielded from the inside by the wall, then, after a silent countdown, reached out, depressed the lever and shoved the door inward.

Jack threw himself against the jamb, sawn-off at shoulder height.

It was a small, pokey room, but there was sufficient light from the corridor to illuminate it. The window at the back stood ajar – the wind maybe – though just below that, the light showed a figure crumpled against the wall, head hanging forward. It also showed how that head was lathered in a glutinous red slop of blood and brains, courtesy of the two or three brutal blows that had left a yawning crevice in the middle of it.

For half a second, Jack struggled to make sense of what he was seeing. Even the large, heavy-bladed machete sunk at a mocking angle into the wooden side-rack, where normally the spare toilet rolls would be kept.

2: IMPLEMENTS OF TORMENT

Twenty-Four

'You realise it's partly your fault that Dekko's dead?' Donaldson said.

'Partly, yeah,' Jack agreed. 'But how much is it also down to the guy who sent him on to the roof? I mean he had to be a real dumb-ass to go, but even so . . .'

Donaldson made no initial response as they strode side by side along the paved path leading to the staff quarters. As former cops, they weren't unfamiliar with gruesome scenes, but O'Hare's death had hit them in the gut. So much so that, for a moment, their innate hostility to each other was muted. The rain had ceased at least, but ahead of them the bushes tossed on either side of the path. It had crossed both their minds more than once, since setting out from the hotel, that the killer might be lurking somewhere along the four-hundred-yard route they were now taking, which was why Jack had his shotgun at the ready.

'I presume you're going to apply the same zealous scrutiny to everyone else that you did to us two?' Donaldson said.

Jack didn't respond, his thoughts askew. Of them all, only he, Claudia and Ray Donaldson were in the clear for Declan O'Hare's murder. But were any of the others credible suspects? There were many circumstances where an adult female could kill an adult male, even face to face and armed with a blade rather than a gun.

But O'Hare had been a six-foot-six bruiser. Most men would have struggled to overpower him, let alone a woman.

That left Harry Wayland, Jonas Pugh and maybe, with her martial arts skills, Gabby Milburn. All three were possibilities, but what would their reason be? What could they gain?

'We ought to have given some thought earlier to this bastard, Beck,' Donaldson said. 'He's a smooth customer. Too fucking smooth, if you want my view.'

It was true, Jack conceded, that they only had Lucas Beck's own word for it that he was a respected hotelier. Then there were the three Albanian women. But if they were on St Dunstan with murder in their hearts, they could have done it more easily than this, by simply poisoning everyone's food and drink.

'Let's just get everyone together, like we said,' Jack replied.

It seemed like a cliché, but the only way forward from here was to gather everyone in one place, preferably the hotel, which was more spacious and better supplied than the pub, and make a base of operations where they could watch each other, along with every door and window. That would include the four members of staff, whom Jack and Donaldson were now en route to speak with, and Harry Wayland and Jonas Pugh, whom Claudia and Gabby Milburn, the former armed with the Beretta (though they still hadn't told anyone else it was empty), were going to rouse. It hadn't seemed like a plan, splitting the group up again, but needs must. Even then, the one rule they couldn't afford to break was that everyone needed to be accompanied by someone else.

'Winds don't feel as strong,' Donaldson commented.

Jack wasn't so sure. From the ongoing distant roar of surf, heavy waves still pounded the coast. No relief boat was arriving any time soon.

'Fuck!' Donaldson stumbled to a halt.

The staff accommodation on St Dunstan was a new build, but in appearance resembled an old-style barn conversion. It was built from weathered granite, with a thatched roof, its downstairs windows fitted with neat diamond-paned leading. It sat amid private gardens of its own, which were hedged off from the rest of the island but accessible at the front through a white-painted wrought-iron gate. The two ex-cops had already passed through this, having assumed it stood wide open because of the wind. The many flower beds in the staff gardens were denuded of petals, the various fruit trees straining in the heavy gusts, their own blooms and leafage ripped loose. But now, as the duo approached the front door, the fact that this too stood open seemed ominous.

Especially as the frosted glass panel in its upper section had been smashed.

There was a light on inside, but no sound.

'Fucker's had a busy night,' Donaldson said, half to himself.

They stopped a few yards short. The wind gusted again, more branches clashing and clattering. An item of plastic garden furniture tumbled across the pathway behind them.

'You're the one who's tooled up,' Donaldson said. 'You go first.'

Jack levelled the weapon in his right hand, pushing the door inward with his left. There was a small reception area behind it, containing a desk. No one was present there, and the various items on top of it lay undisturbed. However, a door on the right also stood open, and the light came from here.

'Mr Beck!' Jack called. 'It's Jack McGurn.'

'What the fuck are you doing?' Donaldson hissed.

'We don't go in armed without shouting a warning.'

'We're not in the job anymore, dickhead!'

'Yeah, and if these people are hurt or frightened and come running at us with cutlery, what do I do then?'

It was always the same question, even when you were part of an official raid. Most people, crims included, would throw themselves on their faces when they heard 'Armed police!' But not everyone was always in their right mind in these situations, especially if something awful had just happened. And even the best-trained firearms cops weren't always able to distinguish friend from foe in the half-second it might take an unknown person to charge at you, screaming.

Shotgun ready, Jack went through the next door.

Into a communal living area that had been wrecked.

The big-screen TV on the wall had spiderwebbed with cracks and hung from a single screw. Furniture was overturned, ornaments lying shattered. The French windows at the back stood open but sagged from twisted hinges. On the wall alongside there was a smeared crimson handprint.

Jack called out again, his voice echoing eerily. They ventured into the kitchen, seeing more destruction: drawers pulled out, smashed crockery . . . and blood droplets trailing across the tiled floor.

From here, they ascended a narrow staircase, also spotted with blood, to the first floor, where seemingly, there were quite a few rooms to check. In fact, there were two separate passages. Jack took the left, while Donaldson took the right. The first thing Jack noticed were the fragments of female underwear scattered in front of him. That set alarm bells ringing before the red smears on the walls did. Warily, he proceeded.

Most of the doors were locked because their rooms were not yet in use, but three of them, all on the left side of the passage, stood open. The first was relatively small and contained a single bed, a wardrobe, a lamp and some drawers. Again, it was in disarray. Clothes strewed the floor, and the quilt on the bed had been pulled off, exposing a slashed mattress. The next room was the same, though there was blood spatter on the walls and the bed.

As Jack's eyes roved the grisly mess, he heard a long, slow creak from somewhere close.

He stepped out into the corridor, but it was empty. Listening, he heard nothing else. With an open door still remaining, he advanced stealthily, weapon cocked. Repellent thoughts bounced around in his head: Declan O'Hare's sundered skull, Alan Rothermere nailed by the wrists and ankles.

He halted at the next entrance, the Remington's barrel slick in his moist grasp.

This time, he heard a soft rustling from within.

Heart thudding, he kicked the half-open door so that it swung inward. As it did, he threw himself across the corridor, jamming his back to the wall, shotgun levelled at shoulder height. But beyond the open door lay only another wreckage-strewn room, this one with a damaged window, several shards of glass having fallen out, leaving holes through which the stiff breeze penetrated, setting the curtains rustling. He went in to appraise it properly – more blood, more mess – before retreating again, forehead damp. As he backed down the passage, the door to the first room moved, clearly under pressure from another draught seeping through the broken window. It did so with a protracted creak.

Frustrated with himself for getting spooked, Jack rounded the corner at the end, crossed the top of the stairs and entered the right-hand corridor. All the doors off this one were closed, apart from one at the far end, which stood wide open. Even from this distance, the space beyond it looked roomier than the others he'd seen. There was even a bigger window in there. Beck's room, perhaps. As the senior manager on the plot, he'd get the best digs. Meanwhile, where the hell was everyone? And where was Donaldson?

Jack advanced, trying every door as he passed, but all were locked. More prickles of unease ran through him as he approached the end room, where he halted. No sound at all.

He went inside.

It contained a double bed and a double wardrobe. The latter hung open, revealing several sets of smart clothing: blazers, shirts, pairs of pressed slacks. There was even a TV, smaller than the one downstairs, but perched on the bedside cabinet. In terms of destruction, there wasn't as much as in the other rooms, but the bed was disordered, and the pillow blotted crimson.

He backed to the doorway, firearm lowered, wondering what it would take for a lone assailant to overpower four people near enough all at the same time. It wasn't impossible if you attacked them while they were asleep, he supposed.

Was that what had happened here? But if so, where were the bodies?

He was so engrossed in this grim conjecture that he didn't notice the next door along the passage open quietly and a figure come out and stand directly behind him.

His awareness was only sparked when he heard the heavy breathing.

Spinning wildly, he raised his shotgun.

'Fuck!' Donaldson jumped backward.

A stagnant smell wafted from the room he'd just vacated. Only now did Jack realise that he was listening to the sound of a toilet flushing.

'Seriously?' he said, voice shaking. He lowered the weapon.

'It's easy for you. With your luxury en suite. Some of us poor fuckers have been cooped up in a bloody attic.'

They were halfway back down the stairs when they stopped, listening again.

A muffled but lengthy groan ascended.

Jack hurried on down, Donaldson blundering after him. The ransacked kitchen was still deserted, and when they glanced into the living room, it was the same.

Another groan sounded. Directly behind them. They whirled around, Jack zeroing in on the handle of one of the compartments under the worktops, from which hung a single droplet of blood.

'Suppose there's no point asking if you want to open that while I cover you?' he said.

'Ask away,' Donaldson replied, 'but you're right, there's no point.'

Nerves prickling, Jack squatted, reached for the bloodstained handle, gingerly hooked his finger around it and yanked the door open. Before he could jump away, Lucas Beck fell out.

The T-shirt and pyjama pants he'd been wearing were torn and bloodied, his face so badly bludgeoned that it looked less like human flesh and more like pulped fruit.

Twenty-Five

'Well, I've done my best,' Cheryl Baxter said. 'But I was only a police first-aider, not a qualified nurse.'

Lucas Beck lay very still on the sofa bed in the private office at the rear of reception. The entire upper part of his head, including his eyes, nose and ears, was swathed in bandages and surgical pads. His lower left arm, which was broken, Baxter said, was splinted across his chest with a long-handled steel spoon from the kitchen. She pulled the quilt up to his chin and peeled off her latex gloves.

Beck lay still, but at least he was alive, as his shallow but regular breathing indicated.

'Okay, well . . . we've all done what we can,' Jack replied.

Harry Wayland, dishevelled from having been dragged out of bed so early, stood in the doorway connecting to the staff corridor, hands shoved into the pockets of his army surplus trousers.

'We should speak to the others,' Jack said.

Wayland nodded and followed him into the corridor, Baxter close behind. Not far along, another door opened into the hotel's main lounge, which they'd decided on as their base of operations. Jack had discarded the tracksuit from earlier, as it was streaked with Beck's blood, had donned jeans and a sweatshirt, and was wearing the Remington in its shoulder-rig, the gun hanging openly under his left armpit.

They went through into the lounge. It was a large, comfortable room, nicely carpeted, filled with cosy furniture. The rest of the group, most still only half dressed, were scattered untidily around it, watching and waiting with tired, haggard faces.

'I thought we were all supposed to be sticking together,' Sally Jakeman said, after he'd explained what they'd done with the latest casualty.

'It's only through there, Sal,' Cheryl Baxter said. 'If there's a problem, we can be in there in a jiffy.'

Jakeman snorted and got up from the sofa she'd been sharing with Donaldson. 'So long as he doesn't need nurse-maiding. That's one thing I never signed up for.'

'Pity our new benefactor didn't come here early enough to get trapped in the storm with us,' Jack said. 'He'd have loved seeing what a catch we all are.'

Jakeman flipped him the bird as she went to a sideboard occupied by coffee-making equipment and already littered with torn sugar sachets, spilled grounds and splashed milk.

'What did he say happened?' Claudia asked.

Jack shrugged. 'It was difficult getting anything out of him, but sounds like he was asleep in his bed when someone started hitting him. He didn't see or hear them come into his room. Didn't even get a look at them while they were battering him. It was too dark.'

'How many?' Claudia asked.

'He thought only one.'

Gabby Milburn stood with arms folded. 'What was the weapon used?'

'A fist,' Jack said. 'Perhaps wearing a knuckleduster.'

Milburn grimaced. 'It's a miracle he didn't die.'

'The fact his assailant thought he'd died is probably what saved his life,' Jack said. 'By the looks of it, the bastard encountered the first of the three women downstairs, overpowered her there, then went upstairs, ransacked her room and attacked the rest of the staff while they were sleeping, Beck first. In an uncharacteristic error, he didn't finish that job before he went on to the other two women. Maybe he'd heard one of them stirring. Either way, it was only after the nutcase had moved on to the women that Beck made it to the top of the stairs. Got down to the kitchen, half made it to the living room, but then realised he wasn't going to get any further. Went back into the kitchen and hid.'

'While the women were being attacked?' Varada Rathour sounded shocked.

Jack shrugged again. 'His head was spinning. Don't think he really knew what was what.'

'Absolute hero, eh?' Donaldson chuckled. 'Ta, my love,' he said, as Jakeman settled back on the sofa with two large coffees, one for herself and one for him.

'At least we've now got a live witness,' Baxter said.

'Who says he didn't see anything,' Jakeman retorted. 'Very useful.'

Rathour jumped to her feet. 'What in God's name is this!' Her voice had turned brittle. 'Is there some maniac on this island, who we disturbed when we arrived?'

'We're not the first people on here, Varada,' Claudia said. 'There've been building crews on site for months. Why didn't he just attack them?'

'Maybe he's a native islander. Maybe he hoped it would all go away. Then, when he saw the first guests arrive, it was more than he could take.'

'You know we're in the Scilly Isles?' Jakeman scoffed. 'Not the fucking Bayou.'

Rathour glared at her. 'There happen to be madmen everywhere. In TacOps, I did a course on geographic profiling . . .

plotting the movements of violent offenders. You'd be amazed some of the nice little villages where murders happen for no reason.'

'Murders that genuinely happen for no reason are rare,' Wayland said. He'd been subdued thus far, seemingly lost in thought.

'The hell they are,' Donaldson scoffed. 'Get among the blaggers of Manc, and you'll find looneys who'll swing a pickaxe handle at your head for the slightest reason.'

'Yeah, but there's still a motive,' Wayland countered. 'They want the money from the job. Or they want to get away clean.'

'Maybe it *is* a gang,' Baxter said.

'Maybe this island's their secret hideout,' Rathour suggested. 'And they're terrified that we might have discovered them.'

'Jesus, Varada!' Jakeman snickered. 'Your plan to keep your hideout secret is to start murdering people there? Good job you were a civie. That'd be the final proof the modern brass'll let anyone in.'

'All right, let's ease off on the insults,' Claudia intervened. 'We're all on the same side.'

'Really?' Jakeman snorted again. 'That didn't stop you putting Declan O'Hare in the attic.'

No one initially responded. The matter of O'Hare was now a source of confused guilt among them. The fact he still lay in situ, that room crudely taped off, made them uneasy in itself. No one had wanted to do that, but you never wanted to do it with murder victims out in the real world either, and yet sometimes you had no choice. On top of all that though, there was a collective disquiet about their having arbitrarily decided that O'Hare was a prime suspect and having treated him accordingly.

'Look!' Jack said. 'There's one big question here, which for some reason no one's asking.'

'You mean . . . who put *you* in charge?' Jakeman's lovely green eyes were as hard as glass. 'That's the main question as I see it.'

'I'm not really in charge, Sally.'

'Well, you could have fooled me.' She rose to her feet. 'I mean, if it's a matter of rank . . . shouldn't it be Ray who gives the orders?'

All gazes diverted to Donaldson lounging on the sofa, who, seemingly less affected than most by the horrors of the day, responded by slurping his coffee.

'None of us holds rank anymore,' Jack said quietly.

'Oh, I see.' Jakeman adopted an air of understanding. 'So . . . *you're* the one with the big gun, and that's the whole thing, is it? Anyone steps out of line, you just shoot them, yeah?'

'No one's going to shoot anyone,' he said tautly. 'Unless they try to kill more people.'

'Well, that's reassuring.' She turned to the others. 'Here's another question. We keep trying to work out who it is . . . but why are we even bothered? Why don't we just hunker down here in the hotel? It won't even be that long. The storm's already abating.'

'Doesn't matter whether the storm abates or not,' Wayland said. 'No one in the outside world knows we're in trouble, and we've got no way to tell them. So, no one's going to come here until the end of the week. As scheduled.'

'Hardly a disaster,' she replied. 'It's not like we haven't got easy access to a toilet, food and drink in the kitchen.'

'Two of our colleagues have just been murdered,' Claudia said. 'Maybe a whole bunch of civies too. And you suggest we just sit here?'

'At the very least we should go and look for Beck's staff,' Milburn added.

'The three Albanian women?' Jakeman looked startled by that. 'Why? We don't know them. They mean nothing to us.'

'For God's sake!'

'For God's sake, nothing! We all agreed we're going to use this place as an HQ because we can easily secure it. But that only works if we stay put.'

'We can't just leave those people out there,' Claudia said.

'They're already dead. Look what happened to Rothermere.' Sensing that she wasn't winning them over, Jakeman became more conciliatory. 'Look, why risk it? The best thing we can do for these poor unfortunates is ensure *we* survive this ordeal, so we can provide witness testimony when the real investigators arrive.'

A silence followed this.

In fairness, it wasn't an unsound opinion. Given how isolated and ill-equipped they were, maybe it *would* be better if they put all their efforts into protecting themselves.

Except that, to Jack's mind at least, it wasn't that simple.

'It sounds great,' he said, 'until we consider the possible motive for these attacks. Like Harry said, there's nearly always a motive. And on this occasion, it clearly wasn't just about ridding the world of a child-abuser. It's no leap now to assume that *everyone* here is a target. There must be a reason for that, which brings me to the question I was going to ask before. Could these deaths be something to do with the Crew?'

The silence that greeted this was the longest yet.

'Yeah,' Jack said slowly. 'I thought that might have been lurking at the back of a few minds. I first wondered about it earlier on when Ray here dropped them into the conversation while we were looking for Alan Rothermere.' He watched them carefully. 'The plain fact is we've all, directly or indirectly, done business with the Crew.'

It was easy to say that word, 'Crew', though in itself it didn't quite capture the full meaning.

Initially formed by old-style underworld firms pooling their resources to resist the incursion of foreign gangsters into Britain during the 1980s, the Crew was now, after several blood-soaked decades, the controlling power, in fact the apex predator, in northern England's vast criminal network. Though headquartered in Manchester, the Crew's writ ran from Liverpool on the west coast to Hull on the east, and Newcastle in the north. There was scarcely a racket they didn't have a finger in, barely a gang they didn't either own, underwrite or tax. Well known these days for their alliance with the Russian mafia, they were second only on the UK mainland to the Corporation, who controlled London and the south-east, and whose own numbers and profits had leapt since they'd got into bed with the Albanians.

Like all successful crime syndicates, the Crew were mainly about business. They liked things to run smoothly and peacefully, but on their own very extensive patch they alone were the malign power behind drugs, prostitution, gambling, sex trafficking, robbery, extortion, bribery, murder-for-hire, and just about any other money-spinning obscenity their board of directors fancied taking a cut from.

Who else could have guaranteed Tyrone Baxter's safety while he was in prison?

Who would have benefited more from so many major police enquiries going south thanks to Sally Jakeman's indiscreet liaisons?

Though Jack and Claudia had never met senior Crew members face to face, they'd known who lay behind the drug-dealing gangs they'd sold confiscated narcotics back to. To inexperienced observers it might have seemed odd that a criminal superpower would stand by and allow a couple of two-bit cops to in effect blackmail their proxies, but the Crew were savvy businessmen. They'd have seen greater gain in cutting their losses by buying their own gear back at half the price than in stirring a wasps' nest by clipping a bunch of serving police officers.

'What's the real story behind our mysterious benefactor, Harry?' Jack asked. 'Does he even exist?'

Wayland eyed him carefully. 'As far as I'm aware. Like I say, I've never met him. Only been contacted by email or telephone.'

'You actually spoke to him?' Claudia said.

'Only to one of his reps. Mostly it was a woman called Maxine, who said she was part of his legal team.'

'Did you receive any cash?' Jack enquired.

Wayland shrugged. 'Wages, I suppose you'd call them.'

'Wages?'

'Well, I was recruited, wasn't I? To set this whole thing up. Wasn't going to happen overnight and for free.'

'How were the wages paid?' Jack asked.

'How do you think? BACS transfer. All above board.'

Donaldson snorted with laughter. He mopped a big hand through his sweaty, messy hair. 'I'm sure the Crew have made the odd legit payment in their time. Fuck, eh? The bastard Crew! All those jobs we did, and this is our reward.'

'Wait up,' Wayland said. 'Just wait a mo.' He looked thoughtful. 'There're a couple of flies in this ointment.'

'Go on?' Jack said.

'First of all, if it was the Crew . . . the Crew for Christ's sake, why go through all these theatricals? Why not just send a kill-team packing automatic weapons?'

It was another good point.

'You said there were two flies,' Claudia replied. 'What's the other?'

'Jonas Pugh.'

'Whoa, that's right,' Rathour said. 'Pugh was Essex. He wouldn't have had any contact with the Crew.'

Jack wasn't absolutely certain about that, but there was no denying that an Essex cop's underworld paymasters would more likely have been the Corporation.

'Where's Pugh now?' he asked.

Claudia looked awkward. 'Pissed. We couldn't rouse him.'

'Well, that's not good enough. We need him here. At least so we can keep an eye on everyone.'

'I'll go and get him.' The unexpected offer came from Donaldson, who climbed lazily from the sofa. 'All I need from you, Machine Gun, is your 12-bore.'

'I'm not giving you this weapon, Ray,' Jack said.

Donaldson smirked. 'Still don't trust me, eh?'

'I don't trust any of you. But you can trust me.' Jack glanced round at the others. 'You *know* you can. Because if you couldn't, I'd be blasting away right now.'

'Enough of this finger-pointing bollocks.' Sally Jakeman stood up too. 'I'll come with you, Ray.'

It was something of a surprise, given her unwillingness to cooperate much thus far, but it wasn't unwelcome. Especially not to Donaldson, who grinned broadly. The unlikely pairing sauntered towards the lounge's swing doors. 'If the rest of you want to be useful, get some breakfast on,' Donaldson said over his shoulder. 'We can't run on coffee all day.'

'Wonders never cease,' Claudia said, as they vanished into the vestibule.

'Agreed,' Jack replied, 'but let's not look a gift horse in the mouth.'

'What about the missing women?' Milburn asked again.

'I'm inclined to agree with Jakeman,' Jack said. 'Those bedrooms were a bloody mess. I mean, we'll go and look . . . but first let's make this place fully secure, yeah?'

The lounge itself, despite being a large, comfortable room, was also easily defensible. It boasted four tall arched windows on its north side, looking out on to the hotel grounds, and any one of these could be broken, although, as they'd already seen from garden items blowing against them during the storm, they contained reinforced glass, so it would take an attacker considerable effort, and the noise would arouse those inside. In terms of other access, there were two doors. One connected with the staff corridor, which could be locked, though there was no need for that. The corridor connected at one end with the small office, where Lucas Beck was now confined to his sickbed, and then reception, though the door to reception could also be locked and was. Further back along the staff corridor there was a staff toilet, which was obviously useful, a small staff common room, another back office, and an exterior door. The exterior door could also be locked, and again, it already was. This basically gave them a suite of rooms to occupy for the remainder of the week, and though it would be necessary to continually patrol them, checking mainly on the windows, it would hardly cause a problem given that there were nine of them and they could take it in shifts.

The only weak point was the lounge's main entrance, which connected with the vestibule. This was a pair of double swing doors which could not be locked, though they could be prevented from opening easily by inserting a broom through their two pull bars. It would have been possible to secure this entrance further by building a barricade there from spare furniture, but the refuge seekers themselves would need to pass these doors at least a couple of times a day to gain entry to the kitchens. They'd already brought several crates of bottled water and soft drinks through, though the food itself would need to stay in the refrigeration units.

'If we're going looking for those women, we can't just disperse across the island again,' Claudia said. 'We need a plan.'

Jack nodded. 'To start with, I'm inclined to wait till full daylight.'

They mulled this over as they made rounds of the perimeter. Varada Rathour, by the window, commented that the weather finally seemed to be improving. They glanced out into the spectral light of dawn: the hotel's greenery was still billowing, the lawns strewn with twigs and ragged leaves, but there'd definitely been a reduction in ferocity. Furniture wasn't rolling like tumbleweed anymore.

After that, they checked out the staff-only areas, ensuring that all the appropriate doors and windows were barred, then returned to the reception back office, where there was no change in Lucas Beck's eerie ongoing slumber.

'He's been unconscious a long time,' Claudia said.

'Think he's just sleeping,' Cheryl Baxter replied.

'Or on the other hand it could be brain damage,' Wayland said, standing in a corner, hands again jammed into his pockets. He looked tired and disconsolate.

Jack didn't say it, but he was surprised at how ineffective the former homicide ace was suddenly proving to be. DCI Harry Wayland had won huge acclaim for his investigation of the Dogman murders. His small, handpicked team had worked tirelessly in their pursuit of Jimmy Cornwallis: a guy who never used a gun but was nevertheless an expert killer; he knew the streets, he knew his hand weapons, he was strong, agile and fit, and he planned his attacks in minute detail and executed them with precision. No one who knew about police work had blamed Wayland for the maniac's astonishing thirty-victim scorecard because the victimology had initially been so difficult to pin down, the Dogman's targets ranging across the sexes, ages and races, from hookers to drug dealers to muggers, thieves, addicts and other petty offenders, the sorts whose deaths most folk wouldn't even notice, or if they did, would write off as the outcome of a dysfunctional lifestyle. It was only later on, when the guy had started writing gloating letters to various press outlets, that many of the crimes were linked together. But in the end, the public were simply glad the madman had been dealt with, even if it had been done with a police bullet. In some quarters it was even seen as appropriate that it had been Wayland himself who'd fired the fatal shot, he having emerged as the public face of the enquiry; an inevitability when the Dogman's letters called him out by name, challenging him to change sides and help 'scour the vermin from the streets'.

It hadn't been that long ago. A mere decade. But time had clearly sped up for Harry Wayland since his disgrace, and possibly because of it.

He was still a loose-limbed kind of guy; when they'd first met, he'd exuded confidence, cockiness and know-how, even to the point where he'd despatched the Quincannon firm without a punch thrown. But right now, under pressure, he seemed a shadow of the human dynamo he must once have been. It was also likely that he'd sunk into a state of despondency because, whoever it was persecuting them here on St Dunstan, it was obvious that this would not be the swift route back to a normal life he'd envisaged.

Before anyone could say more, the wind dropped again, to be replaced by the muffled grind of an engine. It was somewhere outside, and initially, when they exchanged glances, they assumed it was one of the quad bikes. But then, as Jack and Claudia glanced at each other again, now thinking the tone of the engine was different, Varada Rathour came dashing in.

'There's a boat on the harbour,' she shouted. 'At first, I only heard it, but then I went out to the front, and I *saw* it . . .'

The entire group broke into a run, all concerns for their own safety discarded as they stumbled through the lounge, along the vestibule, past reception, and out through the front doors, where they halted. Gabby Milburn was already standing there.

'It's the dinghy from the harbour boatshed,' she said.

Far below, a small craft cut a zigzag course across the heavy waves in the harbour. It was travelling out to sea, but it wasn't making much headway.

'Donaldson,' Jack said with disbelief. 'He's doing a bloody runner!'

Twenty-Six

'You know what this'll be,' Claudia shouted, as they hurried through the village. 'You mentioned the Crew . . . that'll have spooked him.'

Jack glanced at her distractedly.

'Donaldson knows the Crew,' she said, as they entered the esplanade. 'He probably did more business with the Crew than the rest of us put together. If they're the ones behind this, he'll know it means we are well and truly screwed.'

Even so, it was a hell of a risk the ex-super had taken.

It was true that the storm had lessened, but the sea in the harbour still rose and fell in endless foam-capped mountains, surf breaking over the pier and quayside. Two hundred yards from the harbour wall, the buoy danced and swung, its bell clanging, while just beyond that, the grey dinghy tossed and turned like a leaf. There were two people on board, both packaged in waterproofs, but though a significant distance from shore, they weren't so far away that Jakeman's flame-red hair and Donaldson's ungainly bulk didn't reveal who they were.

Milburn's jaw had all but dropped. 'This is bloody insanity!'

'We've got to do something!' Rathour said.

They scanned the whole harbour, but even if there'd been a life ring available, which there wasn't, the endangered duo was way too far out of reach for it to be thrown to them.

Instead, Wayland spun away, mounted one of the quad bikes that they'd left outside the pub, gunned it to life and curved around in a tight U-turn, before rocketing along the esplanade and swinging on to the stone quay. Jack did the same, mounting another of the quads and throttling it in pursuit. It was towards the south side of the harbour, the quayside, where the dinghy was now being beaten by the relentless swell, though as Jack approached the end of the stone causeway, it became clear that the small, flimsy craft wasn't close in real terms. It had passed the buoy and was bound for open water, but there was another couple of hundred yards to go first, and it was a hundred yards, at least, from the quay. However, the vessel was evidently in crisis, leaping and bouncing, threatening at any second to dislodge its passengers.

Jack leapt off his ride, leaving it so late to brake that the vehicle almost went over the end of the stone promontory, and ran to join Wayland.

'You pair of lunatics!' the former murder man shouted. 'Get over here!' But his cries were lost in the wind and spray. 'I know Donaldson's a dickhead,' he said, 'but what the fuck is Jakeman doing with him?'

'Haven't you heard?' Jack replied. 'She's got a thing for senior officers.'

It must have sounded stingingly unsympathetic, but the more he'd got to know the former honey-trap girl, the less he'd liked her. Self-interest had been high on her agenda even by this group's standards. If nothing else, he'd admired her instinct for self-preservation. Until now.

'Can't have a brain in her head,' Wayland said. He raised his voice again, cupping both hands to his mouth. 'Donaldson! Get your arse over here! Before it's too late!'

But in truth, it already was too late. Not least because the two panicking figures on board had no control. If they'd ever had oars or paddles, they'd lost them now. Donaldson clung to the tiller, but the motor at his rear wasn't exerting enough power to drive them clear of the harbour. In addition, it looked as though the dinghy itself was deflating, its taut rubber structure rippling, bellying inward.

'Fuck!' Wayland said in slow disbelief. 'Bloody thing wasn't even seaworthy!'

'Or maybe *he* had something to do with it?' Jack pointed along the harbour's south shore, which extended far westward of the quay. It was basically a natural embankment of jumbled, barnacle-covered rocks, running all the way to the edge of the ocean before curving out of sight. But a hundred yards along it, a tallish figure, clad head to foot in green camouflage, stood about twelve feet above the exploding waterline. He wore some kind of head covering, which concealed his face, but his focus was clearly on the unfolding disaster in the harbour.

For several helpless moments, Jack's attention was torn between the mysterious figure and the collapsing dinghy, though increasingly it was fixed on the latter, which was now shrinking in on itself, withering away before their eyes, Donaldson and Jakeman floundering in the flood, splashing like children.

It was impossible just to stand and watch, but it was equally impossible to do anything else. The waves hitting the quay seemed gargantuan; Jack and Wayland were sodden with spray. Again, Jack glanced along the southern shore, where the figure in khaki had turned and was loping back up the rocks with animal agility. It seemed to be carrying something, some kind of lengthy implement, though Jack couldn't make out what it was.

'He's on his way!' Jack hit Wayland's shoulder, pointing.

Wayland looked but was immediately torn back to the dinghy, or rather its passengers, both now adrift, going under again and again. Donaldson, in physical terms the lesser of the two, went under more regularly and for longer periods than Jakeman, who now attempted a front crawl in the direction of the buoy, though with forty yards to go it seemed unlikely she'd manage it.

An engine thrummed to life somewhere above them. They stared again up the embankment of rocks. There was no sign of the camouflaged figure, but they knew what they were hearing.

'Quad bike,' Jack said.

Still, they were frozen in place, unsure what action to take, but knowing there was nothing they could do where the swimmers were concerned. Jack thought of them as 'swimmers', but Donaldson had submerged again and this time hadn't resurfaced, while Jakeman's red hair was visible on and off, as the waves surged over her. Above the rocks, meanwhile, the sound of the quad bike engine dwindled.

Unexpectedly, Wayland grabbed Jack's shoulder, spun him and hauled him back to their own bikes. 'We've got to get the bastard!' he said. 'This may be our only chance.'

They glanced again towards Jakeman. She was ten yards short of the buoy, still striving hard, but it now looked as if she was drawing a reddish trail behind her. She'd been injured.

'McGurn!' Harry shouted, wheeling his machine around. 'This is it! We've got him!'

Jack nodded, thoughts whirling. As they hurtled back along the quay, he spied a commotion on the esplanade, Claudia and the others darting back and forth, trying to work out what to do next. All he and Wayland could do was leave them to sort that out.

The ex-murder cop drew ahead as they swerved between the silent cottages, throttling up as they hit the grassy slope. They halted on the Quad Track, engines rumbling.

'Where did the bastard park?' Jack said. 'Looks like he was out on a headland.'

'Must be a path leading out there,' Wayland replied. 'But you've seen enough of this island to know its most efficient transit route is the Quad Track.'

They rode southward along it, bypassing the entrance to the hotel drive, the village and harbour falling behind them. The gorse thickets south of Porth West soon gave way to the beach, and indeed, as Wayland had forecast, ahead by about five hundred yards, travelling southward over the sands, but veering towards the Track, was another quad bike. It wore orange livery but was more notable for the camouflaged figure hunched over its handlebars.

Wayland throttled up, spearing onward.

Jack accelerated too but already found it unnerving. According to his speedo, he'd just passed forty-five, and he was acutely aware that he wasn't wearing a helmet. With his machine jumping and jolting on the firm but uneven Track, it struck him what an irony it would be if, in chasing the murderer, he ended up killing himself.

Wayland had no such qualms, accelerating all the more. This surely was a throwback to earlier days, a momentary glimpse of the Harry Wayland who once was.

Ahead, it looked fleetingly as if the orange quad bike would come unstuck. In line with the Track now, it thrashed its way uphill through dense hanks of thorns and other beachside foliage, and then hit a sudden steep incline. The camouflaged rider made no apparent adjustment to his speed or angle, and yet he made it, he and his machine vaulting upward, briefly flying, before crash-landing on the Track, skidding across it, veering around on two wheels, and resuming his headlong flight.

◆ ◆ ◆

'You can't be serious,' Gabby Milburn said to Claudia. 'You're going to *swim*?'

Claudia, who'd already kicked her trainers off and stripped down to her shorts and T-shirt, knotted the rope around her waist. 'If I run into trouble, you guys can pull me back out. It's not a problem.'

Milburn exchanged glances with Baxter and Rathour, who seemed equally astounded. Even Jonas Pugh looked startled, and he'd only recently awakened from his latest drunken stupor and had come staggering on to the esplanade to see what the noise was about.

They peered over the rolling, grey water. The buoy rode it chaotically, bell clanging, but it was the figure clinging on to it that they zeroed in on: the sodden mop of bright red hair, the white arms wrapped around the weed-encrusted metal pyramid atop the float. The waves pounded the girl repeatedly, and yet she hung on. It was life or death. You could summon up remarkable reserves when everything depended on it, though that didn't seem to apply to Donaldson, who'd been lost to sight for minutes now.

Milburn took up the rope, still protesting. 'Go out there, there's no way you survive.'

'There's no way Sally Jakeman survives if I don't,' Claudia said. 'I just need to get away from the harbour wall. I'll take a running dive, so you guys keep a loose grip till I'm clear.'

More spray swept them as another surge boomed against the esplanade.

'If I need you to pull me back in, I'll make this symbol.' Claudia crossed her arms above her head, both fists clenched.

The other women regarded each other with horror. Pugh picked up the rope, but only seemed to half comprehend what was going on. Claudia meanwhile, paced backward twenty yards. 'I'll need to hit it straight after a wave strike, so the backwash carries me out.'

'Claudia!' Rathour pleaded. 'You're not a copper anymore. No one'll thank us for anything we do here.'

Claudia shook that thought from her mind. She wasn't doing this to win brownie points. Her eyes roved the roiling, crashing surface, closing again on the tiny dot of ember red, the desperate Sally Jakeman still riding the great torrent as it continually engulfed the buoy. She was doing it because this was what she had signed up for all those years ago. To be more than just a useful member of society; to be its protector. She couldn't believe how she'd sleepwalked into something so diametrically opposed to that.

She exhaled slowly, and as the latest mountain of foam came rolling at the harbour wall, lurched into a furious forward sprint.

Twenty-Seven

Jack and Wayland drove neck and neck along the Track, travelling at just under fifty miles per hour. The wind was hard, not just in their unprotected faces, but from the sea too. But if nothing else, their target was still in sight, now no further ahead than three hundred yards. They'd gained on him, presumably because, though he'd jack-knifed up from the beach in the sort of high-speed stunt Steve McQueen would have pulled in a 1960s action movie, it hadn't been as smooth as it looked and had delayed him a little.

The problem was that they weren't closing the distance between them now.

Jack glanced to his right. Atlantic breakers still struck the beach and though only a narrow expanse of sand was visible, indicating a high tide, the beach itself was receding from view, more foliage filling the gap between them. He knew that the Quad Track veered inland before coming alongside the castle, and guessed this was happening now, because the eroded Tudor structure, fully visible before, was no longer in sight, trees screening it.

Left of the Track meanwhile, the open woodland speeding by was a greenish blur. Jack swore. If their quarry veered off somewhere ahead, and they didn't see where, there were any number of places he could conceal himself and his vehicle.

Jack was tempted to throttle up more. He was especially tempted when he saw the Track bending out of sight, their target constantly vanishing as he got ahead of the curve.

He shouted to Wayland that they needed to get a move on.

Wayland glanced at him, nodded and lurched ahead. Jack attempted to accelerate as well, only to feel the mechanism judder underneath him. Judder and cough.

It started losing speed.

Glancing down and behind, he saw puffs of black smoke spewing from his exhaust.

What the fuck! Now? Seriously?

He was staying in this chase. He was adamant about that. Not least because he was the one carrying the firearm. But try as he might, and his options were limited, he couldn't get any more power out of his ride. Its engine changed tone continuously as it slowed and jerked and chugged.

'Sodding thing!' He glanced down again, pointlessly, because with his untrained eye he wouldn't have been able to spot a mechanical problem anyway, though it almost sent him spinning into oblivion. With the Track curving sharply inland, and deep thickets of pinewood springing up left and right, Jack was fleetingly so preoccupied that he almost went hurtling into it. He adjusted at the last second, the quad bike travelling two-wheeled before righting itself.

Frustrated at having dropped behind, he stood up as he rode, to try and see properly. Because the route continued its long, slow bend towards the island's interior, he'd lost sight of their main target, but it was more irritating that he could now only just see Wayland. The ex-homicide dick forged ahead but continued to glance back. Jack waved him onward, indicating that he was having engine trouble. Wayland nodded, accelerating again. He'd easily pushed past fifty now and was rocketing far, far ahead of his associate . . . at which point, he jerked once in his saddle.

As his head leapt from his shoulders.

It was that simple.

Harry Wayland's head had come off.

Jack's jaw dropped, his vision shifting out of focus as it was torn between the pink, roundish object with the grey mop on it, blood spurting from its stump as it bounced towards him, and the truncated form suddenly slumped forward over the machine in front, which was swiftly losing speed, though not so much that it didn't sail clean off at the next bend, hurtling into the trees with much crashing and banging.

Even in the chaos of his thoughts, Jack still spied the glittering metallic wire pulled taut between two fast approaching pines, one on either side. It still thrummed from the recent impact, its central section glinting crimson.

Though running at less than thirty, Jack rode straight at it.

He threw himself sideways, hitting the hard-packed sand with bone-jarring force, and the next thing was cartwheeling into the trackside foliage, where his entire body struck a solid upright, a pine tree no doubt, with sledgehammer force.

Claudia was startled by how breathtakingly cold it was. Even in June, the North Atlantic was no swimming pool. The other thing was its elemental power.

As planned, she got caught in the backwash, and as she broke the surface, was propelled way out, froth boiling around her. She dived back under, breaststroking forward through a void of swirling sand and whipping kelp. Under the surface, of course, it was impossible to measure progress. The undertow was terrific, and her main fear was that even at this distance – thirty yards or so – it still might hurl her back against the harbour wall.

She kicked forward. As she broke the surface again, it swelled tremendously, carrying her high and dropping her low. Switching to a front crawl, her strongest stroke, she motored onward, only once risking a backward glance. She was surprised and pleased to see that she was already some fifty yards out from the esplanade. Through clouds of erupting spume, she saw the others arrayed like a tug-of-war team as they paid out the rope behind her.

She turned frontward again, where another wall of foam came at her. She ducked under it, emerging on the far side to glimpse the upper portion of the buoy: the swinging, clanging bell. It was still fifty yards ahead at least, but she churned through the surf, driving herself like a torpedo. She was the best swimmer she knew. She'd learned when she was four years old. She'd won multiple medals. She'd passed her police life-saving course with honours. But there was turmoil underneath her. The angle of the harbour bed deepened, the undertow strengthening. Again, the swell was fantastic, carrying her high, then plunging her down into fizzing depths now darkest green and shuddering with ocean thunder.

It didn't deter her. She resurfaced with force, thrashing onward, the swinging bell close. She caught glimpses of Sally Jakeman's milk-white arms as still, incredibly, she clung to it.

There was something else now, though.

As more waves gushed over the desperate young woman, the foam that came with them was red. Deepest red. She was hurt. Badly.

It didn't matter, Claudia told herself. It was to be expected. She front-crawled onward, tireless, steely. Until – suddenly and violently – she was tugged backward and down.

Beset by the dissonant roar of ocean waves, she fought back to the surface, riding it like a roller coaster as she glanced behind. If the rope had snagged on something on the harbour bed, that could be catastrophic . . .

But in actual fact, it was worse.

The rope was clearly discernible, pulled taut above the water . . . all the way to the harbour wall, from on top of which the tall figure of Gabby Milburn waved frantically.

Claudia's heart sank. This was all the rope they had.

She swung back around. Twenty yards off, the wounded Sally Jakeman hung on by a single arm, the pipe-cleaner limb hooked agonisingly around hard metalwork. The girl's rich red hair glimmered under the surface, but only then amid ballooning clouds of crimson.

Twenty-Eight

As Jack stared dazedly up through a lattice of green branches, there was no doubt in his mind that he'd broken something. He also knew that he couldn't lie here for long. Because, groggy though he was, he had a vague awareness that something awful had just happened.

Though his entire left side was numbed by pain, he tried to jam both hands under his body to lever himself up into a sitting position. The resulting agony knocked him dizzy, made him want to throw up. He persevered nevertheless, finally making it. A second then passed, before he rolled forward on to his knees, planting his right hand down in front of him. Again, the pain rip-sawed along his body, but he was sufficiently compos now to identify its origin.

Damn, broken collarbone. Not the end of the world. But Christ, it hurts . . .

He panted hard as the pain subsided. It didn't vanish altogether, eventually receding to a nagging throb, which was just about tolerable. He felt at the holster by his side to ensure the Remington was still there. It was. Now that he thought about it, the ribs on that side also felt bruised and tender. Bloody weapon was doing more harm than good so far. He raised his head, blinking the sweat and grime from his eyes.

Open woodland on all sides. It mainly comprised pines, but this wasn't the north of Britain. They weren't clumped together. There was plenty of daylight here, not to mention plenty of breeze. He was inland now, but strong currents of air still funnelled through the foliage, rattling the heavily needled boughs.

He struggled to get his thoughts in order. And then . . .

Harry . . . oh God, Harry.

Glancing back, his eyes alighted on the Track, a dozen or so yards away, though only partly visible through the greenery.

With another mighty effort, using the tree he'd slammed into as a prop, he swayed upright. Briefly, he stood as close to the trunk as he could. Only now was he thinking about the killer. The killer who'd clearly known they were coming. In fact, who'd lured them into a pre-prepared death trap. There was no doubt in Jack's mind that, had his own engine not failed him, he too would be lying decapitated.

The constant motion of the wind made it difficult to establish whether there was anyone else lurking in the nearby undergrowth, but knowing that he couldn't stay here indefinitely, Jack lurched forward, venturing towards the Track, where he halted again.

To the right, he saw the wire.

Still pulled taut at neck height. Still stained crimson.

He hesitated to go further.

Step out there, son, and you're a clear target.

'But I'm armed too,' he told himself. 'And I can't stay here.'

Steeling himself, Jack drew the Remington, hefting it one-handed as he stepped into the open. Intense pain rippled through him. He struggled to stay upright, his consciousness ebbing. *Shock*, he told himself . . . *it's just shock.*

Glancing leftward, the Track lay bare, save for the gruesome trophy in the rough vegetation alongside it. It was about forty yards away, and from this distance he was mercifully spared any close detail: just the mat of iron-grey hair dabbled with blood. More blood trailed along the Track towards it. A meandering path of glinting crimson droplets.

'Good God,' Jack breathed. 'Good God almighty.'

◆ ◆ ◆

It was a crazy decision. But Claudia knew she had no other option. It was the sight of Sally Jakeman, semi-conscious at best, finally losing her grip on the buoy, her pale arm sliding from sight, that prompted her.

Treading water amid the whitecaps, Claudia tugged at her crude rope harness, loosening the knots, struggling free. Even all this way out, she could hear the cries of consternation from her comrades, which she ignored as she knifed her body downward, plunging deep. Even down here the currents tossed and buffeted her, but now, as she arched around, breaststroking forward, she gained a clear visual on the spreadeagled form of Jakeman, descending slow and ghost-like, thick clouds of blood swirling around her.

Claudia pumped her way forward. In almost no time, she was grappling with the cold, leaden form. It was unclear what state the casualty was in, but Jakeman's head lolled, and her eyes were closed as Claudia wrapped an arm around her, and with more massive frog-kicks, lugged her towards the towering bulwark of the harbour wall. In the furious fight for survival, the young woman had lost her waterproofs and running gear; she wore only a sports bra and knickers, but she still proved cumbersome, not least because blood was literally throbbing out of her. If she didn't drown, she would bleed out.

Casting all delicacies aside, Claudia took a firm grip on the woman's hair, swimming strenuously upward, hauling the deadweight to the surface. She only needed to break it sufficiently to draw breath before she went back under, heading shoreward but slanting back to the harbour floor. It was a shot in a million, the remotest chance, especially as the floor was a good ten feet down, but by a miracle it paid off, the long black thread of the discarded rope still lying on the sand.

She snatched it up, frog-kicking to the surface again, though it was harder than she would ever have believed with the unresponsive Jakeman in tow. When she broke through the foam, she gasped for air in a spasm that almost turned her lungs inside out.

The problem now was how to give the signal. She'd told Gabby Milburn that she'd cross her wrists above her head, but that would involve both arms, neither of which were free. Thankfully though, Milburn, dancing about on top of the harbour wall like a demented cat, spied her again. Shouting incoherent orders, she and the rest of them pulled on the rope.

Despite the heaving sea, Claudia and Jakeman travelled landward with remarkable speed, that great battlement of stone soaring towards them. Yet, far from feeling encouraged, Claudia was agonised, every muscle strained to breaking point as she was dragged over and under, pummelled again and again by the mighty backwash.

Only when the harbour steps teetered above her did she dare to think she might survive. She gazed up the dizzying height of brine-soaked stairway, so torn with pain that she thought she was going to faint. Gabby Milburn hurried down towards her, splashing in waist-deep to assist. Claudia released her burden but continued to ascend, still drawn upward on the rope, the unyielding edges of the steps biting into her, banging her ribs, barking her shins and knees.

She released her grip near the top, slapping down on to stonework. As she did, Milburn dragged the still inert form of Sally Jakeman past her, and it was only as the casualty's naked left leg bumped through Claudia's close vision that she saw the thing sticking in its thigh.

Not just sticking in it: pinning a shred of grey rubber there while deep inside, as evidenced by the blood still pulsing out, having breached the femoral artery.

◆ ◆ ◆

Jack found his quad bike not far from Harry Wayland's. Both vehicles had travelled past the neck-wire by fifty or so yards, leaving the Track at the next curve, the pair of them ploughing deep into the woodland.

Jack's machine had come to a halt about thirty yards in, having collided with a tree, the whole front of its engine and suspension caved inward. Some twenty yards to the left, Wayland's machine had finally succumbed to the thick mesh of vegetation that had wrapped around its wheels and axels, though that too had collided with an unyielding object: a large rock, against which it rested skew-whiff. Wayland's vehicle had boasted blue livery, all of this now spattered with congealing gore, as was the slumped body of Wayland himself.

The vehicle might still be roadworthy, but Jack wasn't going near it.

This was when he spotted something else, perhaps fifty or so yards further on: a glint of orange deep in the greenery. He stiffened.

Was that the maniac's ATV? He'd been riding an orange machine.

Jack raised the Remington as he edged over there. But it didn't offer great comfort. Firstly, with only five cartridges available overall, he'd need to be stingy in their use if he wanted them to last. Secondly, he was physically lopsided by the pain of his fractured collarbone. Just walking around was difficult and exhausting. Thirdly, if this was their assailant's machine, it very likely meant that he himself was around here somewhere.

Jack clicked back the hammers as he cautiously advanced.

The problem with a shotgun of course was the wide spread when it fired. Up close it was devastating, but over a distance much less so. As a cop, Jack had been an authorised firearms officer. A basic requirement for AGI. But he'd trained with the Glock 17, a modern lightweight pistol with an effective firing range of fifty-five yards. You couldn't have done better when executing clandestine ops in the asphalt jungle that was Manchester's gangland.

In comparison to that, what he carried now felt like something from the Stone Age.

A twig snapped to his left. He spun as much as his injury-encumbered body would allow, pointing the Remington straight-armed.

At nothing.

Just an empty gap between the two nearest trees, the ferns beyond it swirling and twirling. He pivoted round. Empty glades on all sides. He proceeded uneasily, his own ATV, useless hunk of metal though it was, falling behind. Instinctively, he gave a wide berth to Wayland's remains.

Another loud *snick* signalled a twig breaking.

He spun around again, almost toppling over. Just keeping the Remington levelled was difficult. Sweat spangled his eyebrows as he scanned the woods. Still nothing.

When he looked frontward again, the orange ATV was clearly visible. From what he could see, this one hadn't struck anything. It looked as if it might have been driven off the road deliberately and parked.

Unable to raise his left arm, Jack had to use his right to mop the sweat from his eyes. Feeling increasingly vulnerable, he pressed forward.

It wasn't impossible that their assailant's own mechanism had become faulty as well and he'd simply abandoned it. But it still seemed more likely he'd dismounted to view the effects of the neck-wire. It had been supposed to kill both of them. If that was the case, where on Earth was . . . ?

Jack heard the twang of a high-tension string and the whistle of a shaft travelling at lightning speed just before he was struck across the left side of his face with such force that it sliced his cheek open. He tottered, astounded more than initially hurt, because the glancing blow had deflected the missile to his right, where it now stood quivering in the trunk of the nearest tree.

Jack didn't know much about living in the wild, but he knew a hunting arrow when he saw one.

Twenty-Nine

For a few minutes at least, adrenaline overrode all pain.

Of course, Jack didn't know where he was going as he blundered pell-mell through the coastal woods. There were no direction markers. The sky was a roof of low, rushing cloud, the sun hidden. He could hear the ocean, but he couldn't see it. One mass of evergreens hit him after another. All the way, every thirty seconds or so, a wooden arrow, smartly fletched and armed with a lethal bodkin point, came whistling after him, thudding into the sturdier trunks or splitting saplings wide apart.

He panted and gasped, but stumbled on, zigzagging. He wasn't sure if this was why he was still alive or whether it was down to the tree cover. Evidently, the maniac wasn't getting too close because he'd seen that Jack was armed. At some point though, if Jack continued to resist returning fire, he'd draw the conclusion the gun was empty or at least that ammo was low.

Jack glanced back repeatedly, but his pursuer remained invisible, though on one occasion he was just in time to see another feathered missile winging towards him. He threw himself sideways as it whipped past, colliding with a young fir tree, the pain almost knocking him senseless. Head swimming, frothing at the mouth, he charged on, tangling in brambles, thorns raking him, before breaking out on to open ground, which suddenly tilted downward.

He halted, sobbing for breath, face bleeding copiously.

The terrain sloped away from him, and he realised that he could now see the grey swell of the ocean through breaks in its foliage. He didn't know what good that would do, but at least it gave him a sense of direction. The trouble was that if he continued downhill from here, he'd be on open ground, with only a few tree trunks to impede the vision of anyone who came up behind. He'd be a clear target for as long as it took him to reach the denser vegetation far below.

He glanced back again. Wind rattled and thrashed the leafage. Could it be masking the approach of his pursuer?

Maybe, if a lesson needed to be taught, now was the time.

He levelled his Remington at shoulder height – he was one-handed, but he could still fire it – training it on the depthless mesh of evergreens. Focusing on the point that seemed to be thrashing the most, he fired, the storm of shot blasting through, chopping down a cascade of twigs and leaves. The recoil was massive in one hand, the sawn-off swinging upward as his arm hinged, almost clubbing him in the face.

He waited and watched, breathing hard, fresh blood streaming from his slashed-open cheek. Wind still moved through the undergrowth, but – and whether this owed to his imagination, he couldn't say – perhaps not so frenziedly.

Had the lesson been taught? Had the bastard been driven to ground, or even killed?

Jack couldn't wait around to find out. He turned, slotted the weapon back into its rig and hurried downslope, digging his heels into the needle-covered earth, which, thanks to the recent rain, was soft and yielding. Fleetingly, through the trees on his right, one of the upper parapets of the castle came into view. It was some distance off and he was now seeing it from a different angle, but it briefly distracted him because he thought there was a light in one of the empty apertures of its windows . . . only to realise that it was nothing more than sunlight reflecting through the hollowed-out interior. At which point another arrow whistled past, missing by inches, kicking a chunk of bark from a nearby trunk. Jack diverted behind it, where he stood upright, sweating, gasping, hoping that it shielded him.

'You see I'm armed!' he shouted hoarsely. 'Be under no illusion, pal . . . I'll kill you if I see you! You also need to know that we've got a boat coming. Your number's up if you don't get your arse away from here.' He paused to catch his breath. 'It'll be no easy ride in jail, I'll tell you that. We may be dirty coppers, but we know people in every clink in Britain. For the right money, they'll bust you up morning, noon and night.'

He waited, listening. The wind droned on, Atlantic rollers crashing. But no sound came down from the higher woodland. Likewise, no further arrows.

There was no chance that a few loudmouthed threats had done the trick. This guy had been killing people in torturous and spectacular fashion like it was some kind of hobby. He wasn't going to be warned off so easily. But most of the murderers Jack knew were big on self-preservation. If nothing else, the shotgun might have made him think twice.

Taking another breath, he scuttled on down the slope, fighting forcibly into the deeper greenery near the bottom, regardless that the gradient was steepening. Steepening so much in fact, the ground so loamy and wet, that it disintegrated under his feet. Jack threw himself on to his back. It was a hefty jolt, and it went through his broken torso like a spear, but the next thing, he was tobogganing downhill without a toboggan. Bushes whipped at him as he bounced over humps and rocks, dirt flying into his face and eyes. Even then, an arrow slanted past, closely missing.

¹ As the slope levelled out, he scrambled back to his feet, tottering forward on rubbery legs. He'd left the real thickets some distance up the slope, and now the ocean lay in front, but before that, the ground sloped again, and a few feet down it he saw the roofless remnant of what looked like a farm cottage.

He stumbled downward, seesawing in pain. It was no more than a shell. There were a couple of square windows on the landward side, but no door. He edged around it, leaning on the age-eroded granite just to stay upright. If the sea was to the west, that meant the entrance he finally located was in the north gable. He went through it into a mass of fallen slate and broken timber, and a jungle of nettles. There was no higher floor. Literally just four walls, though there were glassless windows on all sides, which of course meant that, even here, he hadn't found the perfect redoubt.

As if proof were needed, an arrow came rattling through. Jack hurled himself against the wall between the two landward windows. Fresh sweat broke all over him as he listened, eyes darting around the interior.

The cottage had possessed only a single room and one entrance/exit. That was the good news. It meant it would be harder for his opponent to sidle in here unnoticed. But the windows were a problem because they were so numerous. It wouldn't be easy moving around in here. Those on the ocean side were less troublesome, because on that side the ground tilted away again, descending thirty feet or so to the waterline, which at present was all rocks and heaving spume. The bastard couldn't hit him from that side, but the others were another matter.

As Jack waited, his energy flagged and his pain flared.

He sucked in lungfuls of sea air, trying to impregnate his blood flow with fresh oxygen so that he wouldn't faint. His left arm was dead wood, literally useless. The limb itself was uninjured, but thanks to his collarbone, he couldn't move it an inch. If he'd had the time, he'd have removed his sweatshirt and tried to lash together some kind of sling, but more important now was to slot a new cartridge into the empty barrel, so that his Remington was fully loaded.

Of course, he could only do this by cracking the damn thing open, placing it down, digging into his pockets to find what he needed, and getting the job done single-handed. It was fiddly and difficult, mingled sweat and blood dripping freely from his face as he struggled, but he managed it, jerking the breech closed.

He waited again, listening. The impact of the waves only added to the noise of the wind in the branches. There could be a whole army out there, under cover of the foliage, and he wouldn't know it.

Then there was a sudden crackling in the underbrush, very close to the cottage. By the sounds of it, close to the entrance. Jack spun to face it, levelling his weapon.

He focused on the empty doorway so unblinkingly that his vision blurred. Only slowly did he realise that, just beyond that open doorway, perhaps five or six feet away, a couple of young hawthorns struck each other whenever the wind gusted, their spiky branches entangling noisily.

He lowered his weapon and hung his head. Only to hear another sound from the other side of the building. Again, he pressed himself into the wall.

Still, nothing happened, no one appearing at any of the apertures. As the minutes dragged by, Jack tried to work things out rationally.

If *he* were the bowman, he would definitely stay up the slope, out of sight, waiting for his prey to move past one of the windows. But he'd need to be an excellent shot, on which subject Jack was now wondering how much of a marksman his adversary actually was. He'd loosed off twenty arrows at least, and hadn't once hit his target. Okay, the circumstances had been difficult: a foot chase through overgrown woodland. But even so, didn't that suggest that he wasn't quite the dead-eye Jack had feared?

But was that a chance he could take?

The bastard might simply be waiting on a high perch, well rested, well hidden, comfy in the knowledge that his injured target was certain, at some point, to make a run for it.

But then again . . . ?

Jack searched mentally for things that might lend him advantage. He'd estimated that the guy had expended twenty arrows. That couldn't be too far wrong. So, how many arrows did the bastard actually have left?

Jack knew nothing about archery. He'd seen the quivers that sports archers used, and they never seemed to contain more than ten or twelve shafts. Of course, that still didn't mean the guy was out of ammunition. He could have been collecting his spent missiles as he went along, but they wouldn't all have been easy to find. This was woodland. Many, he'd never see again.

But he might also have other weapons at his disposal.

Jack resolved to wait a little longer.

Except that this plan didn't work either.

It was just after two now. So, there were many hours to go before darkness. But what happened after that? He wouldn't be able to see his hand in front of his face. And yet that didn't necessarily apply to his opponent, who'd set mantraps and clearly knew his way around. Was it a stretch to assume that he'd also have the means to light his way after nightfall?

Bastard might even have night-vision goggles. He's playing this whole fucking thing like it's a commando fantasy. Why the hell not?

'Okay,' Jack said to himself.

He had to get out of here before dark. The question was how would his opponent respond? Most likely, he'd have calculated that he simply had to wait. But would he have the patience for that?

And would it not interfere with his plan? Because he clearly had a plan, and it involved eliminating everyone on this island before his time ran out.

Jack wondered if the bastard had heard his shouted lie that there was a boat coming. Again, he tried to put himself in the other guy's shoes. If it were him, he'd have been discomforted by that. He'd assume his quarry was lying, but he couldn't be certain. Perhaps it might encourage the maniac to speed things up? Did that mean an attack could be imminent? An attack Jack might repel? He tensed again, and as he did, heard something that sounded like footfalls. Heavy footfalls, as though someone was descending the slope on the landward side. Jack raised the Remington, listening.

Was this his moment? Turning to face the wall, he sidled along it, and a foot short of the nearest window, leaned sideways, the top-left corner of his head and his left eye sliding past the edge of the window frame.

But there was no one on the slope.

That didn't compute. He could still hear the damn footfalls. And now undergrowth was thrashing too. And only then, to his horror, did he realise what was happening.

The slope from the higher woodland didn't just lead down to this cottage. It continued south, the full distance along the coast, and even from this window, even if he leaned dangerously out, he couldn't see all the way along it. So, between here and the window in the south gable wall, there was a complete blind spot. But he'd glimpsed it earlier: though there was initial open space around the immediate exterior, on the south side it was all foliage.

'Crap!' Jack swung to face the south window, at any moment expecting a camouflaged figure to appear there, bow at full stretch.

Again, nothing.

He lurched across the interior, half tripping on the rubble. Coming swiftly to the aperture, he made no effort to hide as he peered out, Remington at the ready.

At first, he was again startled to see no one. But then he blinked the grimy sweat from his eyes, zoning in on the nearest wall of vegetation, which was only a handful of yards away, and realised that a well-disguised figure had merged into its lushness.

The camouflage gear he'd envisaged? Check.

The head covering? Check . . . an olive-green ski-mask.

There was even military-style webbing, which looked to be loaded with lethal weapons; Jack glimpsed a hefty commando knife, a mallet, a hand-axe, a bundle of cord. More importantly, the bastard's bow was down in front of him, half drawn, arrow nocked. Even semi-concealed behind leafage, it would have been nothing for him to raise it and loose, hitting Jack square on. Except that Jack's Remington was already cocked and aimed.

Jack fired.

The semi-visible figure spun away as the hail of shot scythed through the undergrowth. It must have hit some part of him, but already he was out of sight, leaves hanging shredded and quivering behind him.

'Bastard!' Jack bellowed.

The fucker must be wearing Kevlar under his coveralls, which in its turn meant that he might be looking to resume the battle from a little further away. Jack peered harder, eyes penetrating deeper into the greenery.

Was *that* him? That human shape that was just about distinguishable, standing some twenty yards further back, taking aim once more?

Jack fired again, the rain of death blasting through the vegetation. As it did, an arrow hurtled towards him, but awkwardly, turning in the air, broken mid-stem.

Jack withdrew from sight, breaking his gun open, digging into his pocket for his last two shells, shovelling them into the barrels, snapping it closed. He risked another glance into the ripped and smoking verdure.

Nothing moved, either near its surface or down in its depths.

Had he got the bastard?

He'd been on the right track; he'd deflected the arrow.

Another thought struck him. As the half-seen figure had reeled to get away, he'd seen something that looked like a quiver, hanging on his back. More to the point, that quiver had been empty.

Jack had been right all along. The maniac was out of arrows.

'Okay, you fucker,' he muttered. 'This is it. You pull that big knife – oh God, I hope you try it . . . I'll turn your head to fucking Swiss cheese.'

He stumbled out through the front door, and along the length of the cottage on its seaward side. When he reached the south-west corner, he hesitated, eyes scanning the devastated undergrowth.

Were there still hints of movement in there?

It was likely down to the sea wind. But what if it wasn't?

He cursed. That bloody knife, not to mention the other weapons . . . they wouldn't seem so inferior to his sawn-off if he got lost in that leafy tangle.

He ventured in anyway, tense and wary, finally coming to the trunk of a young hawthorn, which had been gashed by shot. Glancing back, the window in the south gable was just about visible. It must have been around here from where the bastard had loosed his final arrow. It couldn't have been much further.

Then his foot touched something.

When he glanced down, it wasn't as he'd hoped: a severed limb or blood-drenched ski mask. But it was maybe the next best thing. Jack hunkered down, nudging the item with the Remington's muzzle. Unless he was very much mistaken, this was what the firearms guys in the job had referred to as a 'compound bow'. It looked impressive, and in fact it probably was, but now it was broken, its drawstring snapped, and central handgrip shattered, so that it lay in two parts.

Jack retreated towards the cottage, gun still levelled.

It was discouraging that he hadn't even winged his opponent, though it was some consolation to know that while he was trudging back along the Quad Track towards Porth West, he'd be in less danger than before of being shot down from sixty or seventy paces.

Thirty

Once he'd found his way to the Quad Track, which wasn't easy as initially he'd had to get uphill and back through the woods, which again were filled with storm shadows and rippling and rustling in the breeze, Jack estimated that he had about a mile to travel on foot, and that would be a hard trudge in his current condition.

He started walking. But it wasn't just the pain and fatigue that nagged at him. As long as there were pinewoods on either side, he kept the Remington drawn, loaded and cocked, but couldn't help feeling that he'd lost a little confidence in it. Twice now, he'd blasted the bastard, and both times he'd failed to make an impact. Okay, the explanation was body armour, but all this meant was that next time, Jack would need to go for a head shot, and that made the outcome even less certain.

He constantly scanned the trackside verges, looked repeatedly over his shoulder. Even when he emerged from the woods, and the sea lay to his left, he was nervous. He couldn't travel a hundred yards without the sudden conviction that a masked, camouflaged figure was running silently up behind. Again and again, he spun around, firearm levelled, but there was never anyone there.

It was a palpable relief when the hotel came into view.

When he reached the bottom of its drive, the temptation was to go straight up, assuming that everyone would now have taken refuge there. But he was equally intrigued to know what had happened down in the village. He crossed the Track and peered over the rooftops. The harbour wasn't quite the cauldron it had been, but the sea was still surging in, the buoy rocking wildly. There was no sign of the dinghy, though a light shone from one of The Salmon's upper windows. It implied the activity was still around the harbour area.

He slotted the Remington back into its rig, before limping down the steps and threading through the network of passages to the esplanade. But before he had a chance to enter the pub, he spotted two figures lying motionless at the top of the harbour steps, both of them draped with canvas.

Jack walked slowly over there. One by one, he uncovered their faces. The first was Ray Donaldson. His blank features were white, his lips blue, his eyes glazed and only half open. The second was Sally Jakeman. She lay in a similar state, though in her case, some unexplained object jutted upright about two thirds of the way down her body. Puzzled, he pulled the covering away entirely.

An arrow, still with fragments of the rubber dinghy attached to it, had transfixed her left thigh.

'She bled to death,' a voice said.

He turned. The pub's front door stood open, Gabby Milburn approaching.

Jack nodded. 'I can also see why the boat went down.' He dropped the canvas back in place. 'How'd you retrieve them?'

'Claudia swam out and got Sally . . . but it was too late, she'd already gone.'

He glanced at her. 'Claudia *swam?*'

'Amazing, isn't it, what people will do to atone for their sins?'

'What about Donaldson?'

Milburn stood with hands on hips. 'Washed up next to the steps an hour later. Full of contradictions, the ocean, don't you think? Quite often it *does* give up its dead.'

Jack shook his head. 'This is some body count.'

Milburn appraised him, taking in his filthy, bloodstained clothes, his wounded face. Then reached behind her back and pulled the Beretta into view, levelling it on him with the tactical two-handed grip that all SFOs were taught until it was second nature. 'Stand still, Jack.'

He froze. 'What're you doing?'

'You're in a mess, mate. And where's Harry?'

'Harry's . . . Harry's dead.'

'Is he indeed. How?'

'Gabby . . . how did you get Donaldson's gun?'

'Claudia left it with her trackie top when she dived in. Guess she forgot about it after that. She went through quite a lot out there. Half dead herself when she got back. Had to carry her upstairs. Put her in the bath myself. She's still there . . .'

He glanced towards the pub. If nothing else, that explained the light he'd seen from the upstairs. Movement at the door distracted him. Cheryl Baxter, Varada Rathour and Jonas Pugh had come out and were warily approaching.

'Think I had a fight with Harry, eh?' he said.

'What would you think?'

'We were chasing someone. You *saw* that.'

'Yeah, but we don't really know what's happening on this island, do we? Or who's with who.' She kept the pistol trained on him. 'So, what happened, Jack?'

Tiredly, Jack relayed the events of his and Harry's journey to the coastal pinewood, up to the point where he'd finally plodded homeward on foot.

'And that's how it happened?' she said, sounding unimpressed.

'If I have to, I'll take you back along the Track,' he retorted. 'You can see the neck-wire for yourself. Being honest with you, I don't like the idea of leaving Harry's body out there for the birds to pick at, anyway.' He started forward. 'We should put him with the others.'

'Stay where you are!' She levelled the pistol again. 'And while you're at it, take that sawn-off out. Two fingers on the stock and toss it away.'

He walked forward again. 'Don't be bloody ridiculous . . .'

'*Do as I tell you!*'

He halted. 'Gabby, why would I be killing people here?'

'I don't know, Jack. Maybe the Crew are paying you?'

'Back to the Crew again, are we? I thought we'd agreed that because of his lordship over here,' he jabbed a finger at Pugh, 'the Crew are unlikely to be involved.'

'Yeah, but that was before we knew Pugh was on the Crew's payroll too. Or so he's just admitted.'

Jack looked at the ex-CSI. 'An Essex copper?'

Pugh reddened. 'Only a short time, you understand. Technically, I worked . . . well, mostly I worked for the Corporation. But . . .'

'But . . . don't tell me,' Jack said. 'They've got some kind of truce with the Crew?'

Pugh shrugged. 'Part of the deal was . . . talent sharing, I suppose.'

'Talent sharing? Okay.'

'The Crew had some business round Colchester way, you see. The Corporation played ball.'

'For a price, I'd imagine?'

Pugh shrugged again. 'More than we could ever earn, I'll tell you that. But . . . well, they got *me* into the bargain.'

'And whatever disgusting horror they perpetrated,' Jack said, 'you sent Essex Major Investigations the wrong way by royally fucking up the crime scene?'

Pugh reddened even more. 'We're none of us bloody proud of ourselves!'

'It seems Jonas here is another loose end the Crew have decided to tie up,' Milburn cut in.

Jack glanced from one to the other. Pain still gnawed its way through his body. He was damp and filthy, and for some reason still standing here in the wind.

'Good,' he said. 'Hoo-fucking-ray! At least we now know why we're all going to die. In the meantime . . .' he lurched forward again, 'I need a cup of coffee and a bag of nuts.'

'Stay where you are!' Milburn snapped. 'Hands where I can see them . . .'

Jack walked towards her. 'It isn't loaded, okay. I thought as an SFO, you'd have worked that out by now.'

She lowered the weapon as he passed. Highly likely she'd noticed it felt light but had probably hoped there'd be one or two rounds left.

Inside the pub, all was quiet, firelight sparkling in the large mirror on the bar's back wall, glimmering through the bottles on the glass shelves. Claudia sat at the counter alone, head bowed, hair hanging in a mass of sodden ringlets over a glass of what was either whisky or brandy. She seemed to have found an old sweater and a pair of canvas trousers from somewhere.

'What the bloody hell do you think *you've* been playing at?' Jack demanded.

She jerked upright as though half asleep. 'Oh, erm, Jack . . .' She gawked with shock. 'What happened?'

'Got into a scrape with our homicidal mate.' He joined her at the bar. 'Wanted a coffee, but now I wouldn't mind a double whisky.'

'Yeah, sure . . .' She jumped from her stool and scurried round to the other side.

'What do you think you are, a bloody mermaid?'

Claudia said nothing as she grabbed a bottle.

'Make it a treble, yeah?' he said.

She did so and placed it on the counter. 'Where's Harry?'

Jack threw his drink down in a gulp. Outside, they could hear the others conferring loudly.

'Jack!' Claudia said again. 'Where's Harry?'

'Harry's not coming back.'

To her credit, she remained calm while he explained. Her eyes were already moist and sore with salt, so it wasn't possible to tell whether tears had appeared there.

'We're in a real spot, here, Claudi,' he said. 'Whoever this guy is – and I think it is only *one* guy – he really knows what he's doing. To start with, we should all be back in the hotel, in that secure base we made for ourselves.'

She produced a first-aid kit from behind the bar, unzipped it and pulled on a pair of disposable gloves. 'Let me look at that face first.'

He leaned over, while she cleaned his sliced cheek with an antiseptic wipe. 'Jesus, Jack . . . this needs stitches.'

'We haven't got time. Did you hear what I said? We should be up at the hotel.'

'Yeah, I know.' She rummaged in the ziplock bag again, found an extra-large plaster and carefully applied it to the wound.

'I can't believe you're all still here,' he tutted.

'It's warm, cosy, there's booze . . . it was convenient.' She rooted in the bag again. 'Think there's a sling in here, for your arm . . .'

'Never mind the bloody arm . . .'

'We can't never mind it, Jack!' She glared at him. 'If that collarbone's broken, it needs to be immobilised, or it'll get worse . . .'

'Things can get worse?' Gabby Milburn said, coming inside, the others close behind. She threw the empty Beretta on to the bar top. 'Good job I didn't actually need this, isn't it!'

'Yeah,' Claudia replied. 'Sorry.'

'You never mentioned that thing wasn't loaded. Why?'

'Same reason you just pointed it at me,' Jack replied. 'We don't really know anyone here, do we. Though I think it must be safe to say, that with only six of us left, we need to throw caution to the wind and club together.'

'We should all go back to the hotel,' Milburn said.

'My thoughts too.'

'Wait a bloody minute!' Pugh pointed at Jack. 'He said he was going to show us Harry's body . . . and this neck-wire, to prove he's on the level.'

'For God's sake,' Baxter replied. 'We've just agreed to stick together, and you want to split us up already?'

Pugh shook his head. 'The only person I knew here was Harry Wayland . . . and now he's dead? Or so *you* say, McGurn.'

'Well, I don't need another trip out,' Baxter said. 'I'm going back to the hotel.'

'Me too,' Rathour agreed.

'Is it really important we retrieve Harry's body now?' Milburn wondered.

'We can always get it tomorrow morning,' Baxter said. 'In daylight.'

'It's not dark yet, and it won't be for ages,' Pugh replied. 'We've got the quad bikes.'

'It'll mean we get separated again,' Milburn warned.

'But not for long,' Jack said. 'And the alternative is I have to spend the whole night with everyone looking at me sideways, wondering if I'm the guy. That said . . . if we're bringing Harry's body back here, we'll need that golf buggy thing from the backyard.'

'Those things don't go very fast,' Claudia warned.

'We'll take a quad bike too.'

'Whatever you're doing, will you do it quickly?' Baxter steered Rathour towards the rear corridor, where they halted. 'I don't see any sense in bringing Harry back now, but if you insist on it, fine.' She eyed Jack's gun. 'I must say, though . . . I don't understand why we're letting you keep that weapon, McGurn. Not when we've only got your word for what happened out there.' She glanced at Milburn. 'It's not like we couldn't disarm him seeing as he's hurt his shoulder.'

Milburn seemed to be on the verge of agreeing with that, so Jack raised his good hand.

'You don't need to.' Stiffly, he unfastened the gun harness. 'You're right, I'm hurt. So, it makes sense to give ourselves a shotgun rider.' He handed the rig to Claudia, who regarded it with worry and uncertainty.

'Jack, I don't know . . .'

'If we're going out there again, I need a wingman I can trust,' he said.

'Very well.' Baxter sounded mildly mollified. 'But understand . . . we're not just going up to the hotel, we're locking the place down as soon as we get in. So, don't drag this hare-brained mission out any longer than you need to.'

Jack's eyes met Milburn's. 'You'd better go with them.'

Milburn still looked unimpressed by the plan, and now seemed surprised too. 'You want someone to ride shotgun and you don't ask the only real shot in the house?'

He threw a glance at Baxter and Rathour, both of whom were demonstrating bravado, though neither were anything like real fighters. 'I think you can do more good at the hotel, don't you?'

Milburn sighed and nodded towards the hefty shillelagh. 'Pass me that, yeah?' Claudia did so. Milburn swung it. 'Better than nothing.'

'Bar yourselves into that lounge area, and you likely won't need it,' Jack said.

He went upstairs, grabbed some bedsheets, and when he got back down, they moved as a group into the pub's yard, where the trolley-car with the trailer waited.

'I'd say can you give us a ride as far as the hotel gates,' Milburn said, 'but I suspect we'd be quicker walking.'

'Can we just go?' Baxter urged her.

Milburn shouldered her shillelagh and set off on foot, Baxter and Rathour scampering in pursuit. Jack, meanwhile, climbed behind the trolley-car's steering wheel and turned it on. Claudia, who'd fixed the gun harness in place, climbed into the passenger seat, while Pugh accommodated himself behind. They drove out on to the Back Lane, travelling with a ponderous lack of speed, which was probably a good thing, as Jack was already struggling to control the vehicle single-handed. As an automatic, it only had two gears to manipulate, forward and back, but the wheel was heavy.

'You say you shot the bow out of this guy's hands?' Claudia said. 'It has occurred to you he might have another? He could have weapons stashed everywhere.'

Jack was grim-faced. 'I'm not leaving Harry out there. For a brief time, I suspected his motives. Even wondered if he'd set us all up. Couldn't have been more wrong, could I? Least I can do is bring him back and put him under canvas with the others.'

'Okay . . .'

'Why do you sound sceptical?'

'You sure you're not just going back along this Track for round two?'

'What?'

'You forget, Jack . . . I know you. You're not the sort to let things go . . . who'll sit in a hotel lounge for the rest of the week.'

'I thought you said it was needs must that we catch this bastard.'

'Yeah, but maybe not to take risks like this.'

He shrugged. 'Go and wait in the hotel with the others if you want. But I think you'll find round two's coming whether we like it or not.'

Thirty-One

'You reckon that little girl with her big gun's gonna give us adequate cover for this?' Pugh grunted as he drove.

'I trust Claudi with my life,' Jack replied.

'It's not *your* life I'm bloody worried about, boy.'

They had ridden the trolley-car together, but once they'd got to the bike shed, Jack had realised that he wouldn't be able to drive the vehicle much further with one arm in a sling, and so had swapped seats with the former CSI.

They were now en route again, but the Quad Track alongside the sea was proving a tough surface for the flimsy electric vehicle, which constantly rocked and jolted. Seeing that it could only reach a top speed of fifteen miles per hour, Claudia, who now wore the harness and the Remington, raced ahead on her black and green striped quad bike. The plan had been for her to act as scout, but given the discrepancy between their velocities, she was finding it difficult staying close.

'We're going to get the blame for all this, aren't we?' Pugh said.

He was a jittery mess, his shirt crumpled and stained, his hair a lank mop, his entire person reeking of booze and sweat.

'Don't you think I'm responsible anyway?' Jack replied.

'Fuck it.' The ex-CSI dug into his pocket, pulled out his hipflask.

Irritated, Jack snatched it and tossed it into the scraggy vegetation left of the Track.

'Hey, you bastard!' Pugh shouted.

'Fuck's sake!' Jack retorted. 'What bloody good are you if you're soused all the time? Don't you get it? We're in a fight for our lives here.'

Pugh scowled but drove on. His anger soon faded; he looked tired, despondent.

'In a way it's true that it's us to blame,' he said. 'Outfits like the Crew want the best. The ones who can do most damage to the justice system. That was us, boyo. It's coming back to haunt us now because we were so damn good at what we did.'

'They used us, abused us and now they're chucking us away,' Jack replied. 'But we could have said no at any time.'

'Say no to the Crew?' Pugh snickered. 'Some planet you live on.'

Claudia came rumbling back along the Track towards them, circled round and decelerated so that she could ride alongside.

'Just found Harry's head,' she said, glassy-eyed.

'Okay,' Jack replied, queasy at the thought of setting eyes on it again.

'That's all you've got to say?'

'I'm just glad it's still there. This bastard's more than capable of removing the evidence, trying to make me out a liar, cause more division among us.'

'Best just to be objective about it, eh?'

He shrugged. 'Unless you know a better way.'

'Crying's not going to fix his head back on,' Pugh added.

Claudia said nothing, just accelerated ahead of them again.

'Well, it's true, isn't it?' Pugh asked no one in particular.

'Mr Beck's gone!' Rathour shouted, stumbling into the hotel lounge.

Milburn looked around from where she and Baxter were piling chairs and tables against the swing doors. 'What?'

'He's not in his sickbed anymore.'

The two older women glanced at each other, Milburn checking the broom was back in place between the pull bars, before hurrying across the room towards the staff corridor.

But it was true.

The sofa bed, though its pillow was stained with dried blood, was now empty. The rest of the small office was equally bare of life.

'He hasn't stumbled down to the bathroom, or something?' Milburn said.

'No, I looked.' Rathour's voice verged on frantic. 'There's no one there. Or in the other office further down the corridor. He's completely vanished. But . . . surely if the murderer had taken him, there'd be signs of a fight?'

Milburn's eyes roved the orderly office space. 'I agree.'

Baxter joined them. 'The back door's still locked.'

'So's reception,' Milburn said.

'If he's wandered off, he must have gone out through the lounge,' Rathour put in.

No one argued. The lounge doors connecting with the hotel interior had been left unsecured when they'd hastened down to the harbour, along with the hotel's front doors of course. They went back through the lounge to look, but no obvious telltale signs were visible.

'You patched him up,' Milburn said to Baxter. 'How bad was he?'

'He'd been severely beaten. Does that mean he couldn't walk out of here on his own? Probably not.'

'So, do we go and look for him?' Rathour asked.

'No, we bloody well don't.' Milburn was sure about that at least.

'But if he's in a daze, anything could happen to him,' Baxter protested.

'Look, Cheryl . . . I didn't even want us to split up so they could get Harry's body. I'm damned if *we're* splitting up too.'

'Excuse me?' Baxter said. 'If I want to go and look for Mr Beck, which would be the right thing to do, I *will*. And there's nothing you can do to stop me.'

'No, but I can stop you coming back in.' Milburn stalked to the barricade. 'Because I'm finishing this thing, and I won't be dismantling it until the others get back.'

Baxter looked aghast. 'You'd lock me out there? Are you mad?'

'Are *you* mad? Hunkering down in here with every door bolted is the best idea we've come up with since we arrived. It's the one sure way to keep us all safe until help comes.'

'Cheryl, don't go out there,' Rathour pleaded. 'We don't even know this guy, Beck.'

Baxter glared at her. 'And that makes a difference?'

'The hell with it,' Milburn said. 'If the perp's dragged him off to do vile things to him, that's just tough. We need to survive and we're only going to do that by looking out for ourselves.'

Baxter looked as if she wanted to argue further, but relented. After all, she'd originally been as keen to come up here and lock herself in as the other two. She moved huffily away, sitting down with arms folded.

'Why would he come back for Beck?' Rathour asked, as she and Milburn continued dragging items of furniture and stacking them against the swing doors.

'Obviously wanted to finish the job,' Milburn said.

'How did he know he hadn't already done that?'

'You mean is he watching us? Well, yeah . . . definitely. He's known every move we've made all the time we've been here.'

'If he's that good,' Baxter said tersely, 'a broom handle and some armchairs aren't going to keep him out.'

Thirty-Two

'Keep watching the woods, yeah?' Jack told Claudia as he and Pugh manhandled the hefty shape along the Track. Wayland's body was swathed in bedsheets, crimson patches blossoming all over them. Though missing a head, he was still a solid lump of bone and muscle to carry a hundred yards back to the wire. It was especially difficult for Jack, with only one fully functioning arm, but it still made more sense for Claudia to have the weapon, as getting a clean shot at their adversary would be the most vital contribution anyone could make that day.

Claudia remained abreast of them, Remington levelled as she scanned the encircling pinewoods, now dim with shadows, twigs and foliage twitching in the wind. How much she was actually seeing she couldn't be sure. She'd thrown up twice since arriving here. Firstly, at the sight of Wayland's severed head, and secondly when they'd wrapped it in a bedsheet and placed it in the back of the trolley-car. The heavy, bony thud as Jack put it down had hit her deep in the gut. And now the rest of him was here and she was determined not to look.

Inside of course, she was ashamed. The tears and vomit had demonstrated weakness, and yet, like many cops, she'd long taken pride in not being weak, in becoming hardened to the ugliness of life. They did that job because they *could*, because they were a different breed to whom feeble emotions like fear, shock and revulsion were unknown. But now all that inner mettle seemed to have melted away. It was unsurprising given what she'd been through, but this was hardly the time to find out.

Or it could simply be that she'd grown to like Harry Wayland, to view him as a trusty friend, so to see him beheaded and left by the roadside like trash was more than she could take.

'Has it occurred to you we're interfering with a crime scene?' Pugh grumbled.

'This whole island's a crime scene,' Jack replied.

'Wonder what the Devon and Cornwall crime scene manager will have to say about it.'

'I hope he says it to my face. I'm just in the mood to punch someone's lights out.'

A sharp crackling of foliage spun them round to the other side of the Track.

Again, the greenery fluttered, the darker spaces within visible only in shifting, semi-opaque patterns. Anyone could be there, camouflaged or not, and they wouldn't easily be seen. Jack thought about the bow and arrow. Did the lunatic have another one?

Claudia clicked back the shotgun's hammers.

'Go easy with that thing, eh?' he advised. 'Our ammo's limited.'

She gazed into the swirling undergrowth. 'I'm sure I heard something.'

'Christ's sake!' Pugh pushed forward again. 'Let's just get out of here!'

They ducked under the wire, lumbered to the trolley-car's trailer and laid Wayland's body next to his bloodily packaged head.

Claudia watched the woodland as she mounted the quad bike.

'Stay close, girl,' Pugh instructed her. 'Don't go speeding off again like the bloody Road Runner.'

'You need to relax, Jonas,' Jack said, climbing into the front passenger seat.

'Relax, he says.' Pugh slid behind the wheel. 'It's a long way back travelling slower than a council workman on fucking overtime.'

'Yeah, but we've got the gun,' Jack reminded him. 'It's the ones who haven't who should be worried.'

◆ ◆ ◆

The swing doors to the lounge thudded twice.

The women looked up from their armchairs and sofas. Rathour got to her feet. 'Was that the wind?'

Milburn watched the barricaded entrance. 'Could've been.'

The doors thudded again. Loudly. Silence then followed.

Milburn reached to the coffee table in front of her, picking up the shillelagh. She listened and watched. It was difficult to ascertain how massive an obstacle the heap of furniture in front of the swing doors would prove to be if someone made a determined effort to get through. It would certainly hamper them, in addition to which they'd first have to snap the broom handle. The doors creaked, as though non-violent pressure was being exerted from the other side. Milburn rose to her feet. The doors creaked again, bowing inward slightly, definitely being pushed.

She walked over there, the shillelagh at her shoulder.

'Jack?' she called. 'Claudia?'

The pressure on the doors relented. Another silence followed, but there was no question in her mind that, whoever it was, they were still there, listening.

'Jack McGurn?' Milburn shouted. 'Are you guys okay out there?'

No response.

The other two women had stood up too, Rathour wide-eyed. Milburn made a calming gesture as she edged towards the barricade. Belatedly it occurred to her that whoever it was, they might be armed, might even have taken possession of Jack's Remington, so she stepped to one side to avoid being shot through the woodwork.

From left of the barricade, she listened again.

With a thundering *bang*, a huge weight struck the doors. They swung inward an inch, the broom handle visibly bending.

'Just keep it up, mate!' Milburn shouted. 'When you get in here, I'll hammer that damaged brain clean out of your fucking skull! D'you get me? You won't know what day it is, pal!' The force relented again. 'Yeah, that's it. Who do you think you're up against, eh? Fucking gangland moron!'

The silence beyond the doors stretched out. Milburn wanted to clamber over the chairs and tables, to plant her ear against the gap, but she was still thinking shotgun.

Now, however, she couldn't help wondering if the tone of the silence behind the doors had changed, as if whoever it was simply wasn't there anymore.

She glanced towards the others. They watched her tensely, Rathour glinting with perspiration. Milburn listened again – and now, from further away though still inside the hotel, she heard a dull, repeating, clumping sound.

Was this Jack and the others returning?

Possibly. But probably not. There was no conversation. Meanwhile, the curious sound came closer. Only when the first blow landed did Milburn realise it was some kind of battering ram. She jumped back at the jarring boom. Rathour squealed.

Another impact followed, and another. The pile of furniture dislodged slightly. The broom handle was taking a pounding, but still held.

'It's simple maths!' Milburn shouted. 'You come in here, and I'll kill you. I was an SFO in Liverpool. Specialist Firearms. I dealt with punk-ass shit-for-brains wannabes like you all the time.'

The impacts ceased again. Interminable seconds followed.

Milburn felt emboldened enough to approach the left side of the barricade again. She was sure that if this bastard had managed to get hold of Jack's shotgun, or even had one of his own, he'd have unloaded it through the middle of the doors by now to blow away the improvised bar. Of course, if he didn't have a gun, she was wondering why she was cowering in here. More to the point, she was increasingly certain there was only one of them out there. More than one, and she'd have heard them whispering.

'What's happening?' Baxter asked, venturing forward.

Rathour remained where she was, rigid.

Milburn backed towards them. 'I've a feeling he's regrouping, rethinking his strategy.'

'He must be confident if he thinks he can smash his way in and take on all three of us.'

'That's what's puzzling me,' Milburn said. 'Stealth is the only real way to overcome more numerous opponents. It's worked for him so far, but suddenly he seems to have given up on it.'

'Doesn't rate us girls, you mean?'

'Either that or he thinks he's reduced us to a manageable number.'

'What's he doing now?' Rathour asked.

Milburn held up a hand for silence. She'd heard something beyond the door again, though it sounded further off. Another clumping thud, as if whatever hefty item had been used to attack the doors was now being dragged away.

Another thud followed, and another, the noises diminishing.

'Sounds like he's retreating,' Baxter said, hopeful.

'Maybe,' Milburn replied. 'But why take his battering ram with him?'

'You mean he's going to smash one of the other doors?'

Milburn didn't say anything, because that was exactly what she meant, and neither the reception door, nor the outside door connecting with the staff corridor, would be anything like as sturdy as the swing doors in here. They'd been locked but neither had been barricaded.

'What do we do?' Rathour whimpered.

Milburn waved for quiet. 'Let me think . . .'

'We need to block those other doors surely?' Baxter said.

'Yeah, but they're single doors. The outside one's at the far end of a corridor, and I'm not sure how easily we can get any of this heavy furniture down there.'

'We can block the reception door at least,' Rathour said.

'You can try.' Milburn turned to the swing doors. 'In the meantime, I'm going after him.'

'W-what do you mean?' Baxter stammered.

'It'll take ages to block off those other doors as well.' Milburn eyed them coolly. 'For whatever reason, he's decided we three in here are no opposition at all. I think someone needs to correct that viewpoint, don't you?'

'What about everything you said before?' Rathour stuttered. 'About sticking together?'

'I know, but maybe this is our chance. He won't expect one of us to go out there after him. He thinks we're scared . . . But . . .' she showed them the shillelagh, 'I've got *this*.'

Baxter looked unimpressed. 'That's just a club, Gabby.'

'A club, a staff, a truncheon . . . that's all the generation before us ever had on the streets. They didn't even wear stab vests and they still controlled tougher inner cities than we've got anywhere in Britain these days. Look . . . if it bothers you, get some stuff . . . try and block those other two doors off.'

'Gabby,' Rathour whispered, 'he's going to kill you.'

'Loads of fellas have thought that over the years, and I'm still here, aren't I?'

Milburn didn't wait to debate it further, but began lugging the armchairs and tables away from the swing doors.

'For God's sake, Cheryl, talk some sense into her.'

But Baxter had now adopted a more thoughtful look. 'She might be right. I mean, look at her . . .' Milburn's muscles rippled as she cleared a way through the heap of furniture. 'Would you want to take *her* on?'

'But this guy's a killer!'

'So am I, darling,' Milburn said over her shoulder. 'That's what they used to pay me for.'

'And did you kill anyone?'

Milburn hesitated to respond. 'I . . . could've done.'

'See . . . she *could* have.' Rathour's voice turned shriller. 'Except that she *hasn't*. She bloody well *hasn't*. And this madman *has*, over and over . . .'

'Keep your voice down!' Milburn hissed. She'd now cleared room in front of the doors and extracted the broom handle. She glared at the girl. 'I'm going out, okay? I'm going to end this problem here and now.'

Baxter took hold of one of the tables. 'We'll block this up again once you're out, but only temporarily . . .'

Rathour's gaze shifted from one to the other as if she could scarcely believe what she was hearing. '*In God's name!*' she shrieked. '*This is bloody ridiculous!*'

Baxter slapped her cheek. 'Stop acting like a useless little girl!'

The younger woman looked astounded. 'You . . . you hit me.'

'Don't you get it? This guy is going to slaughter us like cattle. *All of us*, Varada. Unless we get him first.'

Rathour stood blinking, fingers pressed to her tingling cheek. Baxter switched her attention to Milburn. 'Don't hold back,' she said.

Milburn nodded, shouldered the weapon and slowly opened the left-hand swing door. Glancing out, she was satisfied to see a deserted vestibule.

She winked at them. And stepped outside.

Thirty-Three

Milburn felt painfully exposed in the vestibule. At her back, the lounge swing doors, now closed and barred again, were visibly scarred by several huge semi-circular indents, the carpet scattered with flakes of varnished wood. But there was no trace of whatever had caused such damage.

She kept the shillelagh at her shoulder and initially stayed close to the doors, glancing the full length of the vast chamber. Nothing moved or seemed out of place. On the right, a few dozen yards away, was the reception area, another possible point of attack, but there was no sign of anyone there. Across the way, directly facing her, stood the closed double doors to the kitchens. On the left, the vestibule led to the exercise area and swimming pool. On the left side of that, just past the lounge, was the open archway into the hotel bar.

There were many other entrances and exits from the vestibule. Milburn didn't know where half of them went. There could be a route to the great outdoors behind any one, but if their foe was planning to attack the exterior door to the staff corridor, it seemed most likely that he'd have left by the hotel's front entrance.

Steeling herself, she detached from the wall, heading in that direction, only to hesitate again. It would be an obvious ploy: to pretend that he'd left, when in fact he was lying up somewhere close by.

'Shit,' she breathed.

Had he second-guessed them?

She glanced over her shoulder just to ensure that he wasn't padding up from behind. And though the vestibule was clear all the way down, she saw a curtain twitch.

She didn't know why the curtain was there, or what it covered, but it filled a single doorway on the right-hand side of the vestibule at the point where it narrowed into a corridor.

It twitched again.

'Okay,' she said quietly. 'Okay . . .'

She advanced towards it, taking reassurance from the shillelagh. It was a clumsy, clunky piece of kit, but it was sturdy. If she got this right, she'd only need to hit the bastard once.

The curtain twitched again. She was about thirty yards away now and slowed down, glancing behind her. It was a shock to see Baxter leaning out from the lounge, watching. Angrily, Milburn gestured for her to go back inside.

When the swing doors closed, she advanced again, even more stealthily.

The curtain was about ten yards ahead now. As she approached it, she noticed another pair of double doors on the other side of the corridor. They stood partly open and she could see through them into what looked like a miniature ballroom: white-painted chairs around the edges, a polished wooden dancefloor. A wedding venue maybe? That was exactly the sort of service posh hotels provided these days.

Perhaps more unexpected was the huge wrought-iron table lying on its side in the middle.

Milburn regarded it with fascination. The bastard must have brought it in from outside to batter at the lounge doors. It would have taken some doing. The iron structure was solid and heavy.

She glanced again at the curtain in front of her.

It was crimson velvet. She wondered if there was a cloakroom behind it, part of the wedding suite. Or was this a trap? She swung round again. Was the madman about to launch himself at her from inside the ballroom? She crossed over and kicked the double doors open, exposing the entirety of the space beyond.

It was empty.

She focused on the curtain again, shillelagh in hand.

Clearing a room of dangerous suspects had once come second nature to her. But always then she'd been part of a team, she'd been well armoured and wielding either a Glock, an MP5 or a Kurz sub-machine gun. It felt like pure insanity to be doing the same thing now with a piece of wood. But Milburn was damned if she was snuffing it today. Not after some of the dig-outs she'd emerged from unscathed in the past.

Taking a big step away from the curtain, the weapon in her right hand, she reached out with her left, grabbed the material and yanked it back.

If there'd been anyone hiding behind it before, there wasn't now.

It was indeed a cloakroom, a small counter on the left, a rack of empty coat hangers. A frosted glass door stood partly open on the other side of it. As Milburn watched, it moved slightly, a breeze whispering past.

She pushed it open properly. Behind it lay another staff area, similar to the office behind reception, though showing no sign of ever being used. Another open door waited on the far side of this.

She glanced behind the coat-check counter just to be sure no one was hiding there, then went through. Past the office, another corridor led on, though this one ended abruptly at an exterior door, which also stood ajar. Milburn crept towards it.

Outside was a small tarmac yard, marked as a parking zone, probably reserved for the trolley-cars. On the right, next to a row of dumpsters, a pair of steel doors stood closed; if her mental picture of the hotel's layout was correct, these would link to the kitchens. The narrow, tarmacked slip road by which the trolley-cars arrived led around the side of the building. Everything seemed normal, until she spotted the figure lying face down about halfway along it.

At first, she thought this must be Beck. In his injured state, had he wandered out here and collapsed? She started warily along the slip road, conscious that things weren't always what they seemed. Ex-army lads in the firearms unit had told her of dead bodies in Iraq and Afghanistan wired with IEDs.

There was no sign of anything so obvious here: the body lay out on an open flat surface. But it didn't seem straightforward either. For one thing, Beck had been wearing pale blue pyjamas when they'd brought him from the staff quarters, whereas whoever this was wore dark clothing. As she drew closer, she saw that the figure was lying at the corner of an annex to the hotel. She halted and glanced up. The annex ended two storeys overhead at a stone balustrade, heavy pots filled with summer blooms arrayed along it. An upstairs terrace. Probably for outdoor dining. It was a convenient place to leave a body as a trap, because just around that corner someone could be lying in wait.

She crossed to the other side of the slip road, the hotel wall now a good ten yards away. If someone did leap out, she'd get at least one good swing in with the shillelagh. But there was no one round the corner. Just a section of lawn, squared off and with flowers around its borders and closed French windows.

She crossed back over, close enough to the body now to see it was a bulky male in a dark coat and trousers, some kind of sackcloth bag pulled over his head.

'Crap,' she muttered.

If nothing else, it clearly wasn't Beck. And then, very abruptly, the sunlight was blotted out. A black shadow engulfed her. Milburn just had time to look up – at the massive stone flowerpot tumbling towards her.

Thirty-Four

The trolley-car was easing to a halt on the hotel forecourt when Jack and Jonas Pugh heard a tremendous impact from the south side of the main building, a belly-juddering crash of exploding masonry. Jack stumbled from the passenger seat, but no additional sounds followed. Pugh remained behind the wheel, as if this snail-paced holiday transport might provide an excellent getaway car.

'Fuck's going on?' Jack said.

'Be my guest and find out,' Pugh replied, resolutely not moving.

With a growl of her four-stroke engine, Claudia braked alongside them. Jack was about to explain what they'd heard, when she glanced past him, registered something, and grabbed for the Remington. Jack spun round. A figure had emerged around the hotel's south-west corner and stood leaning against the whitewashed brickwork. It was Gabby Milburn. She was shaking violently and struggling to stay upright.

Claudia dismounted and hurried towards her. Jack hobbled over as well, Pugh climbing from the trolley-car and following more slowly.

'What happened?' Claudia asked.

Milburn wiped a trickle of blood from her brow and gestured weakly behind her. 'Shrapnel wound . . .'

Claudia glanced along the south side of the hotel, noting the figure lying prone on the ground, a jumble of soil and masonry all around it.

Milburn still struggled to speak. 'Walked into a trap. Idiot that I am. Pure luck it missed me.'

'Who's that down there?' Jack asked.

'Didn't get a chance to look . . .'

Claudia took Milburn's face in her hands, to examine the injury. 'You've got a gash just under your hairline. Couple of inches long, but it doesn't look deep.'

Milburn nodded her gratitude, but still seemed dazed. 'Flying fragment.'

'You bloody did get lucky if someone tried to drop a pot on your head,' Pugh said. 'Straight out of Poirot, that, eh?'

Jack stared up at the annex roof. 'You see anyone up there?'

Milburn shook her head. 'Just legged it. I know I screwed up, but I didn't know if he had anything else he could lob down.'

'No one there now.' Jack shielded his eyes to make sure. 'Anyway, you're alive, aren't you? You're more use to us that way than dead.'

'You're all heart,' Claudia said. She turned back to Milburn. 'You need to sit down or something?'

'I'm fine. Just knocked me a bit dizzy.'

Jack meanwhile had started along the path. 'Let's take a look.'

The others followed, Claudia aiming the Remington upward, both barrels cocked.

They were ten yards short of the bag-headed figure, when Jack realised who it was. 'Shit . . . Pasco.'

They scrambled forward, Claudia hanging back, still gazing at the parapet along the sawn-off barrels. The hefty plant pot lay in smithereens, a huge gout of black soil having exploded in every direction. A nasty divot had been gashed in the tarmac.

Jack squatted next to the body and lugged it on to its side using his one good hand, before pulling the sackcloth away. Ted Pasco's features were white but mottled blue, his lips black, his distended eyes bloodshot.

'Garrotted,' Pugh observed. A very obvious ligature, fishing twine perhaps, was wrapped several times around the victim's neck and cinched so tightly it was mostly buried in the discoloured flesh. 'Knows every method in the book, this boy, doesn't he . . . ? Wait a mo.' Pugh leaned closer. 'Is this supposed to be the harbourmaster here?'

Jack glanced at him, puzzled. 'There's no supposed about it.'

Pugh straightened up. 'That's Milo Crindle. I'd recognise that sad fucker anywhere.'

They glanced at each other.

'Milo Crindle?' Claudia said.

'Small timer from the East End. Had the odd contact with him when I was in uniform. Spiv, conman. Never a harbourmaster.'

'Conman?' Jack repeated.

'Played a range of different characters to get money out of nice old ladies.'

Which explains the exaggerated Cornish accent . . . maybe.

'How come you didn't spot him before now?' Milburn asked.

Pugh made a casual gesture. 'Didn't see much my first couple of days here. Had no close dealings with him, anyway.'

'You're telling us this guy's a professional conman?' Claudia said.

'Not a very good one. Remember him getting locked up a lot.'

'Organised crime connections by any chance?'

Pugh shrugged. 'It's possible, but . . . more a fall-guy type, I'd say.'

'Which is evidently what's happened here,' Jack said.

Milburn glanced at him. 'They gave him this job because he was dispensable?'

'Had to dress the place up somehow.'

Claudia looked shocked. 'He thought he was on the inside, but he was in line to get chopped as well?'

'Says a lot about their killer, doesn't it?' Jack said. 'They can't control him. So, they've just unleashed him instead.'

Even with the ghoulish recent events, that put a new chill through everyone.

'Where're Cheryl and Varada?' Claudia asked.

'Still in the lounge,' Milburn replied. 'I hope.'

'We need to get back there,' Jack said. 'Right now.'

Milburn led them indoors via the shortcut through the wedding area. 'Beck's gone walkabout, by the way. Either that or he's been abducted.'

Jack put a hand on her shoulder to stop her. 'Beck's gone?'

'While we were down at the harbour,' she replied. 'Maybe Mr Pugh can look the reception office over and tell us whether Beck left of his own free will.'

Pugh grunted. He didn't sound keen, but at least the surly drunkard of earlier had been replaced by someone who, if only for his own survival, was now taking a more active interest.

They moved on into the vestibule, where, hearing their voices, Baxter opened the lounge swing doors.

'I take it no one's tried to get in since I left,' Milburn asked.

'Quiet as the grave,' Baxter replied. She noted the sticky red stain in Milburn's hair. 'What happened out there?'

They went inside, where Claudia filled her in.

'Good Lord,' Baxter said, on hearing about Pasco. 'We're being whittled down like a First World War platoon.'

'You've kept a running check on all doors and windows?' Jack asked her. 'All still secure?'

'Of course.'

He turned to Pugh. 'You gonna help us out with this or what?'

Pugh nodded and walked through to the reception office with Jack, Baxter tagging behind. Claudia began re-stacking the furniture against the swing doors. Rathour came over in an addled state.

'That was definitely Mr Pasco you found out there?' she said.

'Yeah,' Claudia replied. 'Except that's not his real name.'

The younger woman became tearful. 'That's only one thing I can't get my head round. I . . . I came here for a summer holiday . . . and now someone I've never met before wants to kill me. Really and seriously wants me dead.'

'He wants to kill us all, Varada.'

'But you were all police officers. You must have dealt with this before.'

Claudia glanced at Milburn, who'd sunk into one of the armchairs and briefly looked too weary to participate.

'This is new to us too,' Claudia said.

'So, how are we supposed to deal with it?'

'We're not. These are standard terror tactics. This is what terrorism is all about.'

'God help us.' Rathour seemed incredulous. 'I thought it was bad enough we were facing a hitman. Now apparently, he's a terrorist too.' She walked away, seeming dazed.

You're haven't heard the best part, Claudia thought. *Wait till you find out he wasn't sent here but was unleashed.*

Unleashed.

That had been an unusually grim turn of phrase, even from Jack. Gave the impression they were dealing with a wild animal. Except that no wild animal would have clocked up half as many kills as this.

Thirty-Five

'Well, there's no sign of a fight in there,' Pugh said, emerging from the reception office. 'No smears of blood, stuff knocked over.'

'Beck was in no condition to fight anyway,' Baxter said.

'Okay.' Jack headed back along the corridor. 'Let's have ourselves a powwow.'

'Let me guess,' Pugh said, 'we're sending out a search party.'

'We're not, are we?' Baxter sounded surprised. 'I thought we'd agreed we were fortifying ourselves in here?'

Jack glanced back. 'Cheryl, we're in a real battle here. And battle is a fluid situation.'

'The way I see it,' Jack said, standing in the middle of the lounge, 'we've got to go and look for Beck. Not to mention the three Albanian women.'

'What?' Rathour exclaimed. 'What happened to us locking down?'

'Varada, we didn't get a chance to look for the three women last time. Now, we've got someone else missing. That's four people in total who may not yet be dead. If nothing else, if we just hide in here, it's not going to look good.' He paused. 'Look, wherever we go, we should be safe so long as we stick together.'

'Unless he's got another missile weapon,' Claudia replied. 'Like another bow.'

'From what you told us, the three women are almost certainly dead,' Rathour countered. 'And Beck was badly beaten. Even if he wandered off on his own, he's not going to last out there. Why should the rest of us keep risking our lives? We're dropping like flies.'

'It's the rest of us I'm thinking about,' Jack said. 'Look, Beck can be of use to us. He's been on this island longer than we have. He knows his way around.'

'We don't need to know our way around if we stay put,' Claudia said.

'So, *you* don't want to go looking for him either?'

'I didn't say that, Jack. But you've got to be honest with us. We all may live or die depending on the decisions we take here.' She paused briefly. 'Beck's your prime suspect, isn't he?'

Baxter looked surprised. 'Beck was badly injured.'

'So you say,' Jack replied. 'But you're not a doctor.'

She looked shocked. 'He had multiple head and facial contusions, plus a broken nose and a fractured radius. He'd also suffered a severe concussion.'

'First of all, you didn't have an X-ray machine handy,' Jack said, 'so he could have been faking the fracture. Likewise, the concussion.'

'And his face?'

'Come on,' he said. 'We've all known prisoners headbutt walls on their way into custody suites, so they could claim police brutality. Anyone's capable of that if it gains you an edge. On top of which, Beck did his disappearing act while we were all down at the harbour, which just happened to be when the perp appeared . . .

you know, the guy who shot the dinghy, while we all stood around like spare pricks at a wedding.'

'That could have been a coincidence,' Baxter said.

'Could have been. But it makes Beck a person of interest. Especially as we haven't seen him since. Look, he was on St Dunstan before us . . . for God knows how long. He's had time to recce the place, set up deathtraps like that neck-wire.'

None of them seemed convinced.

'I thought he was a hotelier, this fella,' Pugh said. 'A civilised guy with professional credentials.'

'We've never seen his credentials,' Jack replied. 'And it's easy to pretend you're civilised.'

'He could be in cahoots with the Albanian women,' Claudia suggested. 'There's a lot happened here for one man to have done it all alone.'

'Can't dismiss that,' Jack agreed. 'And the Albanian mob are connected to the Corporation, and now we find a London criminal posing as the harbourmaster. It's possible. But have you ever heard of a pro-kill team that wasn't equipped with firearms?'

'Maybe they are, and we just don't know it yet.'

'I think we would,' he said. 'If they're in it with Beck, that's four against six. And if they're armed, what's holding them back? Even without guns, we've already said they've had ample chances to poison us.'

They mulled these possibilities over.

'I'm with Jack,' Milburn finally decided. 'The best form of defence is attack. Whether Beck's a lone assassin or part of an outfit, we need to strike first.'

'We can't go scouring the island,' Claudia said. 'We've got one gun between us . . . and only two slugs left. And there may be more man-traps out there.'

'Let's check Beck's quarters again,' Jack said. 'If he's not there, we can turn the place over . . . we might find something that'll tell us who he really is, what we're dealing with. The staff digs are only four hundred yards east of here, but if we're going, we're going together.'

'Let's have a show of hands,' Milburn said. 'Do we check out Beck's pad?'

She and Jack stuck their arms in the air. Baxter followed, then Pugh, more reluctantly.

Jack glanced at Claudia. 'What's wrong?'

'You sure this is the best course of action?' she said. 'Or are you just dying to solve the case and show the world you're still the best bloodhound in the pack?'

Baxter's hand half lowered again.

'Nothing can undo what we've done,' Jack said, 'but maybe, if we sort this out ourselves, we can salvage a little pride.'

'To do that, you've got to stay alive,' Milburn added, 'and I still think this is the only course that's open to us, so my hand's staying up.'

Baxter raised her hand again.

'Makes sense,' Pugh said with a shrug. 'It won't be easy staying boxed in here for the next five days, anyway. Plus, our perp's going to come for us, isn't he? He's not going to let us survive just by hiding.'

Claudia looked from one to the other, her eyes resting on Jack a tad longer, then she slowly lifted her hand. This left Rathour, who, looking more like a scared rabbit than a person, finally, very unwillingly, put her hand up too.

◆ ◆ ◆

Even traversing the four hundred yards between the rear of the hotel and the staff quarters looked problematic. On one hand, as there usually was safety in numbers, they could clump tightly together and move along the path like a rugby scrum. On the other, if the perp still had missile weapons, grouping closely together would make it easier for him to strike multiple targets.

Pragmatic to the last, Milburn said that, whatever they did – and there was no guaranteed safe way to do it – they should at least arm themselves first. She was still wielding the shillelagh, while Claudia had the Remington. From the kitchens, Jack had now taken a cleaver, Pugh a meat tenderiser, and Baxter and Rathour a knife each.

'Just remember,' Jack said. 'If it comes to it, strike the head or the limbs. Preferably the head. Our killer is wearing body armour.'

They nodded grimly and set out along the path.

The storm had abated considerably by now, but there was much wreckage in evidence, garden furniture, leaves and torn-off branches scattered across the lawns. On the upside, this also meant there wasn't much greenery left intact behind which an aggressor could lurk.

'You'll see we're packing!' Jack shouted, holding his chopping blade in the air.

'Christ,' Claudia muttered, but she didn't try to shush him.

'Try anything,' he added at the top of his voice, 'and you'll get cold steel up your jacksie.'

'Well, if he didn't know what we were doing before, he does now,' Baxter said quietly.

'He knows what we're doing,' Milburn replied. 'You think he hasn't had eyes on us all the time we've been here?'

The wind picked up again, sending shivers through the undergrowth nearby. Claudia trained the shotgun on it as they passed.

'Pity about Beck, eh?' Milburn said. 'Always the nice-looking ones who turn out to be absolute bastards.'

'Pity about Jack,' Claudia grunted.

Milburn glanced at her. 'What do you mean?'

'You may have noticed that he's on a bit of a power kick.'

Milburn considered that. 'You don't want to live through this?'

Claudia frowned. 'Serious question?'

'You and Jack were key parts of an anti-organised crime outfit. You're the best chance we've got of getting through. It isn't good if you're at loggerheads. We can't just lie low and hope for the best.'

'I guess you were a bit more proactive in Specialist Firearms.'

'Bloody right. We took the battle to the enemy . . . but you lot did too. Or you used to.'

'That was Jack's style,' Claudia agreed. 'He was good at it too. Supervised some great takedowns. You want the truth, I was glad when he first grabbed this bull by the horns. He'd been drifting, even talking about topping himself. But the way it's going now, it just shows he's never accepted what we did was wrong. This thing was always going to be a challenge he couldn't resist. He even admitted that he brought that shotgun because he didn't buy the Damned Rankers cover story. Didn't buy it, but he came anyway . . . because he thought there might be a win in it for him somewhere. I can't get it through to him that whatever we do here, we're not going to get our jobs back.'

'For my part, I don't need *the* job back,' Milburn said, 'but I need *a* job. And I don't mean stacking supermarket shelves. So, if your solution is we keep our heads down, and hope the world's a bit nicer when we get back to it . . . count me out.' She strode off ahead.

Claudia watched her go, surprised, wondering if she was being hard on Jack. She'd chided him before they came here for adopting a fatalistic approach. And now, when he seemed to have rediscovered his old self, she was being critical of him for that as well. But this wasn't a game. Did he understand that? Did he fully comprehend the potential outcome of one wrong decision? Or was he so wrapped up in redeeming himself he was blind to the danger? She'd taken risks since arriving here. But more and more people were dying. Was it really worth trying to turn the tables on the killer when they could simply lock themselves away?

Up ahead, the staff quarters came into view: a rambling barn conversion-type structure, which would take some searching. Even from the gate, she could see that its front entrance stood wide open.

In front of her, meanwhile, Jack was organising everyone.

'Jonas . . .' He pushed the gate open. 'You're the ex-CSI, so I want you upstairs with me. We've got four potential crime scenes. Cast your eye over them before we start pulling out drawers and ripping carpets up, yeah?'

Pugh made some incoherent comment.

'Claudia, you come with us. There're other rooms up there supposedly locked and untouched. Can't think of anywhere better to conceal evidence. Gabby, you and the others do the downstairs. They're mainly communal living areas but give them the best going-over you can.'

'Be my pleasure,' Milburn said.

Pugh gave the upstairs murder scenes his professional once-over.

'Beck's bedroom I'm not so sure about,' he finally said. 'Says he was beaten while he was asleep, barely able to resist. It's not inconceivable that's what happened, but it's hard to be sure either way. The women's bedrooms though . . . they look like the real thing. The patterns of blood spatter, the general disarray . . . if they're mock-ups, they're good ones.'

It was now late afternoon and given that he'd been sober for that whole day, Pugh seemed more and more the analytical investigator. He was still a physical mess, of course, and visibly stressed, but that applied to everyone.

'Okay.' Jack knew he had an important decision to make. He glanced at the other two as they waited expectantly in the upstairs corridor. 'Okay . . . if you feel those are bona fide crime scenes, we leave them be. But we should search the other rooms up here.'

'Beck's bedroom too?' Claudia asked.

It was a fair question. Technically, Beck's bedroom should also be preserved, but Beck was the main suspect. It wouldn't make sense to turn everywhere else over and avoid his inner sanctum.

'We'll save that till last,' Jack said. 'Do the other spare bedrooms first. We're looking for anything personal that might have belonged to Beck: documentation, diaries, electrical gear – iPads, tablets, phones, laptops, any clothing, particularly of the outdoor variety. Any weapons, but also tools, ropes, spools of tape . . . you know the drill.'

They got to it, working through one empty bedroom after another, throwing off blankets, turning pillows inside out, kicking at the skirting boards to ensure none of them were loose.

It was the same story downstairs, the other group, marshalled by Milburn, going at it with gusto. Jack was on his way back down to join them, when he heard Milburn calling.

'Jack! Something you might want to look at.'

Joining her in the kitchen, Jack saw the entrance to the cloakroom standing open, and alongside it a square section of flooring propped up against the wall. Beneath it lay empty blackness and the top part of a ladder.

'Thought it weird there was nothing else in here 'cept coats and boots,' Milburn said. 'Usually, you get all sorts in kitchen closets.

Mops, buckets. I only needed to stamp around, and it sounded hollow.'

'I wonder what's down there,' Rathour said.

'What do you usually find in rat holes?' Pugh replied. 'Most likely a large, very objectionable rat.'

'*I'm* not going down to find out,' Baxter said.

Claudia shook her head. 'No one's going down there on their own.'

'Someone's got to go first though, haven't they?' Pugh replied.

'Such are the privileges of rank,' Baxter said. 'Eh . . . ex-DI McGurn?'

Thirty-Six

'I'm not even debating it.' Milburn clambered on to the ladder before anyone could stop her. She nodded at Jack. 'He might be able to climb down there with one arm, but if there's trouble at the bottom how will he handle that?'

Jack wasn't going to argue. Even if he'd had two arms functional, you only needed to look at Milburn to know she was by far the more athletic.

'Besides,' she said, 'I've got this.' She showed them the shillelagh.

'Take this as well.' Claudia offered her the Remington, stock first. 'I'm right behind you, but you'll be down there on your tod for a second or two, and it's pitch-dark.'

'Thanks.' Milburn shoved the shillelagh into her waistband, then took the gun and started down.

Trying not to think about the mutilated flesh she'd seen so far, Claudia positioned herself to descend in pursuit. 'Wait.' Jack offered her the cleaver. 'Just so you're not unarmed either.'

She nodded.

'It's not that far down,' Milburn's voice carried up from below. 'Hang on . . . what's this?'

With a click, an electric light flooded up. A telling silence followed, those in the kitchen staring at each other, tingling. Claudia waited on the ladder.

'Gabby, what've we got?' she called down.

'It's, erm . . .' Milburn responded in a curious monotone. 'You're going to have to come down and see this for yourself. Jack, it's okay for you to come down too. No one else, though. There's barely any room as it is.'

'Suits me.' Pugh moved away from the cloakroom door. Neither Baxter nor Rathour seemed disappointed either.

'No danger,' Milburn said. 'But steel yourselves.'

No longer expecting a fight, Claudia laid the cleaver aside before going down. Jack followed, clasping the ladder with one hand, descending into a small, subterranean room. Apparently dug out of the building's foundations, it had a beaten-earth floor, which had been laid with plastic sheeting, while the walls were breeze block, and the ceiling made from heavy boards braced by cross-beams. None of it was dirty or cobwebbed like a normal basement – it was probably too recently constructed for that, though it was crude and basic. Not that this had stopped someone trying to make it partially habitable.

A naked bulb hung overhead. It was this that Milburn had found the switch to. Its light revealed an office chair partly sunk into the dirt, facing a small table pushed against the right-hand wall. There were several large, buff envelopes on top of this, dog-eared and crammed with what looked like aged paperwork, while propped up so it faced whoever sat there was a noticeboard, the sort of thing you'd find on the wall in a school corridor.

But the cellar's most eye-catching feature was a macabre tableau, comprised of three figures, again all swathed in plastic sheets, each one held with twine fastenings to an upright wooden post, the three posts then propped against the left-hand wall. Though the figures were indistinguishable through plastic covers now rendered even more opaque by thickly clotted gore, there was no question in Jack's mind about who they were. However, just in case of doubt, each gruesome package had been tagged with a paper label handscribbled in green felt tip.

'"Collateral damage",' Milburn read aloud, plucking off the first one. '"Killed for a higher cause",' she read from the second.

Claudia pulled off the third. '"Casualty of war".'

Neither of them were concerned about interfering with a crime scene. Not anymore. The immediate priority was finding out if Mariela or her two daughters might still be alive. However, as Milburn and Claudia lowered them one by one to the floor, working hurriedly at the twine knots, tearing away plastic, gasping at the injuries exposed, Jack found himself backing towards the desk.

They were dead. He knew it. Everyone who'd gone missing on this island so far was dead.

He glanced sideways at the noticeboard, firstly at the curious word, written in green felt tip, and attached to the top:

UNDERBARROW

Then at the twelve photographs arrayed neatly underneath it.

There were various styles: some were snapshots taken in the street, others clipped out of newspapers or lifted from websites. But each one depicted a single person.

Milo Crindle, Harry Wayland, Sally Jakeman, Jack McGurn, Claudia Crayford, Cheryl Baxter, Varada Rathour, Gabby Milburn, Ray Donaldson, Declan O'Hare, Alan Rothermere and Jonas Pugh, though the images of Crindle, Rothermere, Wayland, Jakeman, Donaldson and O'Hare had a small X added in green to each topright corner.

Beneath the pictures, occupying the majority of the noticeboard, there was a large map portraying an island, presumably St Dunstan, though the map itself was old and crinkly, and evidently pre-dated the current occupation. The Quad Track was absent, though someone had drawn it on in green. Other sites which the map owner clearly considered important had also been marked with the same felt-tip pen: the harbour at Porth West, The Culraven Arms Hotel, a coastal prominence not too far north of the village which Jack guessed was Hangman's Point, and further south along the coast, at the end of the beach, a larger structure, presumably the Tudor castle.

None of this gave him any clue what the word 'Underbarrow' referred to, but glancing down, his gaze now fell on the bundle of envelopes. He should be wearing gloves, but he couldn't resist. They were all in aged, battered condition, but they weren't fastened, and when he opened them, were packed with what looked like magazine cuttings. As he drew them out and rifled through them, he was struck with a new level of horror, not just because of what he was seeing – in truth, there was nothing here explicit (none of these images held a candle to the mangled red carcasses in the corner of his vision, from which Claudia and Milburn were now rising stiffly to their feet) – but it was what they implied.

'Good God!' Milburn said in a nausea-thickened tone. 'This isn't the work of a hitman. This is the work of someone who's mentally ill.'

'And I know which one,' Jack said. 'Think about it . . . a killer with the ability to move quickly and without being seen, either day or night, to lie low in town or country, to take his quarry by complete surprise. A killer who seems to eschew the use of firearms but is happy to utilise other implements of torment.'

'"Implements of torment"?' Claudia said. She'd heard that phrase before.

'That's how he referred to his arsenal of hand-weaponry,' Jack said.

'You know this guy?' Milburn asked.

'I know *of* him.' Jack looked again at the noticeboard. 'I mean so far we've had, what . . . a neck-wire, a garrotte, a machete, a hammer and nails?'

'Who is he?' Milburn demanded.

'It was never mine or Claudia's case,' he said, 'but it's got plenty to do with us now.'

'You're not . . . ?' Claudia spoke tentatively. Cogs were turning, small, previously unconnected details falling into place. 'Jack, you're not talking about the Dogman?'

He regarded her solemnly. Milburn glanced from one to the other, bemused.

'It can't be!' Claudia said. 'Jimmy Cornwallis died ten years ago.'

Jack handed her a pile of cuttings. She flipped quickly through them. Some were colour, some black and white, but all were old, frayed and ragged along the edges They displayed a range of faces, both men and women. A significant number looked like police mugshots, thin, sallow features, ratty hair, trashy tattoos. In all cases, a green felt tip had been used to add a small X to the image's top right-hand corner, though some also had a caption scribbled at the bottom in green.

One read: *Sold poison to school kids. Traced, stalked, slain.*

Another: *Trader in human flesh. Now his flesh is grass.*

Another: *Knowingly spread disease. Cured.*

'Dogman victims,' Jack said. 'Bank on it. I've not counted, but there's a good forty or fifty in here. Harry's task force totalled the vics at thirty, but admitted there might be more.'

Claudia emptied out another envelope. This one mainly contained photos of places. Many were closed off by crime-scene tape but were almost entirely the sorts of dismal backstreet locations that all cops were familiar with: disused yards, burned-out garages, urban waterways that were more like open sewers.

'Check this out.' Jack handed her a newspaper clipping that was much larger than the others.

It was a centre-spread from the *Daily Mirror*, depicting an assortment of weapons, various knives, a Molotov cocktail, a home-made javelin. Across the double-page spread, the headline read:

IMPLEMENTS OF TORMENT

'His weapons were always simple, but cruel,' Jack said. 'And he used them all. It was in one of his deranged letters that he coined this memorable phrase.'

'I remember seeing this,' Milburn said, voice tight with recognition. 'In Liverpool, the Dogman killed a married shoplifting duo who'd just filled their car with stolen goods . . . He fire-bombed them through the car's open window when they got home. He used that same term when he wrote to the *Echo*, claiming responsibility.'

'There's an item referring to that incident right here.' Jack indicated another tatty clipping. This one reported the Liverpool attack and included an excerpt from the Dogman's letter.

Cockroaches like this are changing our national life beyond recognition . . . so I did the same to them. There are more vermin, but I have implements of torment for each and every one . . .

'But Harry Wayland shot the Dogman dead,' Claudia protested. 'Everyone knows that.'

'What was Harry sent to jail for?' Jack replied.

'Framing criminals for the crimes of others,' Milburn said.

Claudia was incredulous. 'You're saying Jimmy Cornwallis was framed for the Dogman murders, then executed?'

Jack shook his head, not wanting to believe it himself. 'Cornwallis was a war-damaged veteran, a right-wing obsessive known for making comments about cleaning up the streets . . . what better fall guy could Harry have found?'

'But why would Harry do that? The Dogman was a serial killer. Nothing to do with organised crime.'

Jack shrugged. 'Surely a more pertinent question is why would the Dogman be here? If he survived because the wrong person got clipped, why not take the chance to retire? Why court danger again by coming after the cop who hunted you years ago?'

'And why go after us?' Milburn wondered.

Claudia still seemed astounded. 'Are we thinking these murders have nothing to do with the Crew after all?'

'I wouldn't rush to that conclusion,' Jack replied. 'But look at who the Dogman went after.'

'In his own words,' Milburn said, 'the worst of the worst.'

'And let's not beat around the bush,' Jack said, 'in his eyes . . . that would be us.'

Thirty-Seven

'Are you seriously trying to tell us that Lucas Beck is the Dogman?'

They stood together in the staff quarters kitchen. Cheryl Baxter's face was a picture of disbelief. Jonas Pugh chuckled to himself.

'The evidence suggests it,' Jack said, having come up from the cellar with Claudia.

'Seriously?' Baxter's voice was barely a whisper. 'The same Dogman who left that trail of slaughter?'

In truth, they could not be facing a more terrifying opponent. For three years the whole of north-west England had struggled to cope with the Dogman's outrages. Yes, the killer had supposedly only targeted 'those who deserved it', but who had made *him* judge, jury and executioner? In towns and cities like Manchester, Liverpool, Bolton and Blackburn, people had locked their doors once darkness fell, terrified by a faceless predator who came and went like a phantom, leaving nothing behind save his latest butchered atrocity. Though his targets were nearly always 'people of the night', as he called them, no one had felt safe. He'd once gone after a suburban family man who'd been acquitted of murdering his wife, that same man later found hanging on a meat hook. But the scariest thing about the Dogman wasn't just his warped sense of morality but his total proficiency. Thirty victims was the official tally, though by Harry Wayland's admission there were probably more. Few other killers in British criminal history could boast such a body count, even though for reasons best known to himself, the Dogman had never once used a firearm.

Baxter shook her head. 'If Beck *is* the Dogman, how is it that Alan Rothermere was marched away at gunpoint?'

'We surmised that he was,' Jack said. 'But a blade in the hands of a specialist like the Dogman would serve just as well.'

'But why is he *here*? On an island no one's heard of?'

'Maybe he came here to get even with Harry,' Rathour said, 'then felt he had to do us as well . . . leave no witnesses.'

'How did he know Harry would be here?' Baxter asked. 'Hasn't this whole thing been arranged on the QT?'

'We don't know how Harry's arranged it, do we?' Jack said. 'He told us not to say anything, but did *he* follow the same rule?'

Pugh leaned on the kitchen cabinets, still snickering. 'Harry, eh? Sly old dog.'

'A sly old dog who's going to get us all murdered!' Baxter snapped.

'A lot of this is still supposition,' Claudia reminded them.

Jack nodded. 'Yes, but Harry brought us all here.'

'Did he bring Beck as well? Install him as hotel manager? Fabricate a past career for him? I can't see Harry managing all that on his own.'

'We're still talking about the Crew?' Baxter said.

'Course we bloody are!' Pugh blurted, suddenly exasperated.

'And they signed Harry up to bring us here?' Baxter grimaced. 'You mean he knew in advance that these killings were going to happen?'

'Unless the Crew pulled the wool over *his* eyes too.' Claudia sounded hopeful but looked doubtful. 'And he genuinely thought Damned Rankers was a thing.'

'It's got to be the latter,' Rathour said. 'I can't believe Harry would betray us like that. Not the Harry Wayland I knew.'

'*Thought* you knew,' Jack corrected her. 'I think he might have had a wobble earlier today. Maybe as the reality of what was happening kicked in. Was okay seeing a nonce and a Robbery Squad bully boy get theirs, but the thought of the rest of us going the same way might have started to bother him. Then he saw Donaldson and Jakeman doing a runner, and he remembered there was work to be done.'

'But Harry tried to help us catch the killer!' Rathour protested.

'Play acting,' Pugh said. 'You never heard of that?'

'It was convincing,' Baxter replied. 'He even came face to face with Lucas Beck and played it so cool we were all persuaded he'd only just met the guy.'

Rathour looked even more appalled. 'Harry knew Beck was the killer all that time?'

'Obviously,' Pugh said. 'Jesus, woman! Aren't you supposed to be some kind of genius?'

'Easy, Jonas,' Jack warned him.

But Pugh had now become animated. 'Listen to you all! Harry stitched innocent men up for crimes they didn't commit. And what about this Cornwallis boy? Harry didn't just fit him up. He popped the poor bastard. One shot to the heart, one to the head. Talk about making sure . . .'

'To protect Lucas Beck?' Rathour still couldn't believe it.

'Or preserve him,' Jack replied. 'For some other purpose.'

'But Harry's dead too.'

Pugh snickered again. 'The Crew didn't tell him about that part.'

'Harry was another loose end,' Claudia said. 'He just didn't know it.'

'But what's all this got to do with the Dogman?' Baxter asked. 'Why is *he* here?'

Milburn now ascended from the cellar. 'Because he's on a mission of his own.'

She moved across the kitchen, laying out various newspaper cuttings. She and Jack had already agreed they were going to return as a group to the hotel – their fort, as they considered it – which meant there'd be nothing to stop the Dogman coming back and burning every scrap of evidence. So they were taking as much as they could.

'Seen the back of these?' Milburn passed around the photographs from the cellar noticeboard. The rear of each one bore scribbled green handwriting.

Harry Wayland: *False witness*
Ray Donaldson: *Racketeer*
Declan O'Hare: *Thug*
Sally Jakeman: *Blackmailer*
Alan Rothermere: *Child pornographer*
Jack McGurn: *Drug dealer*
Claudia Crayford: *Ditto*
Gabriella Milburn: *Traitor*
Jonas Pugh: *Drunkard*
Varada Rathour: *Hacker*
Cheryl Baxter: *Double agent*
Milo Crindle: *Thief*

'Oh my God,' Rathour whimpered.

'We need to kill him,' Milburn said simply. 'We've got no choice. He's got the drop on us all along because he's been planning this for weeks. We've got to strike back, or he'll finish the job.'

'But we don't even know where to look for him,' Baxter said.

'Gabby, let me have the map,' Jack said.

She handed it over and he flattened it on the worktop. His finger followed the green squiggles until it came to rest just south of Porth West. 'This is the only place marked where he hasn't yet killed someone.'

'The castle?' Baxter said. 'Harry said it was a ruin, a no-go zone.'

'All the more reason to check it out,' Milburn replied.

'Even if he's not there, it might be a better redoubt than the hotel,' Jack said.

'A ruined castle?' Baxter sounded astonished.

'It's a stronghold. Its whole purpose is defence.'

'And how do we get there without exposing ourselves to attack?'

'The same way we came here. Together.'

Baxter shook her head. 'If we're going to take such a risk, there has to be a better reason than maybe he'll be there, or maybe it'll give us somewhere to hide. Too many maybes, Jack.'

'Could be his weapons stash,' Jack suggested. 'If so, we could really tool up. And there's something else . . .' He glanced at the window. Outside the wind had dropped and the clouds were clearing, though the sun lay low on the western horizon. 'This is a long shot, but just before I hid in that cottage on the coast, I caught a glimpse of the castle from its south side. There was a light in one of the upstairs windows . . . I assumed it was the sun reflecting through the various rooms and passages. But, thinking about it, there wasn't any sun. We were in the eye of the storm and the cloud cover was heavy.'

'Electric light?' Milburn asked.

'Maybe.'

'So, he's got some kind of generator?'

'Which, if he's got a bit of kit to hand, might also mean he has a radio.'

Jack paused to let this sink in. They didn't need to think about it for long.

'What are we waiting for?' Pugh said.

'Wait . . .' Jack raised a hand. 'We need to be sensible about this. First off, we go back to the hotel and pick up the quad bikes.'

'How many are left?' Claudia wondered.

'There's one still on the hotel forecourt, but the other four are all now back in the bike shed. That leaves us one short, but we'll think of something.'

'We need to go now,' Pugh said. 'It's early evening. We don't want to be over there in the dark.'

'Well, we're going to be,' Baxter replied. 'Don't you guys think we should do this in the morning?'

'And give him the whole night to reorganise?' Jack said.

'And if he does, how can that hurt us?' she asked. 'Once we're in the hotel, we're more or less secure. We've got to go back there anyway. We need food.'

Now that she mentioned it, Jack couldn't remember the last time he'd eaten.

'Not a bad idea,' Claudia said. 'We go to the castle now, it'll still be daylight when we get there, but we don't know how long it's going to take us to get inside, or what might happen when we do.'

Jack glanced at the others. He wasn't happy at the thought of spending another night in the hotel while the Dogman prowled around outside. But that castle, which was supposed to be dangerous even without a killer lurking there, would be no place to mess around in after dark.

'Okay, but when we're back in the hotel, we take turns keeping watch,' he said. 'And whoever's it is, they patrol the whole perimeter of the area we've secured: the lounge, the reception rear office and the reception staff corridor. Door to window, window to door.'

Baxter shrugged. 'No arguments there.'

◆ ◆ ◆

They made it back to the hotel without incident, but as they approached it struck Jack as having a sinister air. There was nothing in particular, but the place had been left open and unattended for a couple of hours, which meant their opponent could easily be inside. It was also getting dark, the hotel's windows gradually filling with shadow. They went in by the wedding suite again, the interior now much dimmer, but only when they entered the darkened vestibule did they realise something was wrong.

Baxter crossed to a row of light switches and flipped them all. To no effect.

They glanced at each other. She hurried to the lounge and in the fading daylight hit a row of switches there. Nothing.

'Fuck me sideways,' Pugh said. 'He's only gone and done the power.'

'Where are the generators?' Claudia tried not to sound as alarmed as she suddenly felt.

'Apparently, there's one installation,' Milburn replied. 'It powers the village, the pub and hotel. Least, that's what Beck said when I asked him on our first day here.'

'Where is it?'

'All I know is it's an outhouse somewhere.'

'It won't be hard to find, will it?' Rathour said, sounding absurdly hopeful.

'You *have* noticed these grounds are extensive?' Pugh said. 'What if it's down in the village? We can't get into half those buildings.'

'We must have light!' she said, panicky again.

'We'll find the generators,' Baxter assured her, without conviction.

'Someone grab a torch or something!'

'If there *is* a torch in the hotel, he'll have moved it by now,' Claudia said.

'My God, he knows every yard of this place!' Rathour's voice had risen to a scream.

'Varada, calm down,' Baxter said.

'And now we're going to be stuck here in the pitch-black!'

'*I said shut it!* We've got to think . . .'

Rathour stumbled away, one hand clamped to her mouth. The others exchanged nervous glances. This place was going to be difficult enough to defend at night. But without lights? Especially if the Dogman was already in the hotel.

'You genuinely think there might be some electrical kit in that castle?' Pugh asked Jack.

'I can only say that I saw a light,' Jack reiterated.

'So, a radio's not out of the question?'

'I don't know, but he's got to be getting his instructions from somewhere. Or at least have some way to log his updates.'

Pugh mulled this over for a second, and made for the swing doors. 'The castle it is.'

'Wait up,' Jack said, thinking there might be something they hadn't yet considered.

Pugh glanced back irritably. 'It's past eight o'clock. Every minute we wait, it gets darker.'

Jack looked at Claudia, who shrugged and nodded.

'This should be straightforward,' Jack said, as they headed along the vestibule together. 'The Quad Track'll take us most of the way there. Varada can ride with me. She's the lightest.'

'We'll be out in the open again,' Baxter said.

'There's no way we can do this without risk, Cheryl,' Milburn retorted. 'What's the alternative?'

They went out of the hotel on to the concourse, where they avoided even glancing at the bloody blanket-wrapped packages in the trailer attached to the trolley-car.

'I'll take this one.' Claudia mounted the black and green striped quad bike. 'Meet you down at the shed.'

Jack nodded, and as she roared away, the rest of them continued on foot.

'You realise if we catch this fella and end up smoking him, that'll only be the start of it,' Pugh said quietly. 'There's still a functioning justice system out there.'

Jack's eyes roved the surrounding gardens as they descended the drive. 'Once we've dealt with Beck, we need to gather as much evidence as we can.'

'They'll never believe us, whatever we show them. Fucking Wayland, eh?'

'When the Crew lean on you, Jonas, they lean on you.'

When they got to the bike shed, Claudia was waiting there astride her machine, engine rumbling. The shed door was open an inch or so.

'The other quads still in there?' he asked.

'Don't know,' she said. 'Haven't looked.'

'But the shed's open.'

'It's been open all along.'

'Come on.' Pugh marched past.

'Jonas . . . wait.'

Pugh glanced back. 'Now what?'

Jack wrinkled his nostrils. 'Is that petrol?'

'It's a bike shed. What else would it smell like?' Pugh shoved the door inward, every one of them then hearing the sharp, protracted *scritch* as a dozen matches slid across a striking surface. A small but searing flash of firelight lit up the shed's interior.

'Down!' Jack launched himself at Claudia, dragging her from her machine, slamming her to the Quad Track surface. The rest dropped too, instinctively.

Except for Jonas Pugh.

Whatever wick had ignited, it was a quick burner. Immediately after the fleeting flash there was an immense *boom* and a dazzling glare as a massive fireball exploded from within.

Thirty-Eight

There was no need to check whether Jonas Pugh was dead. All that remained of him was a shrivelled, smoking mannequin. The bike shed meanwhile and all the quad bikes inside had also been reduced to blackened ruin. Aside from a scattering of charred, burning timber, the flames had mostly receded, but a cloying, stinking fog had sent the others stumbling away, leaning on each other as they coughed and choked.

They found sweeter air at the bottom of the hotel drive, where they collapsed on their haunches, and regarded each other with gaunt, grimy faces.

'Explosives?' Rathour spluttered. 'He's using explosives?'

'Petrol, matches,' Jack replied wearily. 'That's all you need to blow someone up.'

'Poor Jonas!'

And poor us, Jack thought. *The frigging bikes, our one means of speedy transport, all kaput save one.*

Claudia got to her feet, staring back along the track, palls of smoke drifting down the slope into Porth West. The smell of burned meat was pungent in her nostrils.

'What do we do?' she asked.

No one initially responded. Even Gabby Milburn was blank-faced with shock, but also fear and incomprehension. 'In the absence . . .' she stuttered, 'in the absence of any other ideas, we should do as planned. Go to the castle, see if we can blag ourselves some comms.'

'The castle?' Rathour sounded incredulous. 'On foot?'

'The only alternative is a night in the hotel in the pitch dark,' Milburn replied. 'That would definitely hand the advantage to the enemy.'

'God's sake!' Rathour exclaimed. 'It's just one man . . . and there are still five of us. Surely, we can best him in a fight?'

No one gave the obvious answer: there wasn't going to be a fight, not when their foe could pick them off guerrilla style, at random, never showing his face.

Claudia looked at Jack, who'd also got to his feet. 'What do you think?'

It took a moment for him to realise he was being addressed.

'I, erm . . . I think Gabby's right.' He pointed south. 'If we can get to the top of one of those towers . . . only one way up, one way down. That'll be easier to guard than the hotel.'

'No, no, no!' Rathour insisted. 'We can't go to the castle now.'

'The castle's our best chance of lasting till morning.'

Claudia gazed along the beach towards the distant edifice. 'Let's go,' she said. 'I recommend you travel southward along the beach. It's all open there. No one can sneak up on you.'

'What about *you*?' Rathour said.

'We've got one quad bike left. I've got used to handling it, plus I've got the shotgun. I can ride a defensive guard along the Quad Track. If anyone suddenly springs out of the inland undergrowth, I can get to him before he gets to you.'

'Good plan,' Jack said.

'Gabby's the ex-firearms officer,' Baxter sniffled. 'Isn't she better suited to that?'

'Gabby's also the best fighter among us,' Jack said. 'If our friend confronts us out there, she's the best protection we've got.'

He looked at Milburn. She seemed tired and strained but nodded.

They continued southward along the Track, a weary, bedraggled, smoke-sullied band.

'Everyone draw weapons,' Jack said. 'He's doubtless got eyes on us right now . . . it might dissuade him.'

'I suggest we approach the target in stick formation,' Milburn said. 'You know? Like the military do. Single file, ten yards between each person. I take point and watch nine o'clock to twelve. You walk behind me, Cheryl, and watch twelve to three. You go behind Cheryl, Varada . . . watch three to six. You bring up the rear, Jack. Six to nine.'

Jack nodded. It made sense and even cheered him a little. Professionalism; it helped.

'I don't understand what any of that means,' Rathour said. She was easily the most fatigued among them and by far the most frightened. She trudged along, shoulders slumped, knife held loose by her side.

'I'll explain when we get on to the sand,' Baxter said, the gorse thickets now passing by on the right, gradually giving way to dunes.

The Atlantic rolled and crashed, though minus the ferocity of the previous day. The sole remaining quad bike rumbled as Claudia rode it up from behind. She clutched the handlebars with her left hand, brandishing the Remington in her right.

She decelerated, to ride alongside them.

'Look,' Jack said awkwardly, 'I'm thinking I'm detecting some disapproval on your part. Like, maybe we're overplaying our hand? That I'm not thinking straight? That we're not coppers anymore, and haven't got the backup and resources . . . ?'

'Jack, it's okay,' she said stiffly. 'You're being a despot again. But when you're under fire, leadership is good.'

'Okay,' he said. 'Well, you know the drill?'

'Yeah. We're going to kill the Dogman.'

◆ ◆ ◆

In AGI Claudia had occasionally carried firearms on duty, though she'd never discharged her weapon at a person. She didn't feel she'd have any problem doing that now. She'd seen what this guy was capable of, though she didn't understand him. She'd been involved in the arrests of several underworld murderers, but their motivations were obvious. It was always about power and profit. If someone had to die, they were usually rivals or traitors.

But what did this killer gain from his rampage?

It had been easy to picture the Dogman when she'd thought it was Jimmy Cornwallis, a guy who was indeed more like a terrorist than a serial killer, a politically motivated fanatic who'd lost all sense of restraint. But this guy, Lucas Beck – clearly, he was some kind of vigilante. But his kills were so vicious that he had to be insane, and yet she'd met him and spoken to him – and there had been no hint of madness. That thought alone was bone-chilling.

She'd parked the quad bike down the Track, so that she could watch the others as they progressed along the beach. At the same time, she eyed the open woodland behind her. Long dark shadows speared through it. She was certain she'd see or hear someone creeping up. Except that this guy was something of a specialist, a commando. She scanned deeper into the verdure. Was he in there now, merged with the leaves and undergrowth, maybe very close, staring right back at her?

She hit the ignition and rode on.

Thirty-Nine

Only the topmost portions of the castle were exposed to a sun now setting, and so were burnished a fiery red. Conversely, the trees below were deep in shade. Jack wondered again if it made sense to have come here. Some distance along the beach, Gabby Milburn turned and peered back towards him.

She signalled that they needed to get a move on, and he nodded. The sand was soft and clumpy, and they kicked it up in clouds as they struggled along, their legs like lead. By the time they reached the southern end of the beach, the sky had turned indigo and the sea was dark. They could still see through the trees to the outer stonework of the stronghold, but it was a tangle of shadows. The perspective had changed, the upper parapets now hidden.

Claudia, who had parked at the point where the Quad Track swerved inland, came down to join them on foot.

'We should go from here in a skirmish line,' Milburn said. 'Five or six yards between each one of us.'

Jack glanced at Claudia, who shrugged. 'Let's do it,' he said.

In this fashion, they ascended to the higher ground, which was treed and so comprised proper soil carpeted with old leaves and pine needles. Claudia glanced behind them for the eighth or ninth time, but there was no sign of anyone else. It was a numbing thought that their only certainty of survival lay in keeping constantly out of the killer's reach.

They emerged from the trees alongside the castle, which up close was a faceless ruin. There was nothing majestic or atmospheric about it. They walked along an outer wall, its fissures thick with moss, and finally came to an entrance that was tall and broad enough to admit men on horseback riding side by side.

Beyond lay a huge open space, though it wasn't a courtyard. It looked as if it had once been roofed, that roof having now collapsed, because a rubble of fallen, mildewed stone lay everywhere. High on all sides, ragged cavities yawned where once there had been rooms. At ground level, multiple doorways led into darkness.

'Where did you see the electric light?' Milburn asked quietly.

Jack thought about it. 'Somewhere on its south-east side, which I guess is over there.' He pointed and they trooped across the open space, skirting mounds of weed-grown masonry. Jack suddenly halted, raising his hand. The others stopped too. 'Thought I heard something.'

They glanced at each other, listening. The only sound came from the distant rollers.

They continued, finally coming to an arched entranceway.

'We're actually going inside?' Rathour asked nervously.

'Any good stuff he's got is inside,' Milburn replied.

They entered warily, proceeding along a dank corridor, the little light there was outside diminishing behind them, footfalls echoing. They constantly paused to listen, hearing nothing. A flight of narrow stone steps, but a main staircase judging by the way the feet of generations had worn it down, appeared in front of them. The light Jack had seen was high up, so they ascended.

There was more daylight on the upper floors, though for the most part these were labyrinths of empty chambers, vast broken holes in their outer walls as though massive, Elizabethan-age cannon balls had exploded through them.

'What's that?' Claudia said.

She pointed along a side passage. Jack backtracked and stared down it. A faint pall of greenish light was visible at the furthest end.

'Doesn't look natural,' she added.

He agreed.

'Is it shining down from the next floor up?' Milburn asked.

'Let's see.' Jack ventured down there.

They were on the third level of the structure, but it was increasingly dim even up here, dusk finally having settled.

As they approached the end of the corridor, they saw that the green light, which was no optical illusion, was shimmering down from another stairway.

Jack made to go up.

'Jack, wait!' Milburn caught him by his good shoulder.

He stopped while the others trooped up behind.

'Let me go first,' she whispered. 'This might be the Dogman's hideout.'

'I thought we'd already found his hideout,' Rathour hissed.

Milburn shook her head. 'A real operator would have more than one. Plus, this is an artificial light source. That means he *has* got some kit here. So, it's not going to be a base he never visits. All right, Jack? Let *me* go first.'

No one raised an objection. Claudia handed over the Remington again. Milburn nodded her gratitude and, shoving the shillelagh into her waistband, sidled up the steps, halting at the top, where the green light was much brighter. The others watched, cold sweat seeping through their ragged clothes. On cat-like feet, gun cocked, Milburn disappeared around the corner.

Tense seconds passed before she returned. 'It's okay. Come up.'

'What is it?' Jack asked.

'See for yourself.'

They ascended, entering another upper-floor corridor with several rooms leading off it. In most cases they were empty or filled with piles of fallen rubble. However, the whole passage now glinted with the greenish light, which appeared to emanate through a barred metal gate.

'Check this out,' Milburn said, getting there ahead of them.

The first thing Jack noticed was that the gate was a recent addition, made from solid steel, and fastened closed with a heavy-duty padlock.

He tested it and found it secure. 'Nothing Tudor about this.'

'Or this.' Milburn nodded through the bars.

He glanced through, the others crowding behind him, all now bathed in glimmering green. This room was wider than it was deep, and at one end some kind of workbench had been placed against the wall. On top of this stood an upright metal box, the size of a small fridge. An array of emerald lights indicated it was functioning, while a range of insulated antennae projected from the top.

'Is that . . . ? Good Lord!' Rathour sounded hopeful rather than frightened. 'Is that a signal jammer?' She became excited. 'I think that's a jammer . . . you know, for blocking phone and internet traffic. My God! That's why we can't get any calls out.'

'Must be powerful,' Milburn said, 'to cover this whole island.'

'It'll pack a punch. But St Dunstan isn't *that* big.'

'I'm impressed,' Jack said. 'We know this killer's organised . . . but I had no clue he was *this* organised.'

'Varada,' Claudia said, 'are you saying that we only need to deactivate this thing, and we *can* get calls out?'

'Yes, of course.' Rathour clapped her hands girlishly. 'I don't know about the internet, but we can make phone calls. We can call the Coastguard. They could have a boat here in a couple of hours, couldn't they?'

'All well and good,' Milburn said. 'But who's got their phone with them? Mine's back in the hotel. I didn't think I'd have any use for it, so I left it in my baggage.'

The others exchanged glances. With no facility to make or receive calls, or to access the internet, and no real desire to immortalise their time here in photographs, they'd all left their phones in their rooms. With the sole exception of Baxter, who, with something of a flourish, produced her iPhone from her pocket. 'Always keep mine with me. Force of habit, I guess. And it's still got juice.'

'Thank God,' Rathour said.

'Don't let us stop you, Varada,' Jack told her. 'Get to work.'

'I need to get in there first.'

Claudia rattled the bars. 'Okay, this might be the next problem.' Milburn tried the gate as well, to no avail.

'If we can't get in there, maybe we can get to the generator?' Claudia said. 'He must have one here. A portable thing. Put that out of action and it'll have the same effect.'

But no cables were visible leading out of the room or anywhere else.

'Okay, so we search,' Claudia said. 'It'll be somewhere close by. It has to be.' She was ready to hurry off, but Jack stopped her.

'We don't know much about that contraption in there,' he said. 'It could easily have a storage capacity. We disable the generator, and it just carries on working . . . at least until such time as miladdo comes up here to fix it.'

'Shit,' Baxter said. 'There must be a way.'

'Shoot it,' Rathour blurted, sounding frantic again. 'Surely you can hit the jammer from here. Fire through the bars.'

It seemed an obvious solution, except that when Milburn stuck the shotgun's muzzle through the sturdy steel uprights, such was the positioning of the jamming device that the angle was hopelessly wrong. She couldn't even get close to hitting it.

'Wasn't stupid when he located it there,' she said.

'Shoot the lock off the gate,' Baxter suggested. 'Once we're in, we can deactivate it manually.'

Claudia glanced at Jack, both then glancing at Milburn. All three were thinking the same.

'We're down to our last two cartridges,' Jack said. 'This is a Remington 12-bore, but even from close range, there's no guarantee that even both of them, fired one after the other, will pulverise this lock sufficiently. And if they don't, we're out of ammo.'

Rathour glanced at Milburn. 'Is that for real? A shotgun wouldn't blow this lock off?'

'I don't know.' Milburn checked the lock again; it was a chunky piece of metal held in place by a sturdy length of shiny new chain. 'I suspect this rig is chrome steel. It might be able to resist two blasts even at close proximity. And of course, close proximity will be extraordinarily dangerous for whoever the shooter happens to be. There'll be rebounds all over the place.'

'Surely it's worth a try?'

They looked at each other again, weighing up the risk.

'It's something we may have to do,' Jack conceded. 'But let's exhaust other possibilities first. *That*, for example.'

He pointed through the bars. Again, he had to stand at an awkward angle, but just to the right of the jamming device, the room contained a single window. It was tall, rectangular, and located in a recess, but probably just wide enough for a normal-sized person to slide in through it. Even so, there was a dumbstruck silence.

'You kidding?' Baxter said. 'That aperture must be ninety feet off the ground. How's anyone going to get up there?'

'We don't know what's on the other side,' Jack replied. 'Suppose a tower collapsed and there's a mountain of rubble. Maybe we can just walk up to it. We need to look.'

'He's right,' Milburn said. 'Let's not piss our ammo away until we're sure there are no other options.'

They went back along the corridor, checking the other rooms. Most were pitch-black and empty. Only one had a window, though in this case, rubble had collapsed from overhead, three-quarters filling the embrasure, leaving only a tiny gap at the top. The slimmest among them was Rathour, who, after receiving a boost from Milburn, climbed up warily, lumps of broken rock tumbling around her. At last, she was close enough to the gap to peek out.

'There's a terrible drop,' she said. 'I can't see the bottom.'

'Is it sheer?' Jack asked.

'Wait a sec.' She wormed her way forward, getting as close to the gap as she could.

More rubble clattered down. Claudia glanced uneasily overhead, worrying about the integrity of the overall structure. The chamber itself, whatever it had once been, looked solid enough, its ceiling still securely mortared. But it was the upper part of the window recess that had collapsed. Rathour pulled more debris down so that she could stick her head outside.

'Quiet everyone,' Baxter said. 'Thought I heard something.'

They listened. Nothing sounded from any other part of the castle.

'An echo?' Milburn suggested.

'It could have been. I don't know.'

'Let's focus on this,' Jack said. 'Varada, can you get your head out any further?'

'I think so.' More pebbles tumbled. 'It hurts, this stuff. Like climbing on broken glass.'

'It's for a higher cause, I promise you.'

She now pushed her head outside properly. 'It's too dark to see the ground, but I think there are fallen stones down there. You know, like bits that have come off the top.'

'Is it climbable?' Jack asked.

'Doesn't look like it . . . oh wait, hang on. There's a ledge about five feet down.'

'A ledge?'

'A stone shelf. Horizontal. Seems to be running along the whole wall.'

'Does it pass the jammer room?'

Rathour turned her body, so that she could look properly. 'Goes all the way along the side of the building. So, yes . . . I'm guessing it does.'

'How big is this shelf?' Milburn asked.

'About nine . . . ten inches.'

'As wide as that?' Jack said, flinching at the mere thought. 'Nothing to worry about then.'

Meanwhile, Claudia had moved to the room's entrance and stood listening. Baxter went over to join her.

'What's the matter?' Jack asked.

'Thought *I* heard something this time,' Claudia said uneasily.

'He can't let us sabotage his kit,' Baxter whispered. 'He *has* to try and stop us.'

They listened again but heard nothing.

'What did it sound like?' Jack asked quietly.

All had now gathered at the door. Rathour joined them, beating the dust off.

'A bang,' Claudia said. 'A clatter.'

'This floor? The floor below?'

'I don't know. Didn't sound *very* distant.'

'Look, guys,' Milburn said. 'We can't just stand around here. Not when we're *this* close to turning his machine off.'

'What options have we got?' Rathour replied.

'We've got that ledge.'

'Christ,' Baxter muttered. 'Seriously?'

'We've got to find a way on to it first,' Jack said dismissively.

'Correction, *I* have.' Milburn's gaze roved across them. 'Who else is more qualified?'

No answers were forthcoming. Milburn was by far the most athletic here, but no one else was prepared to volunteer anyway.

'I don't like it,' Jack said. 'Let's keep looking. There may be a better option . . .'

'The longer we do that, the darker it gets.' Milburn handed the Remington back to Claudia. 'Let's see if we can find a window I can climb out through.'

'In the meantime, I'll go downstairs.' Claudia hefted the shotgun. 'We thought we heard something, and we can't afford to ignore it. And I've got *this*.'

'I'll come with you,' Baxter said. When Claudia gave her a querying glance, she brandished her kitchen knife. 'It isn't much, but two are better than one.'

Claudia considered, then nodded.

'If you run into him,' Jack said, 'remember it's a headshot. And don't hesitate. Because *he* won't.'

Forty

'You sure you want to do this?' Jack asked Milburn.

Unable to find an exit on to the ledge from the main corridor, they'd now turned a corner and were checking more rooms, though again, none had windows.

'If he's in the building,' she said, 'I'm safer out there.'

'I'm half hoping we won't find . . . oh crap!'

They'd entered another room with a rectangular window. There was just enough space for Milburn to slip out.

'Rather you than me,' Rathour said. 'We must be a hundred yards from the jammer room by now.'

'A hundred, ten . . . it's all the same if you keep your nose to the bricks,' Milburn replied, 'and take it one step at a time.' Even so, it was only with some reluctance that she climbed into the embrasure and, leaning forward, poked her head out. 'The ledge is here. Let's get cracking, eh?'

'You don't have to do this,' Jack said. 'We can try the Remington. Blow that lock off.'

'It's fine, we don't want to waste the cartridges.' She glanced through the aperture again. 'It's a good ten inches wide. More than enough room.'

'Fair enough.' Jack showed her his good hand, which she stared at nervously, almost as if he was offering a goodbye handshake, and then realised that it would be her anchor when she clambered down on to the ledge. She clutched it, tightly, before sidling out through the tall gap, holding position for a moment, then lowering herself to her knees, burying her right hand claw-like into the stone of the window's right edge, and swinging down out of sight.

Rathour watched from the other side of the room with unblinking bug-eyes.

'How you doing?' Jack asked, grimacing.

He wasn't bearing her entire bodyweight, but it was agony all the same, the intense strain spasming through his twisted, injured torso. With only one hand, he couldn't latch on to anything else, and was forced to jam his body against the right side of the recess, his foot against the other. 'Gabby, how you . . . ?'

'I'm there,' her voice came back. 'It's okay. I'm on the ledge. You can let go.'

He gasped with relief as their grip broke.

And then, from somewhere else in the building, a cacophonous boom sounded. Like a cathedral door swinging closed.

'What was that?' Milburn asked from below.

'Don't worry.' Jack scrambled down. 'Head to the jammer room. We'll be waiting there for you.'

He and Rathour paused in the corridor, listening.

'Was that Claudia and Cheryl?' she asked.

'Probably.' But Jack's face was prickling with sweat.

'Wasn't a gunshot, was it?'

'I don't know,' he said. And he genuinely didn't.

It wasn't a gunshot. All Claudia could think as she lay groaning was that Harry Wayland had warned them about this building being structurally unsound. Rather than heading down to the ground floor, they had ventured a little way along the third. But the next thing Claudia knew, a section of wooden floor had collapsed underneath her.

'Good God . . . are you all right?' came a voice from overhead.

Claudia was too groggy to at first respond and was enveloped in choking dust as she lay on her back. She coughed, dragging herself to her feet, warily prodding at the various points of her body that hurt. Thankfully, all seemed to be intact. Looking up, she saw Cheryl Baxter's concerned face framed in a jagged hole about ten feet overhead.

'I'm okay,' Claudia replied. 'Do you want to try and make your way down?'

'Erm, yes . . . I'll go back to the stairs.' Baxter withdrew from sight.

Claudia spied the Remington lying close by and picked it up, checking it was undamaged and thankful that she'd thought to let it go. If she'd accidentally fired the thing, they'd be down to a single round.

She turned, trying to work out where she was. There were two possible exits: a window on the left, which, when she approached it, looked down on what had formerly been the castle's interior, the main hall or whatever, and a broad flight of steps on the right, ascending out of sight.

She opted for the steps. But at the top, found herself at a small T-junction. On her left a short passage led to the main hall again, where once it might have opened into a minstrels' gallery, though now it ended in a sheer drop. Going right instead, she saw a passage with a couple more side entrances and at the far end, a door standing ajar.

On the other side of which, she now spied movement.

Claudia went still. The shotgun was in its holster; she didn't draw it, but clicked back the hammers. The evening light had faded to a dull lilac, filling the space beyond that half-open door, but as she watched, something again moved past the gap, the evening twilight briefly winking out.

'Cheryl?' she said quietly, but she knew that it wasn't.

Jack and Rathour stood at the top of the stairs.

In addition to the echoing boom they'd heard, they thought a brief exchange of shouts between muffled female voices had followed it. After that, there was silence.

'What do you think?' Rathour asked.

Jack shook his head, perplexed. If he called down to check that everything was okay, he'd alert the maniac to their presence on the upper floor. The chances were he already knew, but Jack was reluctant to stack the odds against them further. Besides, Claudia was armed, and it was questionable how much extra assistance he and Rathour could provide.

'We're going back to the jammer room,' he said.

She looked surprised. 'What about Claudia and Cheryl?'

'Varada . . . Gabby's edging her way along that outside wall right now, okay? She'll need you to guide her through the deactivation process.'

They walked back along the upper level, where the darkness had thickened to near impenetrability. Conversely, the green light shining from the chamber at the other end of the passage had intensified, the brilliant emerald glow reflecting from their sweaty faces.

'She could probably just pull the plug,' Rathour said.

'Yeah, it might be that simple. But you're tech backup. *You need* to be there at least.'

They reached the gate to the jammer room. Beyond it, the machine's glittering green array filled the enclosed space with light. But through the narrow window the purple sky was fast turning black.

Forty-One

The secret lay in not looking down. This much was obvious to Gabby Milburn. Though she doubted she'd be able to see much anyway, given how dark it was getting.

At least she could see the stonework in front of her nose. She kept her eyes trained firmly on it as she edged sideways along the shelf. The good news was that, though she called it 'a shelf', it was actually the upper edge of a lower section of wall which projected outward, meaning it was sturdy. Also, ten inches meant that she wasn't balanced on the balls of her feet, which doubtless would have put huge strain on her calves. She could move along flat-footed, though constantly in fear of overbalancing.

The wind had died down, but sometimes whipped past her. All she could do then was flatten herself against the rugged surface, which, scoured by the Atlantic weather for centuries, afforded plenty of finger-holds. She hooked into these gratefully, though none felt as if they'd support her should she suddenly lose her footing. But keeping calm was everything. Even breathing too hard threatened to topple her backward.

After what felt like twenty yards of ledge, her leading foot suddenly slipped, kicking at emptiness. Fleetingly, she was lopsided, sliding bodily down the wall. She dug her fingers in all the harder, her whole body drenched with sweat, whimpering with terror.

When her foot finally regained its perch, she probed around with it. This section of shelf was slick with some slithery, oily substance. She couldn't think what it might be until her vision cleared, and she focused on the black and white streaks on the stonework in front of her.

'Birdshit. You serious? Death by birdshit? Come on, Gabster . . . that's no way for a former shot to go out.'

She continued, moving with extra caution due to the slime underfoot. Once she was past it, she felt better, though she'd only made another five yards or so before her right hand groped past a vertical edge and grasped at thin air.

Her thoughts whirled. *What in God's name . . . ?*

And then she realised it was the building's corner.

She turned her head. The structure's edge was just ahead. Beyond it, the vastness of the night filled her vision. The stars blurred as sweat trickled from her brow. She blinked hard. It stung her eyeballs. She blinked again. It cleared a little.

'Good God,' she muttered, in a voice she wouldn't have recognised. 'Like this isn't hard enough.'

There was a final vestige of light visible around the half-open door, so it was difficult to see whether the motion on the other side persisted.

Claudia came to a halt. She listened but heard nothing. She didn't even know what was through there. Was it a passage or a room? Levelling the shotgun, she nudged the door with her foot. The wood was old and scabby, and initially it seemed to jam in place. There was no sound from beyond it, though she knew she'd seen movement.

Remember it's a headshot. And don't hesitate.

Jack's last words before they parted company. Claudia's heart thumped.

Remember it's a headshot.

It struck her again how, back in AGI, on those occasions when she'd participated in armed raids, they'd gone in behind the specialist firearms team. She'd never needed to shoot at anyone.

Remember it's a headshot . . .

Her thoughts lingered on Rothermere's mutilated corpse, O'Hare's sundered cranium . . .

She threw her shoulder against the door, slamming it open, shotgun aimed.

And found herself alone in what looked as though it had once been a guard room: a smallish cell, built from basic bare stone. There was a large embrasure on the right, where the wall had crumbled away, and a smaller aperture high up on the left, a viewing port of some sort. But what had she seen moving?

She edged first to the embrasure. It was about twenty feet to the ground and all she saw on peeking down were the outlines of large stones in the summer grass. No one could have jumped from here. Looking behind her, she spied two cavities just below the viewing port. The bricks and mortar had fallen out, creating two cubbyholes, but as Claudia moved towards them a mass of sticks and straw exploded. The room was filled with flapping wings and shrill cries as the two seagulls beat their way past her, tearing out through the larger embrasure.

◆ ◆ ◆

Milburn was in such darkness now that she couldn't see the perilous drop beneath her. She eased her body up against the ninety-degree angle, a sense of vertigo sending her dizzy.

'Please . . . God,' she said, reaching around the corner with her right foot, and when she found the ledge again, planting it firmly.

Taking a massive breath, fingers burrowing into eroded stone, she inched around to the other side.

From here, it was easier. She shuffled along so speedily that she had to force herself to slow down. Imagine coming all this way only to slip or trip at the last moment. But then there was further encouragement. She turned her head, squinting to try and work out how much distance remained, and spotted, firstly, an upright aperture only a few yards ahead, and beyond that, by thirty or forty yards, a second one with green light shimmering out.

The first aperture was likely the room where the window embrasure had fallen in. Thinking that she could rest there, as the broken stonework would afford her a proper grip, she sidled determinedly along. The lower half of that first window was still cluttered with debris, except that there seemed to be more space above it than she remembered – almost as if someone had been decluttering it.

Pity we didn't do that before. I'd only have had to go thirty yards instead of ninety.

It wasn't initially clear why they'd tried to make some space there, though it then occurred to her that, once she'd got into the jammer room to deactivate the device, she'd be trapped behind a locked gate. The obvious way out would be back along the ledge, but at least this other window would afford her a quicker route back inside. She edged up to it, where, as she'd planned, she stopped. The half-cleared rubble only came up to her chest, and she was able to stare into the empty blackness of the room. She relaxed a little, though with hands clamping the uprights on either side. At which point she realised that whoever had cleared the space was still there. Gazing back at her. She tried to speak but didn't manage a word before the gloved fist thudded into the middle of her face. A blow of such brutal force that she lost all four of her grips.

Both her hands.

Both her feet.

Forty-Two

It was too dark in the guard room for Claudia to see the body come whistling down past the embrasure, but she heard the heavy impact on the stones below. She'd been in the process of groping her way out at the time.

Moving back to the embrasure, she peered down. She couldn't see anything, but it didn't need a genius to work out what had happened. Claudia suddenly knew that she had to get out of the castle. She wanted to shout up through the building, but some sixth sense kept her lips sealed. Pulse racing, she felt her way to the door, and blundered along the passage.

She edged out through the first aperture on the left, weapon lowered, one hand in front. But only when she felt the breeze on her face did she realise she was approaching another break-point in the structure. She slowed down, fearful that she'd step over some unseen edge. And indeed, that was almost what happened, the floor abruptly ending. She halted, smelled the sea wind, and realised that the hefty masses moving back and forth about forty yards in front were the upper boughs of trees. Dropping to her knees, she felt her way along the paving, and on the left, located the top of a narrow flight of steps. These were just visible, paler than the darkness as her eyes attuned to the starlight. She descended on her backside, one step after another, ultra cautious. She reached ground level successfully but was now struggling with which direction to take. The vast, looming mass of the castle soared upward on her right, so she worked her way along it, her back to the wall, until her shoulder came hard against another lower wall, this one only about ten feet tall, but running transverse to the main building. Some five yards along this, she encountered a narrow entrance, a postern gate. As she passed through it, a half-moon slid into view around the shoulder of the main building, casting a dim radiance over the rugged ground ahead.

A human form lay broken amid the scattered remnants of fallen masonry.

Claudia hesitated. She could already see enough: the awkward angle at which the body lay, the fantastic rearrangement of its limbs. There was still the question of who it was, though this was answered when she ventured closer. Gabby Milburn's handsome face, upturned in the moonlight, was unblemished save for a single bloodied nostril.

Claudia reached for the carotid artery, but there was no sign of a heartbeat. She rose to her feet, her spine an ice-cold streak down the middle of her back, and yet an eerie calm had settled over her: that stiff ambivalence that all police officers hide behind when confronted by death.

By Claudia's reckoning, there were four of them remaining. And one of those four *must* survive. They *had* to make it back to civilisation to tell everyone what had happened here. That was the sole priority. And neither grief nor panic nor shock would help.

She turned, wondering what was the best route back to the main staircase. This side of the outer wall was clearly visible in the moonlight, while the postern gate was a black rectangle. But as she moved towards the latter, a light appeared, a thin-beamed torch. Claudia froze.

Remember it's a headshot. And don't hesitate . . .

She raised the shotgun, two-handed.

'Wait, it's me!' came Cheryl Baxter's frantic voice. 'It's me!'

'What the hell are you doing?'

'I'm sorry, I didn't recognise you. You're filthy. I didn't realise it was you.'

Slowly, Claudia lowered the weapon. That collapsing floor. The dust had swamped her. She must be a real sight.

'What are you doing out here?' Baxter asked, voice querulous.

'I should ask you the same.'

'I was looking for you. After you fell, I couldn't find a way to get to where you were, so I ended up in the main hall. All I could do then was make my way round the building.'

'Yeah, okay. Well . . .' Claudia's anger ebbed. 'I've got some bad news.'

'Oh God . . . What now?'

Baxter didn't cry when Claudia took her to see Milburn's body, just stood staring, her pale face expressionless. She switched her phone torch off to hide the more gruesome details. Finally, she said: 'I don't suppose we know whether or not she was successful before this happened?'

'Only one way to check,' Claudia replied, 'and you're the one with the phone.'

Baxter seemed to struggle with this logic, but then raised her device, unlocked it with her thumb and punched a few keys. 'Still no signal.'

'Shit.' Claudia headed back to the postern gate. 'Come this way, yeah? I need you to help me.'

They went back up the side steps and into the guard room. Here, with several hard blows courtesy of the Remington's stock, they loosened the wooden door. Several planks broke in the process, but ultimately, they were left with a shapeless slab of splintery wood, roughly five feet by three.

'You plan to use this as a shield,' Baxter said, as they descended the outer steps.

'If I'm going to shoot that lock off, I'll need to get close. It can't hurt to have a chunk of timber between me and the point of impact.'

Following Baxter's directions, they returned to the main staircase and re-ascended.

'Do you think Gabby fell by accident?' Baxter wondered. 'Or was it something else?'

'I don't know.'

But that thought alone was enough to make them pass every dark doorway with extreme caution. When they finally got back to the upper floor they found Jack and Rathour still waiting by the barred gate, bathed in green light.

'Where the hell have you been?' Jack asked.

'Give it a rest.' Claudia propped her makeshift shield against the wall and slumped down. 'Gabby's dead.'

'Told you,' Rathour muttered, voice weepy and tired. 'I told you it shouldn't have taken her this long . . . that something must've happened.'

Jack's eyes moved from Claudia to Baxter and back again. 'You're sure?'

'Christ's sake, Jack . . . we've seen her body,' Baxter said. 'If nothing else, it was quick.'

'Fuck!' Jack hissed. 'Christ . . . I don't believe this.'

'We don't know whether she fell or was pushed,' Claudia said.

Jack glanced sharply at her, then past her along the corridor. Even with the green light, it was so dark they couldn't see as far as the top of the stairs.

Rathour got to her feet. Suddenly, she looked less grief-stricken, more frightened. 'So, he could be up here with us?'

'We . . . don't . . . know,' Claudia said forcefully, tired and irate with saying the same thing over and over.

'Okay, sod this.' Jack spoke with cool urgency. 'We'll have to try and shoot the lock off.'

'Way ahead of you.' Claudia got to her feet, hefting the wooden shield. 'I can squat behind this when I fire. Might give me some protection.'

Jack, Baxter and Rathour retreated a little way along the corridor as Claudia shuffled forward on her knees, shoving the wooden shield into an upright position. When she was a foot from the padlock and positioned just to the right of it, she adjusted the timber so that it was in front of her, holding it in place with her left hand, and levelling the Remington over the top with the other. She lowered her head sideways, so that only her squinting right eye was over the rim.

When she fired, the flash was momentary, but the *boom* deafening.

As the dust settled, Claudia leaned on the timber, the surface of which was riddled with hot fragments. She wafted the smoke aside.

'Okay,' she said slowly. Then, with relief: '*Okay!*'

The padlock remained intact, but the chain hung loose. She yanked it off and the barred gate swung inward.

The others came forward, Rathour going into the room and over to the jamming device.

'What do you think?' Jack asked from the doorway.

'It's . . . it's incredibly simple.'

She hit a couple of switches and the machine deactivated, plunging that entire upper section of castle into opaque darkness.

'Hang on,' came Baxter's voice. There was a rustling sound as she fumbled in her clothes for her phone.

'Hurry,' Claudia said. 'Hurry, hurry . . .'

This was the most frightening moment so far. Impenetrable blackness. The perfect time for a predator to strike. When Baxter's phone torch sprang to life, Claudia half expected to find a couple of them missing, but all four faces reappeared, gathered tightly around, glinting with sweat.

'Have we got a signal?' Jack asked her urgently. 'Come on, check.'

Again, Baxter used her thumb to unlock her phone. And then shot them a look of astounded relief. 'I *have* . . . I've got a signal. It's not strong, and I've not got a lot of juice left—'

'Call someone!' Rathour cut in. 'Anyone!'

'Okay . . . just wait.' Fingers rattling the keypad, Baxter put the phone to her ear, backing away from the group. 'Yes, hello . . . hello? Oh, thank God . . .' Her voice almost broke. 'Yes . . . erm, we're on St Dunstan. We need assistance straight away. No, we're on St Dunstan . . . yes, St Dunstan. In the Scilly Isles. Look, please send the Coastguard or someone. We're in terrible trouble here. We've had a number of fatalities . . . There's a man trying to kill us. Look . . . what? No, I don't know who he is, but we're almost out of ways to defend ourselves . . . just get someone here, please. Please! We've got injured personnel too, so we need a casevac as well as armed support . . . yes, you heard that right, armed support!'

Jack was tempted to grab the phone and give whoever was on the other end hell, but Baxter was getting the message home clearly enough.

'Yes, please . . . quick as you can, please,' she said. 'No . . . I can't stay on the line. My phone hasn't got much power left and we need to preserve it. You can call me back on this number if you need to, but we have to keep things brief. No, we're not in immediate danger at this moment, but . . . look, just . . . just get someone here, yes? Thank you. Thanks very much . . .'

'999?' Claudia asked.

Baxter nodded. 'They're getting straight on to the Coastguard and Police Comms at Plymouth. Apparently, the Coastguard should get here first, to take us off.'

'How long?' Jack asked.

'Two hours. Maybe three.' She looked at them all. 'So what do we do? Hole up here? Find a room with only one entrance?'

'We'll need to do better than that,' Jack replied, adding in a lower voice, 'we've only got one slug left.'

'We can't stay here anyway,' Claudia said grimly. 'The Coastguard will go to Porth West. They won't come here. They probably can't even anchor near here.'

Rathour looked crestfallen. 'So, we have to go back to the harbour?'

'Don't see we've any choice,' Claudia said.

'Let's not fuck around needlessly,' Jack cut in. 'We know help's coming. All we have to do is get back there. It's a straight run along the Quad Track.'

'But it's over a mile,' Rathour exclaimed.

'Yeah, plus there's cover on the inland side of the Track,' Claudia added. 'He could still jump us.'

Jack shrugged. 'We go along the beach.'

'Over sand?' Rathour said.

'Varada, there's no easy way to do this. One last effort. That's all that's needed. Then we can barricade ourselves into the pub. It's not ideal, but we can hold out long enough till help arrives.'

'Jack's right,' Claudia said. 'On the beach, no one can sneak up on us.'

'And this time we don't split up,' Jack said. 'We go back together.'

'So no one takes the ATV?' Baxter said.

He shrugged again. 'We stick together, with the gun.' No one argued. 'So . . . what the heck are we waiting for?'

They went down the stairs with only the paltry phone light to navigate by. At least once Jack glanced back up and thought he saw a figure on the landing: tall, featureless, black all over, staring down after them. He encouraged them to go faster, which was a risk on old, age-worn steps. Once they were out in the open it was even more difficult. The debris covering the hall floor hindered them. Rathour tripped, but snapped when Claudia tried to help her up. 'Let's just go! Let's just bloody fucking go, please!'

Outside the main gate Jack brought them to a standstill at the base of the outer wall. For half a second he harboured a mental image of some fiendish presence on the battlements waiting to drop a block of stone on them. When he voiced this concern, Baxter switched off her phone light. They made a whispered count of three, then dashed into the trees. It was a blind charge, Jack bouncing off a pine trunk, which struck his fractured collarbone full on and sent him gasping to his knees. Claudia hauled him up by his waist. Moments later, they were stumbling down the slope to the beach. From there, the half-moon lit their way only intermittently due to the fast-moving clouds, though it gave them a clear path ahead through the sand. Thanks to a high tide, the sea's foaming edge lay some fifty yards to their left; the Quad Track, perhaps a hundred yards to their right, was hidden in darkness.

'He could be up there,' Claudia panted. 'Keeping pace with us, staying parallel . . . and we wouldn't know.'

'So long as he's not down here,' Jack replied.

They kept going, but it was far from easy. The scenery barely changed: sand, sand and more sand, breaking waves to the left, clouds scudding across a black sky.

'Like wading through treacle,' Rathour whimpered.

'Keep going,' Baxter said.

'I can't . . .'

'You've got to.'

Right on cue a dazzling light sprang to life on the Quad Track. Its piercing beam spilled across the sand like a searchlight. They stumbled to a halt.

An engine growled and Jack realised it was one of the quad bikes. It didn't really matter which. It could be the one they'd left behind near the castle, the bastard having hot-wired it, or it could be the one on which Harry Wayland had died, which probably still had the key in its ignition.

With an angry rumble, the light jolted forward and down the short, steep slope towards the beach.

Forty-Three

'Run!' Jack shouted.

Baxter and Rathour lurched forward, finding new energy.

'Claudi, this is your chance!' Jack retreated to create space between them. Claudia understood, moving away to create more.

The light leapt and bounced over the sand towards them. They could just about distinguish the bulky human form riding behind it. Claudia shouldered the Remington, taking aim at the approaching orb, clicking back the final hammer. Both she and Jack were caught in the glare and perhaps that explained why its rider seemed undecided about which one to attack, veering in neither direction but coming in a straight line as though to pass between them. He was already twenty yards away and closing. Ten yards . . .

'Shoot the bastard!' Jack shouted.

Claudia moved further back, hoping the headlight would veer towards her, but it came on in the same straight line. 'Okay, that's it!'

She unloaded as the quad bike throttled past, from near point-blank range, fire spurting, the boom not quite so thunderous on the open beach, but the payload striking, flinging the figure on to the sand. Riderless, the vehicle ploughed on past, sloshing deep into the waves before coming to a halt. Claudia lowered the weapon, the breath tight in her chest. She'd hit him; no doubt about that. But had it been in the head?

It didn't matter. She advanced, Jack coming from the other side, wielding his cleaver. Even if they'd only wounded him, this was their chance to finish him off. But the first thing they saw when they got close was that 'he' was actually a dark-green blanket stuffed with cushions and tied into shape. The head, which had received the bulk of the shot and was burst wide open, was a single cushion wrapped in a towel.

'Oh my God,' she breathed.

'He's split us up again,' Jack said slowly.

He's also got you to fire off your last shot, you dumb fuck!

From somewhere up ahead, out of sight now because the quad bike's headlamp was submerged, a wail of horror came back to them. They stumbled towards it, Claudia clinging on to the Remington for all the good it might do her. Perhaps she could use it as a club, she thought bitterly. It was one of the greatest ironies of this entire experience, that they, the hunted, had possessed a gun all along, while the hunter apparently did not, and yet it had proved itself next to useless.

A smaller light was now visible ahead – Baxter's phone again – lying on the ground.

Jack swore through gritted teeth, as they got to the scene of the latest crime. A figure lay prone, arms outspread. But it wasn't Cheryl Baxter, it was Varada Rathour.

At first it wasn't clear to them what had happened, though she wasn't moving, and Baxter was kneeling alongside her, frozen with shock and confusion. Jack hunkered down, seeing immediately that the younger woman was dead, and not just because of her glazed eyes, but because of the thin cord wrapped several times around her throat with such force it had induced immediate asphyxiation, though if that hadn't done the trick, the two hefty lumps of stone, one tied in place at either end, had struck brutal blows to her skull.

'A bolas?' he said, stunned. He'd underestimated the bastard, for sure. But a bolas? A home-made one at that?

And of course, if the lunatic had improvised one, he could improvise more.

'Everyone, down!' Jack dived at Claudia, dragging her to the sand, jarring his injured collarbone in the process, biting down on the pain.

Baxter didn't react so quickly, still kneeling, stricken with shock. A second bolas came swishing down from the Quad Track, but aimed at Claudia, the one with a gun and therefore the most dangerous. It scythed closely over her head, slashing into the sea.

'Move it!' Jack shouted, levering himself painfully to his feet.

Claudia got up quickly, helping him. They ran, Baxter alongside them, though her phone light had winked out and everything was a blur. Only ripples of moonlight on the sea's surface gave them a sense of direction. They drove themselves on, hearing what they imagined were faint swishings of air as more lethal missiles twirled after them.

And then, mercifully, the sand tilted upward into dunes crowned with spiky marram grass. It made the going harder, but it also meant they were at the north end of the beach. Soon afterwards they plunged into ripping, tearing foliage, the gorse thickets, which rent clothes and flesh as they fought their way through. Of course, what hampered them would also hamper their pursuer. Jack took heart from this, especially as in this deepening mass of vegetation they'd be harder targets. Only when the gorse broke into clumps were they able to make speedier progress, but almost immediately after that the ground sloped down in front of them, and they knew they were approaching the harbour.

'This way.' Jack pointed to his right.

The trio, who'd briefly become separated in the greenery, now stumbled back together, heading inland.

In a small clearing, Jack dropped to his haunches, heaving for breath. The others did the same, gasping, wheezing. In the feeble moonlight it was possible to see that all three were now covered in trickling blood. They'd certainly have wounds to show from this battle if they made it back alive. No one could argue they hadn't been through hell.

They listened, confidently expecting the sounds of frenzied pursuit. And yet, as always with this guy, it was even more sinister to hear nothing at all.

'He knows what he's doing, this fella,' Jack panted. 'He's all about the ambush. He's equally about not being ambushed himself.'

'Poor Varada.' Baxter dabbed her eyes with her sleeve. 'She was the least guilty of all of us, and the most frightened, and now she's just lying out there . . .'

'We mourn later,' Jack said brusquely. 'We've a war to win.'

Baxter made an effort to get herself together. Claudia meanwhile was still listening. 'Can't believe he'll just let us creep away,' she said quietly.

'So we keep heading landward,' Jack replied. 'Following a rough north-east path, yeah? That'll take us down to the quayside. From there, it's a quick run round the harbour.'

'We're going to the pub?' Baxter eyed him uncertainly.

He shrugged. 'Returning to the hotel would mean going back through the village, along the Quad Track and up the hotel drive. There're any numbers of points along that route where he could jump us. Okay . . . everyone got their second wind?'

Baxter chuckled bitterly. 'I'm on my fortieth or fiftieth.'

They travelled on, veering inland, but now keeping low as the gorse thinned out. It still seemed likely the Dogman would try to snuff them out before they got somewhere defensible. But when they descended through the last vestiges of thorny scrub on to the quayside, it was empty of life, the harbour deserted in the moonlight.

They hunkered down. From where they crouched, they could see the pub's open front door, and a dim red light inside. The power was out, but the pub's gas fire, a recent installation, functioned on a battery-powered switch. In any case, the appliance had been switched on before the power cut, and gas was still flowing from the tank, so its real-flame display continued to provide light and heat.

They lurched out of cover, all three finding last reserves of energy as they hurried along the quayside, looking frantically around but seeing nothing. It wouldn't have surprised Claudia if, just as they got close, they spotted the bastard on the roof of The Salmon armed with a whaler's harpoon or something. They rounded the harbour corner, hammering across the esplanade, encroaching on the door. This was surely the moment he'd strike with another of his ghastly implements. A poisoned dart from a blowpipe? A razor-edged boomerang? This wasn't her imagination. He *had* to stop them.

But he didn't, and the next thing they knew, they were inside the pub, Jack closing the door behind them, throwing the bolts top and bottom.

'I don't believe it.' Baxter panted hard. 'We made it.'

'Not quite.' Jack eyed the interior, lit by reddish flames but still an unfamiliar world of twisted, shadowy shapes.

'You think he got in here first?' Claudia whispered.

'I'm not saying that exactly,' Jack replied. 'But he's always been one step ahead.'

Forty-Four

Jack gritted his teeth as he ventured down the pub's darkened rear corridor, closing slowly on the door standing ajar at the end of it. At any second he expected it to explode open in front of him, or maybe a brutal attack to come unseen from the lavatories as he passed them.

But neither of these happened.

He shouldered the rear entrance closed and bolted it up and down, hopes growing that their adversary was still outside, though that wasn't a given as yet. When he got back into the taproom, the two women had circled the rest of the downstairs area and checked all the windows. 'Good stuff,' he said. 'You guys still got blades?'

Baxter showed hers.

'Never had one in the first place,' Claudia replied. 'But given the Remington's no use anymore, how's this?' She crossed to one of the pillars and took down a pirate's cutlass.

'Probably break on first contact,' Jack replied.

'So long as first contact is with Beck's skull, it doesn't matter, does it?'

'Depends which breaks first. My money's on that thing.'

'For God's sake.' Claudia tossed the cutlass on to the bar and went around it and into the pub's kitchen, re-emerging with a paring knife.

Jack nodded. 'Okay . . . we've still got to do the upstairs. Secure every door and window. Once we've done that, back down here . . . we load all the spare chairs and tables against the two main doors.'

It meant more work, especially for three bodies now battered and bruised beyond belief, but no one was arguing. They searched, not just checking windows, but hauling out the contents of wardrobes and cupboards. When they were sure there was no one hiding anywhere and that all portals were sealed, they returned to the taproom.

'Just had a text from the Coastguard,' Baxter said. 'ETA one and a half hours from now.'

The other two nodded as they humped items of furniture against the front door.

'I'm sure we can stick it out until then,' Jack replied.

'And we've even time for a drink.' Claudia went around the bar again. Without power, none of the pumps were working, but there were plenty of bottles. She took some tumblers from a side shelf. 'Care to join me?'

'In a mo,' Jack said, taking a side table down the rear corridor.

'Don't mind if I do.' Baxter swayed over there.

'What's your poison?'

'This time of night? Brandy.'

Claudia selected a bottle of Rémy Martin. 'This do?'

'Absolutely.'

Claudia pushed the bottle and a tumbler towards her. Baxter poured a good four fingers.

'You guys are not going to get wasted, are you?' Jack asked when he returned. 'We may still have a battle to fight.'

'If our friend had any sense, he'd leg it,' Baxter murmured.

Claudia poured herself a similar-sized measure. 'I'm inclined to agree. He wanted to get us all and he hasn't succeeded, but a body count of twelve is good going even for a spree killer.'

'You think he's satisfied?' Jack said, sounding sceptical.

Claudia took a sip. 'I'm just saying maybe he'll cut his losses.'

'Maybe, maybe not. Shit, I'd love to know more about this guy.'

Baxter yawned. 'I'd be fascinated to hear why, given that we already know the main thing – he's a bloody killing machine. But there are a couple of beds upstairs that look too comfy to resist.' She examined the label on the brandy bottle. 'I'm taking a nightcap with me.'

They watched as she poured another couple of fingers, and then left the bar, trudging towards the staircase, creaking her way to the upper floor.

'Sleep wouldn't be a bad idea,' Claudia said.

Jack shook his head. 'One of us has to stay awake.'

'Surely, they'll honk a horn or something when they get into the harbour?'

'Maybe, but before then our guy could still try to force entry. The least we can do is post a sentry.'

'You know, Jack, he's probably gone. He must have a boat somewhere. He knows help's coming, so he'll take to his heels.'

'I'll stay awake, just in case.'

She gave him a long, level stare. 'You mean as a penance?'

He shrugged.

'None of this is your fault, Jack. You didn't even want to come here.'

'I tried to take the bastard down . . . and courted danger for all of us.'

'We had no choice. It was him or us.'

'Yeah, but . . . I know it seems self-centred, Claudi. But in some ways, I almost saw it as an opportunity.'

'It'll make you famous again, that's for sure. We'll have a great story to tell.'

'I was thinking about telling it in book form.'

She arched an eyebrow.

'Could be that Old Mother Hubbard upstairs has just given us the title,' he said. 'How does *Killing Machine* grab you?'

'Are you serious?'

'There. I knew you'd hate the idea.'

'Oh, hell . . . Jack, you are who you are. And you thinking you might, I don't know . . . write a true crime classic . . . well, that's better than talking about topping yourself.'

'You could write it with me. You know me, my report-writing was always the worst thing about me.'

She finished her drink. 'I still want to do what I said before. Just go . . . leave it all behind.'

'Won't be as easy after this.'

'Can't worry about that now.' She came around the bar. 'Seeing as you're volunteering to watch, I'm getting my head down.'

'Choose your bed.'

'The armchair in the snug will do. Don't worry if there's a problem. I'm a light sleeper.'

After she'd gone, Jack stood alone for a few moments, before choosing a chair with a good straight back. He placed it in the middle of the taproom, facing the front door, and settled in it.

The heat from the gas fire was intense, almost soporific. He thought about turning the flames down, but that would reduce the light. Instead, he got up and lumbered stiffly to the bar, where he grabbed himself a couple of cans of Pepsi from the fridge. He resumed his seat and drank them down, though drowsiness was still sneaking up on him.

He kept pushing himself upright, but his eyelids continually drooped closed. When he opened them for the fifth or sixth time, he glimpsed the outline of what might be a face peering in through the pub window. He leapt to his feet, heart suddenly racing.

There was no one there.

Stumbling across the taproom, he peeked outside, but still saw nobody.

He patrolled the interior again, his body aching, checking all the downstairs windows, only returning to the chair when he was sure he'd been mistaken. Seated again, he could discern the slight distortion in the window's glass that had created the false impression.

He relaxed at that, allowing the heat of the fire to steal over him.

When another face appeared, it was probably the same one, only in a different window. He told himself there was nothing there. When this face withdrew, a lumbering outline seemed to make its way along the pub's front, Jack watching sleepily as it passed one pane after the next. But only when he spied another figure at the same time heading in the opposite direction did he know he was dreaming.

Or was he?

He bolted upright again, eyes snapping open.

For several seconds he sat taut and sweating, blinking hard.

But everything was as it should be, the fire still blazing, the wavering red shadows filling the room. Nothing stirred beyond the dark, empty windows. Cursing his imagination, he levered himself back to his feet and went over there, cleaver in hand. Outside, the harbour lay in near-total darkness, the moon, having shifted position, no longer reflecting from its lapping waters. It would have been nice to see the distant spotlight of an approaching vessel, but there was nothing on the horizon. It wouldn't come from that direction anyway. He walked around a bit more, wandering into the snug, where Claudia lay slumped in the armchair, deeply asleep. He looked for some kind of sheet to drape over her but found nothing.

Going down the rear corridor, he opened the doors into both sets of toilets. All their windows were closed and locked. However, whereas the pub's front door was stacked with tables and chairs, only the single side table had been pushed against the back door. It wasn't much of a barricade. He contemplated lugging a few other items of furniture down here, though surely there wouldn't be time for that before the rescue boat arrived?

He sloped into the taproom. If nothing else the walkabout had sparked him back to life. He was now thinking about all the freebies they'd been promised, few of which he'd actually taken advantage of. He lumbered to the bar, placed his cleaver on the counter, reached over to get a tumbler, and poured himself a large measure of the Rémy Martin. Returning to his chair, he pulled up a small table on which to put the drink down.

How were they going to explain all this in a convincing way? In his efforts to get everyone here, had Wayland left any kind of trail an investigation team could follow? Or would Jack and the two female survivors always be regarded with suspicion? The idea of putting it all on paper appealed to him. Get it in writing that someone else was responsible for all this death and destruction, someone who knew the island, someone who murdered with cold efficiency, never leaving himself open to attack or capture. But it wouldn't be easy persuading them it was the Dogman. The original Dogman, the one Harry Wayland was supposed to have shot dead. That would open a real can of worms.

Jack took a large swill of brandy. His eyelids were leaden, the combination of physical and mental effort overpowering him. He tried to fixate on the barricaded front door and the windows to either side of it, but all he could see was the firelight reflecting in the glass.

And the tall, featureless shape encroaching on him from behind.

Jack tried to jump from the chair, but before he'd left the cushioned padding, the ligature was across his throat and round his neck, once, twice, and pulled so tightly it cut off his air supply. He struggled and fought, kicking out, the chair dancing on two legs. But the man behind him – the thing, the monster – was built from steel. Jack gagged and choked, sputum flying everywhere. He clawed backward with his one good hand, to no purpose. Tried to grab the small table but latched on to the tumbler of brandy instead. Sensing that he was about to slam the glass backward, his assailant twisted him round on his seat, all the time cinching the neck-cord tighter.

Jack thought his head would explode, his eyes burst from his sockets. He felt the blood on his cheeks as capillaries ruptured and his vision faded. Then he spotted the bar, and the mirror and the glass shelves behind it. He flung the tumbler as hard as he could.

It spun through the air, impacting with tremendous force, the entire display collapsing, the mirror cascading in shards, shelves and bottles falling.

Despite the roaring in his ears, Jack heard Claudia call from the next room.

Distracted, the killer loosened his grip. Jack sucked a sliver of air into his chest and lurched sideways. The killer went with him, still at his rear, twisting his tourniquet again.

'*Jack!*' Claudia was in the room now.

She stood rigid, unable to compute what she was seeing: the tall figure clad in camouflage gear and military-style webbing; thick gloves on; an olive balaclava covering his head; the twine, or baling wire or whatever it was, looped around Jack's neck; Jack's face the colour of beetroot, eyes like duck eggs, mouth slathered with vomit and spittle.

She stumbled forward, but the maniac had spotted her. Presumably because the last time she'd had a gun, he swung Jack round as a human shield . . . only to see that she was clutching a knife instead.

Turning Jack again, he dealt him a ferocious headbutt in the face, sending him sprawling backward, before rounding to meet Claudia.

'*I'm warning you, you bastard!*' she shrieked, assuming the combat pose, knifepoint to the fore. '*I'm a sixth dan!*'

It was untrue, but he didn't come straight at her, holding his ground . . . just long enough to loosen another weapon from his harness.

It looked like a hatchet or wood-axe.

Claudia tried not to show her terror. But he sensed it anyway, and came on, raising the weapon over his head, only for Jack to scrabble after him across the floor and rugby tackle his left leg from behind, wrapping his one good arm around it. The killer glanced back and tried to kick himself free, allowing Claudia to strike first with her paring knife, slashing as hard as she could across his cloth-covered face. Grunting with animalistic pain, he staggered away as far as the pool table, blood welling through his fingers as he clutched at his mask. Jack was now back on his feet, working the cord loose from his neck, close to the bar . . . and the shiny shape of the cleaver.

He grabbed it and lurched around.

Fleetingly, they formed a triangle, Jack by the bar, Claudia by the snug, the Dogman at the pool table. It was a toss-up between Jack and Beck as to which of them was in the worse state.

Jack now sported a broken nose as well as everything else, but the lower half of the killer's mask hung off, along with what looked like a huge slice of face. As the Dogman delicately peeled the wool away, it was sodden with blood. The handsome features beneath, already self-brutalised, were now entirely and gruesomely misaligned, Beck's wound running deep into the tissue, stretching from the left side of his mouth to the lobe of his left ear.

Despite this, he regarded them both with baleful eyes. Slowly, he drew another weapon, a huge horrifying commando knife, which he weighed in his right hand while hefting the hand-axe in his left.

'You might be a walking fucking armoury . . .' Jack gestured with the cleaver, 'but it won't work, buddy. You've got one way out of this. Drop those weapons, and any others you're carrying . . . and you won't get chopped to mincemeat.'

Beck's cold eyes were chips of metal amid swollen flesh. They darted from one opponent to the other, taking stock of what he faced.

'You really fancy your chances against two of us?' Jack said.

Beck suddenly looked amused, focusing on Jack's distorted body. 'More like one and a half, Mr McGurn, wouldn't you say?'

'What the hell's wrong with you?' Claudia demanded.

'What's wrong with *you*?' he retorted. 'Guardians of the law . . . turned into its worst abusers. And not even for a noble cause. For monetary gain.'

'A noble cause?' Jack said, bemused.

'A shock to you, I'd imagine,' Beck replied. 'That you haven't been able to leave your dishonourable pasts behind. But no one understands that better than me.'

'Who the hell are you?'

Fleetingly, Beck's attention was elsewhere. They wondered if the blood still streaming from his slashed-open face was taking its toll. He breathed deeply, eyes lidded. 'I thought I could outrun my days in Night Patrol.' Then he fixed them with another intense stare. 'But . . . no. Of course not. Nobody can.'

'Night Patrol?' Claudia said. 'What, were you some kind of cop?'

'Ignore him, Claudi,' Jack said. 'Can't you see he's crazy?'

'Some kind, yes,' Beck replied.

A slow understanding dawned on Claudia. '*Private* police? That's big money in South Africa, these days, isn't it?'

Beck sneered. 'You think your homeland's overrun with crime. You don't know the meaning of that.'

'Look, Beck,' she said, 'just because your country has a tragic past . . .'

'It's *your* country where my tragedy lies,' he countered. 'Where my life ended.' The sneer became a snarl. 'And all thanks to the likes of you . . .'

He took a step towards her, throwing the hand-axe.

It crossed the taproom in a blur of steel. Claudia just had time to dive, the weapon embedding itself in the panelling behind. A split second later, he launched a second missile. It was one of the pool balls, and it smacked her clean on the left temple, the impact like the *whop* of a shuttlecock on a racquet. It left her motionless on the carpet.

Jack was startled by the speed of the attack, especially as the maniac now came straight at him, knife first. Jack struck with his cleaver, but it was a backhand sweep, and clumsy, and Beck ducked it easily. Jack swung it back, but Beck parried it with his own blade, sending it twirling loose. Jack grappled with him one-armed, but was punched under the jaw, which knocked him back against the bar, and then took a blow in the lower body, and then another and another . . . and it was only on the third when he realised that it wasn't a fist striking him.

The shock went through his guts like iced water. His knees buckled and he crumpled where he stood, clutching at the bar top to stay upright.

Beck stepped back, watching, bloody-faced.

Jack stared at him with outraged disbelief.

Not like this. Not without landing a single glove on the basta . . .

With a final monumental effort, he reached back across the counter. There had to be something there – anything, a glass maybe – only for his fingers to close on something better.

Beck's wounded face hardened, his fevered gaze burning into Jack's, as if willing him to die more speedily. Which is maybe why he didn't react in time when Jack's one good arm suddenly arched towards him, fast-bowler fashion, ramming the corkscrew into his left eye.

Squealing like a flayed pig, Beck tottered away, clawing at the steel implement hanging from the punctured jelly in his left socket, fresh blood pulsing down his face, along with streams of black ichor.

Jack sagged all the way down on to his side. His body shuddered uncontrollably, seemed to be freezing from the inside out. He barely even saw Claudia when she scrambled over to him, grabbing him by the collar, trying to slap some life back into his lacerated face. 'Jack, come on, come on . . .'

He managed a very faint smile.

'Jack, we'll write that book together. Soon as we get home.'

He mouthed a single word, which she felt certain was 'Sorry', before his eyes went still.

A hideous cold sank through her as she lay on top of him, drenched in his blood.

From the corner of her eye, meanwhile, she spotted Beck, his own face a grotesque ruin, his left eye a gory hole, lurching towards her, still wielding his butcher-sized blade.

'*You fucking lunatic!*' she screamed, rising to meet him.

She had a knife too, and she thrust it at his midriff. But for all that he was maimed, the madman still had the strength and dexterity to swat her blade aside with his own and catch her face with a furious backhand. Bells rang as she tottered sideways and fell. He followed through with a brutal kick to her belly. Claudia scampered away on all fours, adrenaline overriding the pain. Scrambling to her feet, she struck at him again with her knife, though again he parried the blow, this time with such force it flew from her grasp.

Clutching her throat with his huge hand, he swung her round and slammed her down backward on top of the small table, holding her in place. As he raised his steel to impale her to the wood, it was the face of a devil that peered down at her. Once angelic, now mangled to horror. And of course, half blinded.

Which is why the first gunshot took him by surprise, knocking him backward a yard; the second knocking him back again; the third tearing a huge chunk, like a divot of turf, from the top of his head. The commando knife slipped from his fingers as he stumbled in a slow, grisly pirouette before dropping to the pub floor.

For several nightmarish moments, Claudia lay gasping on the table, heart juddering. She thought she was having a coronary. Then, as her breathing steadied and her pulse settled, she forced herself to sit upright, and then stand, all the time staring down at Beck's broken form, a ghastly lake of blood forming around his imploded skull. Numbed, her focus slid across the taproom to the door connecting with the rear corridor, where Cheryl Baxter, clad head to foot in waterproofs, stood in tactical pose, a pistol held two-handed in front of her.

'Remembered to go for the headshot in the end, eh?' Claudia said dazedly.

Baxter approached, still pointing the firearm at the body. Claudia recognised the Beretta that had caused such problems for Ray Donaldson. 'I aimed for the head all three times,' Baxter said. 'Guess I'm not that great a shot. Good job he never saw me coming, eh?'

'Where'd you get the shells for the Beretta . . . ?'

'But I'm good enough from this distance.' There was a snap in Baxter's voice as she swung the weapon on to Claudia. 'So, you stay where you are, Claudia. You hear me?' Any response caught in Claudia's throat. She watched, perplexed, as Baxter went first to Jack's body, still keeping the gun trained in her direction. 'McGurn's definitely dead?'

'I . . . I . . .' Claudia felt a pang of agonising sorrow. 'I think so.'

When Baxter kicked the prone body, it didn't move. She kicked it harder. Still nothing.

'Hardly a respectful way to treat a friend,' Claudia stuttered.

'He wasn't my friend. And you aren't either. So, like I say . . .' Baxter moved to the pub's windows, to peer out, 'you keep your pretty backside over there, where I can see you.'

'Or what . . . you're going to shoot me?'

Baxter turned an expression on her that she simply didn't recognise. It was the same face, except that now it was carved from granite. 'I don't want to, but if you force my hand . . .'

'Cheryl, what the hell is this?'

'You haven't worked it out?' The woman's mouth curved into an unamused smile. 'Bit slow for a former ace detective, aren't you?'

'You're . . . you're *part* of this?'

'I'm the key part. I mean, I came to St Dunstan just like the rest of you. A disgraced ex-cop. But I also came here as the Crew's fail-safe.'

'You're still working for them?'

'Not through choice.' Baxter remained by the window, but kept the gun on her captive. 'Once I wasn't useful to the Crew anymore, who was going to keep my son safe in prison? After the job kicked me out, I couldn't feed them the intel they needed, so I had to offer a different service. I went to see them personally. Said I'd do anything they wanted. And it was the Crew who came up with Damned Rankers . . . which, as you've probably guessed, is not a support group, but a death list.'

That reality was obvious enough now, but to hear it put in such blunt terms was still a jolt. The woman deserved an Oscar for her convincing portrayal of a decent citizen.

But Baxter was still talking. 'There's something new on the cop-land horizon, you see. It isn't widely known. I didn't even know about it until I was told by my contact in the Crew that the Organised Crime Division . . .'

'Scotland Yard?'

'The same,' Baxter scoffed. 'Dodgy customers, themselves. But part of the National Crime Group, who basically know what they're doing. They're currently developing a new strategy. They call it Operation Underbarrow.'

'Underbarrow . . . ?' Claudia remembered the word from the noticeboard in Beck's den.

'I know,' Baxter said. 'I was a bit worried when the dickhead Dogman left that code word on his cellar wall where anyone could see it, but thankfully none of you were sufficiently clued-in. It's pretty well need-to-know, but in a nutshell it amounts to the wide-ranging prosecution of senior organised crime figures across the UK.'

Claudia frowned. This was her neighbourhood, but though she and Jack had broken a good many firms, they'd mostly been small to mid-ranking. The big guys were all but untouchable.

'I mean the Crew, the Corporation,' Baxter said, as though she'd been reading Claudia's mind. 'All those smarmy top-dog shit-heads who think no one can touch them are mostly right about that. But everyone's got an Achilles heel. For Al Capone it was tax evasion. In our version, it's the widespread bribing of public officialdom. And not just cops. Judges, barristers, civil servants, politicians, bigwigs in the media . . . every posh scrote you can think of. The Crew have been lining these worthless bastards' pockets for years.'

'And Operation Underbarrow is the solution?' Claudia asked.

'Not least because it would be calling in the many former police officers who'd been jailed or dismissed for corruption to provide witness statements and name names. In return for full amnesties of course, and lifelong protection.'

Slowly, inevitably, it fell together.

'So, all the bent cops on the Crew's payroll had to go?' Claudia said.

'The important ones, yeah. The ones who'd made a difference.'

'How was Alan Rothermere part of that?'

'Who do you think provided the illegal porn to frame him with?'

'Oh my God . . . Alan was innocent?'

'No one here was massively guilty, Claudia. Not when you consider their eventual fate. But the Crew didn't want it to look as if these guys had simply been killed by underworld hitmen – that would have exposed their own intel sources at Scotland Yard.'

Claudia hung her head. 'And that's where Harry Wayland came in?'

'Correct again. Not to mention the Dogman.'

Claudia stared at Beck's corpse. The image of that ravaged face bearing down on her would haunt her forever.

'You've already got some idea where he came from,' Baxter said.

Claudia nodded. 'The Night Patrol.'

'The Night Patrol, yes . . . that was the icing on the cake. But before then, our Mr Beck, real name Deon Scheckter, started out in the Recces.'

'The what?'

'First Reconnaissance Commando. South African special forces.' Baxter kicked at Beck's legs, just to ensure he was dead.

'Saw plenty of action as a sniper. When he left, he wanted to join the cops, but there was more money in the vigilante corps.'

'The private-hire police.'

'Don't sound so disdainful. Some of them are almost respectable. But the Night Patrol Bureau . . . well, they were a law unto themselves. You think he learned the "search and destroy" tactics he's deployed here in the Recces? Not totally.' Baxter backed to the window again, still diligently training her weapon on Claudia. 'When the real law finally caught up with them . . . looking to solve God knows how many murders, the whole Night Patrol made a dash for it. The one place they *didn't* want to end up in was a South African prison. Our friend, Scheckter, having made some very good connections – because you know, a team like that only really looks after the interests of the super-rich – was well supplied with all the fake credentials he needed to get himself and his wife over to the UK.' She looked at Beck. 'But he wasn't too keen on the inner-city shit-hole they wound up in. Hatchwood Green . . . one of the worst estates in Crowley, which I'm told is the part of Manchester God forgot the most. Not only that, Mimi – his wife – was pregnant. They soldiered on for the sake of the baby. Until Mimi got attacked. Mugged and severely beaten on a late-night shopping trip to buy baby formula.'

'Let me guess,' Claudia said, 'she died?'

'Bang on.'

'And our friend went vigilante again.'

'Only when our lot, or rather, *your* lot – Greater Manchester Police, not West Yorkshire – failed to lock anyone up for it. Not only that . . . you failed to catch Scheckter after he topped the bastards he decided were responsible. Of course, no one knows whether he got the right people, but the die was cast. All low-life scum were suddenly fair game to our shell-shocked refugee from the Night Patrol. He'd picked up where he left off at home, and now he remembered how much he'd enjoyed it. Then Harry Wayland came along.'

Claudia frowned. 'But Harry spared him. Stitched up Cornwallis.'

'Jimmy Cornwallis, the deranged ex-squaddie, the fall guy. A total fantasist. His only real crime was wasting police time with those letters he wrote. Ten out of ten for imagination – he was the one who invented the nickname "Dogman". But he took the whole rap and died for his trouble, while Harry, as part of his arrangement with the Crew, handed the real killer over to them. They were going to punish him for the damage he'd done to their street operations. But seeing him as a mad dog they might someday make use of, they recruited him instead.'

'And reactivated him to capsize Operation Underbarrow?'

Baxter nodded. 'Under a false pretext – namely, Damned Rankers – all the potential witnesses would be brought in secrecy here to Porth West, an unfinished holiday resort, one of numerous legitimate enterprises underwritten by the Crew. Then the Dogman, already installed here, would be allowed to continue his one-man war against . . . undesirables.'

'Okay, we're undesirables. But the Crew are worse. Why would he play ball with them?'

'Get real, darling. Scheckter's still got a young daughter . . . She'd go straight into the care system if anything happened to him. That was all the leverage they needed. He'd dance to any tune they wanted to keep himself alive.'

Baxter produced her phone. She also glanced out of the window again, very eager it seemed – too eager? – for the rescue boat to arrive. Which now made no sense whatsoever.

'You haven't thought this through,' Claudia said. 'No Scotland Yard detective worth his salt will fail to consider the possibility the Crew are behind these killings.'

'What killings?' Baxter replied. 'There won't be any proof they ever happened. Or that any of you were even here. The Dogman was never going to leave this island alive either.'

'*Your* role?'

'Partly. The Crew guaranteed my son's safety for the rest of his sentence if I would come on to this island as a Damned Ranker. Not even Harry would know my real purpose, which was to ensure the Dogman was successful.'

'All along, you've been doing your bit to help him, haven't you? You pretended Beck was more seriously injured than he was. You framed Donaldson and O'Hare with that Beretta, which presumably the Crew gave you . . . along with the ammo you held back until the end.'

Baxter smiled. 'I felt Donaldson and O'Hare would be the most dangerous opponents, so I tried to separate them from the rest of you. But in doing that, I underestimated you and Jack McGurn. In fact, you two were making so much headway in your little enquiry that I had to intervene again.'

The silence between them stretched taut.

'Which ones did *you* kill?' Claudia asked quietly.

For the first time, Baxter looked tired. As if this was one weight that had genuinely been wearing her down. 'Jonas Pugh wasn't the intended target in the shed. I rigged it as a massive Molotov cocktail because I increasingly felt the ATVs were giving you an advantage. But if someone died in that fireball, so be it.'

'You cold-hearted bitch.'

'You don't know the half of it. Gabby Milburn was proving a nuisance too. She was in tip-top physical condition. On top of that, she'd bought fully into your investigation.'

Claudia's hair prickled. 'You . . . you pushed Gabby off that ledge?'

'I told you!' Baxter turned defensive. 'Scheckter wasn't making the progress I anticipated. I even had to open one of the upstairs windows to let him in here tonight. There's a lesson there, Claudia. Never hire a madman if it's a job you can do yourself.'

'And you're not mad?'

'My son's safety is all that matters.'

'They won't let you live either. You surely realise that?'

'That's a chance I must take.'

'Even if the Crew *do* keep their end of the deal, no investigation team will believe the Dogman caused this carnage on his own. And they'll never believe that so many potential witnesses in Operation Underbarrow would gather here together unless they'd been lured.'

'I've already told you, no bodies will be found here. First of all, the Coastguard are *not* coming. Surely, you've realised I faked that phone call? In actual fact, I was alerting a Crew clean-up team, who are now approaching in a boat equipped with a refrigeration facility. Every crime scene on the island will be professionally scrubbed. There'll be no trace of any of you. In a few months' time a thousand holidaymakers will be here, so it won't matter. Your bodies meanwhile will be dumped at appropriate locations around northern England, along with the documentary evidence produced by Scheckter.'

'The eventual inference,' Claudia said, 'being that a lone madman went initially after the corrupt cop who framed Cornwallis for his crimes, and then moved on to fellow corrupt associates as a matter of course?'

'Bravo.' Baxter gave another humourless smile. 'Which brings us, at last, to you.'

'I'm surprised you've let me live this long.'

'It's not by choice, I assure you.'

Claudia started edging across the room. 'It's because the Dogman never shot his victims, isn't it?'

For the first time, Baxter seemed vaguely nervous. 'The Dogman never shot his victims in the UK because as a former sniper in South Africa, he wanted to put distance between himself and an identifiable past. But that doesn't mean he couldn't have used a gun if he'd needed to.'

'But he never did. I imagine it was okay for you to shoot him, because his body will just disappear. But aside from that, there's an illusion to maintain . . .'

'Stay where you are, Crayford!'

'To mix my body up with all the others, I need to die as they did . . . by blade, ligature, whatever.'

'Don't count on it. *Stay where you are!*'

But Claudia continued to drift. 'And you don't fancy getting so close and personal, do you?' She reached the bar, where she stopped. 'You're waiting for your mates to get here. So, they can help you.'

Baxter advanced, the Beretta levelled, but at the same time changed position to keep a clean angle on her target. 'If need be, I'll do it.'

'And I'm just supposed to wait for you to pluck up the courage?'

Baxter halted by the gas fire. 'You won't have to wait for long.'

And with eerie synchronicity, a siren-like horn blasted out a single piercing note from down in the harbour. Baxter was distracted, glancing towards the pub's front windows, which suddenly were filled with artificial light. It was fleeting. But it was all the time Claudia needed to grab the half-full brandy bottle from the bar top and fling it past her into the flames, the glass exploding forcefully and an immense fireball ballooning outward, enveloping Baxter from behind. Seared and screaming, she tottered away, spinning, beating at herself.

Claudia grabbed the pirate cutlass and launched herself forward, ramming it into Baxter's body. The blade was ancient, but the tip still penetrated the waterproofs on Baxter's lower left side, Claudia thrusting with such desperate force that the whole thing slid in deeply, well past half its length, before snapping off at the hilt.

Baxter's gasps of shock and pain became shrieks, her face draining white.

Claudia had never been the sort of police officer who enjoyed hurting people. She'd rarely used violence. But now she had no hesitation in throwing herself on to the wailing, cavorting figure, wrestling the Beretta from her weakened grasp, turning it around and firing twice, blowing her opponent back against the bar counter with jackhammer force.

Outside the pub meanwhile, right outside the main door, there were male voices. Still wielding the pistol, Claudia backed towards the rear corridor, scuttling along it to the pub's back door, only to hear voices on the other side there too, and then for the first hefty blow to land. The door shuddered in its frame. Another blow landed, and another. It was apparent that neither of the two bolts would hold for long, nor the single table barricade.

Panting, she raced back into the taproom. Now they were banging on that door too. Dim figures beyond the windows. A gloved fist struck glass. It shattered.

Ice-cold despite the intense heat of the fire, Claudia retreated slowly into the pool table area. It was more by instinct, but this was the furthest corner from the pub's entrance. The front door banged in its frame. Barricade furniture fell.

Claudia clutched the gun hard.

A Beretta 92, its clip normally carried nine rounds. That meant she could have as many as four remaining. But by the looks of things, not even four direct hits would turn the odds here.

Instead, she gazed across to where Cheryl Baxter's iPhone lay alongside her body. It would have locked itself by now of course.

But Claudia had seen the woman unlock it at the castle with a simple thumbprint. And she wasn't doing anything with her thumb right now.

Another window shattered; one of the door's hinges flew.

Claudia dashed across the room . . .

Epilogue

Charlie Quincannon was in a private members' bar in Manchester's Northern Quarter, when it came on the news again. Aside from one of the barmaids, who was busy mopping the bar top, he was alone. It was early evening, midweek, so it had never been likely to be full, but on top of that it was August, so lots of regulars were away. It didn't bother him too much. It meant he could safely crack a smile as he watched the news item on the big-screen TV, snickering at the sight of the police cordon at the entrance to the quarry just off the M62, the forensics tent on the other side of it, the investigators moving around in CSI coveralls.

One of those older, pompous-looking senior coppers in a uniform so pristine it suggested he rarely went outside his office was being interviewed. He wore a theatrically grave expression as he spoke to a journalist.

'It is true that Jack McGurn and Claudia Crayford were former members of the Greater Manchester Police,' he said, seeming to consider every word carefully before uttering it. 'But any stories linking their two deaths, which we are now treating as murder, to the reason for their joint dismissal from the police service are purely speculative. We are, as has already been stated, pursuing a different line of enquiry at this time.'

'Did you know the two ex-officers personally, sir?' the journalist enquired.

The senior cop seemed hesitant to answer. 'I knew them, erm . . . only in their capacity as serving officers. I . . . I had no connection with them, otherwise.'

Charlie snorted into his double Jim Beam and ice. It was hilarious watching the bastards wriggle.

Normally at this stage of a murder enquiry, with nothing useful to report, they'd be falling back on the usual platitudes, saying what good people society had lost and how they hadn't deserved to die in this violent fashion. But all that would have sounded pretty rich given that characters like this cartoonish specimen here had recently drummed McGurn and Crayford out of the force, refusing to hold back on the scathing criticism.

Hearing someone enter behind him, Charlie turned and was surprised to see his father. When Peter Quincannon came and stood alongside him, Charlie made some jocular comment about it not being like him to start early, but the older man ignored him, watching the TV.

As Manchester firms went, Peter Quincannon and his family were about midway down the city's criminal strata, but not so far down that they didn't pay their dues and owe their loyalty to the Crew, whose grip on the northern English drugs trade was all-encompassing. Peter Quincannon was still a player, though. And right now, he didn't seem happy.

'Tell me you had nothing to do with this,' he said. Very quietly.

Charlie glanced at him, puzzled. 'You know I didn't.'

'I don't *know* you didn't. You *told* me you didn't.' His father looked round at him, meeting him eyeball to eyeball. 'Tell me again. Persuade me.'

Irritably, Charlie glugged his bourbon. They'd already had this conversation at least twice. It was about time this old bastard saw what was coming a few years down the line.

'It's that nutcase, the Dogman,' he said.

'The Dogman's supposed to be dead.'

'The cozzers have decided they'd got it wrong . . . they popped an innocent bloke.' Charlie pointed at the screen. 'See, they're still talking about it.'

Briefly, the TV depicted the bearded, wild-eyed visage of the original Dogman suspect, the deceased Jimmy Cornwallis. Unmoved, the older Quincannon regarded his son with a hard, bleak stare. 'You definitely had nothing to do with this?'

In truth, Peter didn't actually believe that Charlie could have been involved at any level. The kid – he thought of him as a kid even though he was going on thirty – was a huge disappointment. It was true that he and his mates could easily be relied on to beat twenty colours out of anyone who needed it, perhaps in a backstreet somewhere, but anything that required an nth of planning, forget it.

'Look . . . we threatened them, sure,' Charlie said. 'And we were going to give them a kicking. But we wouldn't have gone any further without you okaying it.'

'Because obviously, this is the last thing we fucking need.'

'You weren't saying that a couple of days ago. You were laughing, saying those two bits of scum got what they deserved.'

The piggy little eyes behind Peter's bottle-thick lenses never blinked. 'I didn't need to be sure then that you haven't done something totally fucking out of line.'

'It was the Dogman!' Charlie protested. 'Didn't they find Harry Wayland's body too? Down some backstreet a couple of weeks ago. Minus his head. Very Dogman-ish. He only goes after low lifes, so now his sights are on corrupt police . . .'

Peter Quincannon pondered this. It was true that other dirty coppers had been turning up these last few weeks, wiped out in gruesome ways. With the best will in the world, there was no chance his dimwit son could have managed all that. But it didn't make things easier.

'See!' Charlie pointed at the screen again, where the camera had zeroed in at the foot of one of the scruffy letters written to the press during the original murder spree, which had ended a decade ago, and signed off by someone calling himself 'the Dogman'. 'D,' he read aloud, 'O-G-M . . .'

Peter rounded on his son. 'Will you get it through your thick skull! What the cozzers say and what they actually think are two different things!' He let that hang, glancing behind him to check how close the barmaid was, but she'd gone through into the back room.

'Okay, what's happened?' Charlie asked nervously, the penny finally having dropped. 'Something must've happened.'

Peter hesitated. 'Let's just say there've been whispers.'

'Whispers? From where?'

'From well above your pay grade.'

'About what?'

Peter's gaze narrowed on the screen, where a pair of photographic stills had appeared, facial images of their two least favourite ex-coppers. 'Seems that Crayford got a message out just before she got topped. On someone else's phone, would you believe.' He shook his head in disbelief. 'Rang a fucking relative. A sister, I think. Apparently, the sister's a snotty-nosed cow. Didn't recognise the number, so didn't answer. Didn't even bother listening to the message. Not till the bodies were found.'

Charlie shrugged, blank-faced. 'She couldn't have named *us*. We didn't do it.'

'No one got named. Sounds like the message was all scrambled . . . only lasted twenty seconds. It was all about saying goodbye and that. But she still had enough time to give the date of the murders, the time of the murders, the place where the murders happened and the motive for them.'

Charlie swallowed uneasily. 'So, where was the place?'

'All I know is it wasn't round here . . . and it was nowhere near that quarry where the bodies were found.'

'And . . . what's the motive?'

'No one's shared that with me either – I'm like you, the shit on some people's shoes – but it doesn't sound like it's got much to do with some retired serial killer going back to work.'

Again, Peter let that hang, offering his son a chance to figure things out for himself.

'Look!' Charlie blurted. 'Those bent cops were into all sorts of crooked shit, weren't they. We had it in for them for old time's sake, but there are plenty others they were doing bent deals with.'

'Yeah, and lots of those others are higher up the food chain than us. Which is why the Top Table's panicking like fuck.'

Charlie felt another pang of concern. Shit rolled downhill in this business. Always had.

'This is kosher? Yeah?'

'No, I'm making it up . . . you know, just for larks.'

'I mean, it's come from a good source?'

'What do you think?'

Charlie didn't need to have asked. The Crew had as many good sources of intel inside the police as the police had inside the Crew.

'Look,' he said, 'I still don't see why *we've* anything to worry about.'

'Do you not? Well, try and think it through while we're heading abroad.'

Charlie frowned. 'Abroad?'

His father nudged the drink in his hand. 'Finish that and get your shit together.'

Charlie was astonished. Clearly the old guy meant *now*. 'You mean we're really going?'

'There are certain kinds of people, Charlie, who don't do time. Certainly not full-life sentences. Instead, they send other people to do it for them.'

'Surely it wasn't just us who made threats to Crayford and McGurn?'

'I doubt there were many others who did it as openly.'

'There's other ex-coppers dead. They can't blame us for those.'

'Oh, don't worry . . . there'll be repercussions across the board. Lots more heads are going to roll than ours.'

There was something in the humourless certainty with which his father said this, the subtle fear etched deep in his hardman face, that persuaded Charlie Quincannon to throw down what remained of his drink and slip from his bar stool.

But still the younger guy resisted. 'Where are we going to go?' he asked petulantly.

'We'll find somewhere.' The older Quincannon glanced back at the TV screen, but then noticed that his son was still hovering. 'Jesus, must I spell this out? All these dead ex-cozzers were in a position to help their former colleagues build a case against the Top Table. So, appropriate action was taken. But now their former colleagues know exactly what kind of action and where. So, they're going to build a murder case instead. That won't be easy for them of course . . . but especially not if the Top Table muddy the waters by throwing them some easy fall guys as alternatives.'

Charlie's shoulders sagged. Now that he considered it, his father's firm weren't just expendable, they were also the obvious candidates for these two latest murders. And it didn't matter that they hadn't done it. If there wasn't enough evidence already pointing to them, more would be provided. 'I'm going,' he said, throwing a baleful glance at the TV again. 'Who'd have thought it, eh? Pair of bent bastards like them two. And now even the Crew are running scared.'

'Bent bastards?' the older Quincannon snorted. 'Don't you believe it.' The face of Claudia Crayford – beautiful but tough, clearly photographed at some past police function, but written with defiant confidence – gazed back at him from the screen. 'Once a copper, always a copper.'

About the Author

Photo © C. Finch

Paul Finch is a number one eBook bestseller and a top-ten *Sunday Times* bestseller. He first worked as a policeman in the north-west of England and then as a journalist.

His writing career commenced with episodes of the hit television drama *The Bill*, and since then, he has written extensively in the horror, fantasy, historical epic and sci-fi genres, including for *Doctor Who*. He is a two-time winner of the British Fantasy Award and a recipient of the International Horror Guild Award. However, Paul is probably best known for his dark crime thriller novels, including the Heckenburg and Clayburn series. In this capacity, he has twice been shortlisted for the Crime Writers' Association Dagger Awards.

The Island is Paul's first novel for Thomas & Mercer, and is based on an idea he had while holidaying in the south-west of

England. At the time he was contemplating new, different locations in which to set his action thrillers rather than the more familiar inner city, and suddenly found that the answer lay in front of him.

Paul lives in Lancashire with his wife and business partner, Cathy.

Follow the Author on Amazon

If you enjoyed this book, follow Paul Finch on Amazon to be notified when the author releases a new book! To do this, please follow these instructions:

Desktop:

1) Search for the author's name on Amazon or in the Amazon App.
2) Click on the author's name to arrive on their Amazon page.
3) Click the 'Follow' button.

Mobile and Tablet:

1) Search for the author's name on Amazon or in the Amazon App.
2) Click on one of the author's books.
3) Click on the author's name to arrive on their Amazon page.
4) Click the 'Follow' button.

Kindle eReader and Kindle App:

If you enjoyed this book on a Kindle eReader or in the Kindle App, you will find the author 'Follow' button after the last page.

Printed in Dunstable, United Kingdom